CROSSING THE LINE

Crossing the Line

S. Howard

Crossing the Line

the third volume of the Mayflower Trilogy

Published by Hodgers Books.

First print edition.

Copyright © 2023 S. Howard. All rights reserved.

The characters and events portrayed in this book are fictitious. Any similarity to real persons, living or dead, is coincidental and not intended by the author.

No part of this book may be reproduced, or stored in a retrieval system, or transmitted in any form or by any means, electronic, mechanical, photocopying, recording, or otherwise, without express written permission of the publisher.

To my family and friends

Our lives are girt by boundary walls,
Snakes and ladders, risky falls.
Yet lest we take some slides and jumps
We never learn from any bumps.
And those too scared to sally forth
Beyond their comfort, south to north,
Will never taste discovery
Nor test their rims of bravery.

T.R.S. Hayward
Crossing Lines (Verse 2)

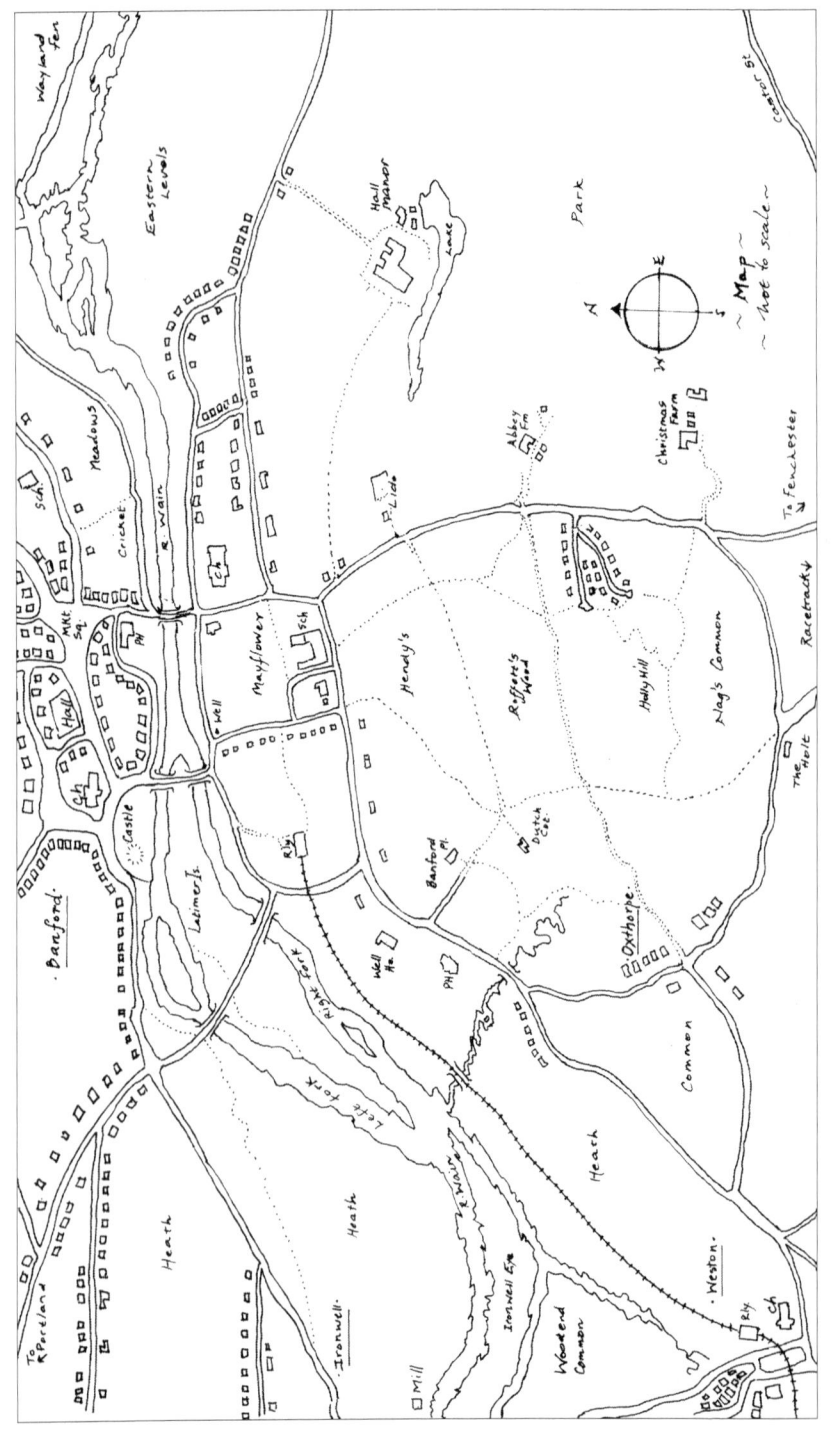

1.

New blood

There were two candidates for the recently vacated post of First Form teacher – a mimsy-looking woman of fifty who took one look at Mayflower school on the day of the interview, shuddered, and withdrew. The other was Miss Isabella Delgado, a probationer from Fenchester Teacher Training College.

"Did you not wish to remain at college an extra year and gain one of those new Bachelor of Education degrees on top of your teaching certificate?" Mrs Clark, the headmistress, asked her.

"No. I chose not to, as I need to be out in the world, earning some money. I could complete it later, of course. My mother recently passed away."

"Oh, I'm so sorry."

"This is my second interview. I tried for a school in Fenchester last week."

"I see. Wouldn't Banford be rather a long way for you to travel each day, if you live there?"

"No. I am actually lodging here temporarily, with my Aunt Eliza, while I look for a job. She is Miss Eliza Muggeridge. She lives in our old home in Wag Lane. I was born in Banford and went to Dane Street Primary, so I'm local." The candidate smiled. "She's my great-aunt."

Guy Denny nodded. He and Julia Scott, the vice-chairman of the governors, were helping Mrs Clark with today's interviews. Not that there was a mob of applicants beating down their door. He liked this girl, though. She didn't look too bad.

"Isabella…" began Mrs Clark.

"Bella please. Everyone calls me Bella."

"Bella, then. As the advert said, the position is for a general class teacher for our six year olds. We would like someone who is also interested in taking girls' games across the school, and maybe a little music from time to time. I see from your supporting letter that you play the piano and also enjoy sport."

"Yes, I do. I trained for the five-to-eleven age range. I like sculpture and pottery, I play the recorder too, of course. What games do the girls play here?"

"Netball, rounders. Tennis. We have two softball teams, too – glorified rounders, some say. The children swim at the Lido in the Summer term."

"Could the girls possibly be offered some of the boys' sports too? Like cricket and football?"

Guy nodded again, happily. That was a super idea, he thought. "I don't know whether the boys would want to play netball in return, though," he said doubtfully. "Maybe a little basketball."

Bella felt this was sounding rather hopeful. "I swim most days if I can. Or ride my bike, or go for a run. I like to keep fit."

"The Lido pool is just across the road," Julia chipped in. She liked this girl too. She was young and keen. "Everyone here swims. Clay-work is such fun for children isn't it? But there's no pottery kiln or anything. Maybe we could look into that, Mrs Clark?"

Skipper Clark hesitated. 'No More Frivolous Spending', her secretary had told her forcibly only last week. But how wonderful it would be for the children to make some simple coil pots and clay figures. "Yes, maybe soon," she smiled. Bella was a breath of youthful fresh air and enthusiasm.

They sent their candidate out of the room while they made a show of deliberating, but as there was literally no contest Miss Delgado it was. She would do perfectly. Skipper, Guy and Julia were mightily relieved to have Mayflower fully staffed before the new academic year began.

Bella was thrilled too, and felt her life had suddenly taken a much-needed turn for the better. It had been a very hard year so far, what with her mum being so ill and dying, and her dad so upset. She was grateful to have found her first permanent position, one she knew she would enjoy. At least the uncertainty of where and how she was to earn her living was finally over.

Guy showed their new recruit around the main building while Julia Scott hurried home to feed Pongo the poodle, and Mrs Clark filled in a pile of paperwork.

Bella was pleased with her new classroom. It was spacious and light, comprising the entire upper floor of an old Victorian terraced house linked to the main school building by a short first floor corridor. She ran her fingers over the upright piano's keyboard while Guy explained about bats and balls and books and where they were all kept.

"There are these connecting stairs going directly down to the kindergarten room," he pointed out. "And the first floor loos are just along the landing that way. Mrs Nesbit, the kindergarten teacher, is very nice and helpful, and the lower school aide – Carol Moore – is a star. You're in good hands. I suppose Mrs Nesbit will be your mentor for your probationary year. You couldn't ask for better. And you can come and ask the rest of us if you need to know anything else. You've joined a really friendly team."

Guy's pride in Mayflower was evident. "It's a small school, but beautifully formed," he joked. "The kids are pretty good – well, for the most part. We get the odd one or two, but mostly they're fairly normal and compliant. Learning support is first rate, parents are super. Coffee can be a bit questionable, but that can change. Come on, I'll find you the Summer newsletter and show you the rest of the place."

"Aunt Eliza said if I landed this job she'd be thrilled. It will be hard to leave my dad on his own, but I'm sure he knows I have to move forward. He has work, anyway. I must start looking for a flat of my own to rent now, I suppose. In town. Have you any suggestions?"

"No, but I'm sure some of the other staff will. Between us we'll try to get you somewhere reasonably priced, don't worry. Now then, I think that's it, you've seen it all. Is this your bike? Right then, I'll say cheerio. See you September first at nine-thirty for our initial staff meeting of the year."

"Oh I'll be in long before that," laughed Bella. "I want to set up my room and get used to the feel of the place. I'm so happy to be starting here at Mayflower!"

Guy waved the girl off, remembering that very soon his own eldest daughter would also be leaving home. She was off to university in October. I bet Bella's dad is feeling pretty miserable, he sympathised. We're going to miss our Debbie dreadfully. He closed the school's front gate and went back indoors.

The hot Summer sun beat down on the old Georgian building, causing it to creak in the heat and blanch and twist a little more. It lay dreaming contentedly, catlike, awaiting the tidal resurgence of life to flood back over its threshold once again. A trickle had already begun.

Down to work

The first day of September was golden, as if everywhere had been steeped in Summer honey. The liquid light flooded the lawns and drenched the drowsy flowers. Around the rim of the playing field the horse chestnut trees had begun to crisp and turn brown. Leaves as big as hands wafted lazily down into the acres and acres of untended school wilderness and pile in drifts on the playground. Reg Green sighed and began his Sisyphean task of sweeping them up.

A caretaker's life is never done, he told himself. Just when you've tipped the last blessed shovelful into the bin, the drains want raddling. Then the bike shed roof needs a nail, and the dratted back fence wants another coat of paint. Or all the blessed doors and gates start squeaking, and some teacher or other is kicking up a fuss over how many spiders have nipped indoors to find a lady-friend and taken up residence in their book cupboards. You deal with all that and you're right back to leaves and drains again. Never mind the polishing. Never mind stoking the boiler. Or fixing its blasted pump.

All Reg needed was the kids to pitch up now and he would be back in his usual routine. Gone would be the pottering in his vegetable garden and taking Ivy to the seaside for an ice-cream.

He glanced over at an oddly dressed woman who was bustling across the yard towards him. She was leading a fat donkey and encouraging it by clicking her tongue. Miss Winstanley, the local artist who owned the fat donkey (which had spent the Summer nibbling the greensward of the school's sports field) hailed him cheerily.

"Morning, Mr Green," she chirruped toothily. "Alright if I take Persephone home today?"

"It is. Round as a ruddy barrel, that donkey's grown this Summer. She's kep' my grass nice and tidy though, I'll say that for 'er. And provided me with some decent manure for my vegetable plot." He had grown quite fond of Persephone during her stay. Reg walked with them.

Miss Winstanley grinned. "She's the perfect manufactory," she commented. "In one end and out the other."

Mr Green nodded, not caring to pursue this indelicate topic. He opened the car park gate for Mr Denny's Rover to enter, and to let Miss Winstanley and Persephone out.

Guy drew up between a dusty MG and the librarian's new little boxy Renault runabout. Toby, the deputy head, had raised the MG's soft top against the falling leaves. Ernest Chivers' new car was parked askew, taking up far too much room. He was not yet very adept at parking. Miss Delgado's racing bicycle was in the bike rack, nice and tidy, alongside Cathy Duke's brand new shopper with its shiny little wheels. Charlie Tuttle crunched in and slotted his blue Cortina behind Guy as Reg slowly closed the gate. Toby Tremayne shouted a cheery hallo to them all as he walked up the path from school to see where the late-comers had got to.

"Am I last?" Charlie called out. "Sorry, Toby, had to drop Tim round at his friend's and the kid's mother simply wouldn't stop asking about Fiona. I've only just managed to get away."

"Not a problem, old man. We haven't started yet. How's the wife keeping?"

"Very well indeed, thanks. These last few months are a bit of a trial, but she's packed up work already, so I suppose she can get a little more rest from now on. Where are we meeting?"

They left Reg to tidy up the haphazard car parking, and strolled into the shady school, along the polished corridor and down to the gym hall. Toby flipped the latch down on the school's front door behind them. The staff didn't want to be disturbed while they gradually brought themselves back up to speed after the long Summer break.

Mrs Clark, fresh from what she described to herself as a naughty weekend away, was handing round doughnuts and fresh coffee. The classroom teachers and other staff were arranged around a set of lunch tables upon which had been placed packets of important information all neatly clipped together by Toby. The two secretaries and the cleaner were already there. Reg sidled in from the playground. No member of the Mayflower team was left out.

"Where's Jimmy today?" Jean asked her friend May.

"With Grandma Dora, bless the kind soul that she is," smiled Miss Fisher. "She's looking after Shelley too, as they get on so well together. I think Dora's planning a picnic in the garden."

"It's nice they chummed up this Summer," murmured Jean quietly. "Shelley always seemed an odd little fish to me."

May agreed. Shelley's mother, Pru, was the school cleaner and sitting only a few yards away. "I think she looks upon my Jimmy as a little brother. It's nice for him too."

Jimmy was her foster-son, taken in when his mother had been killed by a hit-and-run driver a few months ago, leaving the child an orphan. He had always caused his teachers concern, having serious health and learning problems exacerbated by neglect. However, since going to live with 'Auntie May' he had finally begun to show signs of improvement. He was making friends too.

"Did Ernest and Mike ever take him on that trip to the seaside or hasn't there been time this Summer?" asked Charlie, pulling his chair up beside May.

"They did, bless them. Well Ernest had promised, so he made sure it happened. Jimmy and I both went, in that funny new car of his with the horizontal gear-lever. It was a splendid treat for both of us."

The only little holiday I'll bet you've had in a long while, thought Charlie. Like young Jimmy, he adored May Fisher. There was something about her which always made you want to try your very best, and earn her approval. You wanted to catch her eye and please her. She reminded him of his own Auntie Gwladys. Both ladies were inveterate knitters, and the wisest old women he knew. "Is that a new pullover?" he asked. "Bit small for me, you know."

May held up the knitting. It was indeed a new piece of uniform, what they called nowadays a 'tank top', she told them. It was green with a smart yellow line around the v-neck.

"Fit your left hand, Charlie," chuckled May. "Jimmy's never had any new clothes at all, really. People have very kindly handed me down plenty of bits and pieces for him though, especially Mrs Hodges next door. She's given him wellington boots and shirts and all sorts. Other Mayflower parents have been incredibly kind too. And Chloe sent a whole parcel of dungarees and shirts from America. I can knit him things too, of course. But some items simply *have* to be bought, don't they? Like socks and underwear and so on. My heaven, aren't children's shoes expensive?"

She had bought Jimmy sandals and playshoes and slippers. He had arrived at her house with nothing May considered remotely suitable, and had required outfitting from the skin up. If it hadn't been for the donated clothes and a little extra cash provided by the children's social services May's August household budget would have been severely stretched, especially as she also had to track down particular foodstuffs for his very restricted diet. It had been a huge relief to discover Mr Singh's large delicatessen newly opened in Castle Square. It stocked almost everything on the child's dietary list.

Charlie whispered in her ear, "Don't forget. If you need a little extra money for Jim, you've only to say. Just to tide you over, you know. We're hanging on to everything Tim's outgrown too, for when he's bigger. Be a few years, but it's all stored away, ready."

She gave Charlie a look of such gratitude he had to get up and find another doughnut.

Mrs Clark rapped on the table with her teaspoon and smiled around the room.

"Well now, here we are again," she cried, happily. "Welcome back everybody. And, if you're all sitting comfortably, I'll begin. Let me start by introducing our newest recruit – Miss Bella Delgado."

Bella settles in

Her first day in her first proper job. No more teaching practice, no more essays to write. No more being watched over by anyone. She was considered competent enough to fly solo. Bella looked at her small class of six year-olds and smiled confidently. It would be harder keeping her own butterflies in check than managing these babies this morning. They looked angelic – possibly sizing her up before ripping her throat out. She was not entirely convinced.

Bella's three teaching practice periods had been spent in the west of the county, in tough schools with kids who knew she was only a green student-teacher, and had played up accordingly. She had quickly learned to yell and scowl and act the disciplinarian – and develop all the skills that had not been included on the formal curriculum at training college. She rapidly discovered that becoming a schoolteacher was the next best thing to becoming a thespian. Both jobs required you to stand confidently in front of a captive audience and project an authoritative persona. There might be no script to learn but the right words and the appropriate delivery, she found, flowed naturally once you got started. Having grasped these facts everything became much simpler, and no matter how badly the children behaved or how ill-prepared her written plans might be, she struggled successfully through – anticipating and diffusing trouble – always confidently in charge. 'Never forget,' her education tutor had joked to her once, 'that you are bigger than they are.' It was the soundest advice she had ever been given.

Mayflower's returning children all looked extremely appealing that first morning. Mrs Moore had helped Bella bring her class in from the playground and up the stairs. They hung their coats and satchels up, changed into 'indoor shoes' and shuffled off to find their names on their desks. The best seating arrangement had been discussed last week with Mrs Nesbit, who had suggested which children would work well together and who would do better apart.

"I'll leave you to it for a bit," whispered Carol Moore with a wink, knowing Miss Delgado was eager to be alone with her charges, and not under the eye of another (albeit sympathetic) adult. The children watched her leave with round eyes. Bella took a deep breath, smiled, and began.

"Now then, let's start with a song today, shall we? Mrs Nesbit tells me you know 'Twinkle, Twinkle'. Alright, stand up where you are and sing along."

The upright piano stood against the back wall, a Victorian mahogany beauty complete with polished candle-holders. How it had ever been carried up there was a mystery.

The children clattered to their feet and gave the nursery rhyme their all, letting go their pent-up anxieties, and once again beginning to feel part of their particular Mayflower group.

"You play nice, Miss" commented Matthew, after they had sat back down.

"Why thank you, Matthew. Do any of you play a musical instrument?"

"Leo does," piped up Kelly. "His mum takes him for piano lessons."

Leo grinned sheepishly.

"Now, I will call out your names from the register, and then we will go down to assembly. When we come back we will have a True Talk."

"What's that?" enquired Mungo.

"A chat about real things. I might ask you to tell about what you enjoy doing at home, and so on. And then you can ask me something. How does that sound?"

"Will we get reading books and pencils and stuff?" asked Leo after the register had been called. He didn't want school to be all talk and singing.

"Oh yes – in good time. Now then, in a minute – when I tell you – you will stand up, push your chairs in and make a line by the door. Leo, you're the leader today, and Vicky you be our sheepdog at the end of the line. Make sure our classroom door is closed properly and that everyone keeps up in a nice tidy line. Alright? Stand up."

"Shall we take hymn books, Miss?"

Bella had forgotten about those. "Yes, each take one from the box as you leave the room. Now then chairs under and line up."

Form 1 was off to a splendid start.

The old routine

Thanks to the steady work of the decorator Mr Ted Jolly, during the Summer holidays most of the interior walls of the building had received a fresh coat of white paint. Even Mrs Clark's gloomy study looked slightly less funereal than hitherto, with some beautiful William Morris willow wallpaper hung above the oak half-panelling. It complemented her heavy curtains rather beautifully. Unfortunately Jolly had drawn the line at whitewashing the wainscotting, which was what she had requested. He told her it would be a desecration, so she was still stuck with the dark oak trim, whether she liked it or not. Not to worry, she told herself, the school in general is in much better condition than last year. New flat roofs, new water-pipes, even a brand new glass roof over the Iron Duke stairwell thanks to the new academic year's budget, so hopefully no more rainy-day dribbles. She felt temporarily satisfied as she inspected her domain.

The initial two days of term were enough to re-establish classroom routines and school-wide habits. Exercise books were handed out, pencils stashed away and brown paper covers fitted to old textbooks. Names were written on inside labels, desks neatly organised. It all took time, but these were sociable activities, allowing staff and pupils a chance to get the measure of each other. The regular timetable resumed after the weekend and everyone felt as if the world of school had finally returned to its normal clockwork reliability.

The photographer turned up for his initial visit of the year.

"What ho!" called Toby Tremayne as he saw him arriving at the school gate. He knew Mr Simms quite well by now. They had had many a chat about modern cameras and lenses over a pint at the Yeoman during the Summer holidays. The bloke might be only a provincial but he knew his business, Toby thought. "Is it individual portraits today?"

"Yes, for your record cards, I believe. I must say, I've mentioned this idea to several other schools who seem to think it an excellent innovation." Mr Simms opened the boot of his car and started unloading equipment bags. Toby helped him carry them down to the gym hall.

"We were wondering whether you would have time to take a snap of our governing body today. That's if you can fit it in. They are all coming for lunch, lord help us. The lads will set the group chairs up on the stage so as not to interfere with our usual dinner tables."

"Yes, I can't see why not," said Mr Simms. "Shouldn't take long, should it?"

"We'll treat you to lunch too, of course," added Toby with a grin.

"What, mince and mash and spotted dick on a Monday morning? Thanks, but if it's all the same, I'll forego that particular gastronomic delight. All the more for your governors to guzzle, eh?"

The governors were not nearly as dismissive of their free lunch as Mr Simms. Lady Longmont and Julia Scott, the neighbourhood representatives, were often in school as they both loved to help out any class for an afternoon. Rev Bill, the vicar, turned up – as did the new parent-governor, Mr Henry Benson a local architect. He had two sons at Mayflower and was very eager to be involved in as many aspects of their school life as he could. Betty Nesbit was the teachers' representative this year alongside the headmistress. They were a knowledgeable and energetic group and Skipper felt additionally pleased that Sir Hugo Chivers would be there again to lead them forth. He had been abroad for much of the previous school year. None of these worthies turned their noses up at Ivy Green's lunch either, however modest the menu. By lunchtime they were shuffling self-consciously about in the corridor, waiting to have their picture taken and savouring the scent of lunch as it drifted on the air.

"Why don't you sit there – front and centre – Mrs Clark?" asked Mr Simms as he fussed with his camera tripod. Would they never settle?

Mrs Clark patted her greying hair and perched herself on the seat between Sir Hugo and Julia Scott. She always did her best not to appear too dowdy, but next to Sir Hugo she knew it was a contest she could never win. He was so well-groomed she always felt like a washerwoman. She folded her hands in her lap and smiled slightly.

"Ankles crossed, please, ladies in the front. Gentlemen, feet together. Now then hold still. Smile! And another – there. All done, thank you very much."

Mr Simms was tired and wanted a fourth cup of tea. Unfortunately nobody was offering him one so he packed his gear away and returned to his studio. Perhaps, he thought, I should have stayed for lunch after all. It had been a long morning and that mince smelled mighty good.

After the photo session, and just prior to lunch being served, Sir Hugo Chivers nipped upstairs to Toby Tremayne's study. It was a bright, pretty room with its white paint and yellow curtains. A couple of rugs lay on the polished wood floor beside a small fireplace. A black cat raised its head as the man entered.

"Hello, Nicky," said Sir Hugo, and soon had the cat purring.

"Ah, Hugo," said Toby, entering with an armful of exercise books and stacking them on the desk. "It's lunchtime. Are you staying?"

"No, not today – just thought I'd catch you. Shut the door a minute. We have a new special guest arriving tonight. With an escort."

"That's not typical. How come?"

"I think our American cousins want to verify our – er – transit camp is operationally secure, after all the recent ups and downs. So they've scheduled themselves to pick up the latest man at the coast and accompany him the rest of the way, via us here. Which means there will be a party of two – a defector and a minder."

Toby grunted. He had been told this might happen. It was bloody rude of the Yanks, but as they were footing most of the bills for the safe house there wasn't much to be said.

"Alright. Leaving again tomorrow, presumably? Via the airbase or the train? You know, I think I will use this as a test run to exercise my sole remaining lookout. See if she's still up to the job."

"Bicknell?"

"Mmm. See if she spots anything untoward. Are the Buntings prepared?"

"They are. Both the Lodge and Church Road houses are usable." Sir Hugo opened the door to let the cat out. "So we've a choice. You're confident her ladyship is not in a position to imperil anything?"

"I am. Since we alerted her to the fact that we know she assisted Bunting's assailant, and that the Lodge has now been refitted with surveillance, the wind seems to have gone out of her sails a bit. She dodders around her blessed garden most days, or calls in here to Mayflower. Doesn't do much else as far as I can tell. I've prevailed upon Mrs Bick to fit her into her cleaning schedule as of last week, which allows me to know what the old trout's really up to when I'm not around. Gibb hasn't set foot beyond the town all Summer, I'm pleased to say, but I still don't trust her."

Sir Hugo nodded, moderately content.

"She barely even speaks to me," added Toby.

That made Hugo smile. "We will have to find a more permanent solution for Lady Edwardia Longmont one day soon, of course. She's still more than capable of anything."

She was. Toby did not underestimate the old lady any longer. He had spent many a sleepless night stewing over MI5's missed opportunities to uncover the extent of the traitorous old woman's lifetime of spying. At the end of the Second World War his people had suspected her brother Erskine was signalling strategic information to Nazi bombers, and had been on the point of arresting him when he had saved them the trouble by hanging himself. But it had been a very poor show – and an even poorer show since, as Her Majesty's Secret Services had completely missed the fact that Erskine's sister had herself been in the pay of the enemy. In her case it was the communists rather than the Nazis, but it still spelt treachery. She had done it for decades. Their own performance had been unforgivably sloppy. And they *still* did not know exactly how she managed to collect or forward her information either. Sheer luck had brought the old spy to their attention, so they were not about to leave her without surveillance again now. Not on Toby's watch. Interrogation had yielded nothing. Sir Hugo's blackmail only made her cannier. MI5 and MI6 desperately needed to end her operation, and they could only do *that*, they decided, if they gave her some measure of freedom. For her part, Gibb Longmont knew perfectly well she was under scrutiny and redoubled her caution. She had not lasted this long without being as ingenious as an eel.

The representatives of MI5 and MI6 went downstairs together in a sombre mood.

* * *

2.

Dr Legg

"I'd like to see Jimmy Birch before any of the others, please Mrs Duke," Dr Legg told Cathy Duke.

Back to school, for the doctor, meant giving the kindergarteners their initial health check, and reviewing other, more long-term cases. Several anxious mums were already standing in the playground with their offspring, waiting to be called. Dr Legg would have a busy Wednesday morning.

"Jimmy's doing much better, don't you think? I've seen a real change since the Summer," said Cathy. She bustled about with folders and papers and the inevitable mug of tea.

"Oh yes, he's doin' pretty well. I've checked him every week of the holidays, you know," chatted Dr Legg. "He seems happy and settled, but it's still early days as far as his health is concerned. He's not out of the woods yet, Mrs Duke. How's Miss Fisher copin', do you think? It will be hard bein' back at work when they've spent every day of the vacation together."

"Peggy and I will be sure to keep an extra eye on them both, don't you worry. I'll phone the surgery if I notice anything that concerns us, shall I? I must say *we* think they both seem to be thriving on the new arrangement. Miss Fisher's not his form teacher any longer this year of course, which is probably just as well. It's been a massive sea-change for them both, this moving in together, but they honestly seem devoted to each other." Cathy smiled fondly.

"It's not the *love* I'm concerned about, Mrs Duke, it's the catchin' up, as much as anythin'. Jimmy has so much to learn – like sleepin' in a proper bed instead of on a dirty mattress on the floor, and eatin' the right foodstuffs for his stomach troubles. Takin' a bath and brushin' his hair. Doin' his teeth every day. That's a lot. Then he'll be grievin' for his poor mother and comin' to terms with her passin'. And Miss Fisher will have a ton of extra laundry and loads of extra shoppin' and cookin' and carin' to do, which we all know is hard work at the best of times. Taking on a sick child when you're a sixty-year-old spinster is no small matter, Mrs Duke, and a foster child with such difficult health concerns is a huge responsibility."

"She'll cope," said Cathy stoutly. "You'll see, Doctor. May Fisher is old school. If anyone can raise Jimmy Birch to be a healthy and well-balanced lad, May Fisher can."

Afra Legg laughed. "Well, I'm beginnin' to believe you're right, Mrs Duke. And thank you for watchin' over them. You and all the Mayflower folk. Now then, where's my little lad?"

Jimmy came in with a smile and gave her a hug. She was big and colourful and always jolly with him.

"Good mornin', Jimmy my friend," cried the doctor.

The child beamed, displaying the gap in his front teeth. Dr Legg looked surprised.

"What – another tooth gone? And the other one wobbly? I can't believe it. That will please Mr Andrewartha. Can you still drink your milk and eat your vegetables?"

"Oh yes," he lisped. "It's talking that's hard."

Jimmy knew the drill by now and removed his shirt ready for the doctor's stethoscope and gently prodding hands.

"OK. That's good. Turn around. Good. Now tell me, how's Mr Tuttle? Are you settlin' into his class?"

"He's very nice indeed, thank you," answered Jimmy, politely. "He helps me, and so does Mrs Moore. He's got snacks in his desk."

"Snacks? They had better be healthy or I'll be after him with a spoonful of my nastiest medicine! OK, put your shirt back on. I think I will have a chat with your teacher later. Are you keepin' to your no bread and biscuits rule?"

"Yes, Dr Legg."

"No cake or pastries, pies or toast?"

"Yes Dr Legg."

"Good boy. No cramps or runnin' to the toilet since last week?"

"No Dr Legg." That was what she wanted to hear, he knew.

"No wet beds?" She had a whole list of questions. "Oh my! Look at your hair growing in all curly-wurly. Are you pleased with it?"

Jimmy grinned happily. "It won't be as pretty as yours," he said, "But it's getting bushier. Auntie May bought me a proper boy's hairbrush."

This was all very satisfactory. His skin was beginning to look less wizened and more supple and healthy thanks to the cream Miss Fisher rubbed into it every morning and evening. He smelled lovely.

"Is that a new pullover I see?" Dr Legg envied May Fisher's speed with a knitting needle.

"Yep. And shorts and socks with a flash. And lace up shoes, but laces are hard."

"Put your foot up on the chair and I'll help you. There. Now – do you want to ask me anythin'?"

Dr Legg did not usually say this, so Jimmy had a bit of a think.

"Why did Mrs Bicknell give me a picture of my mum?"

That took Afra aback for a moment. "Well now, I heard she found it when she was turnin' out your old home. Cleanin' the place up ready for the new tenants, you know. She thought you might like it."

"I do," answered Jimmy. It was the only image he had of Janey, and while he knew who it depicted, it wasn't how he remembered his mother at all. It was a photo of a girl sitting by a river. "Auntie May and I put it in a frame on the wall of my bedroom."

"Good. I think it is nice to have a photo of your mum. Now then, you had better scoot away as I have a million mums out there waitin' to come in. Alright now Jimmy, bye!"

He smiled his toothless grin one more time. "Bye, Dr Legg."

Dental check

"Who's *that*?" asked the dentist, always one with an eye for a pretty girl. This one was particularly beautiful.

Peggy, the no-nonsense school secretary, gave him a sideways look. "Miss Delgado. New first form teacher. Hands off."

"She's got good teeth," went on Mr Andrewartha. "Nice and even."

Peggy snorted. She ushered him down the corridor into the hall where Reg was setting up the screens and chairs for the school-wide dental inspection. Mrs Duke already sat at a table with a pen and a pile of pre-printed cards and letters to hand out if the dentist decided an individual needed to make a proper appointment at his surgery. It always surprised him how many children had never been seen by a family dentist. He picked up quite a few new customers during these annual screening exercises.

Miss Lomax, his dental assistant, was setting out his instruments. It was a pity she was fair, fat and forty, he thought. He would have preferred someone like Miss Delgado to make the morning go with a swing. Mr Andrewartha sighed.

"How's the family?" asked Peggy, pointedly. The dentist had four children.

"Oh fine thanks. Crispin and Neil are trying out for the rugby team this term and Tracey's in love with her science teacher. Cherry's on the junior hockey side."

"And your wife?"

"Stella's fine too, thank you. Still working in the office up at the quarry." The dentist struggled into his white coat and rinsed his hands in the bowl of water on the table.

"She's been there a while," commented Peggy conversationally.

"Yeah. Still, it helps pay the bills. Now then, am I starting with the tinies?"

Mrs Bailey beckoned Trevor Black over to her side. He was a newly promoted Form 6 prefect.

"Trevor – over to you. Mr Andrewartha is ready to begin. Bring your line in and stand them here. You know the drill."

Trevor did. His dad was a policeman so he knew everything about crowd control. "Yes, Mrs Bailey. Now, then you lot. Line up here along that line, and face front. I'll tell you when to go and sit in the dentist's chair, OK?"

Peggy smiled and left him to it. It looked like Trevor had everything nicely in hand.

Dean and Jimmy break in

Jimmy Birch and Dean Underwood were looking for mushrooms in St Andrew's churchyard.

Jimmy avoided the secluded area where his mother's ashes were interred. It was not a place he cared to visit. The vicar had put Janey there, the boy knew, where she would be safe and out of pain. She was asleep, they told him, and he remembered it had always been best not to disturb his mum when she was asleep. So Jimmy kept away and tried not to think about her too often. Whenever he did, the guilty feeling wormed back into his heart. The gnawing anxiety of those years rose up like water, and with them came the griping pain in his belly. As an infant he had waited hours and hours for Janey to come home at night. After school he had filled the long vacant hours hiking the local heaths and commons, trying to stave off fear, hunger, pain and loneliness, avoiding other people. Avoiding returning to the cold and empty little house in Wag Lane until night fell. Those times had been horrible, he now realised. The strange thing was that since Janey's life had ended, his own had somehow re-started – and was proceeding in an entirely different direction. Since he had been taken in by Miss Fisher, his life had turned right around. He was finally growing stronger. He was safe. He was clean. He had a real bed. He didn't need to walk and walk and walk. He missed the presence of his mother, but not that old, scary life. And he was very grateful that things had changed, but – it was all so *new*. He was not sure he entirely trusted it. So he focused on the future and tried not to walk where ghosts might lurk.

Dean Underwood did not want to go back to yesterday either. He was a graceful child of ten who, like Jimmy, had known a hard previous existence. His early years had been spent in Hoxton with his mother and sister, where life had been a constant struggle to stay out of harm's way. Living conditions had been poor, school had been rough. Now, however, the three of them lived in Ironwell village and were thriving. Mum and Iris had decent jobs, they had a neat little house, and life had become safe, comfortable and predictable. School and his friends meant the world to Dean, and playing outdoors in the local countryside his idea of heaven. It had taken a while, but he had learned to relax. He could now read and write properly, and even speak a little French. He could work sums as well as anyone else his age. This Summer he and his buddy Ryan had swum in the local river and climbed trees to their hearts' content, only now that Autumn had arrived Ryan was at secondary school in Portland, which meant Dean had only funny little Jim Birch or Joe Latimer to roam about with. Today it was Jimmy's turn.

The churchyard was leafy and damp, just the place for a few large field mushrooms, the boys thought. Only they couldn't find any.

"You allowed mushrooms then?" asked Dean.

"Yep. We have 'em for breakfast sometimes. Auntie May lets me do some of the cooking."

"You wanna be a chef?"

Jimmy laughed. That was a thought. "No, I want to be a gardener, like Terry and Olly and Mr Green."

That surprised Dean. "Do yer? Well, that 'lotment of yours at school has got a brilliant load of veggies. Better than mine. I s'pose you been diggin' muck in." Dean knew all about the benefits of good fertilisers. Gardening was an important part of Mayflower's curriculum.

"Yeah, I borrowed Mrs Hewitt's little shopping cart on wheels and collected a 50p bag of horse poo from the stables."

Dean grinned. "I hope you washed it out proper when you took it back," he said. His teacher had been known to wax a little particular when it came to lending and borrowing. "She'd go nuclear if it come back mucky. Maybe we could borrow it again and sell the shit to the kids at school. 10p an 'alf bag. That should be enough for each plot." Dean's entrepreneurial mind was already counting the profit.

They continued happily poking about in the long grass at the back of some forgotten gravestones. This western side of the church was tidier than the rest. Near the war memorial some large flat-topped tombs stood in rows like so many dining tables. The stones absorbed the sun's heat, so the two boys lay belly-down on top of a couple, and peered through the shrubs and shadows towards Longmont Lodge on the opposite side of the main road. The old place loomed large and as impressive as an ocean liner behind its fences and hedges, with multiple jettied storeys and a faux Elizabethan facade peeping through the pines and yews.

A bus eased away from the bus stop on its way down the hill into town. As it moved off, the boys noticed Lady Longmont standing quite still in the shadows. She obviously had a key to the wicket that was set into one of the lodge's double wooden gates, because as they watched she glanced furtively around then nipped through and closed it with a loud click behind her.

"Is that.. ?"

"Yeah. I wonder what she's doing. Come on, let's play spies," suggested Dean. They stood up, slid easily past the churchyard's iron fence rails, and ran across the road into the weedy undergrowth.

"There's a way in just behind here," Jimmy informed his friend in a whisper. He slithered around some bushes and pushed aside a loose plank in the Lodge's otherwise strong oak palisade. They wriggled through just in time to see Lady Longmont unlocking the big front door.

"She's got keys," said Dean in astonishment. "I wonder why."

"Sh!" whispered Jimmy. "Maybe she stole them. Let's go round the back. I know a place we can see inside."

They wormed their way past elder and holly, yew and brambles, around to the edge of the stable-yard at the rear. It was quiet. The back door to the house at the top of the area steps was closed. Climbing on some kind of log store behind a huge and rampant rose bush, the boys crouched listening at one of the kitchen windows. Jimmy fidgeted the lower half of the sash window from side to side, then tried to push it upwards. It was too heavy for him, so Dean helped. They dropped silently inside onto the tiled floor. The sash jammed when they tried to pull it down, so they left it.

Creeping forwards across the empty room, Jimmy pointed to the ceiling. Up there, he mouthed. They could hear voices in a distant room, talking urgently. The miniature spies crept stealthily through the house, up a once-grand staircase, and down a corridor towards the voices. Dean indicated a small side room, into which they slid and crouched down again in the shadows.

"It's a man," whispered Dean. "Why's Lady Longmont in here with him?"

"Might be love. People sneak about when they're in love," Jimmy informed him.

Dean agreed. Grown-ups thought that kind of carry-on was exciting. "Can you hear them kissing?"

Jimmy shook his head. Maybe there was a hole in the wall they could look through. He searched about but there was no crack or hole or opening into the next room, so the boys sat and tried to figure out what was being said. It didn't sound like kissing. The conversation seemed to be about the time somebody else might be arriving. Lady Longmont's voice was bossy and the man sounded cross.

"It can't be helped," the man said clearly. "They'll just have to pick him up on the other side." He was walking up and down, the boys could hear his footsteps on the boards and then on the rug. Lady Longmont spoke so indistinctly they could not really make out her side of the conversation.

"When?" asked the man, and there came another long mumbled reply.

Without warning the boys heard the speakers' footsteps heading back along the corridor as the two left. The meeting was obviously over.

"Well that was boring," whispered Dean. "No snogging or anything. Maybe they've broken up."

"I need the toilet," whined Jimmy.

They waited five minutes after they heard the sound of the front door closing, then they went in search of a working lavatory.

Dean reports

"So you broke in?"

"Yes, Sir," admitted Dean. "I suppose."

"And the man was already there, was he? Which room were they having their meeting in?"

"Like an upstairs sitting room, I think. We were listening next door in a little bedroom. I could show you." Dean was eager to assure Mr Tremayne of the veracity of his report.

"Yes, later. Tell me what was said."

Dean explained the muffled conversation and the words he remembered. "It can't be helped. They'll just have to pick him up on the other side," he repeated. He wished now he had listened harder. He did not mention any snogging.

"Alright, old son. Anything else? No? Well, see me again at lunchtime, please. We'll take a little walk over to the lodge and see where this all happened, shall we?" Mr Tremayne dismissed his informant and sat thinking for five minutes.

Reg Green poked his head round the door.

"Morning, Sir."

"Going to need the keys to the lodge after lunch, Mr Green. I'd like you and the dog to come with me for a little snoop about, if you'd be so kind."

"Aye-aye, Sir." Reg did not like the tone of this directive. "Trouble?"

"Could be, Mr Green, could be. Or it could be the beginning of a turn-around in our fortunes, I'm not sure. Security devices are functioning properly over there, aren't they? Right, that's what I thought. We'll collect yesterday's footage. That's all."

"Very good, Sir," answered Reg.

Yes, thought Toby Tremayne, as he lifted Nicky off his desk and onto the easy chair. This might just be very good indeed.

Expedition to Ironwell

"It's OK, I've got it," said Tim Tuttle. He gripped the canoe tightly as Jimmy climbed into the front and sat down. It was a hard seat and his little bottom was bony. Tim handed him a double-ended paddle and clambered in himself, pushing them away from the bank with one foot just as his dad had shown him. It was easy when you knew how.

"OK, now, one side then the other, like we practised. Great. That's it!" Tim was pleased his small chum had listened and was doing as instructed. "Look, there's a heron!"

Jimmy was too busy concentrating on the paddle to appreciate the heron, but he soon got the hang of it. Left, right, it wasn't so hard. "This is fun," he cried.

Tim smiled to himself. Having Jimmy around was like having a little brother, or a younger version of himself, to play with. He was feeling less miffed about his family expecting a new baby in

November now Jim was around. The kid might be a bit on the weird side but he had grit.

Tim knew Auntie May was glad he had taken her new foster son under his wing this Summer. Miss Fisher was far too old to be having a young kid to look after, in Tim's opinion. She had to be sixty or something at least. Although she *was* kind, and had been very decent to his own mum and dad. Jimmy was OK too, once you bothered with him. And he idolised Tim, which was very flattering.

"Head left," suggested Tim. They turned upstream around Cat Island, and paddled briskly into the deeper waters of Mint Pool from where they could see the back of the pub with its stable blocks. The buildings were quiet and all swept out at this time of year as the horses were all pastured in Hendy's Fields eating their heads off. Mr Unwin, the pub landlord, was rolling a barrel of beer across the yard to his cellar and waved a greeting.

"If we get as far as the mill, we could call on Miss Winstanley," said Jimmy over his shoulder.

"Yeah, good idea. And her donkey with a hat. What's it called again?"

"Persephone." It was an odd name but one that stuck in Jim's mind.

They worked their way steadily forward against the stream as the Wain chuckled over the sand and gravel of its bed like sparkling white wine. Lazy trout and shimmering minnows played and fed in the dappled shade of the overhanging sedges and green willows. It was very peaceful. To their left lay Ironwell Eye, a large, boggy islet that curved like a whale. Banford Heath was to the right, with its acres and acres of open rough land.

Jimmy knew the local countryside very well but was entranced by this new view of it. The sun beat on his left shoulder and was turning his skinny arms brown. He wanted to grow strong and fearless like Tim, and was doing his best to exercise and grow taller. Miss Fisher measured him each month against the kitchen door, and already he had put on a quarter of an inch. His weight graph was also slowly beginning to climb thanks to his new diet, and his belly had deflated to a more normal measurement. Dr Legg was very pleased with him, and he was pleased with himself. At least his hair was finally thickening up even if it was coming in an ordinary curly brown, not crinkly yellow like Tim and his dad's. Jimmy supposed you couldn't expect everything.

"Hey, there's the mill!" he cried.

They paddled on in steady harmony, both boys feeling glad to be alive on this beautiful morning. The cold water slid under them like green silk as it narrowed, and the current grew stronger as they nudged against the old stone dock beside the ancient huge waterwheel. This was firmly chained in a deep pool and had obviously not moved for years. Thick green moss padded its ancient interlocking timbers. Ferns sprouted over the fathomless mill-pool underneath the wheel.

Persephone ambled over to the fence inquisitively, her jaunty felt hat askew. She pushed her head down and hee-hawed at them in welcome.

"Oh I say, visitors!" cried Miss Winstanley, suddenly appearing from her veg patch where she had been plucking spinach. "Ahoy there, sailor boys! Are you coming ashore?"

"Hello, Miss Winstanley! Yes, please," shouted Tim. "We came on a visit. Is it OK?"

"Of course, permission to come aboard any time," grinned Fay Winstanley toothily. She liked the local children who often brought her donkey a tasty treat. "It's Jimmy and Tim isn't it?"

"Yes Miss, Jim 'n' Tim!" laughed Jimmy. "From the good ship Mayflower."

"I remember. One little, one big."

"I'm actually at secondary school in Portland," Tim informed her, seriously. "I'm teaching Jimmy to paddle our canoe today."

"Looks wonderful fun," commented Fay, rather enviously. "This river's perfect for it, I should think."

The boys stood grinning at her while Persephone filched most of the spinach from Miss Winstanley's basket.

"Well come on – there's buttered muffins if you want, and a drink of lemonade."

The boys followed her into the immense and dark kitchen which had apparently not changed very much since the days of George III.

"Jim can't have muffins. Or anything with flour in," Tim explained. Jimmy smiled, sheepishly. It was embarrassing always having to apologise.

"Oh? Well that's a surprise. Allergy sort of thing is it?" Miss Winstanley splashed lemon into a jug and filled it up with water. "I've got… What have I got? I've some biscuits – no, they won't work. I have some popcorn. Do you like popcorn?"

Jimmy had no idea, as popcorn was not something he had encountered before. "Yes please," he said.

It turned out to be delicious. Miss Winstanley had two bags of it, one salty, one sweet. They sat outside by the river, listening to it gurgle over the mill's sluice gate and pour down into the race, as they munched and talked.

"There's a pike down there," said Fay, pointing at the ferny pool. "I don't know what it lives on but it's been there a while. Years probably. You could come and try to fish for it if you want."

Tim's eyes lit up. "Yes please, I'd love that. My dad taught me to fish this Summer. I could teach Jim."

Jimmy gazed at him with more hero worship. It made Fay smile.

"Haven't I seen you roaming about the heath sometimes?" she asked.

He nodded. "I expect," he said. "I used to walk about, but now I play with Tim or one of the others. D'you like cabbages?" Jimmy had spotted a long weedy line of cabbages in Miss Winstanley's garden. "I could help you with those."

He jumped up and started pulling out stray grass and feeling for dandelion roots. "You should keep the plants opened up so the fresh air can get in," he said. "Them carrots too."

Miss Winstanley and Tim sat and watched fascinated as Jimmy worked his way swiftly along the line of vegetables yanking out tufts of weeds. At the end of the line of carrots he straightened up and squinted towards the shimmering heath beyond the garden. It was hard to see where one stopped and the other began.

"Well, I can't thank you enough," said Miss Winstanley gratefully. "You come over anytime you feel like a little extra weeding or fishing practice. Both of you. Well, I suppose I had better get on. Goodbye to you!"

"Goodbye Miss, and thanks," said Tim. He held the canoe steady so Jimmy could clamber in. "We'd better go home, mate. Here, wash your hands in the river a bit. I don't want that paddle all muddy now, do I?"

Nature trails

Mrs Clark often recharged her inner self by walking in the tangled scrub and shrubs beneath the towering trees of the school's extensive wilderness acreage. It was very peaceful there. It was different, separate. It helped put her problems into perspective.

Much of the vegetation had overflowed from the once-manicured gardens of Longmont Lodge, the former residence of the school's founder. The grounds had taken a bomb-hit during the war, and as a result had been locked up and left to their own devices ever since. Decades had passed. The place dwelt undisturbed – blossoming, seeding, renewing itself year upon year. Spreading, thickening. Neighbours mostly ignored the monstrous tangle and Mayflower's schoolchildren merely fluttered around its margins, so it remained mostly an unregulated, isolated, magical place – a wild place in the heart of civilisation. A place in which to dream.

Such an important part of my school ought not to be so inaccessible in this day and age, thought Skipper, not for the first time. I love it, but I must tame some more of it for the benefit of Mayflower in general. We must be seen to be using it more, or the council will requisition it for building or something worse.

She sat under one of the redwoods on a fallen branch in the shade. The nearer parts of the original garden were usable, but the jungly acres further from the Lodge were only rarely seen. Her dreams began to ramble like the weeds, so she rose and traipsed through the long grass and around thickets of yellow-leaved saplings, copses of brushwood, and spinneys of rampant red-gold shrubs, forcing her mind to focus back onto practicalities.

And as she stepped over a particularly wayward briar, the perfect solution suddenly occurred to her. Pathways. Simple, rough pathways. Extend the rough trackways from the peripheral parts and simply leave the rest to its own devices.

How will we do it? she wondered. More importantly, *who* will do it? Reg and Terry can't manage everything. She would ask Toby. He always had bright ideas. A fleeting vision of Peggy Bailey wagging a finger at her, swam briefly across her mind. Funding, the vision was saying. What would paths cost?

Not a red cent, Skipper crowed triumphantly. I'll use what we already have. Surely Reg can *mow* the trails, it shouldn't take long.

Then people could be walking through here this Autumn and enjoying the natural world.

Mrs Clark turned and hurried back to the top of the little hillock known as the Knoll. From there she could look north, south, east and west to Mayflower's perimeter. In dazzling technicolour she now imagined freshly mown trails winding this way and that through her beloved jungle, linking together groups of happy little children who sat and drew, or penned amazing poetry, or who simply lay back and watched the sky through the leaves above.

That is all I want, thought Mrs Clark, swelling with omnipotent religiosity. She flung out her arms. I want this *enrichment*. Come Nature! Come *Real* Education! A tear rose in her eye as she swung round in a circle. I want this – *all* of it – to stay safe. My world is here. I have been given charge of it and I will not fail. She clasped her hands in fervour and gazed at her world.

If only Chloe had still been there. How she would have loved it.

Mrs Clark sighed and came back down to earth. It wasn't a bad idea. It ought to be achievable. After all, if May Fisher and Chloe Shaw could jump off the edge of their worlds into the unknown, so could Skipper Clark.

Junior spies

Nicky, the school cat, rubbed against Dean Underwood's legs. The boy bent down to pick him up. Nicky purred and rubbed his head against Dean's ear in a friendly welcome, then spotted Stringer trotting along the path and struggled to be let free. The child watched the pair trot off together on some nefarious business of their own, and – as no one could see him – waved goodbye.

"Hey," cried Joey Latimer, running up. "Wanna go play cowboys?"

"OK," shrugged Dean, happily.

He much preferred to be the native scout when they played cowboys, sneaking through the undergrowth and tracking bandits. Joey was happier shooting toy cap-guns and cracking homemade bullwhips. Dean played along with Joe though, wondering idly whether his own surname might have influenced his role preference.

The lads clambered over the school railings behind Mr Green's vegetable garden into one of the knottier parts of the wilderness. The smell of damp earth greeted them as they crouched down and forced a difficult path through the lethally healthy stinging nettles and nasty brambles. It was slow going but they eventually came out onto a faint track, probably made by some kind of animal.

"Cor, them brambles hurt," said Joey, licking blood off his arm.

"Sure do. This way, Marshal Dillon. The settlers' stolen beeves may be watering down by yonder river. You might-could-maybe shoot the rustlers from the tree above."

The two intrepid trackers continued cautiously picking their way northwards, deeper into the tangled mass of soggy foliage. They found they were quite close to the perimeter wall that ran along Fen Lane. Several large old ash trees grew here in a straggling line, dipping and swaying in today's breeze. Halfway up one of them sat Jimmy Birch. His attention was on a terraced house across the lane.

"Hey, Jim!" called Dean. He and Joey clambered up to where Jimmy was perched in a fork. "What you watching?"

Jimmy smiled at them. "Just my house. I live there now," he reminded them.

"Why you watching your own home?" asked Joey, mystified.

"You looking to see what Miss Fisher's doing?" asked Dean, also trying to make sense of it.

"Yeah. I used to climb up here before, when I didn't live there. Just to see if she was OK." It was hard explaining, and Jimmy's words were jerky. Even to him his spying behaviour sounded a little odd. "I used to see she'd be home alright after school. Be safe. Sometimes she put the milk bottles out."

"Right," nodded his friends, rapidly losing interest. "So d'you want to come and play with us?"

"OK. Where are you going?"

"Over the common, probably. We're following some evil rustlers. They've stole some cattle and I'm tracking them with Marshal Dillon. We're hot on the trail." Dean looked up into the old grey ash with its multitude of smooth inviting branches. "This is a great climbing tree."

Jimmy hopped down. He wasn't sure he wanted anyone else playing in this tree. It was his. It was his special watching place. Somewhere he could watch and think. It was private.

The three returned to the rudimentary track and ploughed on. It was tough going, but eventually the party emerged at the old well house. They helped each other over the wall and the fence, and brushed themselves down as they finally stood on the public footpath beside the road. The cattle rustlers had temporarily vanished into the wide blue yonder, so they trudged along Well Road to the railway station.

"Morning, boys," called a familiar voice. Mr Tremayne came striding up from the station towards them on his way to Sir Hugo's house. "How's my Observer Corps doing today? Anything to report Captain Underwood?"

Dean grinned. "No Sir. We're tracking rustlers today."

"Rustlers is it? I expect they're up river somewhere." He saw Jimmy was with his local lookout boys today. The small child seemed an unlikely chum for these two. "So, is Jim a new recruit for our little secret team, d'you think?"

Joey nodded happily. "Jim would be really reliable. He goes everywhere and no one ever notices him, you'd be surprised." He turned to Jimmy and explained. "Mr Tremayne has a secret undercover spying organisation going on, and I'm in it. Wanna join?"

"Well, you *are* it," Toby added, for clarity. "Would you like to be part of it too, young Jimmy? Like Dean and Joey? Just come and let me know what's happening around the place, especially anything unusual or unexpected. Comings and goings. I'll slip you a little pocket money from time to time if you agree. There's no need to tell anyone else, though."

Jimmy nodded. That would be fun. He was a good watcher. "Like strangers arriving?" he asked.

"Yes, like that," answered Toby. Hopefully the boy was brighter than he appeared. "I'm glad I've bumped into you, Dean," he went on. "I'd like you to keep an eye on a particular person for me from now on, if you would. Extra special assignment. The lady's old and might not be up to very much, but you never know. I want her specially watched."

"OK," said Dean.

"You remember Lady Longmont?"

"You live with her," answered Dean. "Yeah, we know her. She comes up to school."

"Yes, she used to be a governor. I'd like you to tell me where-ever she goes, and whatever she does. Report as often as you can. When she's out and about, who she visits, who calls on her – that sort of thing. Like you did the other day when she went to the lodge. Think you could?"

"Oh yes," answered the boys. That would be pretty easy.

"Right then, super. OK, I'll let you get on and catch those pesky beef rustlers. See you in school."

"Bye, Sir."

The boys skipped off down the road towards their Latimer Street turning. When they reached it Dean turned to the others.

"I think the rustlers might have left the river and gone up over the mountains to Hendy's. That's right up Dutch Lane by Banford Place."

"Where Lady Longmont lives. Yes," said Joe. "I suggest we go that way, men. OK Jim?"

"OK," said Jimmy. This was fun. No doubt they would have a peep over the wall and see what Lady Longmont was doing. It was great being one of the team.

* * *

3.

Ballbarrow

Toby and Bella

Toby Tremayne had just finished compiling his latest crossword puzzle and was sealing it into its envelope, when Bella put her head round his study door.

"Sorry to bother you," she said. "Is there a film-strip projector anywhere? My library box arrived and there's a rather antiquated film-strip on seabirds included. Hardly cinemascope, but there we are."

"I believe so," he answered. "Probably up in that little media storage room in the attic. Shall we go and take a look?"

The room was stuffed with out-of-date items, from boxes of foolscap paper to deflated leather footballs. There were typewriter ribbons, and dried-up poster paints, and even a stack of lacrosse sticks. Various large mechanical items stood higgledy-piggledy under the window – a sewing machine, an epidiascope and a film-strip projector.

"There!" cried Toby in triumph. "A magic lantern, just as you wanted."

Bella giggled. "It's not *that* bad."

"Yes it is. Who on earth would keep all this old junk?"

"Mr Denny's always going on about wanting a new copy machine. Maybe we could sell off this clutter and buy him one. I must admit a new copier would be a really useful additional piece of technology," said Bella blowing dust off the projector and picking it up.

"Here, let me. Good lord, look at that spider. Yeah, we'll have to see if we can't prise some loot out of Skipper's tight little fist for a replacement for that old Banda one day soon, it seems to be permanently on its last legs. Can you get the door?"

Toby took the projector from her, and they slowly descended to the ground floor. They plugged the thing into a socket in the hall and fussed about with the pull-down screen until they were satisfied with the first dim, wobbly picture of some puffins.

"It might need a better bulb. I wonder if Reg has one in his Aladdin's cave," said Toby vaguely.

"It could just be dust. I don't think anyone has cleaned this lens for decades."

"Oh, I bet they have you know. We don't have the most up-to-date technology here at the old Flower-of-May, but this baby was built to last." Toby tapped the projector setting its dim bulb flickering. It suddenly produced a full strong beam, much to their delight. "See? A little encouragement was all that's needed."

They were laughing together, and Toby was brushing cobwebs off Bella's hair, when Skip hurried into the hall.

"Oh, sorry," she said automatically, surprised and embarrassed. "I...er..." She grew annoyed and not a little confused.

Toby instantly sized up her reaction correctly. "Bella's turning into a witch. Spiders in her hair. Is this the only slide projector there is?"

Mrs Clark pulled herself together. Don't be a fool, she told herself. He's not interested in her – or you. Bella's young and attractive after all. Why shouldn't he brush her hair back?

Bella belatedly caught the mood.

"Thank you for your help, Mr Tremayne," she said. "I'm going to take a quick look through this film strip to get some idea of its content. Might I store the projector in one of these cupboards until Tuesday's lesson, Mrs Clark?"

Skipper couldn't quite smile, but she adjusted her tone with some success.

"Yes, of course. The one with the second hand uniform rail in it has a little space, I believe. But don't move the projector until that bulb's cooled down a bit, or it will explode." She avoided Toby's eye and yanked open one of the hall cupboards. "Yes, there, look. It can stand on that chair. OK?"

"Thank you," said Bella. She was irritated with them both.

"We'll let you get on with your puffins, then," nodded Toby affably, and left the hall closely followed by Skipper. He was amused that Skip could think him a bit of a dog, and walked with a swagger.

Bella stood for a while, looking through the filmstrip and feeling crosser and crosser. Toby was nice, he was kind, but she had no intention of encouraging anyone's romantic attention, if romantic attention was what he had been angling for. She had had quite enough of all that nonsense in college with Crispin.

Crispin had fallen for her hook line and sinker, and she had been only too happy to indulge him, despite his reputation. She realised her friends knew she was having an affair with an older man, a married lecturer, but she had cared little for their opinions at the time. She had been bowled over with what she imagined was love, flattered by his physical affection, and thrilled with the sexy adventure of it all. Illicit meetings, afternoons in distant hotels, telling lies to her parents, using her innocent friends as alibis. Lying to the doctor in order to be permitted the contraceptive pill. It wasn't until her final term, when Crispin showed her his divorce papers and was all for taking her to live in Australia that she eventually came to her senses. Her mother was dying in hospital, and her father was falling to pieces as a consequence. Bella had to start earning a living, and she had to grow up. Crispin was told their affaire was over – the hardest conversation of her life. He took it quite well, Bella thought, merely slamming the door and completely breaking the front gate on the way out. She had been relieved to see him go, although he never repaid the money he had borrowed from her, nor wrote a single letter. He never contacted her again. No, there was no room for any more romantic adventures on Bella's agenda. Certainly not a man of Toby's vintage. She had had more than enough romance to last a lifetime.

'The telephone engineer is here,' said Skip to Toby as they walked back to her study. "I came to tell you. How am I managing the payment for this new line?"

"Up front, if you don't mind. Then I'll deal with the reimbursement, once it's in. Is that OK?"

"Yes, that's what I thought. Fine. I sent him upstairs. Are you still coming round to White Cottage for supper later?"

"Oh yes, if that's OK. Thanks," said Toby, and hurried upstairs to find the engineer. What annoying things women were, sometimes, he thought. Jumping to conclusions. Making you feel guilty. Making something out of nothing at all.

Mrs Clark sat down at her desk and pulled her record book towards her. Calm down, she told herself. I don't have dibs on Toby Tremayne or on anybody else come to that. Hugo and I had a very nice time in Yorkshire this Summer, and Toby is my work colleague, my long-lost could-have-been brother. I'm being foolish. Keep life simple, she told herself firmly.

Joe and Elaine

"Have you seen page six?" asked Dora.

Skipper Clark was poring over the local paper at the dining room table. There was a half-page article and a huge photograph of the wedding of their former school doctor Joe Granger to Elaine, one of the nurses from the cottage hospital, on page six.

"I'm so glad the weather was kind for them," Dora went on, setting down the tea tray and picking up Nicky who was sitting four-square on the table waiting for his supper.

"Honeymoon in Spain, it says here. That's nice." Mrs Clark had once harboured romantic thoughts about Joe Granger. Now she was simply happy that he was happy. Elaine can have him, she thought magnanimously.

Dora sat and sipped her tea. "When was it? Why didn't he invite us?"

"Last Saturday. Well, he can't ask all his patients can he?"

"No, but I'd have thought… Oh well, never mind. Anything else in the news?"

"No. Some people found some more of that old parachute silk buried over near the Greyfriars ruins. Funny thing to bury if you ask me. There's talk of a golfing concern looking to buy the manor."

"Really? All that farmland would make quite a good golf course, I suppose. Probably about three golf courses. It's awfully big."

"I'd have thought they would want some of it kept as fields though, wouldn't you? It's very productive."

"I'm glad those pigsties are gone," said Dora, firmly. "They were jolly smelly."

Skipper was less delighted about that. She had had to make a new arrangement with a contractor six miles away this year in order to get rid of weekly scraps from the school's kitchens. This company was a whole lot less accommodating than Len Kirk at Abbey Farm had been. Mrs Clark decided to call the council next week and see what additional arrangements they might suggest for food waste collection. Why was everything so complicated nowadays?

"It's a nice photo of the happy couple, look. Mr Simms took it," said Skip, reverting back to the newspaper nuptials. Dora thought Elaine could not have looked prettier or more thrilled. Her smile was that of a lottery winner.

"Well, I must get on," said Skip, standing up. "I said I'd go and help June sort jumble for an hour. She'll be wondering where I am. See you later, Mum."

Kay is fed up

Mrs Clark hurried down the lane. It was a lovely evening. The Autumn sun slanted across the Donkey Field and the air was full of drifting seeds. Conkers littered the footpath by the railings and crisp leaves scrunched under her feet. One of her little girls from Form 5 was staring up into the tall chestnuts, obviously intent on lobbing the short piece of dead branch she held in her hand high enough to knock down a fresh, fat, spiky green seedcase.

"Hello, Kay," said the headmistress.

"Oh, hello, Mrs Clark."

"I'd really rather you didn't throw things up into the trees, if you don't mind. Just wait for the ripe ones to fall. You can badly damage the twigs and frighten the birds by throwing things."

Kay scowled and dropped the piece of branch. How come Mrs Clark was patrolling the grounds on a Saturday evening? Telling her off. It wasn't school time.

"I'm on my way to help Mrs Williams sort some jumble for the Church Bazaar. Have you had a good day?"

"Yes, thank you," mumbled Kay. She hadn't. It had been a day of shouting and pouting and being ticked off – which was why she was out and about on her own.

"Here." Mrs Clark felt in her pocket for a particularly large conker she had picked up the day before. She handed it to the girl. "You can have this one of you like. Well, I must be going. Bye-bye."

Kay looked at the massive conker. It really was a whopper and would probably, with the right amount of careful hardening, prove to be a champion.

"Thanks," she called at Mrs Clark's back. The headmistress waved and turned the corner.

Kay went the opposite way and scuffed along the road on her way home, throwing the conker up in the air and catching it as she went. It was a long walk, but she didn't care. They would all be worried about where she was, which would serve them darn well right.

When she finally reached St Mary's churchyard in her own village of Weston, she made a detour under its cool yew trees and dropped the enormous conker down a hole between the snaking roots. There. That took care of that. Planting a living tree was better than creating another weapon of war, wasn't it?

Skipper ploughs on

Mrs Clark smiled confidently to herself. Oh Hugo, she thought in her usual he-loves-me, he-loves-me-not way. You'll be proud of me yet. She was pleased to have made some kind of contact with the awkward Kay Fordam. Perhaps she was turning out to be a good headmistress after all. She liked to think she had a bit of a knack when it came to children. Men too. Maybe she would bump into Hugo this evening. That would make a pleasant end to a productive day. Hugo liked chatting to the Rev Bill, who was a feet-on-the-ground sort of chap, unlike the curate, Theo Wichelow. Skip hadn't seen Hugo for weeks. She could tell him about the grumpy girl and the conker.

June Williams was unfortunately alone in the church hall. No sign of any other helpers at all. There were seven large cardboard boxes of donated jumble lined up on some tables and she was lobbing clothing, item by item, into what appeared to be an old paddling pool several feet away.

"Oh thank goodness! You're manna from heaven," she cried when she saw Skipper. "Could you start pricing up the adult stuff for me? I thought the kids' could be 1p an item, what do you think? Not school uniform, obviously. That will have to be done separately, but well… "

"Hi June. Yes, I'll do that. Is anyone else coming?" Skip cast about the empty room as if expecting a rush of volunteers to materialise.

"No. Ivy couldn't make it. Peg's gone out to dinner, if you please, at the Fox in Portland. Theo and Bill are missing in action – probably busy bee-keeping or just keeping busy and out of hailing distance. Mrs Bicknell and Miss Muggeridge have done an hour of sterling work this afternoon. Mrs Pelham and Mrs Evans seem to have completely forgotten, so it's just you and me. Can you spare this hour? Oh, you are a star."

"Any sign of Sir Hugo?" asked Skipper, as she expertly sorted and priced. "Are these to go over there? Right. We haven't seen him in school yet this term."

June raised her eyebrows, her back turned to Mrs Clark. Why was she asking *her*? The whole town knew the headmistress and Hugo Chivers had been away on holiday together in the Summer. Surely *she* ought to know where he was.

"No," she answered. "Doesn't Ernest have any idea?"

"He never knows anything, poor lamb. Even less now he and Mike live all that way out in the boondocks."

"Boondocks? Oh, you mean out in the sticks. Caster Cottage *is* quite a way out there, isn't it?" Maybe the subject of Hugo could be skirted around.

"I thought you might have seen his porch light on or something," said Skipper hopefully. The vicarage was almost opposite Garratt's Hall after all.

Oh my goodness, thought June in dismay. The woman's obviously quite besotted. With Hugo *Chivers*. I hoped all that silly romantic nonsense was a nine day wonder. You expect a little interest when a new person moves in, but that usually fizzles out pretty fast. Skipper can't honestly have a genuine thing for him, can she? She'll learn a nasty lesson if she does.

June sighed and continued with her task. It was a thankless role, that of the vicar's wife. There was the Mothers' Union, Sunday Schools, Jumble Sales, Coffee Mornings, fund-raising, charity events, parish visiting. You name it, June organised it.

Except, she added gratefully, *except* deciding who received one of Cupid's random arrows. That they can all deal with quite well for themselves.

The manor estate

"Have you heard?" Peggy asked Cathy, one morning at break.
"What?"
"Lord Dexter's definitely selling the manor."
"No!" Cathy was amazed. "Who said?"
"Betty. Well, Ben works for them doesn't he, so it stands to reason she'd know."
"Oh lord, what rotten luck for them. Will he lose his job?"

"Don't know yet. Gamekeepers are two-a-penny, I should imagine, but you never know. Depends who buys it. She said the Dexters are moving down to live in London permanently." Peggy crunched into a garibaldi biscuit and chewed steadily.

"Who on earth would take that old barn of a building on? It must cost a fortune to heat. A hotel and golf course would make most sense. And what about the farms?" Cathy knew the Kirks and Dawkins, the tenant farming families, very well. Simon Dawkins had taken over Len Kirk's pigs after Len had removed himself to Plymouth to be near to his ex-wife and their children. Simon now managed a huge acreage virtually single-handed.

"The whole estate could get scooped up by some big concern, or some foreign investor. They'll probably want the shooting and fishing rights, and everything." Peggy tried to sound as if she knew about such things. "Or build houses on it."

"Well, I just hope the Nesbits…" Cathy broke off as two children erupted into the room.

"Mrs Duke, Bobby Sykes's football hit Alice in the chest! And she's all gasping and hurt her *bosoms*," explained Crystal, a usually sensible girl from Form 4. Mrs Duke put her arm round the tearful Alice and ushered her to the medical chair.

It was not until the next day that Peggy managed to have a proper chat with Betty Nesbit.

"Yes, we've had our marching orders," Betty said, miserably.

"I'm so sorry. What will you do?"

"Well, Ben's ringing round as many of his contacts as he can – seeing if there's an opening somewhere. So far no joy. It's very worrying." Betty was near to tears.

"Could he do something other than gamekeeping? Like – I don't know – working up at the quarry?" asked Peggy.

Betty looked so distraught at that idea, Peggy hurried on.

"I can't see him caring to be indoors, can you? It's lucky *you've* a steady income, working here at school." Peggy did not know how to comfort her friend.

Betty nodded her head and pulled herself together.

"Yes, you're right, Peggy. I do have an income, so we won't be destitute whatever happens. But we'll need a roof over our heads after Lady Day. Living in a tied property certainly has its downside, you know. I've never had to contemplate moving house before. It makes you suddenly very sympathetic to all those poor refugees around the world, it really does. All they want is a safe home. Ben and I don't have a lot of savings, either, what with the girls and everything. So anywhere we do move will have to be cheap."

"Well, we'll all keep our eyes open. I'm sure something will arrive before you cross that March deadline." added Peggy, grimly. "Try not to worry."

She gave Betty a hug and left her to put out the reading boxes ready for afternoon school.

Really, selling up the old manor estate and paying off its dependents might be the future, but it didn't bring the locals any kind of security.

Gibb remembers

Lady Edwardia Longmont let herself into Longmont Lodge again with the secret duplicate key she kept in the teapot on her kitchen mantlepiece, quite forgetting she would trigger the lately-installed hidden cameras. She had been informed of their existence by a very smug Sir Hugo Chivers and Reg Green, who had also told her they knew she had recently met a foreign agent in one of the deserted bedrooms.

Score one to them, she thought angrily. They're sneaky bastards, British intelligence, but also bumbling, amateurish. Male clubmen who agreed everything on a silly handshake. But she should not underestimate them, for all that. She must be on her guard and ramp up her fieldcraft arrangements, particularly as she was becoming aware of how much her faculties were beginning to wane. This was no time to let her enemies gain the upper hand – although, in truth, it was her friends beyond the Iron Curtain she was most in fear of. Moscow was efficient and more organised than ever before. One more under-cover assassin appearing literally out of the blue, and her life could be snuffed out in a second. And it would serve her right. This physical feebleness and mental confusion was spreading through her like a dark fungus, and slowing her down. For the first time in her life Gibb felt frightened. She did not enjoy being a faulty spoke in an otherwise efficient wheel. She did not relish the thought of becoming a target.

So take no chances, especially around that insufferable snake Tremayne, she told herself angrily.

Toby had moved in with her under false pretences, as she saw it. She cursed herself for being a sentimental fool where he was concerned. She had opened her door and welcomed the enemy in. Once she realised her mistake it was too late. He had searched around and found evidence of Erskine's little operation all too easily. Now he was after her. The swine would even inherit her home, quite legally, after she was dead as he had forced her to sign the place over to him. Today her anger was so great she had to get out of the house and try to think. She caught a bus into town and walked back over the bridge to the empty lodge. Only now she was here, the wretched mould in her brain would not let her focus.

Her head felt muzzy, and it ached. Complex thoughts whirled like piranha fish, fussing everything to shreds. The tired old woman shambled down the cold lower corridor of the old house in her long thin shoes, and sank onto a chair in the stark little kitchen, staring blankly, and wondered what it was she was currently cross about.

The history loop of her memory clicked on once more, like a flickering magic lantern show.

Her rather dashing step-papa had not been best pleased at having to bring up another man's daughter when he wed Edwardia's mother. Boys were much more his style. He lavished money on her half-brothers as they arrived, but he deemed his daughter only required a rudimentary education at home. This made Gibb angry and resentful and caused her naturally rebellious streak to grow into a deep and abiding hatred of her step-papa, her suffocating family, and ultimately her entire class-ridden world. By the time Gibb turned fifteen her step-father was sufficiently exasperated with her to finally pack her off to boarding school. She never looked back. At school she did well academically, and a further year at a Swiss finishing school planted the seeds of social and political revolution deep in Edwardia's angry heart. The strappingly attractive and opinionated Mam'selle Gartner awakened her dedication. For Gibb, it quickly became second nature to hide her true beliefs and allegiances – her personal feelings, her political point of view. Her deep and very real emotions. Outwardly (much to the relief of her family), she settled down and conformed to the social expectations of her class. Inwardly she waited and watched, ready for an inevitable revolution.

Kindly providence then washed everything she required to her doorstep.

With her parents and two of her step-brothers dead, Gibb inherited enough money at twenty to launch herself into London society on her own terms. She was like a bear rousing itself after a long hibernation – hungry and very self-assured. Society magazines now contained photographs of young, brilliant, Edwardia Lambert attending this glamorous dinner party, or that gallery opening, competing in this motor-touring race, or flying home after that intercontinental railway journey. Longmont, her handsome young husband – the wealthy lord she had snaffled one evening like some raffle prize – sadly came to grief rock-diving near Cassis a few months into their marriage. Following this temporary hiatus of wedded bliss, she embraced widowed bliss and resumed organising the convivial intellectual social circles she had known before. She was invited everywhere that mattered, and she already knew simply everyone. Her circles included hordes of intense young men and women, from all levels of European and American society, who talked endlessly about modern politics – some with openness and intelligence, some more cautiously, but all with fervent convictions burning in their breasts. They discussed everything – books, medicine, art, sex, economics; patriotism, nationalism, communism, fascism and every other 'ism' there was – in wildly intense free-for-alls. In those days strangers arrived from nowhere, and friends departed swiftly. She remembered the youthful Toby Pelham Tremayne, and Hugo and Hamish Chivers had all come and gone.

I really ought to have paid those reptiles closer attention, she snarled inwardly, but young blood makes fools of us all. I was green in the ways of trust back then.

She had enjoyed hosting her own gatherings of culturati in London, New York, and occasionally rustic old Banford. It had been commonplace to extend invitations to various cabinet ministers and members of the House of Lords, even a few royals. She had appeared to flirt with many a modern political notion, and encouraged plenty of bumptious, over-sexed young men to pontificate about their pet remedies for mankind's ills as they lounged upon her bohemian pillows. They found Edwardia gay yet serious, brainy yet beautiful. She was tantalising, captivating, and she knew it. She considered herself to be far above the bragging, delusional toffs she courted.

Curiously though, her carefully constructed disguise never once fooled the undercover foreign scouts actively recruiting in Europe for the communist cause. One persistent type spotted her very early on and scooped her up in a trice.

When war was finally declared, like many other socialites of her generation, Gibb Longmont espoused a publicly patriotic path. How the busybody press loved it! She rolled up her sleeves, learned how to service buses, took care of the returning wounded and made sandwiches by the lorry load. She threw herself into the allied war effort with gusto, while rapidly establishing her network of contacts in secret. From the earliest days she managed to send a stream of valuable intelligence first north (sometimes south), then eastwards (occasionally westwards), over mountain and ocean, ice and desert, to its final destination deep inside Stalin's Russia.

The end of hostilities found her permanently resident in Banford, living reluctantly with her deeply irritating youngest brother. She grew so intensely weary of Erskine's fanatical fascism (which was little more than extended capitalism in her view), she had been impelled to engineer his suicide – not an especially complicated act. One less delusional little man in the world was no loss, she reasoned. No one really missed him. His demise had the added advantage of convincing her communist colleagues of her continuing post-war loyalty. A double win.

It had taken the war to establish Gibb's unique and highly successful information gathering and transmission procedures. Consistently, during the next twenty-five years, she maintained and refined her activities. Espionage, she reasoned, was generally conducted in cities, close to sources of marketable intelligence, but no one beyond the capital kept a proper watch over the bucolic shires of olde England. No secret service agents scrutinised the leafy lanes and lengthy coastlines of the British Isles in any detail. British Intelligence bumbled along, as complacent and blinkered as a milkman's horse. So, when she settled down in Banford Place as a widowed, provincial, slightly eccentric, occasional-London-visiting aristo fallen on hard times, nobody batted an eyelid. She was in perfect harmony with both town and country. Lady Longmont fitted the image expected of retired country gentry. As she was no longer seen in the glossy pages of the latest magazines, London society soon forgot her. Gibb settled – like a grinning pike in a shady millpool – deep down out of sight. Every so often she would, like anyone else, take the London train in order to shop at Dickins and Jones, take tea at Fortnum's, order new shoes or attend the theatre. Woven between these appointments she would find quiet moments to link up with her diplomatic informants in Kew or Kensington or Kennington or Kingston, after which she would idly ask some passing stranger if they would mind popping a simple postcard into a letterbox for her on their way home from work. Then she would catch her train. Her fieldcraft was elegant in its simplicity. It was simple in its flexibility. She returned to Banford and her garden quite refreshed.

Gibb decided that over the years she had become a genuine gardener in two senses. She not only cultivated a large plot of land, but also tended an ideology, nurtured and toiled over it, so that it too flourished and yielded dividends year in, year out. Husbands, lovers and brothers might come and go, friends too, but her essential harvesting and sowing persisted season in, season out.

Until now.

Gibb rose shakily from the table and drifted unsteadily back down the lodge's chilly corridor, still confused about why she had come to this appalling building. It must be Tremayne's fault.

Fuming, she pushed open a door. A flight of stone steps led down into a dark basement.

As she reached up to switch on the light, a sudden whirling snowstorm rose up in her beating head and an avalanche swept her down and down and down the hard concrete stairs.

Harvest festival

The church was looking lovely for Harvest Festival, as usual bursting with glorious abundance. Rev Bill's wife June had organised the flower rota with extra care so she could include the schoolchildren's jam-jar displays without upsetting any of the regular arrangers. It was always tricky, the flower rota, but she was determined this year to welcome any child who wanted his or her bunch of daisies or roses or sprouting carrot-tops included. One had to encourage the young, after all.

Jimmy took his offering of two fat courgettes to her on the Saturday morning.

"Well! Where shall we put these splendid things?" she fussed, wishing they were slightly more decorative. "Over here by the window, or maybe under the pulpit? Yes, I think here will do very well. Aren't they terrific? Did you grow them yourself?"

Jim frowned at her, trying to be scrupulously truthful. "Well, Auntie May sowed them before I came to live with her. Then she said I could water them, like I do all the veggies in the mornings, and then they'd be mine. We got loads. These are the best, though."

"Wonderful. You must be a very good waterer."

"I am. I can't lift our proper watering can, but my birthday's coming up so I'm going to ask for a littler one. And a barrow."

"A barrow? I might be able to help you there, you know. We are always collecting for jumble sales at the vicarage, Jimmy, and quite a good children's one just happened to be donated last week. Would you like to come and see it? It might suit you."

Mrs Williams led him through the churchyard over to the church hall, which lay at the back of the cemetery. Inside, among a collection of other things, was a small green plastic wheelbarrow with a yellow ball-wheel. Jimmy grabbed the two handles and grinned at her.

"Do you like it?" she asked. "You can have it if you want."

"It's lovely. It's just the right size for me," he said, completely thrilled. He walked it up and down. "See? It has lots of space too. Can I really have it?"

"Oh yes," answered June, amused he was so happy. "There's also a gardening book on that pile you can take, but it might not be suitable. It's by that man on the TV."

"What man? Oh yes, him. Grandma Dora and I watch him on a Friday night. I go to hers on Fridays. We have Chinese food and watch TV. We both like gardening."

"Well, if it's any use to you, take it by all means. It will fit into your barrow rather nicely. And thank you again for the courgettes, they are super. Now, mind how you cross this road, dear. There's a new pedestrian crossing going to be built on the corner soon, but until it is remember to look both ways. See you tomorrow at the harvest service."

Jimmy grinned happily as he trundled off. "Goodbye, and thank you very much," he called. "See you tomorrow."

He let himself in by the side gate to the garden and wheeled his new barrow up to the back door. Auntie May was in the kitchen cutting up potatoes for some soup. She admired the barrow immensely and was tickled by the thrill Jim obviously felt for the gardening book.

"Put it on the kitchen table and we'll have a good look at it over lunch. Wasn't that kind of Mrs Williams to give you those things?"

Jimmy nodded. "Everyone is kind to me," he commented.

Auntie May nodded her wise old head. "Yes, they are, Jimmy. And it is a special privilege to be nice to them in return."

Jim rolled up his sleeves. "Shall I help you with the soup?" he asked as he washed his grubby little hands.

"Thank you, that would be very welcome. When it's ready we can take some round to poor old Lady Longmont who's had a bit of a fall."

"Oh dear. Has she got a broken leg?" asked Jimmy.

"No. But Mr Green said she was very bruised and battered when he found her. She's in bed at home and Mrs Bicknell is kindly looking after her." May was genuinely concerned about the old lady but did not know quite what to take her as an acceptable gift. Jim looked up into her worried face.

"I think she's going to like our soup," he predicted. "Maybe we could take a bunch of roses too. Auntie May, do just look at my book. It's got that man in it." He knelt on his chair and started flipping over the pages, forgetting all about the soup.

Miss Fisher nodded her head and rapidly finished the potato chopping and set the pan on the stove to cook. Wiping her hands, she came over to look at the wonderful book. Some days, other things were simply far more important than soup.

* * *

4.

Causes for concern

"Yes, well I think they're *certainly* an item. They had that time away in Yorkshire, don't forget." Cathy was speculating on the state of the headmistress's love life, yet again.

Peggy snorted. "Pooh. A couple of days in a friend's flat and you think they're engaged?"

"Well, it must have been on the cards, mustn't it? Going on holiday together?" argued Cathy.

"Don't you believe it. Sir Hugo is nothing but an iceberg, if you ask me. She's not his type at all. She might imagine otherwise, but he's no more likely to seduce her than – than Percy Watson the postman."

"Do you think so? No, I mean, really?"

"Really."

Dean Underwood knocked on the door and shuffled in, holding his face which was bleeding on one side. Cathy jumped up. Dean was one of her favourites.

"Oh no, how did you do it?"

"Fell in the brambles. Tripped over that Amy Brown's feet. I didn't see where she was going." Dean perched on a chair while Mrs Duke dabbed at him with witch hazel. "She was playing horses or something." Amy was a tiny little kindergartener.

"You'd better start looking where you're running, Dean. Amy can't have great big enormous gigantic fifth formers tumbling over her every day of the week. You're so tall now."

Dean grinned. "I know. At least I didn't land on top of her. I did one of my twisting flips."

Peggy peered at him over her specs. "And what, pray tell, is one of those when it's at home?"

"Sort of a gymnastic move, Miss. I learned it at my Saturday lesson at the Wool Hall. Mum signed me up. There's no dancing class for boys round here, so she thought gymnastics would be the next best thing. It's not too bad."

"Gymnastics eh? Is it only boys then?"

Dean shook his head. "There's only me and a lad from Sorburn. The rest is all girls. The other boy doesn't like it much. I do though. I can learn dancing later, when I'm at Secondary, Mum says. What's for lunch, Mrs Duke?"

Cathy threw her cotton wool swabs away and told him to go and wash his hands before returning to class. "I really am going to post menus on our door after Christmas," she threatened. "They're always wanting to know what lunch is."

"Mmm," said Peggy. "You could pin up a statement of the headmistress's love-life while you're about it, like a royal bulletin. 'Mrs Clark is currently seeing blank. She is in, not in, considering, falling in love. Delete as appropriate. She is engaged, not engaged, married, living in sin'. Maybe a tick-box would do it."

"Pooh," said Cathy in her turn. She still imagined the headmistress was conducting a wonderfully secret love affair with the handsome ex-chairman of the school governors, and had no wish for her illusion to be dispelled.

Work goes on

Lady Longmont sat in her armchair, brooding darkly as she nursed her bandaged knee and aching bones. She couldn't see to read. She loathed the telly. Everything hurt, although they said no bones were broken. Life was dross. She was bound, like Gulliver.

What should she do? What *could* she do? She must be cautious – so very cautious. That odious caretaker from the school had discovered her the day she fell down the basement steps in the lodge, but not, thank god, the secret keys in her pocket. He had not even searched her, for some reason she could not fathom. It would have been the first thing she would have done. No, Reg Green had lifted her, quite gently, and sat her down until the ambulance came. After that he had disappeared.

Maybe the child could help.

Gibb peered out of the drawing room window wishing she did not feel so ancient. Her mind raced like a steam engine, but her body had become unrecognisable since that fall. It was all most frustrating. She stared at her hands. Whose were these? They seemed to belong to some kind of bird.

Mrs Bicknell knocked and entered with a plastic bucket full of cleaning cloths.

"Can I do that grate now, milady?" she enquired.

"If you have to," Gibb croaked, managing to raise an arm. "Mustn't stop the workers."

Bick pursed her lips and got down to it. Workers indeed. What did Lady Longmont know about work?

"There's some of that nice soup left over, what Miss Fisher brung round," she reminded her employer. "If you're wanting lunch."

Gibb scowled. "Swill it down the sink," she ordered. Then a glimmer of an idea began to shine in her foggy mind. "And bring me that seed catalogue from the hall table before the girl arrives."

Stops and starts

The big grandfather clock in the school library always had to be wound and adjusted last thing every Friday afternoon. It was Ernest's final act of the day. He synchronised the old timepiece with his own expensive Swiss wristwatch (a birthday gift from father) and locked it up again for another seven days. Next week was half term, so for the next eight days the clock would remain an hour wrong. Its face would fib, its voice would deceive. But it did not matter as no one would be there to see or hear. He switched off the library lights and locked that door too.

It was a misty, damp and cold October night. Ernest and Mike drove home from school via Ironwell Mill in order to confirm with Miss Winstanley that she would be visiting in early December to run her annual gift-making craft day. The schoolchildren loved this as they all went home with some fun Christmas presents. Sleet was building up on Ernest's windscreen by the time they left the mill.

"That river looks pretty high tonight," commented Mike as they drove across the bridge and the marshy levels of Woodend Common.

They stopped at the level crossing gates in Weston while the five o'clock train chugged through, then ground slowly up Beech Lane in second gear to Oxthorpe. The night grew even grimmer as they left the hamlet's two meagre street lights behind. Nag's Hill was the usual hazardous pot-holed nightmare it always was, with the burned out ruins of Tremayne's old cottage known as The Holt to the right. The remains of its huge stone chimney loomed stark against the scudding clouds. An old pick-up truck stood by its front door.

"Funny time to be visiting an empty house," commented Mike as they skirted round it.

"Probably some courting couple," smiled Ernest, changing gears and rounding the next bend. "They don't have a nice warm dry cottage to go home to like we do."

He was rewarded by a wide grin. Mike was slowly coming to terms with the recent loss of his beloved mother, and Ernest – for once – acknowledged that he himself had played a large part in that recovery. Both men had reached a point in their lives when they needed to accept who they were and move forward. Ernest accelerated, grateful beyond measure that neither of them had chosen to face a future alone. They had each other.

Even as the sound of the Renault's engine faded and died, the rigid bodies of Sir Hugo's two caretakers – Mr and Mrs Bunting – firmly tied up in sacking, were being tipped down the disused well in the Holt's backyard. Two men – one short, one tall – heaved burnt masonry and other pieces of debris from the fire-damaged property after the two mummy-like bundles, filling the shaft almost to the top. A dim hurricane lamp set in an alcove cast a greasy light on the ghastly scene. The tall man took part of an old roof timber and tamped the contents down hard while the shorter man shovelled in yet more mud and caked ash. They then pulled a heavy flagstone and some rusted corrugated iron on top. By the time they were done the mist had turned to sleety rain and was pelting fast. In no time it washed away all traces of their toil.

The men wiped their hands on the wet grass, picked up the hurricane lamp and the shovel, chucked them into the bed of the pick-up and drove away.

Mysteries

Sir Hugo – like Peggy, rather than Cathy – was not as convinced as he had once been about the headmistress's romantic leanings. As he strolled up from the station he made himself consider the woman.

Skip Clark wasn't entirely *un*attractive. Nor was she completely *un*intelligent. Yet was she still as devoted to him as he believed? There had been a change since their little holiday in the north, although he had not brooded on it very much until now. He had not had to. Hugo frowned as he walked. Wasn't Skip, like every other female he had ever met, driven by the lust for romance and the prize of matrimony in all their dealings with men? He admitted the times they lived in were a-changing, but surely basic instincts were not. In London women were calling themselves 'liberated', whatever that meant, but it wouldn't catch on in places like Banford. He knew a fad when he saw one. Women were simple emotional beings, driven here and there by mother nature. They were, even in their own estimations, *irrelevant* without a man. It was a fact. They worshipped god through men, didn't they? Hugo had noted it himself whenever he saw that adoring, slightly lustful and flirtatious glint spring up in a woman's eye when he paid them particular attention. Their demeanour changed, their voices altered. It was their simple, natural, physiological, psychological reaction. He smirked as he walked, and prided himself on how skilfully he managed all the primitive, skittish little creatures that came his way.

So why had this one gone off the boil?

Hugo stopped smiling and frowned. He reviewed their recent trip to Yorkshire again. Skipper had initially reacted completely predictably when he bestowed a couple of days away together She had been thrilled and flattered and excited. It had amused, not surprised, him to note her flustered happiness. And she had certainly proved willing enough to jump into bed that first night, and to enjoy the fuss he made of her. However, since then, he had the distinct impression she had found their time away together had been – what was the word? – *under-whelming*.

That was irritatingly unsettling, and he racked his brains as to the cause. What had he missed? How had he fallen short? It couldn't be his tried and tested bedroom technique. It couldn't be his impeccable manners. It couldn't have been his amiability. Had he not pushed the boat out enough? He had assumed this gracious little reward for her colluding with his covert safe house operation would cement her future goodwill. Keep her sweet a bit longer. Now he was not so sure.

A tiny, worm-like thought eventually occurred as he stepped over a puddle. Was Mrs Clark being *strategic*? Was that it? Did she imagine she was indulging *him*? Rewarding him for having kept her blasted little school protected from harm? Surely not.

Hugo reached his own front gate and looked up at the house next door. Worrying about Skipper Clark's motivation was pointless. Women were of limited interest at the best of times, and of limited use at others. More importantly, what was he to do about the future of the Banford operation?

The use of Chloe Shaw's old home as their third safe-house had been wound up, and it could now be rented out again as a normal dwelling. That was well in hand. But what on earth should he do with his own place, Garratt's Hall, now that Ernest seemed to be living indefinitely at Caster Cottage with Mike Paton, and he himself would soon be returning to Europe permanently?

Hugo unlocked his front door and went in. He hung his coat in the cupboard and headed for the kitchen where someone had left a plated-up meal and the delivery box full of his clean laundry on the table. Unstrapping it and removing the immaculate contents, he dismissed recent concerns. Priority one was to decommission and close this Banford operation successfully, and priority two was to establish the next – in Europe. Everything personal could wait. He would lock up these two neighbouring empty houses and leave them in the tender care of Tremayne and Green. They weren't going anywhere. After that it would not be very long before he could consign Mrs Skipper Clark, his son, Mayflower School, Lady Edwardia Longmont and the whole of blasted Banford town to history where it belonged.

He's had enough of Banford. It was time to return to Europe where other people would be only too happy to manage his laundry.

Sir Hugo draws a blank

At first, Hugo was merely peeved. He had arrived home to find his house dark and the Buntings nowhere to be found. He was not aware they had been due any leave, so after putting his fresh laundry away himself, he telephoned Reg Green. Next he tried Toby Tremayne and eventually the Lambeth office. But no one had any news of his housekeepers' whereabouts. He conducted a second – more thorough – search of both houses and the grounds, drew another complete blank, then sat up into the small hours, waiting.

The following morning there was still no word. Reg and the dog arrived. Mr Green was still reeling from the dressing down Sir Hugo had given him on the phone regarding the old lady and how she might have managed to gain entry into the lodge and fall down the cellar steps. Picklocks, was all Reg could think of. Not that she appeared capable of using such fiddly things. Keys then? Reg had failed to search her when he'd had the chance, and he knew he deserved his severe reprimand. If the old woman had breached the lodge's security she had no doubt been everywhere else too, added Sir Hugo. The Dutch Cottage outbuilding, Church Road.

Reg was eager to make amends.

"Mrs Bick says last time she spoke with Bunting was last Friday morning, Sir. None of the neighbours has seen either of 'em. Mr Tremayne's three lads ent neither. Shall I let the dog 'ave a sniff about?"

"If you would, Mr Bosun. Do it thoroughly this time."

The Bunting's flat was above Garratt's detached double garage. It was large and comfortable, fully contained, with two bedrooms, a small lift and a private entry. Stringer gave the place a thorough going-over but could find nothing untoward, so Reg put him outside to search the grounds. He was snuffling about in the bushes when Toby Tremayne arrived.

"Anything?" asked Toby.

"Nothing. Dog's drawn a blank, no traces anywhere. Last seen Friday morning. They've vanished."

Toby scowled. This was seriously worrying. Operatives didn't just 'go missing'. "Let's hope they're not in Kirk's slurry pit," he commented, grimly.

"Huh," Hugo grunted scornfully. Who would know about that?

Stringer sat down by the front door and stared at the three men. It was like the Marie Celeste. There was absolutely no sign of the missing couple. No blood, no disturbance, nothing broken. No coats gone from the hall cupboard. No tyre tracks. No keys, weaponry, passports, money or other personal items missing. No messages, no clues at all. The Buntings might have been abducted by aliens.

Arnold was informed, but if he knew of any explanation he was not sharing it. Lady Longmont only looked genuinely bewildered when questioned. The look-outs were quizzed again but there was nothing new. Toby, Reg and Stringer searched everywhere they could think of, but ultimately had to admit defeat.

Arnold ordered them to clear the flat and let it be known the Buntings had retired to North Wales.

A month later Hugo installed Mrs Bicknell in the rapidly redecorated apartment above the garage, where she settled down to a new life as housekeeper for the absent Sir Hugo. She declared she was very happy with her new situation, especially as she was still able clean for Mrs York and Mrs Tuttle twice a week, ladies she had grown particularly fond of, and had almost nothing to do for Sir Hugo. Bick could still enjoy her long country rambles and maintain a watch on the neighbourhood's comings and goings, while enjoying a nice little flat with all mod cons. The only thing she missed from living in Wag Lane, she said, was having Miss Muggeridge to natter to of an evening. Still, as this new living arrangement cost her nothing at all, and Eliza dropped by most days on her way to the shops, she could overlook that minor drawback.

Sir Hugo sold his Rolls Royce and acquired an E-type Jaguar coupé which he drove himself, garaging it in London near his club. He employed a garden service to come and tend the grounds of Garratt's Hall and threw dust sheets over all the furniture before driving off in a cloud of exhaust fumes. With Hugo gone, peace and normality returned to Church Road, marked only by the quarter chimes of St Andrew's clock.

Of the faithful and efficient Buntings, nothing more was said. No trace was ever found – although Reg Green sometimes wondered, in quiet moments, which side (east or west) had been responsible for their disappearance.

Either was feasible.

Jimmy helps out

Jimmy jumped out of Mr Chivers' car and hurried in to see Mr Paton, who was wiping down his kitchen table.

"Ah here you are at last!" Mike grinned at Jim with genuine delight at seeing how well the lad looked. "I swear you've grown another inch taller since last week!"

Jimmy grinned back. "Hello," he cried. "I brought you some blackberries."

Mike Paton peered into Jimmy's paper bag. The juicy fruit looked wonderful. "Gosh, they're huge."

"I picked them this morning over the 'lotments. Before the birds took 'em."

Ernest clattered in and threw his car keys in the bowl on the side by the door.

"Any coffee going? Jim was sitting on the front wall waiting, when I got there. Says he's picked us some blackberries. Ooh, they look delicious. I feel a blackberry and apple crumble coming on, Uncle Mike."

They took their drinks into the sitting room which looked out over the garden. Jimmy had come to advise his new 'uncles' on a plan to restore Mike's vegetable patch, and see how the rest of Caster Cottage's modest acreage could be kept a little tidier with less maintenance. Gardening, planting, sowing seeds were all the child ever thought about these days. Tonight he was being permitted to sleep at the cottage, in the little box-room. It was his first-ever night away from his angel.

"What's Auntie May doing today?"

"She's gone to Fenchester on the bus to see Mrs Harris." Mrs Harris was Jimmy's social worker. "Do you think they'll send me away to live in that children's home again? Or back to Auntie Ann?" The boy's brow furrowed with sudden fear that he might once again lose everything he had grown to love.

Ernest put his cup down and looked the child straight in the eye.

"No one – *no one* – is ever going to take you from Auntie May. You belong to her now and she belongs to you. You're a family –

the judge said so. Even when you're a grown-up man you can still be together. You know this, Jim. We've been through all this. When you're an adult and *choose* to leave, or get married and have a different life, it will be up to you where and who you live with. But right now, while you're young, you are safe. You're home."

Jimmy nodded. He knew it really. The judge would sign the final paper soon. Jim just needed a little reassurance from time to time. He took out a dilapidated exercise book from the school satchel he had brought with him.

"What's this?" asked Mike.

Jim found the page he wanted, and put the book on the coffee table. It showed a rudimentary layout of Caster Cottage's garden with re-dug beds and pathways, a compost area, trees and a pond.

"When did you do all this?" asked Ernest, studying it carefully. "Look, Mike. He's drawn some really good ideas here."

Jimmy stood beside Mike's chair, and they discussed what he had sketched as if it were a piece of homework. The boy's eyes were dancing with happiness again by the time he had explained all his proposals. The men were impressed.

They all went out into the Autumn morning, and Ernest looked at his watch.

"Well, if my job is to mow this blasted field we're calling a lawn, it's going to take me until lunchtime. I'd better get cracking."

"And *we* will make a start on that overgrown veg bed of Mum's," said Mike. "Come on, Capability Birch. Go and open up the shed while I put my gardening boots on. It's going to be a long, busy day."

And so it proved to be, but by the end of it – when they were enjoying blackberries and stewed apple after dinner – the three of them felt it had been decidedly worth it. The garden once again looked cared for, which had not been the case for quite a while. The grass was shorter, the beds dug over and the shrubs clipped into shapes more suitable for withstanding the constant wind that blew across the flat openness. Two new compost heap areas had been cleared and the little patio's flagstones weeded and swept.

Jimmy soaked in a hot bath, washing himself with unfamiliar pink soap, and drying himself on a strange new towel. He brushed his teeth, cleaned the bath, and hopped into his cosy little bed, pulling open the curtains in order to see the sky, as he always did. It was scary being away from his angel, but he knew he would see her again tomorrow. He clutched the comforting little teddy bear she had knitted him, skipped through his prayers, and fell fast asleep. The two adults peeped around the door later, both feeling oddly happy he was there under their roof.

Ernest and Jimmy gave church attendance a miss the next morning and, under Mike's direction, constructed two fine compost containers from some posts and planks that Terry Green had filched from the burned-out remains of The Holt. It was nice to think of them being re-used. After a filling lunch of roast lamb Jimmy was driven home to Fen Lane, where Auntie May stood at the door waiting for him.

"Oh, I missed you!" she cried.

"I missed you too," said Jimmy, hugging her tight. He turned and waved as the Renault hooted and disappeared at the end of the road. "I did say 'thank you for having me'," he informed her, knowing it would be her next question. "It was funny being away."

"But nice too?" she asked as she closed the door and set his little suitcase at the bottom of the stairs ready to be taken up. "Have you had a good time?"

"Oh yes," Jim said as he sat up to the kitchen table on his own cushion on his own chair. "But there's no place like home, is there?" He stared around the room with fresh eyes, glad to see each familiar item was still where it ought to be, and even the cat sitting illegally on the bread board. A deep sense of gratitude and security filled him to the brim. Maybe a night away made life sweeter.

Miss Fisher said nothing. She merely poured hot water into the teapot and set the kettle back to mutter in its rightful place. Just we happy few, she thought, wittily mixing things up, are properly at home on the range.

Half term errands

Jean Hewitt hated going to the doctor, even though it was occasionally necessary to have her blood pressure checked. She chided herself for being nervous, although Dr Legg was cheery enough – and a lot more sympathetic about her anxieties than Dr Granger had ever been. Jean felt she could mention a couple of additional minor female-related ailments that bothered her, without becoming too embarrassed. She knew she was old-fashioned in her reserve, but she couldn't help it.

"So hold off on the sweet things?" Jean asked for confirmation.

"Yes, if you can. Do without a puddin' at lunchtime if that's possible. I know Mrs Green feeds you well at school, but like me, you're often sittin' about and not walkin' it off. You have a little dog, though, right?"

"I do. I should walk him more, I suppose."

Dr Legg rose to see her out. "There's nothin' else to worry about, Mrs Hewitt. I'll see you in six months, unless you see me first!" she joked. Jean Hewitt was a breezy, sensible soul and Afra Legg liked her very much. "Are you goin' out to see your son and his wife in Holland at Christmas?"

"No, I don't think so. Not this year. I'll go next Summer though. They live in a lovely little suburb. It's not quite up to Banford's prettiness, but it's very pleasant. Neat and tidy."

Mrs Hewitt began her new 'more exercise' regime on leaving the surgery by walking briskly into town. The castle loomed high and flung a deep blue shadow across the square to St Peter's church, as it always did at this time of day. Shoppers bustled about with bags of groceries. She was thirsty, so decided to have a cup of tea in the Castle View Café before finally heading homewards.

"Hello, Mrs Hewitt!" called a voice from above.

Bella Delgado was waving to her from a first floor window. Jean looked up.

"Oh hello, Bella," she cried. "Is that your new flat?"

"Yes, I'm over the café. Couldn't be more convenient, could it?"

"Come down and I'll buy you some tea," laughed Jean.

They sat with their teacups looking at the people milling about in the square. It was quite warm in the sun.

"So, have you settled in?" asked Jean. "I haven't really seen you long enough to have a good long talk, I'm afraid. How are you liking our little school?"

"Oh I love it. My class seem pretty easy after a couple of the teaching practices I had," smiled Bella. "And Miss Jackson left wonderful notes."

She certainly looks as though she's coping, thought Jean. She was glad. Mayflower certainly had been fortunate with its new staff. "You're not finding the antiquated building too annoying then?"

"No, not at all. It's quirky, alright, but that gives it character. It's like an extra person – maybe a slightly shabby old grandpa. I like its atmosphere."

Sensible girl, thought Jean. It isn't always the obvious things that make a workplace happy. "Do you think you'll like it enough to stay a few years?"

Bella nodded. "Yes, I do." She looked at her rosy-faced colleague and felt confident enough to explain. "I feel like – well, like I've come home. As if I was meant to be here, somehow. Does that sound too fanciful?"

Jean shook her head, thinking it sounded exactly like the headmistress. "No, it doesn't. I think either you connect with a place or you don't. Many people don't have that sense of place – that *sensus loci,* as Mr Tremayne would say. Others do. I have always loved Mayflower, though I may have to move on one day."

"Oh dear, why?"

Jean sighed. "Well, if my son starts a family, for example, I won't want to be hundreds of miles away will I? He and his wife live in Holland. I can't see them moving back here, alas. I would have to move there if I wanted to be involved with any offspring."

At that moment someone tapped on the window and they looked up to see Sandi Raina's smiling face. She came in and joined them.

"Have you been shopping?" Jean asked her, glad to stop talking about herself.

"Yes. Just collecting a couple of things for my son and daughter's Christmas presents, you know. Raja wants a proper cassette recorder and Nanda a record player. Whatever happened to asking for cuddly toys? Luckily I've managed to get one and order the other. Children, eh?"

Jean and Bella laughed.

Bella said, "They grow up so quickly. You'll have all those joys, Mrs Hewitt, if you do land a few grandchildren."

"Look, isn't that our Jonah Webb with Mr Quincy? They seem to be on their way somewhere. He's got his vet's bag with him." The local vet was striding across the market place with Jonah from Form 6 loping along beside him, trying to keep up.

"It's a long way from the vet's surgery," commented Sandi.

"Yes. I wonder what Jonah's rescuing now?" said Jean. "He's a great one for finding some poor benighted animal or bird and saving its skin, Bella. I think Guy told me he has a Saturday job helping Mr Quincy out. Do him the world of good, that will. The child's parents don't seem to have much time for him and he's so good with animals."

"That's really nice," commented Sandi. "Maybe Jonah will become a vet too, one day," she suggested.

"Yes, maybe. They look pretty intent, the pair of them," agreed Bella. "Now then, would you both like to come upstairs to my new flat and tell me what you think of the colours I've chosen for the living room walls? I could really use fresh eyes on the place before I finally decide. It won't take a minute."

Mr Quincy's apprentice

Mr Quincy was pleased with his new apprentice. He remembered how young Jonah Webb from Mayflower School had rescued a swan last winter. It had been trapped in the ice on the river during a particularly cold spell. The boy had freed its legs and brought it to safety wrapped in his sweater, at no small risk to himself. Walter Quincy admired that bravery and dedication. He also discovered the child had homed some kittens that had been due for drowning, and – most challenging of all – helped one of Lord Dexter's ewes to give birth when it was in trouble. Jonah was his kind of boy, Walter thought. Kind, quick-thinking in a crisis, and good with all sorts of creatures. So the busy vet went out of his way to ask the lad to come and shadow his call-outs at the weekends. Jonah had rewarded him with absolute devotion and never looked back. He turned up clean and tidy at 8am each Saturday morning, and stayed until even the lowliest of jobs was finished on a Sunday.

Quincy, a loquacious man, provided a running commentary on his work as he went about it, affording Jonah a first-hand insight into all aspects of veterinary work. Quincy was an education in himself. Jonah soon discovered that a vet's work certainly wasn't all pretty puppies and chatty budgerigars. It was cold muddy farms, and blood and vomit and pain, sometimes rough and heavy work, always exhausting and always challenging. You had to love it or not go into it in the first place. However, from the moment Jonah first assisted Mr Quincy to mend the broken leg of a suffering cat, he knew this was the work he was truly cut out for. His tender-heartedness never left him, but in the presence of a creature in pain he became level-headed, kind and calm. School had educated him to look at all kinds of problems rationally and reach sensible, balanced conclusions – habits that complemented this delicate work perfectly. He learned fast, which made Mr Quincy believe his young apprentice would grow up to achieve great things. In a short while eleven-year-old Jonah Webb was Walter Quincy's right-hand man.

"He may not read and write that well," admitted Walter to his wife Brydie, one evening as they sat down to supper. "But the kid's dedicated, and he learns fast."

"Like you did," interrupted his wife.

"Like I *do*," he corrected her. "He's not much sense of humour, though. He doesn't get some of my little jokes."

"Yes, well, some of them aren't fit for a child's ears, Walter, so you just be careful what you say." Brydie was well-aware of her husband's chatty disposition. "And I expect you can help him learn to read the important words he needs to know. His reading will improve once he has a reason for it, I expect. Just needs a bit of encouragement. Probably grow up and take over the practice one day, when you retire," she added hopefully. "You never know."

"Now there's a thought," said Walter, shaking salt over his potatoes.

Gibb makes a mistake

Gibb dragged herself out for the walk to the post box. She did not usually mail anything herself, especially from locations so close to home, but the notion of taking a train or even a bus left her exhausted. She waited until the drizzling rain stopped, then buttoned her slippered feet into a pair of galoshes and squelched limpingly off up the road to the pillar box at the corner of Well Road.

Dean Underwood was walking home with his friend Joey. They were planning on checking over their Cub uniforms, and deciding which badges they wanted to work for next. Rev Wichelow, the local scoutmaster, had told them there would be a few new choices coming up soon. Dean thought he would like the ornithologist, and maybe the map-reading badges. Joe decided on home-help. If there had been one for minding animals they would both have aimed for that as, like Ryan Hale, they were already expert dog-walkers. The two crossed over Well Road just as Lady Longmont popped her postcard into the letter box and let out a ghastly shriek.

"Oh no! No!"

"Oh, Lady … er." said Dean. "Is something the matter? Can we help?"

"My keys! I've dropped my keys into the letterbox!"

Dean and Joe stared at her helplessly.

"Um, sorry but I don't think we can get in here." Dean tried to put his slender hand through the slot but it was hopeless. "You'll probably have to wait for Mr Watson or the little red van that empties it," he said.

"Maybe you could go and ask at the Post Office," suggested Joey, feebly. He knew tampering with the mail was a criminal activity. PC Pink had explained it to them one day at school.

Ashen faced, her heart racing fifteen to the dozen, Gibb was so angry she thought she was going to be sick. "It's not my house keys," she gasped.

The boys stared at her. What else? Car keys?

She had been gripping her illegal duplicates of Longmont Lodge's entry keys when she posted today's card to Aberdeen and a few other items, intending to continue up the road to the Lodge for another snoop around, although now she was unsure why she had felt impelled to do this. Stupidly, she had let go of the string of three odd-looking keys and some handy pick-locks, when she dropped the items through the mail slot. Panic now overwhelmed her. If she went into the Post Office asking for their return, all would be discovered and she would be arrested. Tremayne and Chivers' would rub their horrible hands with glee. This was another nail in her coffin for sure – her own carelessness had skittled her again. Now they would finally put her against a wall and shoot her.

Lady Longmont leaned against the pillar box, her head swimming and her bloodshot eyes darting around for the sniper who would undoubtedly be dispatched any minute to finish her off.

"Sorry we can't help," muttered the lads, thoroughly scared by the old lady's terrible aspect. She appeared ready to murder them. Her graspy old fingers were waving at their faces, her mouth hanging open, and her eyes staring as it dawned on her that the children were witnesses. The boys crossed over the street and raced away.

Gibb Longmont finally managed to take her bruised and quivering carcass back home, panting and fuming all the way, devastated by a second botched outing. No more, she vowed. Never more.

Raven-like she crouched in the darkly spinning kitchen until it was time for Tremayne to arrive home from work, whereupon she removed herself to her shadowy sitting room and closed the door.

*　*　*

5.

Toy garden

Clearing the air

The manic half of the Autumn term began in November. Bella Delgado hardly knew what hit her, but she rose to its fresh waves of challenge with a buoyant heart. Even so, it was as if she had been paddling nicely along in shallow waters for a while, and was now suddenly expected to stand up on an ocean-going surfboard in the middle of a gale. It was quite a ride, but with the example of her colleagues and the help of the children, she coped and even began to understand where she fitted into the ever-changing world of Mayflower's annual mayhem.

The headmistress had been noticeably distant since the filmstrip projector incident, causing Bella to work extra hard to dispel any doubts about her dedication to a long-term career in education by publicly and frequently stating her commitment to teaching, with a view to one day running a school of her own. She also let fall the information that although she might enjoy a man's company from time to time, she never, ever, *ever* intended to marry – let alone produce offspring of her own. That raised a few skeptical eyebrows. She tried not to become too repetitious, but the more she voiced these lofty intentions the more she privately began to believe in them. I suppose I cannot stop men wanting to chase me, Bella told herself grandly, but I do not have to be caught. Adopting this pose created an unexpected surge of inner confidence, and the whole of her future began to fall pleasantly, neatly, logically into place. She was surprised at how relieved she felt, and how free. Let them laugh, Bella thought. I don't care.

Toby Tremayne took Skipper out to a distant pub one evening, for what he told her was an overdue explanation of himself. He owed it to her, he said, to come clean. This made Skip nervous. They sat over a pint in a half-empty lounge bar across a grubby table, trying not to look at each other.

He began by reiterating his devotion to her and the entire school team. This made her heart sink even further. Then he reminded her of his other life with MI5. He apologised for the way in which he had wormed his way onto Mayflower's staff. It may have appeared to have occurred by chance, but of course everything had been carefully engineered, he said.

Skipper sipped her beer, hating this. It made her sick to have to admit once again how easily she could be duped. And how often her compliance was taken for granted.

"So, Toby. With Chloe gone you just appeared. And Lady Longmont didn't take you into her home out of the goodness of her heart, did she? You knew about her. It wasn't luck she suggested you were the answer to our prayer for a competent French teacher, was it?." She was growing cross.

Toby remained calm and conversational. "No. But uncovering Gibb's activities was a genuine stroke of luck." He cleared his throat and reminded her she had signed the Official Secrets Act, which made her really angry.

"I'm not likely to forget it, am I?"

Toby ignored her temper and ploughed on. MI5, he said, was overseeing the winding-up of Hugo's safe-house operation. That meant it was his responsibility now. Hugo was required elsewhere.

"He's travelling abroad again?"

Toby nodded and left it at that.

Another thought occurred.

"Were you actually responsible for finding Chloe's new position in America?" interjected Mrs Clark, her mind darting over painful events she usually tried to avoid. If this was to be an evening of laying out all their dirty linen, why not clear up a few other mysteries.

"No," Toby answered, jesuitically. Hugo had been the one to arrange that particular transfer. Toby skirted round the subject by drawing Skip's attention to a few other inter-connected facts it would do no harm to tell her about. The disappearance of the pig-farmer, his wife and her lover. The shifting locations of the safe-houses. The departure of the Buntings. The move of Mrs Bicknell into Hugo's servant's quarters. A little of the extent of Lady Longmont's spying activities.

"So she – is still – a communist spy?"

Toby nodded. "Hard to credit isn't it?"

Mrs Clark gave him a headmistress-type stare.

No, she thought. No it isn't. Old Lady Longmont a spy? Safe houses? Defectors? Why was all this nonsense folded inside her cosy little scholastic world? It was ridiculous. But here you are, Mr Tremayne of MI5, explaining it to me as if it were all next to nothing.

"What about poor Stringer's poisoning? Bella's arrival? Heather leaving? The lead being stolen off the roof? Jimmy's mother's accident? Your own *house* burning down?"

"Nothing to do with the undercover op, I swear. Just accidents. Happenings."

I don't know, she thought. What do I believe? Who? I don't even know the right questions to ask. These men are all beyond the pale. The ones I am attracted to most turn out to be the worst dissemblers of the lot. Hugo, Toby. Dear old Joe Granger. Even Reg only tells me half-truths, and when I *do* finally get told the rest of it, it's always horrible. Or dangerous. Or only half the story.

At least my schoolchildren have never been roped into anything underhand, she thought with relief. That really would be a step over the limit. Hugo promised faithfully, when she first arrived and discovered the goings-on at the Lodge, that her schoolchildren would never be exposed to any harm. She still firmly trusted that promise. No one would ever jeopardise children, after all, would they?

Skip had had more than enough for one evening. Tremayne could see that, so he left it there. It was interesting to note how little Mrs Clark pursued enlightenment when she was busy castigating herself over her own character flaws. Hugo had been right about that. If she was serious about protecting her beloved school she would have quizzed him further. She'd had her chance.

The two drove home in silence, Toby feeling the air had definitely cleared a little. He liked Skipper. He liked her very much, and he privately despised Hugo for having put her unwitting little world at the heart of his shaky operation. Not that his original plan had been an altogether bad one, he admitted. If that Longmont witch had not popped up on their virtual doorstep Hugo might well have been covered in glory by now. As it was, the old woman had scuppered everything, and Toby was left to clear up the mess. It was a great pity. Skip didn't deserve any of this.

The fair sex, thought Toby grimly, as he pulled up outside White Cottage again. They really shouldn't be trusted with too much confidential information. They grew resentful and personalised everything. The headmistress would never have made an MI5 investigations officer.

"Good night," he said cheerily as she closed the car door.

Panto hitches

The busy-ness of Autumn helped restore some of the headmistress's equilibrium. It was difficult to be gloomy or cross when so many distractions and celebrations were on the cards. At least the play season was predictable. Reliably chaotic.

This year the pantomime for the older children was to be a shortened version of Peter Pan. The babies would perform their traditional nativity play, and the middle years the Three Little Pigs – which would allow for a large cast of nursery rhyme characters. Guy had drafted the Peter Pan play, and Ernest the Little Pigs saga. It was a new departure for him, writing a children's show, and he thoroughly enjoyed it.

Charlie and Bella were set to organise the Christmas music concert, which this year would be more of a carol sing-along end-of-term assembly gathering. Skipper had finally put her foot down about having the last assembly of every term in church, saying it was far simpler for the vicar to walk across the road to school than take everyone over to St Andrew's. No one disagreed. Mrs Clark felt gratified she had at least been able to bring about one minor change to Mayflower's world.

Bonfire night was huge fun. Terry and Reg managed to burn up a gigantic heap of rubbish, and the governors forked out for some extra fireworks. PC Pink stopped by on his new moped, to admire the blaze and see everybody was behaving properly. As the rockets roared upwards and burst into dazzling stars in the starlit sky, Toby stood and remembered the terrible night last

March when his cottage had burned down. He shivered. Life was full of unwelcome reminders and recurring images.

The dry weather allowed Mayflower's children to spend break-times out of doors, until a huge gale blew in one night. It broke limbs off several of the wilderness's tallest trees and rattled the TV aerial on the chimney of White Cottage. Skipper was mightily relieved to find the new glass roof over the Iron Duke stairwell leaked not a single solitary drop. Gales and rain storms could be coped with if they did not interfere with indoor life too much.

Toby, Reg and Skipper took a thorough look around Longmont Lodge the day after the storm. Skip was glad the new fibreglass roofing on the dormers was holding up well, and that there was only one tile askew on the house's ornate façade, which Reg said Terry could easily fix. The windows still rattled and there was a chill breeze on the landings, but all things considered the place wasn't as dilapidated as it might have been.

"They knew 'ow to build in the olden days," commented Reg, echoing Skipper's thoughts.

"You know what I've been thinking," Toby said, as he ran his eye along the ornate cornice in one of the bedrooms where he knew hidden cameras and microphones were installed. Reg glanced at him.

"What?" asked Mrs Clark.

"This whole building could be easily turned into a private arts centre one day, once it's finished being so useful to HMG of course. Or a language school, possibly. I reckon I could even run the place – and, what's more, make it pay too."

Reg and Skipper were more than a little astonished. An arts centre? A private arts centre? Reg raised a disbelieving eyebrow and decided the headmistress's enthusiastic flights of fancy must be catching. An arts centre? A language school?

"What kind of language then? Bad language?" he asked.

Toby smiled, and warmed to his subject. "No. English for foreign students. You know – or short courses for travellers going abroad. Maybe French or German or Italian if we could attract the tutors. It's the coming thing. Students could stay in town somewhere and attend by the day or week or term or whatever. We'd need to get properly accredited and hand out a certificate of competence or something to everyone who passes. It shouldn't be too onerous, if it was kept small. It would help our school coffers, and maybe benefit the town too. Foreign currency and all that."

"And an *arts* centre?"

"That wouldn't need much investment, depending on your notions of what constitutes art. I could see a room or two being made available for any local group who wanted to come and draw or paint whatever they wanted."

"No instruction?"

"No, no instruction, necessarily. Just a modest contributory fee to the building's running costs and a space to work together. It would be nice for OAPs or kids to drop by after school. But if you wanted more cash, then classes in sculpting, pottery, dance, theatre, writing and whatnot – whatever a group or a private lecturer wanted, at a proper rate – could be added to the language classes. A cafeteria or a tea machine. That pottery kiln you spoke about. A gallery, maybe, like the Winstanley woman has at the mill."

Mrs Clark smiled broadly and nodded. "You know what?" she said, "I think you could be on to something, Toby.

"It was just a thought, as I said" added Toby. "It's a nice old building. Seems a shame to waste it. It's too big for a private dwelling these days, I suppose. But setting up a private/public arts centre might get the wretched LEA off our backs once and for all. You know what vultures they are. It would be good to have a long-term scheme to shoo them off with. And an arts centre and/or language school would extend what we already are. It could be a new branch of the 'Broadstock Empire'. We'd have to see what Jamal says, of course. Yes, well – you know."

They wandered through the rest of the rooms with a slightly altered view of the place's potential. It could certainly be made useful. Maybe Jamal Raina, the school's lawyer, could provide some calculations to show the governors. As with most whimsies, this one was fast getting a grip on the headmistress's mind.

"I wouldn't let the language school students use the wilderness, Toby. And you'd have to seal up that beastly cellar, Reg, if we converted all this into classrooms or studios," said Skipper, dreamily.

Reg Green grunted. "Don't see why we'd 'ave to seal anything up. You could shove them as don't finish their 'omework down there as a punishment," he suggested. "Or them what don't pay their fees on time. That'd learn 'em."

It would too, thought Skip. She grinned at Toby and took his arm. He was back in favour. She decided to buy him supper and a trip to see the Western that was showing in Portland that weekend.

Remembering

The Wolf Cubs, Boy Scouts, Girl Guides and Brownies were all permitted to wear their uniforms to school on November 11th, the day of the annual Remembrance Service. The children looked very smart and important in their kit as they sat in assembly amongst the usual green, gold and grey. The previous Sunday they had been on church parade, and Joey Latimer had carried the Scout colours all the way to the war memorial. A prouder standard bearer there had never been.

Jimmy Birch's birthday was also on November 11th. To him this year it was a mixed day of astonished delight and confused sorrow. The astonishment started when he came in from the garden for his breakfast at seven-thirty, and was amazed to find several presents wrapped in fancy paper on the table. He looked up at Auntie May's smiling face.

"Are they for me?"

"They are. Happy birthday, darling," smiled Miss Fisher. "Wash your hands and sit up."

He slid into his place. He could not recall a previous birthday that had included gifts, as his mum had only ever handed him a present when she had some money to spare. Then it had been a comic or a packet of fruit gums. Those joyful occasions had been rare, and were usually long after the day itself had passed. Jimmy picked up one of the cards and opened it slowly and carefully.

He had ten cards, and nine presents to unwrap. Jimmy stared at the pile of items he now owned and shook his head while May Fisher gently tried to persuade him to finish his eggs. It was quite a haul for a little gardener, she thought to herself. A trowel, a magnifying glass, a small watering can, a junior allotment membership, a colourful book on plant-hunters and an actual plant in a blue pot. Dean's offering was a Mars bar and Joey's a jar of his mother's home-made jam. Grandma Dora had obviously been collecting items for a while, as in a pretty cloth bag she had gathered a little wooden farmhouse, a hencoop, and a folded cardboard base-mat printed with garden pathways and green and brown rectangular patches. There were models of plastic vegetables in rows, flowers, individual miniature trees, hedges, a farmer and a lady with a hoe, a little silver pond, and two sets of chickens pecking at the ground. Jimmy couldn't believe his eyes.

"You can play with everything after school. Now come on, up you go and do those teeth."

The following day he had to write thank-you letters, another task he was unfamiliar with. But he did not complain as he was so thrilled with his new possessions. The toy house and garden were his secret favourites. He took the whole bagful round to Grandma Dora's at the weekend.

"Is that another new woolly you're wearing?" she asked, giving him a hug. "You look a bit like Rupert!"

"He's got yellow trousers," Jimmy informed her. "Mine are dungarees. It says Oshkosh on this pocket."

"I see. Well, come on into the warm then and you can show me what you've brought to play with. Is this a letter for me? Oh, thank you, I will read it later. Yes, you can set yourself up on the card table if you like and I'll come and take a look when I've made our drinks, shall I?"

All afternoon Jimmy and Dora created garden layouts, setting out the base-board and rearranging the vegetation to their hearts' content. Jimmy was so absorbed in this fantasy world he hardly noticed Mrs Clark and Mr Tremayne come in from an afternoon trip to Fenchester.

"I say, what's all that?" asked Toby, rubbing his cold hands in front of the fire. "Lord it's chilly out there."

"We went to the Guildhall, Mum. There's a fabulous museum inside. I had no idea," Skip told her mother. "Hello Jimmy. Is that one of your new birthday toys?"

Jim looked up. "Yes, Mrs Clark," he said. "Hello Mr Tremayne. Me and Grandma's playing gardens. She give it me."

"That's a great toy for when it's too wet and cold to go outside," smiled Toby, approvingly. "Gosh, is there any tea going Dora? No, no, I'll do it. Shall I bring in another tray?"

"Did you have a lovely birthday?" Skip asked Jimmy.

"Oh yes, thank you."

"Did Shelley come round?"

Shelley Davidson, the school cleaner's daughter, had been a great friend of Jimmy's last term, but no one had seen much of her since she had started secondary school.

"No. I expect she's busy at school," said Jimmy, recalling his old chum. "She wants to be Ryan Hale's girlfriend. I don't mind." Jimmy shrugged and let the memory go. He was concentrating on his model world.

"Ryan? Really? Well, maybe that will be a match made in heaven, who knows?" chuckled Mrs Clark. Dora smiled too. Shelley was an intense sort of girl. Ryan would have his work cut out to avoid her clutches.

"Here we are," said Toby coming back and setting down the tray full of cups and saucers with a rattle. "Budge up a bit, Jimbo. Let me wriggle in here by the fire. Now then, shall I be mother?"

Motherhood

"I'm on my way!" cried Charlie down the phone.

"Go! Just go," cried Peggy, wafting him towards the office door as he dithered. "I'll see to everything." She shoved him in the chest to wake him up a little. "Do you want Mr Tremayne to drive you?"

"No, no, I'm alright. I can drive. Thanks Peg," grinned Charlie, his mad curly hair standing round his balding pate in a panic.

Peggy watched him fumbling for his keys as he rushed through the playground door. She turned and marched down to the staffroom as it was morning playtime, and announced to the gathered staff that Fiona Tuttle was finally in labour.

"Oh, that's wonderful!" said Skipper.

"Poor thing," commiserated Betty.

"Does Charlie know?" asked Toby, sipping coffee.

"Yes, he's headed over to the maternity ward now. What do you want me to do about a supply?" Someone had to take Mr Tuttle's class while he was otherwise engaged.

"I'll do it," offered Toby. "Can you get a message to the secondary school to let Tim know? He's expected to go home with one of his mates when this happens, apparently, and is to stay there until his dad collects him."

"Will do," said Peggy.

After school Toby and Skipper drove over to the cottage hospital. They found a dazed Charlie Tuttle standing at the window of the maternity waiting area, looking out at the surrounding houses.

"It's a girl, Skip! Born twenty minutes ago. They've sent me out to do some phoning."

"Oh Charlie, how wonderful. And are they both alright?"

"They're fine. They're both absolutely fine. Piece of cake, Fiona told me. Six pounds eight ounces. Oh my god, Skip!" he gave her a hug and vigorously shook Toby's hand.

"Congratulations, old man. Here, have a cigar," grinned Toby. Charlie looked as if all his Christmasses had come at once.

"Have you enough coins for the phone?" Toby scooped a handful of cash from his own pocket and deposited it into Charlie's trembling hands.

Skipper, trying to look composed in this alien environment, nodded and patted the new father's arm. "Go on," she encouraged him. "You go and phone. We'll stay here and come and get you if they want you back. Do you have the phone numbers you need?"

Charlie set about his phone calls while Skip and Toby sat side by side and waited – bit-part actors in a domestic drama neither was comfortable with.

May and Jimmy came to see Fiona and her little daughter early the following morning, which was a Saturday. Fiona was looking flushed and happy as she lay in bed with the baby beside her in a clear-sided cot. May kissed the new mother on the cheek while Jimmy stood shyly to one side. He remembered the hospital and didn't like it. It smelled funny.

Fiona beckoned him over. "Look Jimmy. Here's our new little Gwennie. What do you think?"

The boy took one look at the baby's round pink face with her button eyes and rosebud lips and fell everlastingly in love. "Oh!" he whispered. "It's lovely. Is it a baby?"

The women smiled. "She certainly is. Her name is Gwendoline."

"After one of your aunts?" asked May, sitting down on the uncomfortable chair beside the bed.

"My grandmother," confirmed Fiona. "I think it's a pretty name."

"It's delightful. Here, Jimmy, are your hands clean? Do you want to give Fiona our presents?"

Jimmy dragged himself away from scrutinising the baby's tiny features and passed Fiona several packets wrapped in white tissue paper tied with blue ribbon. Fiona was delighted with May's knitted offerings of a matinee jacket and booties. They were as light and delicate as thistledown.

"Oh, thank you very much," she cried. "And what can be in this last one?"

"That's really from Jimmy. He chose it and wrapped it up himself."

"You haven't bought her some baby gardening gloves, have you?" smiled Fiona, unwrapping it. "Oh look at that. A lovely little brown bunny! Thank you, Jimmy. That's her very first toy. Here, you give it to her."

Jimmy slid the soft ribbon loop of the little rabbit onto Gwennie's wrist as she lay blinking at him. He was almost sure she smiled.

"I think she likes it," he whispered happily.

"I'm sure she loves it. It's just right." Fiona's happiness was infectious, and the two visitors departed feeling that their day had got off to a very good start.

"Now then," said May, squeezing her boy's hand as they began the long walk back into town to buy their weekend shopping. "What should we make for Mr Tuttle's tea tonight? I thought we could take round a casserole, then he and Tim can eat the left-overs tomorrow. What do you think?"

Jimmy nodded. "Chicken casserole," he suggested. "With dumplings. I know Tim likes that."

They agreed on the menu and enjoyed their walk home despite the drizzly rain.

"Auntie May."

"Yes, dear?"

"How old will Gwennie be when I'm ready to get married?"

"Er, well, eight years younger than you are. She'll always be eight years younger than you. Why do you ask?"

"That's alright isn't it? So if I'm thirty, she'll be twenty-two. That would be allowed?"

"Yes, it would be alright. Are you planning on marrying her then?"

"Maybe. No, I just wanted to know. She'd have to like me first, wouldn't she?"

"Yes. Why don't you wait and see how things turn out, then see if you still like her when she's grown up? You might change your mind." What strange things this child came out with.

"No. 'Cos Gwennie's just beautiful," Jimmy sighed. Surely it was alright to admire a new rosebud as well as worship an oak tree? He peered up into the face of his one true-love to be sure he had not hurt her feelings. "But you'll always be my best. You're my Auntie May."

Miss Fisher smiled down at him. Yes, I am your Auntie May, she silently explained to herself, as they stumped confidently along together through the puddles. That's who I am. And I no longer feel as if I'm waiting somewhere offstage in the wings of life. You've toughened me up, my boy. Centred me. Given me a purpose in life, my odd little, wonderful little darling duck.

Garden diary

"So I'm to slash my way through this lot as best I can, am I? Where am I heading for?" asked Terry Green, feeling rather like Stanley being sent to search for Dr Livingstone.

His father shrugged his shoulders. That information had not been supplied. "I dunno," he said. "Try goin' where the flow takes yer." He waved his hand forward in an artistic curve.

Terry sighed and picked up his nicely sharpened sickle. Go with the flow indeed. "Send the dog in if I ent back by Tuesday," he said. Reg left him to it.

Terry spent the morning slowly slashing and clipping his way into the wilderness's dying undergrowth and gradually a few short lengths of cleared pathway began to emerge. It was easier in the section where the formal routes of the original gardens had once been, but beyond them he privately felt no one would ever make many sustainable inroads. It was impenetrable in most parts, barring one or two obvious animal runs. Maybe some kind of chemical could kill it all off, but no one had proposed that. He slung the clippings back into the mass of foliage as he went, knowing they would all be absorbed soon enough. Snip, chuck. Slash, chuck. Hack, chop, fling.

At noon he tramped back to find Mrs Clark and Guy Denny standing near the tennis court. He took off his cap and wiped the sickle blade dry with it.

"How did you get on?" asked Skipper, eagerly. "Your hand is bleeding."

"Not so bad," grunted Terry. "Some of it's pretty hard going, Miss."

"I'm sure it is," commented Guy.

Terry went off for his lunch while Guy and Skip edged delicately along a section of one of the new paths, just to take a look-see. It was impressive. A pathway almost three feet wide wound in and out of scrub and shrubs in the direction of the knoll. Wherever a natural space occurred Terry had slashed back enough to make a slightly bigger clearing.

"This is all going to take more than one pass-through with a sickle," commented Guy. "Maybe a heavy lawnmower would help. Or a Sherman tank."

"I know. I'm hoping the children's parents will muck in and lend a hand at the weekends. Which reminds me, did you think any more about that Parent-Teacher Association idea Toby had?" asked Skipper.

"Yes, I think it's a jolly good one," agreed Guy. "Other schools find groups like this can help enormously – raise a few funds from time to time, and generally organise social odds and ends. They allow the teachers time to do their proper job. We've surely plenty of willing volunteers amongst Mayflower's families, haven't we? People love coming in to help with our reading and outings and the fireworks and so on, don't they?"

"Yes, that's true. Right, well, if you and the rest think it's OK we will go ahead. Who did we think might get it up and running? Mr Henshaw, that's right. His Clive is in kindergarten, isn't he? I'll give him a call this afternoon."

They wandered back to school along Apple Alley, both glad that the new pathways were finally initiated, and that a little more assistance in other areas was on the cards.

"Perhaps PTA stands for Pathways To 'Appiness," quipped Mrs Clark, as the playground door slammed shut behind her in the wind.

Guy smiled, privately thinking that whatever happened, however much help they rustled up, the wilderness would always be a major work in progress.

Blues and rhythm

Dean, Jimmy and Joey were hanging around in Hendy's Fields near the rear wall of Banford Place. There was an ancient overgrown hedgerow there, within which was plenty of space to perch and see over into Lady Longmont's extensive garden. A massive Cedar of Lebanon growing in the grounds blocked some of the view, but by no means all of it. The three boys swayed together in the wet branches, wedged for safety and chewing pink bubblegum.

"Can you see her?" asked Jimmy, who was not as tall as the others.

"Nope. But she generally comes out to put bread on the bird table about now," answered Joey. "When she does, we'll go and knock."

It was ten minutes before the old lady emerged from the back door and hobbled down the cinder path to stock the bird table with fresh crusts. She did not appear very steady in the breeze and the rain, but was dogged enough. She wore a long dark raincoat, a bright yellow sou-wester and men's wellington boots several sizes too big. A schoolmate of the boys accompanied her.

"What's that Kay Fordam doing there?" hissed Joey. "I didn't know she knew Lady Whatsit."

"Neither did I," said Dean.

"Maybe she's helping out," suggested Jimmy. "Lady Whatsit won't want us today."

Kay was indeed helping out. Her mother had fallen into conversation with Lady Longmont on the train home from London one day last Spring, and since then often dispatched her difficult older daughter round to Banford Place to run a few errands at the weekends. Gibb Longmont tolerated the nine-year-old's modest help and was secretly pleased to find herself in a position to influence a young girl's mind. Give the child errands to run, she thought. Try to instil a little social conscience. Kay was a sulky type, but Gibb respected that. She had been sulky herself.

The bird table was brushed clean with a stick by Kay, and Gibb strewed their fresh offerings on it. The girl slung half a mouldy old loaf into the bushes, scaring away a visiting tabby, then the two returned to the warm kitchen for a mug of hot chocolate.

The watching boys beat a retreat.

"How do you come to live in Weston, then?" Lady Longmont enquired of her grumpy visitor.

Kay scowled and slopped some of the contents of her mug onto the table. She would have liked to say Mind Your Own Business, and carried on with her perpetual sulking – but she refrained. There was no one else around to eavesdrop or make fun of her, after all. Kay had nowhere else to go today and Lady L was the first person to have ever shown any interest in her point of view, so she grudgingly voiced aloud a few of her deepest resentments.

She had been happy until she was six, she told the old woman, but then her dad had left them to start a new family with his other girlfriend in Ireland. Her mum had found a new boyfriend – the bloke who owned the Old Priory where they now lived. Nigel Armitage, his name was. Kay never saw her real dad any more. She missed him and the flat they had lived in on the fourth floor of a big block in Ledgely. Mum's new boyfriend was a complete berk, but he was quite rich and had bought her mother a car of her very own. Kay still hated him.

"Why?"

Kay shrugged. "I dunno. He keeps kissing my mum. He's always coming into my room and being annoying. Buying stuff I don't even want."

Wearily, Lady Longmont stirred the sludge at the bottom of her cup. Same old story. "Have you talked to your mama about it?"

"No. No point. She's always on his side. 'Oh Kay, you're just being over-sensitive. Nigel is just being friendly. We're so lucky to be with him. Look at the lovely place we live in now, and all the nice things your father never gave us. Just remember your manners and be grateful'. She's always polishing and dusting and ironing his things."

"Useless," commented Lady Longmont in broad solidarity, then lost interest.

"Exactly. That's what I said." Kay looked at the old woman feeling grateful she wasn't being told to simply get over it. They sat brooding a while longer, Kay's angry brain seething, Lady Longmont's a muzzy blank.

As Kay walked home she fell in with her classmate Dean, who was cycling along Oxen Way across the heath. Jimmy had disappeared and Dean had spent the last hour at Joey's house admiring his new boxing gloves. The rain persisted, but he dismounted and walked along beside her to be friendly.

"We were going to come and ask old Lady Longmont if she wanted any jobs doing earlier, but we saw you there so we never," Dean explained.

"How did you know I was there? Were you spying over the hedge or something?"

"Yeah, we saw you do the bird table. She's a funny old bat."

"She's alright." Kay was coming to the conclusion that she was actually friends with Lady Longmont. "She gave me hot chocolate."

Dean grinned, a dazzling smile that lit up his handsome face and completely bewitched Kay. "I would have built her a whole new bird table for some tasty hot chocolate today," he laughed. "It's bloody freezing."

Kay kicked a stone out of her way. "You like building bird tables then?"

"No, not really." He looked sideways at her, wondering why he had never spoken to this girl much. She always seemed cross and silent in school, but she wasn't so bad. "If you can keep a secret, I actually like dancing. You know – tap. Or modern. My mum's enrolled me in gymnastics. It's alright. There isn't a dance class for boys, worse luck."

Kay nodded, taking all this in. "How about ballet? Or ballroom?"

Dean was pleased she hadn't taken the mickey out of him for liking to dance, so he opened up a little more. "I ent got a partner. You need partners for ballroom."

"Oh." Kay wasn't about to offer herself as a potential partner. She hated dancing. It was so showy-offy. "Why d'you like it?"

"Dunno. I can't sing and I can't draw much. I like painting, and I got a great paintbox. But dancing's just – just – well I can *do* it. It makes me happy just keeping in time with the music. Any music. Any rhythm."

"Ha, I see. OK, well, look there's a train coming. Is that making a rhythm you can dance to?"

Dean hadn't thought of such a thing before, but he handed Kay his bike and waited for the Banford train to start clanking over Weston's double level crossing by St Mary's church – clickety clack – thunkety-thunk. Chuff, puff, clank. He moved his feet and hopped and kicked, wishing he had his taps on like Fred Astaire.

Kay's smile was broad, she was genuinely impressed. They went on up the road together, laughing and speculating on what other sounds Dean might dance along to. Grumpy Kay felt quite happy for once.

* * *

6.

Looking after Gwennie

Gwennie, the Tuttle's baby, was a healthy, happy little soul from Day One. She lay in her cot singing and sleeping by turns, she waited for her bottle feeds with eager expectation, and soon learned to recognise her parents and big brother. Having taken the news of a little sister's arrival badly at first, Tim was now completely besotted with her. He would have killed any monster on earth to protect her. She wasn't at all how he expected a baby to be. Gwennie crowed and waved her hands whenever he came near and gazed lovingly into his eyes as he fed her. When his dad wasn't carrying the baby around, pointing out this and that, Tim was fussing over her outfit, seeing she was warm and safe, picking up her stuff. And there was a lot of stuff.

Jimmy Birch walked down the road to see Gwennie whenever he could, much to May Fisher's amusement, and to the genuine delight of Fiona Tuttle. While Tim was off playing football or Charlie was busy in the garden, Jimmy was the busy mother's godsend. Fiona could get on with some housework, prepare the dinner, or take a leisurely bath in peace leaving Gwennie safely to Jimmy. The baby gurgled happily whenever the little boy appeared and seemed to listen attentively to every word he uttered. And he chattered on and on and on – speaking more to her than to anyone in his whole life before.

"When you get bigger and the weather's better," he would tell her softly, "I'll show you the garden. It's where trees grow. You'll like trees. There's willows – they live near the water. And there's oaks out in the fields. There are beech trees up on Holly Hill, and holly of course, elder and ash and pines and fir trees. We have a tree at Christmas. Christmas is when we give presents to our family. I'm going to give Auntie May a jar of the marmalade I made with Grandma Dora for her Christmas present. What would you like?"

And so it went on and on. Fiona would peg the washing out on the line and come back indoors to hear him still explaining the whole wide world to Gwennie. He never grew tired, he was never bored. He never left her. If she grizzled he had a way of soothing her and stroking her face so that she would – quite suddenly – fall fast asleep. Fiona decided he was using some kind of ancient magic and thoroughly approved of his black arts.

He would eventually, reluctantly, depart when it began to grow dark. After all, it would never do to cause his Auntie May any worry. He scampered along Mayflower Road deep in thought, undecided as to which beautiful lady he would end up marrying one day.

The PTA gets busy

The newly established parent-teacher association was only too pleased to have a practical project to be getting its teeth into. Mr Berry, the secretary, was a great enthusiast for the natural world and immediately took over the pathway project, much to Terry Green's relief. Mr Berry and Mr Henshaw the chairman, and a few others, could be found on dry weekends sharpening their clippers and hacking away at the dense undergrowth.

"They're never going to pull them overgrown raspberry canes out, are they?" Terry asked his dad, speaking about a thorny tangle on the far side of the tennis court. They were more than a little skeptical about the PTA's ability to maintain the paths in the future.

"Never," answered Reg. "Not in a month of Sundays. Nine day wonder, all this – you mark my words, Terry me lad. Paths! Next Spring it'll all be so grown over again you'd never know there'd *been* any ruddy pathways." Reg went back to testing the sharpness of his mower blade with his thumb. "Thorns'll be so thick not even old Stringer'll find his way through. Always was a jungle, always will be, you mark my words."

Terry sighed and put away his tools for the day. He didn't mind what he did as long as he got paid. "I'm going over to Pat's to give Phil a hand with that kitchen. You coming over later?"

"Yerse," replied his father. "I'll bring a couple o' them rat traps too for that scullery. Dog's had a good sniff round but he ent caught nothin' yet."

"Must be losing his touch." Terry zipped up his jacket.

Stringer wagged his tail, knowing he was being talked about. Reg ruffled his ears.

"Nah. He's just bidin' 'is time, incher mate? Still a proper little Sherlock 'e is when 'e wants."

Stringer rested his chin on his paws and wriggled his tail. He would wait. He was the master tactician as well as the best tracker in the district. Everyone knew that.

Upheaval

Ben and Betty Nesbit stared at each other in misery. A formal letter had arrived from Lord Dexter's Estate Office explaining that Hall Manor – all its land and all its properties – had been purchased by a London business syndicate and was definitely to be turned into a golf and country club. Therefore Ben's employment as gamekeeper to his lordship was hereby terminated and their home, South Lodge, was to be vacated by Lady Day. Betty burst into tears.

They had known it was coming, but that didn't make the formal dismissal any easier. They would have to leave their pleasant little home of so many years and find another.

"Sign of the times, I'm afraid love," said Ben, hugging her and trying to put a brave face on things. "The old country pursuits like shooting are outdated. Unfashionable."

"Well I don't like it!" cried Betty. "What on earth will we do?" She tried to pull herself together, but seeing their future there in black and white was as if someone had completely unpicked their hopes.

"Well, I'll just keep trying to find another place. Locally if possible, obviously. Or I'll turn my hand to something new." Ben had a more flexible outlook than his wife and was not as daunted by change as Betty. A little shaking up in life could be good – although this was a lot.

"But what else *could* you do? It's a bit late in life to retrain as an accountant," she sniffed.

Ben smiled at her. "Thanks, love."

"Oh, you know what I mean. Who will want to employ you when there's only ten years until you retire?"

"We'll have to see, won't we?" Ben stood up and buttoned his jacket. "Maybe I won't retire at all. Don't write me off just yet, my girl, I might surprise you." He snapped his fingers and Hades ran to the door ready for work. The little Jack Russell was ready for anything. "Maybe I'll become a dog trainer. Or work in a travelling fair on the shooting gallery. Or sell golf clubs to rich players. We have to look upon this as an opportunity, love."

Betty sniffed miserably. "Well I can't. Not just yet, Ben. I'm going to ring the girls and tell them the letter's come." Their three daughters were all grown up with lives of their own, although they phoned every weekend.

Ben hooked his shotgun over his arm and closed the kitchen door behind him. It was a grey day outside, but he decided a long walk round his coverts and over the fields would help him think of something.

November. Not the best month. Winter weather was coming, when folks needed to feel safe and secure. He wondered where next November would find him.

Peg scores points

Nurse Hilary Presley yanked her handbrake on and slammed the door of the Morris Minor shut.

"Here, 'ere," cried Reg Green. "Steady on treatin' that little car like it were a criminal."

Hilary glowered at him from under the brim of her trilby. "I'm late, Mr Green, and I don't care to be late. Out of my way, if you please."

Reg stepped briskly to one side, tickled by the nurse's obvious distemper. She was always in some kind of fret. "Give us yer keys," he said. "I'll tidy up yer parking."

Nurse Presley snorted and thrust her car keys roughly into his hand. She stalked off into school. Bursting into the office like a Valkyrie, she glared at Peggy who was tapping away at her typewriter.

"Oh, good morning, Hilary," said Peggy mildly.

"I know I'm late, Mrs Bailey. I'm sorry for it, but it canna be helped. I'm here now. Has wee Mungo gone back to his classroom already?" Hilary undid the belt of her raincoat and stamped her wet shoes in a little dance.

"Yes, but I can go and fetch him again." Peggy was amused to see the nurse so annoyed with herself. Usually Peg was the one getting it in the neck. "Would you care for some tea?"

"I would not. I'll hang my raincoat up and press on. Do you possess a coat hanger?"

"No. The hook is good enough for most of us," answered Peggy. "If you have a loop on your jacket."

Hilary Presley's eyes glinted dangerously as she set her things out in the medical room.

"A bonny St Andrew's Day on Sunday to you," Peggy wished her, as she set three folders down on the nurse's desk. Hilary Presley looked up, astonished.

"Och, is that this weekend?"

"Well, I should have thought you'd know," answered Peggy, feeling she was scoring points left, right and centre this morning.

"Aye – well thank you, Mrs Bailey. Fancy you remembering that."

Fancy you forgetting, thought Peggy. She returned to her typing. The wall calendar had alerted her to the fact it was the patron saint of Scotland's special day that coming Sunday. The children in Bella's class had drawn some Scottish flags, three of which they had thoughtfully placed in the nurse's office that morning by way of special welcome. If the weather was fine that afternoon, the first formers were to try their hand at playing a game of crazy golf around a course they had devised on the edge of the Donkey Field.

Mungo James, as relaxed as ever, sauntered into the office three minutes later ready for the follow-up inspection of his ears.

His overly-long mousy hair as usual stood out like a dandelion clock around his head, giving him a deceptively alert appearance. Jimmy Birch and Angela Johnson (a girl from the fifth form) joined him, having also been sent-for. Of the three, Jimmy was the smallest. He was always being summoned by visiting medics. The children sat on chairs, waiting.

"What you two in for?" Angela asked the boys, making conversation.

"Lug 'oles," grunted Mungo, who had just learned this interesting nomenclature.

"Dunno," said Jimmy. He did, but he wasn't prepared to explain. Being short and skinny was humiliating enough without having to tell a pretty girl and a kindergartener. When it was finally his turn the nurse was standing up, looming tall and impressive in the tiny little room.

"Good day to you, Jimmy Birch," she greeted him. Usually she disdained frivolous chit-chat in favour of getting on with the job. But she liked Jimmy and knew he was the most medically challenging of her young patients. She had watched over the child since he started school, and was in no doubt as to the part she had played in alerting the authorities to his many problems. She smiled, approvingly.

It had only been a few months since his mother had died – the victim of a still unsolved hit-and-run accident on her way home from work one Summer evening. But since being fostered by Miss Fisher, little by little, his health had started to improve. He was a great deal happier and less anxious too. Hilary Presley felt more than a little pleased to see the bairn had definitely turned a corner.

Jimmy smiled back, trying to hide the gap in his front teeth a while longer. He preferred the doctor to prod and poke and measure him rather than the nurse, but today he had no choice. Nurse Presley wasn't so bad, he reluctantly admitted, trying to be charitable. He removed his shoes and stood with his back against the wall-mounted height scale. He knew the drill.

Nurse Presley checked everything twice. Height, weight, chest, waist, legs, feet, wrists, hands. Ears, eyes, fingernails. She even measured around his head and made notes on an important-looking paper while he carefully re-tied his shoe-laces.

"Well, young man," she announced, rather pleased. "You're finally starting to grow in all the right places. I can confirm your tummy's not so big as it was, and the rest of you is much improved. You're about a half-inch taller than last time I measured you." She looked over at him with another genuinely happy smile on her plain round face.

Jimmy nodded. He could have told her that news himself but he was far too polite to do so. His new corduroy shorts fitted his waist properly, and his skin was less crinkly and cracked. He was warm and clean, fed and rested. Jim knew he was doing much, much better. He asked the nurse to show him where he came to on the scale so he could tell Miss Fisher later.

Hilary ruffled his thickening brown hair, admiring its cleanliness and hitherto unsuspected curls. No sign of nits or dandruff or anything else any more. He had a healthy colour, his eyes were no longer dull, his ears were as clean as a whistle. Jimmy tried to dodge her large hand on his head but it wasn't possible. He remembered his manners and voiced his thanks for the nurse's trouble today.

"You are very welcome," she answered, appreciating his politeness. "Now, did the tooth fairy come to ye?"

She meant she had spotted his missing teeth. Jimmy considered eight was too old for fairies, but he nodded anyway to please her. "Yes. I put them under the pillow each time, and in the morning I found silver money."

"Well, wasn't that exciting? And what does the fairy pay for a tooth these days, I wonder?"

"Ten pee," answered Jimmy who had stuffed the unexpected windfall into his money-box. He was saving up for Christmas presents.

"Excellent! Well enjoy your day, Jimmy Birch. I will see you next month."

Jim beetled back to class as fast as he could, hoping Mr Tuttle wouldn't have started the singing activity they often had at the end of each morning if they'd all been good. Singing was fun, the way Mr T did it and the daily physical activity was helping Jimmy breathe deeper and strengthening his chest. He could tell. He went up the stairs hoping the song-words today didn't include too many s-sounds, because, until his new teeth grew down, he was still a little spitty.

Not OK

"Oh, Kay!" whined her mother, seeing the line of muddy footprints across her recently washed kitchen floor.

Kay snarled "Sorry," and slammed the biscuit tin down on the counter-top.

How she hated her name! It was just a letter of the alphabet. Couldn't they have come up with something more imaginative? Something like a real name? '*Oh Kay*', smirked the children at school. '*Oh, Kay*', cried everyone when they found her behaviour anything *but* OK.

"I'm going round Lady Longmont's," she told her mother who was already down on her hands and knees wiping up the mud with a dishcloth. Kay slammed out of the house and grabbed her bike up from the ground where she had thrown it yesterday. If I made the mess, I should clear it up, she fumed as she pedalled over the double level crossing. Not Mum. Kay had a deep-rooted sense of justice.

Lady Longmont was rootling in the cupboard under the stairs for an old toffee tin she knew to be there. Kay came in with her usual 'Halloo, it's me', and removed her shoes. The stone flagged floor was cold through her socks.

"What are you doing?" she asked.

"Tin. There's a tin. Can you pull it out?"

Kay retrieved the item from the bottom shelf of an old bookcase in the untidy cupboard. It had a picture of some king or other on its square lid. She handed it over.

Lady Longmont clutched the tin to her chest while Kay fed the dogs and changed the water in their bowls, tasks the old lady often forgot these dark mornings.

"What's in the tin?" Kay enquired.

"Never you mind. Nothing. It's private." Lady Longmont squinted at her suspiciously. She prised open the lid and took out a photograph of her brothers, mother and father all in a row on a terrace long ago. She showed it to Kay as they sat at the table.

There were other photographs, all grey and curling at the corners. Some men with moustaches. A wolfhound. An alpine scene. A jolly-looking lady in culottes wielding a cow-bell. The torn front cover of an old Tatler magazine. A young man in a belted swimming outfit.

"Lord Longmont," explained Gibb. Kay lay her head on her arm, bored.

"This is the Queen Mary. This is me at the Dorchester. I came out with some very tedious girls." The old lady pushed the photos away and took out a leather-bound notebook.

"This book is top secret," she told her little friend in a whisper. "It really is. There's people in this town would very much like to get a look at it. It would solve quite a few open questions for them, I can tell you."

"Would you like me to do the bird table now?"

"In a minute, in a minute!" Lady Longmont was tetchy and preoccupied this morning. "That can wait. Here's what I want to show you."

Inside the back cover of the leather notebook was a pocket with a flap, possibly once intended to hold a hiking map. From it, Gibb pulled out several smaller thinner notepads each containing a few wafer-like pages. On each page were hundreds of tiny letters, numbers and geometric symbols laid out like a crossword puzzle with no black squares.

"Lookie here," whispered Gibb, tracing her bony finger along each line. "This is now. Over the page will be tomorrow. They will be expecting this, right here, but I'm not going to be able to… ." She stopped. He eyes glittered as she took a better look at her companion. "Yes," she said. "Yes, you must take it. Take them all. Then *you'll* know what to do." She thrust the pad and book back into the tin and rammed the photos untidily on top. "Yes, there. It's right it should go to you. I'll find a bag."

She rose and pulled out bag after plastic bag from under the sink, finally thrusting the toffee tin into one.

"Quick, before he comes back. Don't let any of them know you have this. But *you* can use it from now on. Go on, take it! I'm done with it all."

Kay gave up trying to protest. She saw the mad glint in the old woman's eye and knew it would be less bother to simply humour the old duck. It was anyone's guess as to what she was talking about. "Thank you," she said politely. "I'll take good care of it."

She rode home later with the bag dangling from her handlebars. What an awful morning. A tin full of boring old photos, stinky dog food to deal with, and a disgusting mess on the bird table. Still, she had sorted it all, and kept out of the way of everyone at home, so that was good. This afternoon she would stay in her bedroom and write a story about the people in the old photos. She might even type it up on the old typewriter Nigel had given her, and sew it into a real, miniature book. Make a cover and everything. That was always fun.

Lady Longmont's old notebooks she chucked in her wastepaper basket.

Flights of fancy

The choice of Peter Pan for the play was proving to be more of a challenge than Guy had anticipated. For one thing people had to fly, and for another nobody could find a top hat. The top hat situation was finally solved when Toby Tremayne discovered one in the attic of Banford Hall. It had belonged to Lady Longmont's step-father and was in a special box with a crest on the lid. Gibb waved him away when he asked if he might borrow it.

Flying actors were the tougher problem. Terry and Reg, and Skipper and Jean stood staring at the stage for an hour after school one dark evening, trying to figure out how it might be done.

"How about rigging trapezes from that beam?" suggested Jean hopefully. There was one central crossbeam high above the width of the stage.

"Like swings? How would they get on them? Trampoline? And 'ow would they move about? They'll just look like a circus act," said Reg.

Terry walked up and down, judging the space in the wings (which wasn't much) and wondering about safety.

"We can't just tie a rope around Peter Pan's waist and haul him backwards and forwards can we? No. He'd likely end up upside down. And what about the rest of 'em in their nighties? Have they all gotta fly, Miss?"

"Yes, but we can't have them all dangling about on strings like conkers. Why on earth we aren't doing Sleeping Beauty or something simpler, I just don't know."

Reg agreed. Flying kids were a bit out of his usual league. However, old sailors like himself rarely admitted defeat. They were an inventive breed. After all, rigging an A-frame to swing stores aboard a moving vessel at sea wasn't impossible. Surely, as the crossbeam was already there they could come up with something. It just had to be safe for little kids. He sucked his moustache and tried to remember whether he had any pulleys in his odds and ends box.

"Elastic?"

"No."

Then Jean had a brainwave. "Why not let them use roller-skates?" she cried.

Skipper stared at her as if she were mad.

"No, hang on. Not roller skates – *tea trolleys*!" Jean was excited.

"What?"

"No, well, some kind of platform on wheels. Peter could lie on it, on his stomach with his arms out like he's flying. Then we could puff smoke round him for clouds. Dry ice. I can get some. Then no one would see the tea trolley. It would be like he was flying through clouds on his way to Never-never land." Jean smiled broadly, so pleased with herself he felt like dancing.

Reg rubbed his chin. Terry looked at his feet. Skipper stood with her mouth open.

"It could work," said Jean, encouragingly.

"You know, it might," said Terry, who couldn't think of anything better.

Reg made a harrumphing noise and started filling his pipe with tobacco. "Tea trolley? You got one strong enough then, Miss?"

"No, but we can find one. They could all have one. Or roller skates. Or, one of those what-do-you-ma-call-ems? *Skate*boards, that's it. Only maybe they wouldn't see where they were going, what with the smoke and everything. Does that matter? Probably will. We ought to try it out first."

They did try it out. Terry and Reg ignored the tea trolley notion and built two small sturdy platforms with ball-like castors which enabled them to be rolled smoothly in any direction. Little Anna Lane who was to play Peter, and Wendy Clarke who was to play Wendy, were brought in. They practised lying on their vehicles and judiciously 'flying' slowly all round the stage. They found the best thing was to keep one foot in contact with the floor in order to turn or stop at will. When Mrs Hewitt added some dry-ice smoke a day later, the effect was surprisingly good. Jago and Jack, who played John and Michael, although deeply jealous of the trolleys, discovered they could both act as if they were flying perfectly well just by running around taking tiny steps in the fog. Tinker Bell did the same. The smoke camouflaged their pattering feet and they had a much greater range, which allowed for more adventurous acting than the trolley girls. Even Mr Green was impressed with the Flying Cannellonis, as he dubbed them, by the time the final rehearsals began. When they all 'flew' in formation through the clouds they looked quite astonishing.

Guy was thrilled. Once the costumes were completed the entire play came together, and everyone had an immense amount of fun, despite the challenging task of ensuring that every child who wanted a part in it was included. Luckily pirates and lost boys could be added to without much difficulty. Alternate afternoons Guy rehearsed his players in the hall for an hour, while Ernest directed his Little Pigs in the library. Other days they swapped. The mornings were set aside for the babies to clomp through the nativity and get used to the echoing space and majesty of the gym hall. Charlie was kept busy with all the musical requirements for the upper years, but had willingly handed over the nativity's music to Bella, who was more than competent. Luckily for Mayflower, the deputy and headmistress were quite happy to help take classes here and there while the thespians rehearsed. It was Guy's toughest, but also one of his happiest and most rewarding times of the year.

The school's Christmas events attracted more and more willing supporters as the weeks trickled by. There was a core of sewing volunteers willing to create costumes. Others preferred to help with props. A few chose to sell tickets, while still others offered to design and print all the programmes and carol-sheets. School could also rely on ex-teacher Julia Scott, one of the governors, to substitute for a day when a teacher was busy. She often brought Pongo her poodle along – much to the delight of whichever class she happened to be in charge of. Stringer and Pongo were great pals and often took themselves off for a run round the field all by themselves. Nicky, the school cat, did not think much of this muddy activity and watched from his perch on the top of the cricket pavilion. When the dogs returned, panting thirstily, he would stretch himself and yawn disdainfully before scampering off to chase up some dinner, or sneak indoors to curl up on the headmistress's hearthrug in front of the small log fire she insisted on being lit every morning.

Sometimes it did not take very much to keep Mayflower's diverse population happy.

Homework

"Auntie May."
"Yes, darling."
"Do worms know they're worms?"

"How d'you mean?"

"Well, I know I'm a boy, but do worms and beetles and birds and trees and lettuces know what they are?" Jimmy was colouring a homework picture and having a bit of a think.

Miss Fisher glanced over from her endless knitting. It had been a long day and she was glad to have her feet up in front of the kitchen fire. She had come across this question, or one very similar, once or twice before in her long teaching career.

"Nobody knows for sure. Worms and things don't speak, do they?"

"Not in words, no", said Jimmy. "But they tell us things differently don't they? Like when worms go deep it won't rain. And if its morning the birds sing. And if its Autumn the leaves fall off."

"Well that's behaviour rather than language communication," explained May.

"I know. But it is a type of talking isn't it? So maybe they understand what they are, too." Jimmy had come to the end of that train of thought, much to May's relief. "I finished."

He held up his homework. It passed muster so he put it safely in his satchel for tomorrow. He slid the milk saucepan onto the range top and set two cups on a tray, making sure the tray cloth was straight. He and his foster mother always had their bedtime milk together about this time, and was one of their favourite moments of the day. Jimmy had already had his bath and was in his dressing gown ready for bed.

"Will Father Christmas know where I live this Christmas?" he asked.

"For sure. Mrs Harris and I discussed it specially. All her forms and documents are up to date and what she knows, Santa knows too." Auntie May remembered that luckily she and the social worker had, in fact, talked about Christmas during one of their recent meetings. May watched Jimmy's face relax, and realized it had been worrying him. If he had been younger she would have given him a big cuddle and told him not to worry, the elves were at work and it was all going to be fine. But although he might look about five he wasn't. He was eight.

"Have you ever been to see Father Christmas in a shop?"

"No."

"Would you like to? We could go to Fenchester on the bus and then you could make sure to remind him of your new address, couldn't you? Just to be sure."

Jimmy grinned.

"Really? In a shop?"

"Yes. In Treve's."

"Oh, yes please," he cried.

Maybe eight wasn't so old after all. Perhaps it was only a matter of sophistication.

* * *

7.

Art Day

Fay Winstanley arrived as usual in a cloud of exhaust on her motorbike – its sidecar stuffed to the gunwales with paper, fabric and craft materials. It was a dark damp morning in early December, and Reg Green wasn't in the best of moods.

"Ahoy there, and a happy-hello to you, Mr Green!" Fay sang out on seeing him hooking back the front door.

Stringer had been bent on having a good sniff around the front yard, but on being confronted by Miss Winstanley and her noxious vehicle, beat a hasty retreat up the stairs and into Mr Tremayne's study where it was quiet and fume-free.

Jumped ship, thought Reg. Can't even trust the dratted dog any more.

"Mornin'," he growled. "Come 'ere to make another fine mess, then?"

"Oh yes," grinned the art teacher, blithely unaware of the caretaker's mood. "Good old Mayflower. Always look forward to this annual treat."

"Free lunch too?"

"Yes, always welcome," she giggled. "What is it today, do you know?"

"Couldn't say, I'm sure. Possibly Spam. Now then, let's get some lads to give you an 'and inside, shall we? I've a couple of good 'n's lined up. Here, Freddy Dawkins. Where's yer mate? Ah, there you are young Trevor. Give Miss Winstanley some 'elp tekkin' this stuff down to the 'all. You'll see what goes where when you get there. And don't drop it all over the shop, neither. Look lively now." Reg began stacking bags in the porch to get them out of the wet. He was eager to relocate the motor bike out of sight round the back, off his gravel entry-way.

Bella Delgado brought her class down for their turn at craft-making at nine-o'clock sharp. They would share the first hour with the kindergarteners. She was thrilled with the prospect of some special Christmas activities for her children, although she did not rule out anybody wishing to make something un-related to the festive season. Perhaps a special flag or a winter-themed hat might be preferable for some. She was disappointed she had not yet managed to get the headmistress to agree to purchase a small kiln so she could begin her after-school pottery club, but it was early days yet. The activities today were a start.

Zoe Smith from Form 2, hoped to make something special for Dean Underwood when it was her turn. He was the heart-throb from Mrs Hewitt's class who had selected her to hand out the school's Christmas gifts last year. She, like many of the other girls, thought Dean was simply wonderful – handsome, kind and funny. She had sung, and he had danced alongside her on several special occasions. He always said hello to her in the playground now – a massive feather in Zoe's cap. And she sensed he liked her too. He was ages older, but that did not matter. Zoe sighed, smitten.

So what should she create for him today? She thought hard all the way down the Iron Duke stairs as the rain drummed on the glass roof above.

"Miss Fisher."

"Yes, Zoe?"

"What do dancers like for presents? Boy dancers?"

Miss Fisher was stumped. "I really don't know, Zoe. Try asking Mr Tuttle."

Mr Tuttle was equally baffled. He and Zoe walked along the line of tables, each already bustling with children cutting and pasting and pinning and sewing. "Is he a *good* dancer?" asked the teacher, feeling he had better at least try to sound intelligent.

"Oh yes."

Charlie suddenly realised she meant Dean. He was the only lad in school who danced without a hint of self-consciousness. "Well if he's *really* top notch, why not make him a gold medal to hang round his neck? Look, there's a place at the air-drying clay table, next to Ronnie. You could make it today, choose a Christmassy ribbon to hang it from, and paint and varnish it in class next week when it's dried out properly. How would that be?"

Zoe grinned. That was a brilliant idea. Mr Tuttle shot up in her estimation.

She spent the rest of the hour creating a round flat circle, piercing it with a single hole, and forming a star-shape on one side. Then she pressed Dean's initials into the other side. Two minutes before time was up she grabbed a length of red, green and silver ribbon from a box on the floor and lined up, carefully holding the still damp medallion in her hand.

"My goodness Zoe," said Carol Moore admiringly. "That's very special. Shall we put it on the window sill to dry when we get back upstairs? I'll take the ribbon for you. Your hands are a bit messy from all that clay."

"Thank you, Mrs Moore," Zoe said politely. "Yes, I'll have a good old wash before lunch. I made this for Dean," she whispered conspiratorially.

"He'll love it," Carol answered. She looked at Zoe's freckled face and Titian locks. She might be only seven, but there was something very self-confident about this little girl. And she would be absolutely gorgeous when she was older. I'm sure he'll love you too, thought Carol.

Exams

"Why do we have to keep doing tests?" asked Kay, annoyed as usual. She sat glowering at Caroline Jacob, who was sitting bolt upright like a puppy waiting for a treat as Mrs Hewitt gave out the exam papers. Kay folded her arms and scowled.

"Now then, Kay," said her teacher, unfazed by the child's attitude. "Don't turn these over until I say. Is everyone quite ready? Good. Then turn over and begin."

Kay zoomed through every exam paper the teacher presented her with. Other children puffed and blew, but Kay Fordam remembered anything she was taught after a single explanation, so it was easy-peezy. Had the child greater personal charm, she might have been considered for head girl next year, sighed Mrs Hewitt. As it was Kay would probably barely make prefect. Her behaviour was rough, her manner surly. She scuffed along with anyone who could put up with her for a few minutes, but in general the other children had learned to avoid her. Maybe Mrs Hewitt should talk to Kay's mother and step-father again.

Caroline collected up the papers after an hour. Kay had been reading her library book for a while, having finished early and checked every answer twice. The fifth form clattered outside in raincoats and scarves for some much needed fresh air. Kay slipped round to the far side of the building to see if Mr Green was in his boiler-room. She had no wish to stay in the playground with the others.

"You come to find out 'ow to fix my boiler then?" asked Mr Green. He cast her a look. This was the one with a big chip on her shoulder, wasn't it? "You know you're out of bounds?"

Kay shrugged. "No one cares," she said.

Reg made a harrumphing sound, then pointed to a pile of discarded offcuts of wood he wanted shifting. "You got time on yer 'ands? Go and get one of them barrers out the toolshed and 'elp me shift this lot down the lodge courtyard then, will yer? Vicar says he wants to build 'isself a sailing boat. Not for ocean-going. A land yacht thing. Like a boat on wheels. Yes, goo on, thass a good girl. Don't tell no-one."

Kay rewarded him with a dazzling conspiratorial grin and skipped off to collect one of the wheelbarrows. A land yacht. That sounded fun. Maybe Rev Bill would like an apprentice yacht-builder.

The tree arrives

The day of the arrival of the school's Christmas tree had been brought forward this year. Mrs Clark felt far too much had been crammed into the last week of term in the past, so this year she had it delivered during the week before the play performances. Reg, Terry, Mr Goodman of the PTA and his son Carl struggled in with it through the french doors of the hall one chilly morning before nine o'clock. It was a tall tree, kindly donated by Mr and Mrs Dawkins at Christmas Farm.

"Wipe yer muddy feet," Reg reminded his helpers. They all duly shuffled over the mats and papers he had spread. It was awkward trying to manoeuvre the long tree in without damaging it. Reg had by far the heaviest job as he bore the thick end of the trunk. They lay it down on the floor, and Carl scampered off to class while Mr Green and Terry clamped a heavy steel contraption (of possibly nautical design and local blacksmith manufacture) onto the trunk's base, then carefully hoisted it upright, where it swayed and settled onto its special mat, dripping.

"Grab the end of this mat," said Terry to Mr Goodman. Together they pulled and slid the tree back into a corner of the hall and turned its most favourable aspect outwards. When they were satisfied, Terry lay stomach-down on the floor and draped some old red velvet curtains artistically over the clunky base as camouflage. By the time he slid back out again the tree began to look festively dressed. The men were pleased with their morning's work. They stood admiring it as rain suddenly drummed hard on the hall roof.

"Just in time," commented Reg, closing and locking the outer doors. He turned round to see Stringer and Nicky trotting down the steps into the hall from the corridor. The two made straight for the tree and lay under it on the edges of the soft velvet curtain.

"Well," said Mr Goodman, brushing stray needles off his trouser legs. "Those two have found a nice dry billet anyway."

Terry grinned. "They'll be there until Christmas, most likely. Tie a couple of ribbons round their necks and they'll be mistaken for a couple of gifts waiting to be unwrapped."

"Don't you believe it," said Reg. "Prob'ly only be there 'til lunchtime, when Ivy brings 'em a bit of dinner. Only there for the present, so to speak. Ho ho ho."

He went off to fetch his mop and broom, whistling. Christmas was actually alright, even if it was a lot of extra work. Only there for the present!

Jingle all the way

Toby was fascinated by all the hoop-la surrounding Christmas in a primary school. It was ages since he had witnessed this much excitement building up day in, day out. He was particularly amused by the lengths the older ones would go to in order to keep the special magic going for the younger children. It was very sweet, very touching, to hear them curtail their own often cynically sophisticated and superior comments when a little person was around. He strolled about on playground duty, listening.

"There, there. Don't you cry, duckie," soothed Philly Roberts as she picked up a first former who had slipped over in a pile of wet leaves on the playground. "Here, let's brush them old leaves off yer skirt. Now come on, we'll do our good deed and help Mr Green sweep them into that corner. Father Christmas won't want to visit round here if it's all messy with dirty old wet leaves, now will he? He likes his sleigh nice and bright. He don't want to land on his bum no more'n you do."

Later, in the wilderness, two big lads were instructing three little boys.

"Come on. Me and Mark'll show you how to make a plate of salad for the reindeer to eat. That's it, put those dandelion bits on that big leaf and we'll show you where we always put out a line of tasty treats for them. Yeah, you can bring a carrot in tomorrow and add it, if your mum says. Here, don't tell no one, but under this hedge is exactly where Father Christmas always lands," they said, completely seriously. "Every year. We seen the marks of the ski-feet on his sledge. S'true."

Toby was most astonished, however, when Charlie Tuttle came into the staffroom chuckling one day.

"What's tickled you?" asked May, looking up from her knitting.

"It's Form 6," Charlie grinned. "I was sorting through the percussion instruments just now and asked where the bell-shaker was. You know, the jingly bells on that hand-grip thing? Couldn't find it anywhere. Turns out, Yulissa and Anna have 'borrowed' it. They're taking it in turns every afternoon to creep past the kindergarten windows just after breaktime when the babies are quietly listening to a story, and jingle them. They've got the little ones thinking Santa's having a few practice runs up and down outside on his sleigh."

Toby burst out laughing and spilt his tea. "Good lord! They're old before their time, our kids. It's rather sweet though."

May nodded as Jean wiped Toby's jacket with a damp cloth.

"It's just Mayflower," she explained.

Paperclips and pirates

The nativity play, like Peter Pan, was not without its challenges this year. The children playing animals were to wear masks. These looked very effective, but one or two of the wearers found the masks slipped up or down during the action making it difficult to see out through the eyeholes. Sarah Fletcher was one such troubled actor. She grew anxious and tearful until Mrs Moore managed to devise a system of paperclips that hooked her donkey mask to the elastic bands securing her hair bunches, rather in the manner of a tent being held secure in a gale by additional guy ropes.

"Swing your head a bit," instructed Mrs Moore, standing back.

Sarah did. Her bunches, and her donkey ears, waggled madly. The mask, mercifully, stayed still.

"It hasn't slipped back down over your nose again, has it? Now then!"

Sarah was delighted. The whole mask felt much more secure and comfortable now, and she could see beautifully. "I'll go and get them other sheeps and oxens and things for you, Mrs Moore. It's the oxens what complains, you know. It's his horns, see?"

Carol Moore did see. The horns were quite a problem as they tended to overbalance everything. Paul Farmer, who played a sheep, seemed to be peering up into the sky most of the time.

"It's a good job we have plenty of paperclips," Mrs Nesbit said to Carol as Sarah trotted off. "Do you have a spare one I could use to fasten Joseph's waistcoat across his chest? He's currently wearing it like an off-the-shoulder ballgown."

Peter Pan now presented another issue. Having successfully solved the mechanics of human flight, the new dilemma was the fight scene between the Lost Children and the pirates. Every player was far too eager to make the battle look realistic, forcing Guy to impose some very strict choreographic rigour on the cast before anyone got seriously hurt. After much practising, the children eventually learned to advance, then fade. They connected, they disengaged. The fight became very stylised and balletic, considerably adding to the dramatic effect. Most children remembered their footwork well.

"Ha-*harrrr*!" snarled Captain Hook, exuberantly lunging forward and nearly pinning Peter Pan to the scenery one afternoon.

"Freddy!" yelled Mr Denny. "For pity's sake be careful! You'll have Anna fall over the crocodile if you push her back that far. Have some sense, do. Colin – can you swing your tail a bit further round? No the other way. We want to see your teeth. That's better. Yes snap them – you're hungry don't forget. Snap, snap. Now Anna, you skip nimbly past him and jump onto the poop deck."

Anna (playing Peter Pan) leapt onto the small stage-block that was doubling as a ship's deck. Hook swung round after her, waving his cutlass and flaring the skirts of his jacket dramatically.

"That's it Freddy – swashbuckle! Now come on Dean, where are you? Right, now drive Hook and those horrible pirates back. Lunge, two three four. Look out, Freddy! You have to watch what they're doing. Now twirl round again, two three four, and... Yes, that's good Colin, grab him! Don't let go. Drag him right off into the wings. Yes, hang on to the curtain with your hook, Freddy, and gasp a bit like that. Pull a few terrible faces – after all you're being eaten alive. Hey that's really good! What do you think, Mrs Hewitt?"

Jean was laughing so hard it took a while to answer him. "Oh my word! That's it, brilliant. Well done Freddy. Do it like that. Oh my!"

Guy was delighted. "Now the rest of you turn and cheer like mad as the crocodile swaggers slowly back across the stage. Yes, look thrilled! Colin sway side to side and burp like you just ate three helpings of Mrs Green's strawberry shortcake. Face front and... curtain!"

A brave face

"Well, it all feels far too close for comfort, somehow," sighed Betty as she safety-pinned Joseph's coat firmly across his front. Paper clips were all very well, but safety pins were better. The Nativity actors were lining up ready for the first dramatic performance of their five-year-old lives, all hot and nervous.

Carol Moore was full of sympathy. "I should hate to have to move out of my house. Still no sign of a job for Ben yet?"

"No." Betty adjusted Joseph's cotton-wool beard and sent him off to stand beside Mary. She was so worried about their future it felt as if she was being stabbed afresh every morning when she woke. This Christmas she felt genuine sympathy for the

Holy Family's homeless plight, although at least both she and the Blessed Virgin had good strong men to lean on.

Ben had scoured the whole county for a position, so far to no avail. His game-keeping colleagues had done their best for him, but the whole world of country pursuits seemed to be shrinking. Ben was becoming more and more withdrawn as each avenue he tried came to nothing. He did his best not to appear too desperate in front of his wife, but she knew he was disappointed. He tried to cheer her up by saying that if all else failed he would turn his talents to fixing bikes, or delivering milk, or hedge-trimming. She wasn't fooled.

Carol Moore watched Betty's face closely. She was grey with fatigue and stress, but trying to be brave.

"Look," she said. "I know your Ben's a dab hand at woodwork and suchlike. I'll ask Paul whether he'll want an extra set of hands come the Spring, shall I? You never know."

Betty hugged her, more than grateful. Lady Day, in March, would be there before they knew it. This kind offer was a tiny little ray of hope, but at this point, Betty would hang on to anything.

If only it solved the problem of where they could live. Even a stable was beginning to look good.

Four-legged friends

The Nativity masks were a huge success as none wobbled or twisted skywards, and every child could be heard speaking their lines beautifully. Even Rev Bill was impressed. The various animals shoved the masks up on top of their heads when the play was finally over to listen to him thanking them and their parents and teachers in time-honoured fashion.

"Now our collection today is for St Andrew's never-ending renovation fund, as you know. The prefects are holding red buckets for your kind contributions by the exit doors. Thank you for coming everybody, and – if I don't see you in church over the holidays – a very merry Christmas."

Peggy and Cathy peered into the buckets later that day and were surprised to see a donkey's face staring out at them. Peggy turned the mask over and discovered Sarah Fletcher's name on the back.

"Why has Sarah Fletcher put her donkey mask in the collection bucket do you suppose?" Peggy was mystified. "Is it her contribution to the church roof?"

Cathy grinned. "Bless the child. She does love anything four-legged, that one. She was telling me Alf Rose is giving up Horace after Christmas."

"No!"

The milkman's horse was a very old favourite with Mayflower's children. Horace had pulled the milk float for years, plodding along and automatically stopping at various gates while Alf clattered bottles, delivered eggs and butter and stacked empty crates.

"Alf's not going to sell him for glue or anything awful is he?" Peggy was quite upset at the thought of old Horace never putting his head through the hedge and waiting for someone to kindly offer him a juicy carrot ever again.

Cathy was shocked. "No, nothing like that. But Alf told me this morning he can't afford to stable Horace at the Mint any more. You know he's had him there in the winter and out on Hendy's Field all Summer for years, hasn't he? Things are getting just far too expensive nowadays."

"So what's he going to do?" persisted Peggy.

"Said he doesn't know yet. I suggested he talk to Miss Winstanley about her little field. The one beside her mill she was going to turn into a car park for her thousands of gallery visitors. Well that idea hasn't materialised yet, as you know. And now she has Persephone, I thought she might want to start a collection of picturesque horses and donkeys. It's just the sort of thing that would appeal to her."

Peggy didn't think much of the notion herself, but she agreed Miss Winstanley might see it differently. "And how's Alf planning on bringing our milk round once Horace has retired?"

"Oh, the dairy's giving him a little electric powered float. They're all getting them, the Banford milkmen. He'll have to get used to driving it of course. Putting the brake on properly and so forth." Cathy opened up her registers and began running her finger down columns of names. "I'm sure Alf will figure it out."

Peggy was not so sure. Alf was not big on innovation, hence his attachment to his horse-drawn vehicle for so many years. Even changing one's regular milk order had him frowning and scribbling with a pencil stub in his tatty order book. Mrs Bailey appreciated consistency herself. It was all very disturbing.

Peggy kicked the Lost Property Box into its corner after dropping the donkey mask into it. That will have to have a good sort out before the end of term, she thought. She turned her attention back to counting the contents of the other collection buckets.

Perils averted and presents

The play performances eventually went off extremely well. Mrs Clark wished her old friend Chloe had been there to see the children act so confidently and have such fun. She vowed to send copies of the photographs Ernest was busily snapping for the school newsletter to her.

"Good lord," breathed Jean with relief, as she sank down onto a chair after the final evening performance of Peter Pan. "I thought Wendy Clarke was a gonner for sure when that trolley wheel slipped over the edge of the stage."

Ernest nodded. He had expected the same. "She was a proper little trouper, though wasn't she? Just stood up, adjust the thing and climbed back on."

"Good kid," agreed Mike. Gratefully, he took the cup of tea being offered him by Cathy. "How were things back here?" The staffroom was used as the off-stage waiting area, there being no real wings to the stage itself. It also had the benefit of a toilet for those with nervous tummies.

Cathy said "Everyone was pretty good. Joey Latimer had a bit of a grump with Mick McDonald over some action figure or something, but once I confiscated the offending object they quietened down."

"I don't know what's the matter with that lad lately," sighed Guy Denny. "He always used to be such a sweet kid. Tried hard and didn't give up on himself." Joey had always needed a little extra help with learning, especially when it came to writing, but had otherwise been a good team player. Maybe puberty was souring his life a little early.

Joey was a nuisance again when Christmas lunch was over and everyone had gathered round the tree for the usual present giving. Roast chicken followed by chocolate pudding were the children's all-time festive favourites, and everyone else was feeling pleasantly mellow and full. As soon as they were all settled cross-legged on the floor and their exalted guests were on comfy chairs, Joe Latimer began kicking at the children in front of him.

"Joe," hissed Guy. "Stop doing that."

Joey scowled and stopped. Then he began again, muttering to a child he had kicked to shove over because he couldn't see.

"Joey, come and sit by me, please," said Mrs Raina, sharply. Joe slid over to her chair and sat with his head down, staring at the floor. "Come on now," said Sandi in a low voice. "Don't spoil it for everyone."

Joey shrugged her kind hand off his shoulder. Why did people have to keep touching you?

The fun gifts were handed out this year by John Larkin, a fourth former who struggled with all academic learning, but who had recently become a regular encyclopedia of gardening information. Zoe Smith (last year's gift deliverer) had selected him for the task because he had helped her plant some very successful potatoes in her allotment last Easter. John was so proud to be the chosen one, he could barely breathe. Red-faced with joy, he handed out tins of special dogfood to Mrs Hewitt, Mr Green, and Mr Tuttle for Sweep, Stringer and Cassius, then a clockwork mouse toy to Mrs Clark for Nicky. There was a bag of biscuits for Mrs Nesbit's dogs. Hammy, the first form's hamster, had died during the Summer holidays but Miss Delgado had nobly replaced it, as she believed children enjoyed caring for small rodents. She was handed a big plastic ball for Hammy Number Two to run around the floor in. The governors, the PTA chairman, the school doctor, nurse, dentist – and even the photographer – were here this Christmas and each was handed a large and personal hand-made card depicting the many ways each one helped the school. Miss Winstanley was presented with a little ceramic donkey and cart. Grandma Dora, that stalwart of the Knit and Nosh Clubs, was given a poncho made of crocheted squares created in secret by the Knit Club members. The school cooks each had a box of chocolate fudge. Mrs Davidson the cleaner, Mr Dawkins from the farm, and Paul Moore the builder were handed tins of fancy biscuits. Cathy and Peggy received hankies in pretty boxes, the vicar a plastic model of a Lancaster bomber as he had once been a chaplain in the RAF. Mr Green was all smiles over a new oilcan, which made the children laugh as they jostled and chattered their way back to class.

Joey Latimer waited until the hall was empty, then muttered a perfunctory apology to Mrs Raina and slouched his way back upstairs. Christmas was stupid. His mum had told him that morning that Uncle Simon was to spend the day with them this year. Joe disliked Uncle Simon. He ate disgustingly and was always wanting to hug everyone. He would make Joe's mum drink wine, and want to play stupid games like Scrabble. Scrabble was all about spelling. He'd want Joe to go carol-singing with the Church choir too. Carol-singing was cissy. You had to muffle up and go out in the dark and get freezing cold for hours on end. You couldn't see anyone properly and then you had to walk home alone.

Joey decided he wouldn't be doing any carol-singing this year.

Dora gives Dr Granger a talking-to

Dora was packing her latest batch of homemade ginger biscuits away in a tin when Dr Granger arrived. Mrs Bicknell let him in, then returned to her hoovering in the drawing room. Dora looked up at Granger's knock on the kitchen door. He peeped round, grinning like a schoolboy.

"Your famous Cornish fairings?"

Dora laughed. "Come on in. I think I can find you a couple of odd-shaped seconds if you're not too fussy."

"And a cuppa? Oh you are the best, Dora York. Just what I needed." He sat down, placing his bag on the floor. The cat came and rubbed round his legs. "Hello, Nick. My goodness you're so grown up these days."

Nicky leapt on the table and lay down with his nose against Granger's hand. The doctor stroked him gently and tickled his cheeks, sending the cat into a roll of delight.

"Hey, Nicholas, off that table!" cried Dora, setting two coffee mugs down and pulling up a chair.

"Now then, are you here to see me or Mrs Bick?"

The doctor sipped and nibbled. "Neither. I just called in to find out whether you were going to the carol thingy in school this morning. I'm a bit early."

"Yes, I was just finishing these before heading off."

"I'll walk with you then," nodded Granger, happily. "Have we time to finish our ten-fifteensies do you think?"

"Oh yes. Enjoy your cookie while I put my shoes on," said Dora.

Cookie. That was a word he hadn't heard for a while. "I wonder how Chloe Shaw is doing," murmured Joe Granger, almost to himself. Dora cast him a look as she tightened her laces.

"You're a married man now, Joe. You can't go pining for a lost love. It doesn't do."

"I know. Yes, I do know. And she's great, Elaine, she really is." Granger looked so – well *forlorn* was the only word Dora could come up with – as he sat there. Dora York closed her opinionated mouth and patted his shoulder. She leaned back against the Aga rail to listen quietly as there was obviously more to come.

Joe sighed. "I dunno, Dora. I don't know what's the matter with me. I don't seem to get any luck."

"How do you mean?" Dora braced herself for some male self-pity. She liked Joe – he was handsome and undoubtedly clever – but since he had returned from Scotland, he seemed to believe there was a malign fate dogging him. She was determined not encourage that attitude. "What really happened when you went out to America?" she asked. Granger had never said a word about his visit to New Mexico to see Chloe.

"Oh," he sighed again. "It wasn't good. She was pleased to see me, then suspicious and finally downright angry I'd come. I didn't see Shane, of course," he tailed off. Picking up another biscuit he dunked it in his tea. "Chloe is doing fine. She has a little school for very young, somewhat socially deprived children. It's right up her street. It's a bit out in the wilds, you know."

Dora didn't but she had seen photos. Chloe's schoolchildren looked about as different from Mayflower's as it was possible to imagine, but was nothing she wouldn't enrich. Dora loved Chloe and had every faith in her new educational mission. Already Bella Delgado's class and some of Chloe's had exchanged pen-friend letters.

"Has she a nice home? Friends?" She wanted to add 'Anyone Special?' but she didn't.

"Yes. A small ranch-style house on the edge of Taos. Big yard. I stayed in a bed and breakfast." Granger didn't want Dora to imagine anything untoward. "Her neighbours are very pleasant."

"So did you tell her how you'd always felt about her?" Time to get this conversation over-with.

"I did. I did, yes. And she was really quite kind after she realised I was on the level. But there's no unhooking her from Max, I think. She's still stuck on him, even though he's gone. Even though she only knew him a short while. Even though… God, I wish…"

"My dear. You have to understand that just because someone is special to you, it doesn't mean you're special to *her*. I'm afraid love doesn't work like that. Chloe can't leave Max behind. She doesn't *want* to. He was the real thing for her – and you – well you're not. I truly am sorry, but I think you will have to put Chloe behind you and be the most wonderful husband possible to your Elaine. She's been jolly patient with you, you know. You are a lucky man to have her wait around so long. Try to block off the past, Joe, and stick to the here and now. Be like our little Jimmy Birch and live in the present. He's a lesson to us all, that child."

Joe Granger finally grinned his wide white smile. "He does live in the moment, doesn't he? I'm so glad he's doing so well these days."

"Yes he is, and so will you too, just you see. Now come on, my dear. Let's get to that carol service assembly or we will be made to stand at the back where I can't see a blessed thing. Little Zoe is singing a solo and we don't want to miss that."

* * *

8.

Stocking

The excitement builds

Jimmy and May Fisher peeped into the cupboard under the stairs. It was alright, Hannibal was still asleep. His box was undisturbed. The last thing they wanted was for the tortoise to wake up and start believing Winter was over when it had barely begun.

"Auntie May."

"Yes, Jimmy."

"Isn't Hannibal hungry or thirsty when he's asleep?"

"No. His body is having a long rest so he's just ticking over."

Jimmy thought this was odd. It was like the tortoise was dead, stuck there in his box. He looked dead. Jimmy's mum was dead. She wasn't going to wake up in the Springtime like a tortoise. The boy sat on the arm of May's armchair and patted some of her soft stray white hair back into place while she knitted.

"Did you enjoy your day?" she asked him. They had spent it in Fenchester buying gifts for their friends – travelling down on the train and returning by bus laden with carrier bags. The undoubted highlight of the day had been the promised visit to Santa in the toy department's dazzling grotto. Jimmy kissed his angel's forehead and slid down beside her into the chair, trying not to squash the ever-present bag of wool.

"I did. It was lovely, thank you. I never seen Father Christmas in a shop before." They snuggled contentedly, each remembering their day. "Oh! I hear singing," cried Jimmy.

Miss Fisher opened the front door to welcome some carol singers. The group concluded "The Holly and the Ivy", then rattled their collecting tin hopefully. Jimmy posted some money into it while Auntie May stood behind him, smiling.

"Thanks Miss," said Red Martinez, one of Mayflower's former pupils.

"Happy Christmas!" called a dozen other well-muffled figures. Joey Latimer stood on the periphery, wishing it was time to run home. He had been made to go and join in by his mother, but had not been happy about it, although he could not explain why. He picked up some snow and started moulding it into a very hard little ball.

"Come on then, off we go. There's quite a few houses down this road and we don't want to be too late at White Cottage, do we?" called Mr Paton, thinking of hot chocolate.

"Did you call at Mrs Hewitt's?" asked May.

"No, she's already left for Holland," answered Ernest Chivers. "Thanks, Miss Fisher! See you on Christmas Day."

"So she has, I forgot she was going this afternoon," said May as she closed the door and drew the heavy curtain back across it. "I hope Auntie Jean had a good journey. I shall miss her this Christmas."

"But you have me, don't you?" Jimmy reminded her. "And we're going to Grandma Dora's for The Day, aren't we?" It was all going to be wonderful, he thought. He had never in his life experienced anything so story-book-perfect as this Christmas was shaping up to be. As it already was.

"Come on, Mister Blister. Up those stairs and jump in that bath! Time for bed."

Jimmy grinned and gave a loud 'cock-a-doodle-doo', just like Peter Pan. He galloped up the stairs on all fours while May Fisher pottered off to the kitchen to warm some milk for their cocoa. It was cocoa tonight – an extra Christmas treat.

And if Hannibal, the hibernating tortoise, heard any Christmassy commotion at all in his safe little cupboard under the stairs, he merely smiled his wise, ancient, reptilian smile and drifted peacefully back to dreamland.

Nests and other magic

It was almost the best fun, crunching back from church through the snow on Christmas morning holding his angel's hand. Except everything else had been the best fun too.

Jimmy had woken early and discovered the large, empty, auntie-knitted sock that he had carefully lain on his toy chest the previous night, was now lumpy and stuffed full. The carrot on the window sill had a toothy bite out of it, and the biscuit plate and milk mug were empty. Thrilled at the feeling that genuine magic must therefore (very recently) have virtually brushed his pyjama sleeve, Jimmy took up the sock and hugged it close to his chest. He peered out into the gloom of dawn and shivered, as a vision of last Christmas morning flashed across his memory. There had been no stocking, no up-coming breakfast to look forward to then. Janey had slept until midday, she was so exhausted. When she finally woke she explained they would probably eat later.

Jimmy tiptoed across the landing and squinted into Miss Fisher's bedroom. His angel was stirring. She beckoned him in and flipped back the feather-soft eiderdown for him to wriggle beneath. It was warm there, and he felt like a baby bird in a nest.

"Merry Christmas. What did Santa bring you?" whispered Auntie May, as excited as he was.

The tantalising joy of anticipation quickly gave way to the overwhelming desire to open the sock.

"Let's find out," he said, as he always did when he could not even begin to guess an answer.

Neatly and carefully, one by one, he undid the various little paper packets. Here was a Matchbox car. Here was a rubber ball. Here a magic drawing slate. A pair of gloves. Cartoon socks. A comic. A giant new pencil with an eraser at the end. A packet of fruit pastilles. Smarties, a sharpener, a comb, a tangerine, a walnut, and a new ten pence piece right down in the toe.

"Goodness, Santa packed lots in there," commented May, looking with motherly delight on her son's astonished face.

Jimmy lay back, flicking the wheels of the toy car. He could not be more content. It wasn't even breakfast and he had already had the best day ever. "I love Father Christmas," he sighed blissfully. "What are we doing today again?"

After matins, as he kicked along in the snow, he recalled everything. That tingling feeling of excitement mixed with cold, then warmth and safety and the rush of delight were all new. The familiar sounds and smells of his new home, of the old church – its clock ticking, the people singing. The old red prayer books, bright candles, smiling faces all around. Could it get any better?

"What's for lunch?" he enquired. Breakfast had been his favourite porridge, but now he was peckish again. A sudden thought occurred. "Oh, will it be turkey?"

"I think so," answered Auntie May, gravely. "You don't have to hold my hand all the way, you know. You can walk ahead."

Jimmy looked at her. "No thank you," he responded politely. "I prefer walking with you." He wasn't going to let his precious foster mother go. She might need him. She might stumble or slip. She might lose him – or forget him. He needed to be ready for anything.

At Grandma Dora's Jim discovered no one was about to forget him. He was the centre of attention and giving him happiness, apparently, was everybody's focus. At first it was embarrassing and he stayed close to Auntie May, keeping quiet, but after ten minutes of everyone laughing and chatting together Jim forgot his nervousness and relaxed. His eyes goggled as he surreptitiously inspected the ground floor of White Cottage. It was a house he knew well, but it had been transformed into a wonderland by Christmas decorations, lights and colour. A vast, lazy fire burned in the drawing room fireplace.

The dining table was laden with more food than he thought existed. Even Nicky was to be given some. There were little extra presents for guests beside their plates and all the best silverware was out. There was an immense golden-brown turkey, blue tureens of vegetables, white bread sauce and rich brown gravy in little jugs that Mrs Clark said were called boats. There were fat crackers. There were even silver coins in the sticky Christmas pudding.

Mr Chivers and Mr Paton eventually, after they had pulled the crackers and sat around in silly paper hats for a while, cleared everything away while he, Auntie May, Mrs Clark and Grandma turned the television on and sat on the sofa by the warm fire. The queen's little talk was a bit boring and he almost dozed off, but after that there was the thrill of yet more gift giving. These parcels were the serious ones to and from each other and it was his task, as youngest, to distribute them from underneath the huge tree. Everyone took it in turns to open their gift and thank the giver.

"Oh my, what a fabulous scarf, May! I love it," gushed Mike.

"Jimmy, did you paint this wonderful pot? My word, it's beautiful," said Skip. He had painted a different flower on a new terracotta flowerpot for every one of his special friends, and wrapped them up himself.

"Oh, I love mine. Look it has a red poppy on it," laughed Dora. "It's splendid, thank you, darling."

"What's in this funny shaped package? Hmm – very mysterious. Oh my word! Well thank you, a shoe-horn-cum-back-scratcher gadget. Two in one. How perfect, Mike." laughed Ernest. "It's just what I need."

Even Nicky had a present, which Jimmy helped unwrap. It was a box of cheese-flavoured treats.

The boy lay on the carpet by the piano feeling as if he were in two dreams – one experienced in minute sensory detail, and one seen only from afar, as if through an echoing mist. A bell brought him back to reality.

Answering the door, Jimmy discovered the Tuttle family, complete with baby Gwennie. If the day could have become any more enjoyable he did not know how. He held the baby in his arms as he sat on the sofa and told her all about everything, while Tim and the grown-ups laid the dining table again for some teatime treats. Turkey sandwiches, Christmas cake, fresh fruit, jelly, and gallons of tea seemed to still be required by anyone who had a chink of empty space anywhere inside them. Jimmy did not. He could eat nothing more. He gave Gwennie her six o-clock bottle and let his mind relax.

This was Christmas as he had always suspected it should be – as he had always yearned for it to be, but had never known. If only his mother had experienced just one day like this! Jimmy's eyes filled with tears.

Tim sat down beside him and tickled Gwennie's tiny toes as they peeped out of the shawl she was wrapped in. "Alright then, boyo?" he said softly.

Jimmy couldn't speak, so he nodded.

Tim stole a sideways glance. "Not your usual kind of Christmas Day, eh? It's OK though, isn't it? A proper family was all you needed. Now you have your Auntie May, and Mrs Clark, and a real granny. Three or four uncles. You can't have too many uncles, you know. Mr Green's like a grandpa to you and me both." Tim put his head a little closer. "Don't be sad. Family's never quite perfect, of course. Bits of it will come and go. Other bits will just be annoying. Sometimes they yak on and on over stuff you do, but there's always pets and food and babies and houses and jokes and lots of other little things all mixed up together that take the edge off. This lot won't stop loving you. Nor me either – nor Gwennie, come to that. Family's like a big old Christmas cake, really. Stuffed with this and that and never quite the same twice, but it's always good. Days like this are something you can hang on to and remember when you're a bit fed up in the future."

Much later, Jimmy lay awake in his own bed in his own bedroom looking out at the Winter moon. Usually he fell asleep as soon as his head touched the pillow, but tonight was different. His mind drifted back over the day's events as he tried to pin down exactly what it was that had made it so magical. Not the gifts themselves. Not the amazing food. Not the jokes or singing round the piano.

It came to him as he finally closed his eyes and snuggled down. It was what Tim had said. It was the whole bunch of people – his family. It was feeling wrapped around by them, like a new baby in a soft shawl. It was like being a baby bird in a warm, safe nest.

Hugo

It was Hugo's birthday, December 30th, and he was missing again. Not for the first time, Ernest wondered whether his father would even remember he had been invited for dinner at Caster Cottage. He and Mike had sent various messages, but had not heard back.

The two friends were now living happily together in Mike's old home, a long way out of town. It was a much humbler abode than Sir Hugo would probably have ever expected his son to call home, but that did not matter. Ernest was genuinely happy for the first time in his life. He had a job, he had a wonderful place to live and an amazing companion. Every day, like Jimmy Birch, he counted his blessings, and for the first time in his life he honestly did not care whether his father showed up or not.

Long after they had decided Hugo wasn't coming, Ernest was wiping down the draining board. He hung the dishcloth over the tap and glanced out of the window. A posh car crunched into their little backyard and doused its headlights. He went to open the door.

His father was in a cheery mood, and brought with him a bagful of expensive wine and a rich assortment of European cheeses. Ernest greeted him warmly, genuinely pleased his old man had made it after all.

"I'm so glad my invitation found you," he cried. "Come on in. Happy birthday! How was your journey? How's the new car?"

"Fine, fine, thank you my boy," chuckled his father. "Ah, how are you Mike? Had a good Christmas?"

They settled themselves down in the cosy sitting room. It was crowded, now Sir Hugo was there, as he dominated the place without trying. He took the armchair and lit a cigar. Urbane as ever, he made no comment on the little home's plain décor or friendly atmosphere, and seemed perfectly at ease with Ernest's new choice of living arrangements, Mike was grateful to note.

Perhaps seeing his son so relaxed is a weight off his mind, Mike thought. Except Hugo would only ever let you read a small part of his mind. Mike had no illusions about Hugo Chivers.

The birthday man was on good form. They dined, then sat smoking while Hugo related anecdotes and memories even Ernest had never heard before. It made the evening race by.

Just as he was pulling his overcoat back on, Hugo turned to his son and said, "By the way. I saw your old friend Jack Murphy yesterday."

Ernest felt as if he had been hit in the face. "Oh?"

"Yes. I happened to drop by that gallery I like in Bond Street. There was a Seago I wanted to take a look at. Anyway, as I was coming out I noticed a bit of a fracas going on a few yards away. A couple of bobbies were trying to get a fellow into a patrol car."

"And it was Jack?"

Hugo pressed the fingers of his gloves one by one, settling them comfortably, ready for the drive home. "Yes. Kicking up quite a rumpus too, I have to say. I had one of my secretaries look into it later on. It seems Murphy's being done for indecent assault on a minor. Looks like he'll be a guest of Her Majesty in the very near future too. There are also other charges."

"Oh my god," said Mike, horrified.

Ernest's face was ashen.

"I thought you'd want to know," commented Sir Hugo, conversationally. "Well now, I'll be off. Thank you for tonight, Ernest. Mike. Happy New Year to you both."

Ernest slowly closed the door.

"My father – he goes through life like someone walking across a beach and picking up stones he will later throw at people. He's a dangerous, powerful, calculating man, is my father."

"Oh, surely he isn't that bad. Surely…"

"You heard him. He waited until he was virtually gone out the door before saying anything about Jack. He does that. He drops a depth charge just when you're nicely sailing along, all unsuspecting. He *knew* that would hurt."

Mike poured Ernest a brandy and stood the fireguard up in front of the grate. He sat on the arm of the chair and waited for his friend to calm down. Ernest was right, but Mike needed him to regain his perspective. Blast Sir Hugo Chivers. He was a lousy father. He was a nasty human-being. With him it was all about power. That was what any relationship was to him, thought Mike, a power play. I'm so grateful my poor old dad wasn't like that.

As he took off his glasses and turned out the bedside light, Mike wondered fleetingly whether Sir Hugo himself had somehow contrived Murphy's arrest. He wouldn't put anything past him.

Tidy up time

Reg and Mrs Bicknell were finishing tidying up No.2 Church Road. Stringer was supervising from an armchair with Nicky curled up next to him. All the surveillance equipment had been stripped out, the holes plastered and painted over, and the carpets cleaned. Most of the furniture was gone. The ghost of Chloe Shaw had vanished too, and in its place there was only a blank air of expectation. The bedrooms dozed. The boiler ticked over. The garden hibernated under a thin blanket of snow.

"Jimmy Birch has settled down alright with Miss Fisher then, ent 'e?" chatted Bick.

Reg grunted. He would rather finish the tidy-up than make conversation.

"Yerse. Turning into a good lad, 'e is." Reg had a very soft spot for Jimmy Birch. He had been teaching him to take Autumn cuttings and how to double-dig his veg plot recently, and was planning on showing him how to sow seeds come the Spring.

" 'Ow's things in Wag Lane?"

"Alright. Liza says your Pat's feller, Phil, 'as done a real nice job with Janey Birch's old home. Done the bathroom up lovely. Put an electric cooker in the kitchen. Second hand of course, but nice. Got a new job too, she says."

"Yerse. Working down at Fox's in Oxthorpe now. It were a shame Chandler's closed down, but times change I suppose. It's wedding bells for our Pat, come the Saturday after Easter."

"Oo, 'ow lovely. Local?"

"Yerse. I dunno all the details, like. My job's just forking over the cash apparently." Reg grunted, trying to be grouchy and not succeeding. He was delighted Pat and Phil were making a proper go of it. He had been impressed by the way the pair had applied for a mortgage, bought and renovated the Birch's old place. Terry and he had helped of course, but it was mostly the couple's own sweat and money that had made the place habitable.

"It'll be ideal for a first home for them. It's got a nice little back bedroom too, in case they need a nursery." Bick was fishing.

"No, none of that for a while. Family planning, my daughter tells me. On the pill. Seems like a much more grown-up approach to married life than when I was wed, if you ask me," said Reg.

"Oh, I dunno. Little ones is always welcome, I say." Bick did love a gossip. "I seen that Jimmy halfway up a tree in the school wilderness the other week. Two or three times. Why does he do that, I wonder?" Bick was polishing hard at the curving mahogany banister rail. It's coming up lovely, she thought.

This was news to Reg. "No idea. Maybe he just likes to climb. Boys do." Reg had been a climber of trees himself and knew the appeal. It was like clambering up the rigging of a pirate ship when a tree swayed in the wind. You had to hang on. You had to know what you were doing. "Bit cold for climbing this weather, I'd have thought."

The weather was indeed frosty. The wilderness trees were hard and slippery, their naked branches clutching and pointing at the sky like hags' hands. All the wildlife was battened down for the season and even the pools of standing water were sealed over with icy lids. The earth could not look up into the sky any more. The sky itself was blind.

"Well, I'm done painting this bit of wall," said Reg straightening up. "You buffed that banister enough yet? I wonder who Sir Hugo will let this place to now."

"Fit for a king, you ask me. Ought to be someone with kids, really," answered Mrs Bicknell. "It's a nice house, this is. Big though. Four bedrooms. It'd do a family." She put her rags away and followed him back to the living room where she tweaked the curtains to please her sense of symmetry. They were American curtains, she remembered, brought here by Mrs Shaw.

Reg clicked his fingers. "Right, you two, orf that chair with yer. Time to go home."

"You sound like Andy Pandy," commented Bick. "Now are you lockin' up or am I, Mr Green? Right then, that's my bucket and clawths. I'll bid you a very good evening."

"Good evening to you, Mrs Bick. Thanks for your help. No, no, that's alright, I'll keep both keys. Come on dog, follow that cat. That's it."

Reg Green switched the lights off, locked up, closed the front gate, and walked home well-satisfied. Except for one thing – he would have to ask Ivy who the heck Andy Pandy was.

Kay and Joey

Half-past ten already. Joey was fed up that his paper round had taken so long, but his mum wouldn't let him start as early as Mr Patel requested, so now half the morning was wasted. So much for Christmas holidays. So what if it was dark when he started? His mum was a fusspot. Joe knew every road between Banford and Ironwell with his eyes shut. He slung his newspaper bag on its hook and hurried out through the newsagent's shop.

"Oy!" someone yelled as he crashed into them. It was Kay Fordam, coming in.

"Oh, sorry. Didn't see yer."

"Well open your eyes, Joe. Gor, that hurt." She hopped around a bit, rubbing her knee where the shop door had bashed it. Her scarf became entangled in the door handle and fell off. "What you in such a rush for anyway?"

"Gotter get home. Mum's found a leaflet about sports clubs down the lido clubroom. She said she thought there might be judo or kick-boxing or something." Joey picked up her scarf.

That was interesting. "For kids?"

"Yeah. I might try out," said Joe. "Wouldn't start 'til the New Year proper, like."

"Do you have to pay?"

"Dunno. I suppose so. Anyway, I'm saving my paper-round money for in case of if you do. Or I could ask Uncle Simon."

"I thought you didn't like him," commented Kay as she followed Joey back outside.

"I don't. Not much. Do *you* like your step-dad?"

"Nope. Not much. I s'pose he's alright sometimes. He just gets on my wick," admitted Kay.

"Mine does too. Well, Mum ent married him exactly, but it's the same thing." Joe unlocked his bike from the lamp post it was chained to. He wanted to hurry home and get his mother on her own so he could persuade her judo was the thing. Or kick-boxing. Or possibly fencing. He would like to run someone through with a sword. There had to be something other than football or chess, surely.

Kay stood beside him swinging her shopping bag. Joey flipped her scarf back round her neck for her and frowned. He never wore a scarf any more.

"You oughta do your coat up," he told her. "It's going to snow."

He cycled off, feeling oddly out of sorts. Girls were silly. Anyone knew you had to put your coat on properly when the weather turned cold. He was sorry he had hurt her knee, but honestly, she shouldn't get in his way.

Then he forgot all about Kay and focused on trying to decide which type of fighting lessons he would like to choose. Yeah, fighting was better than mooning over girls. And carol singing. And scarves.

Party time

Phil Price and Pat Green were not intending to spend one of their rare evenings off on more decorating. Phil had had a wash and brush-up at home then hurried back to Pat's little flat in town to watch while she titivated for hours, before taking her to Fenchester in his new mini. He had only just bought it. Alright, it was a pretty basic model and already three years old, but he thought he might smarten it up with a few go-faster stripes and a leather steering-wheel cover come next pay-day. Maybe even some fluffy dice hanging off the rear-view mirror. He waited contentedly for his fiancée to appear. She was well worth it.

He thought back over the hours of renovation they had put in together on their little house, and couldn't feel more pleased with life. Pat had chosen the colour scheme and had made two fat scrapbooks full of modern ideas and pretty things she wanted to try. Their sitting room would be magnolia with some bright orangey-brown flower prints, their bedroom that avocado colour with purple highlights. All very chic. He had drawn the line at the pink bathroom suite, however, compromising eventually on turquoise. These new colours were a definite step-up from the donkey browns and utility greens he had been used to all his life. His girl Pat knew her stuff. She was the bees knees and smack up-to-date.

She came out of the bedroom dressed ready to party.

"Wow," he breathed. "You look fab!"

"Thank you, kind sir," smirked Pat. "Are you going in that?"

Phil couldn't see what was wrong with his apparel. He'd taken special care to get the grease off his hands too. He ran a hand over his hair and sighed. It was obvious why Pat's dad was often reduced to grunting. She and her mum were two of a kind, he thought, neither of them slow in voicing an opinion. He smoothed down his floral shirt front and undid another button so she could catch a glimpse of his manly chest. Small steps, he thought.

In the car, she talked of this and that.

"So Kevin and Iris are all settled now the baby's on the way," commented Pat happily. It did not do any harm to mention domestic bliss to Phil, and drop a gentle reminder of her own ultimate dream. A baby one day would be the cherry on top, she thought.

"Yep," agreed Phil. It was tricky driving and he wasn't prepared to concentrate on lengthy discussions when there was black ice about.

"Iris says he doesn't like the idea of that new cross-country diesel taking over from the old steam train."

"Had to happen."

"I suppose. Modern life isn't it? But he's not happy, and neither is Mr Polkinghorne. Nor is that Mr Coker."

"Old boys," grunted her fiancé. "Change gotta happen."

"I suppose," repeated Pat, with a sigh. "Be funny though, not hearing that old chuff-chuff."

Phil grunted again. He was all for the new, cleaner engine taking over their local line. Even the quarry up the road was said to be welcoming the change-over. "Dirty old things, steam engines."

"But they're romantic, somehow. Like animals. Dinosaurs or dragons or something. Like they're alive. I prefer 'em, any road up. But I like those new style motor coaches you're driving down at the garage. None of them wheezy old school buses you used to have to drive for Chandler. Shocking old things they were. Must of bin forty years old if they was a day. Mr Fox is a lot more go-ahead."

"Mmm. Old Chandler was alright. He put a good word in for me with Fox, too."

"Yeah, he did. But I'm glad you're there, love. The money's better and we'll have a really good life in Wag Lane, you see. Our kids can go to Mayflower," she hinted.

That made him grin. "Yeah, alright, alright missis, I get the picture. That's us for the next twenty-odd years then is it? Me driving coaches and you raising kids? Well, if I have to, I suppose I can cope with that."

He glanced briefly at the love of his life sitting beside him in her best coat and high-heeled shoes, bright and eager for the new year to kick in. "If we get a few party-nights out during all that time, I won't complain too much. Now hand us one of them lemon drops."

* * *

9.

Fighting

Gloves

It was all very well, but the January sales did not always have what you wanted. The shops in Banford were a bit of a bust, if Toby was honest. He had no idea where to look for what he wanted next. He had visited every place he could think of.

"Good morning, Toby," cried Skipper Clark, spotting him as he hesitated on the pavement outside Coppen's, the draper.

"What ho, old thing," he responded gloomily. "Nippy isn't it?"

It was certainly colder than yesterday. Toby slapped his arms around himself. His nose was red and his hands were devoid of blood.

"Where's your moulting flying mittens?" enquired Skip.

"Lost. I'm hopeless, I know."

She eyed him shrewdly. "You mean you lost them on purpose."

Toby gave a mirthless chuckle. "Guilty as charged, m'lud. Bloody things kept shedding fur worse than a dog with mange.

Still, they were a kind gift." He didn't want to seem ungrateful to his landlady who had donated the offending items to him last Winter.

"What are you shopping for?" smiled Skipper. "Spy stories in the bookshop?"

He grew sober. "No," he said. "As a matter of fact I'm looking for a blanket thing for milady."

"What kind of blanket thing do you mean?"

"You know, one of those blanket arrangements that used to be all the rage. Bright colours, Mexican-looking gear, with a bit of lampshade fringe round the bottom."

"A poncho?" She had not had him pegged as a hippie.

"That's the fellow. A poncho. I thought one of those would keep her a mite warmer in that old barn of a house. I have the devil's own job trying to get a cardigan onto her yesterday, she's that stiff and arthriticky. And she's absolutely *no* help at all. Looks at me like I'm trying to rape her every time I offer. Hates me worse than poison. She would die rather than co-operate. If she had a poncho-thing I could fling it over her head from a distance and leg-it back down to the kitchen in a jiffy. It would stop her turning blue. Keep her nice and toasty 'til teatime."

Skipper had a good laugh over that image and offered to help him find such a garment if he agreed to lunch with her at the Yeoman on the way home.

They walked down Market Street to the castle walls and then round into Castle Square. The cobbles were slippery with ice and they had to tread carefully. There was a bohemian boutique on the left, next to the gunsmith, that looked promising. The sweet scent of weed wafted over them as they raked through its bargain rail items. Skipper suddenly squeaked as she spotted two ponchos draped at the far end. One was crocheted and baggy, the other a thick, stripey affair in blue and orange. Both were rather fetching, thought Skipper.

"That Miss Winstanley, down at the Old Mill Gallery in Ironwell has been supplying us with these," the shop-lady informed them. "Lovely aren't they? So bright."

"Lovely," agreed Toby. Privately he considered them hideous and only fit for Persephone the donkey, but he happily forked out for both garments.

The two teachers staggered back out into the chilly morning clutching their purchases.

"Great! Thanks for your help, Skip. I never would have looked in there in a month of Sundays. Well, that's me done. Have you anything else to buy? No, well, let's toddle off down to the Yeoman then, shall we? See if the new Portuguese cook can find us a spot of something edible."

"Oo, Portuguese? How lovely. I never did get along with endless pies and chips. But first, if we look in at that shoe shop, we might find you a pair of decent gloves."

"No, no. I'm done. I have all I came out for. Have pity, woman, there's only so much shopping I can stomach in a day. Gloves can wait," Toby assured her.

She gave up arguing. Toby might not be able to afford new gloves, she suddenly thought, as she tottered along the frozen pavement. Wait, no, that was nonsense – he must have at least two if not three salaries coming in. Maybe he simply didn't like wearing gloves. Skipper glanced up at him stepping gingerly along in his camel coat and Oxford brogues and concluded he was actually just a bit tight when it came to spending money on certain things. A pity. He could be as sartorially impressive as Hugo if he took the trouble, she thought.

I wonder what those two troublemakers will get up to this year, she sighed. Make more problems for the rest of us, no doubt.

Leaves

There was a large gap between the leaf-clogged gutter and the fascia. It was obvious now he took a proper look. No wonder the rain was coming in. Having cleared the gutter, Reg descended his stepladder wondering whether the school's sports pavilion had ever been properly water-tight in all its history.

"Doubtful," he told the dog. Stringer wagged his tail encouragingly.

They plodded back towards the lodge's stable-yard where Reg stored this particular ladder. Jimmy Birch watched them from up in one of the gnarly trees in apple-alley. His pointed pixie face shone like a little moon caught between the rough old boughs. Stringer gave a short bark of welcome and stretched up the trunk to greet his friend.

"What you up to then, Jim-lad?"

"Nothin'."

"Havin' a bit of a think?" asked Reg. "Come on down and 'elp me with this ladder if you're not too busy doing nothin'."

Jimmy dropped onto the snowy ground. Snow was patchy here in the wilderness, giving the place a black and white ghostliness. He walked along behind Mr Green saying nothing. Reg made him hold the toolshed door open while he returned the ladder to its ordained place, then they walked back over to school together, following the dog who skipped daintily in front. Reg glanced at his silent little pal and decided some straight speaking was in order.

"You had a dust-up with Miss Fisher?"

"No." Jimmy was surprised Mr Green might imagine that. He adored his auntie – always had, and always would. He could never fall out with her.

"Why've you got a face like a wet weekend, then?" Reg stopped and faced the boy towards him just before the playground gate. "Belly ache? Got the after-Christmas blues? Or has someone been 'avin' a go at yer?"

"No." Jimmy hung his head and wept big fat tears, much to his own annoyance. He didn't want to share what he was trying to think about, but the act of speaking caused his eyes to brim over.

"Here, 'ere," soothed Reg. He took the boy's hand and led him away to a couple of fallen logs artfully placed together to form a seat. Reg let go of Jimmy's hand when what he really wanted to do was give the child a comforting hug. He waited until the waterworks subsided. Talk was not easy for the lad, he knew. No rush. Words were sometimes like rusty nails – tricky to pull out.

Jimmy leaned against a tree and opened his mouth a time or two.

"Spit it out. I won't tell no one. You sickening for something?"

Jimmy gathered his courage and took a deep breath. "She never had no nice Christmas like me," he mumbled.

Confused, Reg did his best. "Auntie May? Didn't she have fun? You give her some lovely marmalade. And a flower pot."

"No."

"She's not ill, is she?"

"No. Not her."

Reg blamed the wintery conditions for the slow connections his mind was making today. "Oh. You mean your mum."

Jimmy nodded. Since Christmas his mind had been stewing, churning, as he willed himself to think back. He wanted to remember if his mother had ever once smiled or laughed with him but all he came up with was a blank. He found he could barely recall Janey's face. She was like a character in a story he had once read in a library book and had then returned. He knew nothing about her at all. What had she liked? What had she thought about? Most of all there was nothing in his memory about *her* parents, or *her* childhood.

Jimmy had discovered so much since living with Auntie May. He knew how a childhood was supposed to unfold, who you trusted and why. But what about Janey's life? Had *she* ever felt safe? Had she ever been snuggled and kissed and tickled or listened to? She had loved him, he supposed, but who had ever loved her?

It was his mother's short life Jimmy was feeling miserable about, not his own, and he felt ashamed he could neither remember her clearly nor had thought to ask about her history or her hopes and dreams. He felt as if his head was full of dry dead wood. He tried his best to explain, but his thoughts were only bare twigs without proper word-leaves attached and they kept getting stuck.

Mr Green studied the boy. He knew as much about Janey Birch as anyone else, and although she might not have been his idea of a competent mother, she had been Jimmy's mum. Reg's kind heart saw a little lad missing his dead parent.

"Your mother got by as best she could, Jim. Now she's gorn it's very sad, and we're all very sorry. But my guess is she'd want you to look ahead, not backward. She'd be more than 'appy Miss Fisher's your mum now and that you 'ad a lovely Christmastime. Don't be dwellin' on what's past and can't be changed, my boy. You'll spoil what's 'appening *now* if you go on brooding."

Jimmy nodded, queasy with the effort of trying to talk and relieved Mr Green had missed the point entirely. He was exhausted and embarrassed by this chat, but he knew Mr Green was trying to be kind. He would have to work out a proper way to say what was in his head. But someplace else, and not today. To somebody else.

Mr Green wiped a none-too-clean hanky over the child's face and sent him back into the playground. He clicked his fingers to the dog and made his own way to the boiler-house where it was warm and dark and his third best pipe lay waiting for a refill. School care-taking and the demands of the British Secret Service were easy jobs compared to dealing with bereaved kids, he thought.

"That kid's feeling blue," he informed the dog. "Think I'd better have a quiet word with May Fisher after all."

Kay and Bella

Bella Delgado was admired by all the girls in school and by many of the boys. She was young and energetic, good at sports and smiled a great deal. That was enough for most children. What made her a good teacher, though, was the fact that she also *liked* children. Nobody felt left out when Miss Delgado took their class. Everyone was given a turn at whatever it was, and everybody ended up feeling energised by the end of the lesson. She knew what TV shows they watched at home, she listened to their silly jokes. She knew everybody's name and remembered details about their lives. Her opinions were therefore respected and discussed on the playground as if she were some TV star.

"Yes, but Miss Delgado says… " began many a vigorous conversation.

Kay Fordam silently adored her. She liked her hair, her sportiness, her popularity. Kay's own hair was usually a badly combed tangle, she didn't care about winning, and most children avoided her scathing tongue. It was the attraction of the opposites for Kay at first, but later she began to try her utmost to be like the young teacher. Her dedication did not go unnoticed.

"Your Kay's becoming quite a good little shooter," commented Mrs Elbridge at the next netball match.

"It's the power of love," rejoined Jean, watching her team duck and weave around their opponents.

"How d'you mean?"

Jean explained Miss Delgado's magnetism. The young woman in question could not be there today as she had a dental appointment, which meant Jean was once again standing with her old friend on a damp and chilly netball court with a whistle in her hand.

"Kay has a pash on Bella Delgado," Jean said. "Watch out Plum! That's it, good girl!"

"Oh, the new person? Goodness, times don't change at all, do they? I remember having a terrible crush on our games mistress when I was a kid, too. Dear heaven, I nearly drove my poor mother mad. Come on, Dane Street! Put a bit of zip into it!"

'You and I never seem to attract that kind of devotion, do we?" said Jean wistfully, which made Mrs Elbridge chuckle.

Kay did her best to be chummy on the walk back indoors after the match, just as Miss Delgado would have done.

"That was a really good last shot, Deb," she told her captain.

Deb raised her eyebrows in genuine astonishment. "Er, thanks, Kay," she said.

"Next time we'll thrash their socks off," predicted Kay.

The team giggled, largely at Kay's expense. She didn't care. Miss Delgado would not have cared either. Kay changed her clothes and headed home on the bus, dwelling blissfully on the wonderful qualities her goddess exhibited. She would ride her bike to school tomorrow even if her mother said it was too wet and snowy. Miss Delgado always rode her bicycle.

As she cycled in through the school gate next morning she was thrilled to see Bella already on playground duty.

"Good morning, Miss Delgado," smiled Kay pleasantly.

"Morning, Kay. Golly it's cold isn't it?"

"Would you like me to bring you out a coffee? I expect Mrs Clark has brewed some by now. She always does," Kay informed her.

"That would be marvellous, thanks very much." Miss Delgado blew on her gloved hands and grinned. "Nice to see you riding your bike. Do you live far?"

"No, just Ironwell. It's only a few miles and my new bike has gears. I had it for Christmas."

"So I see. You're a lucky girl." Bella could tell the bike was expensive. Kay walked it to the rack and returned a while later with a mug of coffee. Other girls were swarming around and one jogged Kay's arm so that she spilled the drink down her coat.

"You stupid clumsy pig," cried Kay. She glared at the offender, who was not in the least remorseful.

"Oh dear," smirked the girls. "You'd better take that mug back. Monica's already brought Miss Delgado a drink. Don't cry, Kaysie-wasie. It'll be *OK*. Would you like Miss Delgado to come and dry your tears?"

Kay fled into school, where she spent the next half hour in the toilet known as the Attic Aunt, weeping as silently as she knew how.

On a mission

The Abbey Farm Shop developers had already fenced off the house where Len Kirk and his family had once lived, together with the barns and pigsties. Bulldozers moved in the following week and razed most of them, before levelling the sloping yard. They filled in the old slurry pond and grubbed up the track to it in order to lay pipes and cables. It was fortunate the ground was not yet frozen solid, although more arctic weather was to come according to the BBC forecasters.

Ben Nesbit took a walk down the lane to see what was happening.

A caravan and some portable toilets had been placed near the road entrance to the site and a plastic-covered copy of an artist's impression of the proposed complex nailed to a board. He stood looking at it for a long while, thinking what a useful addition the shops would be to this side of town. There was to be a cafe and artisans' workplaces, complete with craftspeople demonstrating their various skills and selling the results. Ben doubted whether many folks would want to stand watching while someone dipped candles or punched holes into a leather belt, but you never knew. It would be like Santa's workshop.

The wind blew cold. Ben turned and walked back towards town. Just before the Lido, where Dutch Lane met the high road, a girl was kicking along it, bundled up in a hat and furry boots. She waved.

"Hello, Mr Nesbit," she cried.

"Hello. Kay, isn't it?"

"Yep. Hello, Hades! Good dog. I'm just out for a walk." Kay fell in beside him and they marched along together.

"I don't usually come this way," she said, trying to be conversational, just like Miss Delgado. "I've been to see an old lady I know."

"Oh yes?"

"Lady Longmont. I call on her sometimes, to help out and that. Do her bird table."

"That's good of you. Some children try and avoid old people."

Kay looked at him. "I don't know why," she said. "Lady Longmont's alright. Well she was, but to be honest she's going a bit gaga now. It's a little scary sometimes. She keeps giving me things like they're mysterious, or important, and sending me on missions. Photos and bits of paper. Junk really. Today I have to post a letter and deliver some keys."

"Keys? To what?"

"Dunno. I'm to put them in a certain place and not tell anyone." Kay jingled the keys in her pocket.

Ben laughed. "Well, you'd better do it then, double-o seven. A mission is a mission. Don't let the boss down."

"I won't," grinned Kay. "She lost some keys in a letter box a while back, but I asked at the Post Office for her and got them back. She gave me 50p to spend in the sweet shop today as a reward. So I'm going to make sure I complete my duties."

Ben laughed again. "That's a great way to make sure you do her bidding," he said. "Money certainly talks. Well, I'm going to cut down past the rec towards the manor now, so I'll say *adios*. Bye, Kay. Good luck with your mystery mission."

"Bye," called Kay.

She crossed the road and walked on past the school field until she came to Longmont Lodge. It was the work of a moment to wriggle inside the fence and make her way round to the back door.

"Now then, which one?" she asked herself.

The bottom step of the little tiled flight going up to the back door was five tiles wide. The right hand one yielded to her fingers. There was a space beneath it, into which she dropped the keys. She replaced the tile and stood up. It was quite firm, should anyone step on it. No one would know there was a hiding place there.

"Good," sighed Kay. "Though why I'm doing this I have no idea. Now to post that letter and buy a Crunchie. Or do I want a couple of chocolate fudges?"

Fenchester panto fails to impress

"I thought he'd love it," sighed Mike quietly, as Ernest drove slowly home from Fenchester. They had taken Jimmy to see Jack and the Beanstalk at the old Fortune Theatre as a treat. The boy was asleep now on the car's back seat under a tartan rug.

"I know," whispered Ernest, so as not to wake him. "I think the best thing was the choc-ice in the interval."

Jimmy had not exactly jumped up and down with excitement at the prospect of the trip. The men initially put it down to the fact that Auntie May was not going to accompany them. Jim had voiced his gratitude politely enough, but they could see he was less than enthusiastic.

"Maybe it is all a bit overwhelming," said Mike. "You know, the life-style change and all. And it being so soon after Christmas, with all that how-de-do."

"Maybe. He's certainly taken a bit of a dip lately. Charlie was saying as much." Ernest changed gears. "It's starting to snow, darn it. I hate this road in the dark."

"Well, just take it slowly and we'll be alright," said Mike. "Do the same with the lad."

Ernest grunted. "Yeah, you're probably right. Too much excitement all at once. I wonder if this weather's going to stay. We'll have to buy another cord of firewood if it sets in."

"Stop fretting. There's plenty for now. If it stops the Calor gas man delivering, *then* you can start worrying."

"We could always cook on the living room fire," grinned Ernest. "Kippers and potatoes and so on." Mike hated kippers.

They laughed and Jimmy stirred in his sleep.

"Isn't it Burns Night tonight?" asked Ernest after a mile or two.

"So?"

"No reason. Haggis is tasty. We could cook that on the fire. Dangle it on a hook."

"Listen, you concentrate on the driving, I'll worry about the cooking. I'm a dab hand at that primus stove, if the worst comes to the worst. And Jimmy can peel spuds, can't you Jimbo?"

Jimmy had woken up when the car changed gears again to turn the corner into Fen Lane. Home – they were home. He rubbed his eyes.

"Do baked beans come from beanstalks?" he asked.

"Sort of," answered Mike with a grin, turning his head to look at the boy. "Nice snooze? Auntie May will want know all about the pantomime in a minute."

Jimmy pulled his gloves on. "I'll tell her. Maybe we can grow beans next Spring. She likes them, but not magic ones."

"Here we are," Ernest pulled the car into the kerb and opened Jimmy's door. The child thanked them for a lovely time and ran indoors quickly. The Renault pulled away to the road junction.

"Left or right?" asked Ernest. "Yeoman or the Mint? I vote we grab a pie and a pint before heading back through that snow. It'll save cooking."

"Now you're talking," chuckled Mike. "Alright then, I give in. The Mint, driver, and make it snappy."

They turned left, both content with their afternoon's outing and looking forward to their pie and chip supper.

Joey is in trouble again

"Joe Latimer – again?" Mrs Clark despaired. Joe was always in trouble these days. First it was kicking, then it was overly exuberant arm-wrestling, then it was plain-old playground fighting. "What is it this time?"

"Swinging Mick McDonald round by the raincoat belt and letting go. Mick's grazed all down his left leg and ruined his coat. Hit his head on the railings too. Quite a nasty wallop. Might need a stitch."

Mrs Clark sighed deeply. "Wheel him in," she said grimly.

Joe Latimer shuffled in, scowling defiantly.

"Stand over there," ordered Mrs Clark sharply. "Could you get the nurse to check Michael over, please Mrs Bailey? Isn't she in this morning?"

Peggy nodded. Nurse Presley was currently searching for nits in the kindergarten room. "I'll call Mrs McDonald too," she said, casting an angry look at Joe. "And Mrs Latimer?"

"No, I will do that," answered Skipper. Mrs Bailey departed.

The room was warm and familiar. Joe glanced at the headmistress and suddenly felt a good deal less belligerent. He started to cry.

Instead of giving him a royal dressing down, Mrs Clark sat herself in the small armchair by the fire and made the boy sit on the floor next to the cat who was curled up on the hearthrug. She waited. Nicky the cat stirred and put out a paw. Joe stroked his head.

"I'm sorry I spun Mick. We were playing. His belt come undone."

"Playing too roughly," Mrs Clark reminded him. Joey nodded.

"I was mad at him," he explained.

"You were angry? Why? What has Mick done?"

"Nothing."

"Why then?"

"He said… " Joey mumbled something and flushed bright red.

"Speak up. What did Mick say to you?"

"He called me a bad name."

"Why would he do that?"

"Dunno. He called me a pansy. It's not a flower, it's a bad name." Joe was growing cross again. It wasn't right Mick had called him that. He wasn't one. He would never be one.

"I don't like name calling, you know that." Mrs Clark had told her children this many a time.

He did. Everyone did. She was hot on name-callers. Words were as bad as hitting, she always said.

"What ought you to have done?"

Joe had a think. "Come to you?"

"Yes, exactly. Then I would have dealt with Mick, not you. Now you've hurt someone very badly and I have to call his mother and explain."

"And my mother?"

"And your mother. What is she going to say do you think?"

"Dunno." He did though. She was going to be very upset.

"Your poor mum has had to see me about your behaviour several times already this school year, Joey. She's had to stop work and come and get you. You've been rough and unkind to people. It isn't like you. What's going on? Why are you losing your temper all the time and being so mean to your friends?"

"Dunno. I don't like singing."

"*Singing?* What on earth?" Mrs Clark gazed at him in astonishment.

Joey scowled. He didn't know why he hated carol singing. He was all muddled up. "And I don't like wearing my school scarf any more. Mick McDonald's always calling me a bloody pansy. *He's* the one what's a woofter, not me. He didn't ought to call me that."

"Joe, stop saying bad words right now! Both of you were wrong. I suggest you sit there a little longer while I phone your mother to come and get you. You will be going home today, not back to class. You may return in two days, and not before. And I want a written apology to Mick, and another letter for his parents. Let's hope his head doesn't need stitches. And your mother will have to pay for Michael's uniform to be cleaned and mended if necessary. You realise she will have to take time off work now, to stay home with you? Honestly, Joey, I thought with the karate lessons and everything you were managing to get rid of some of this pent up anger inside you. You seem bent on punishing us all for some reason – including your poor mum."

Joey hung his head and started to cry again. "I'm sorry Mrs Clark. I am, I'm really sorry."

"Well I suppose you are. Now sit there quietly while I make this call."

Wag Lane gets new residents

"Here, put me down, you great lummock!" shrieked Pat Green as her fiancé carried her over the threshold. Phil struggled through the narrow doorway and tipped her up to stand on her own two feet.

"There you go, old lady," he puffed. "Can't say I'm not romantic, now can you?"

Pat kissed him on the cheek. "You're lovely, is what you are, though I ent going to keep telling you."

"Here, 'ere, none of that malarky," growled Reg, who was in the kitchen with Ivy, putting out the plates for supper. "Get in 'ere and 'elp yer mother."

It was fish and chips from the van on Merland Road tonight, and no one wanted to eat that cold. They had spent the afternoon putting the finishing touches to the house and were all very hungry.

"You taken our picture, Dad?" asked Pat. She had handed her little camera to him in order to memorialise the arrival. It was the happy pair's official moving in day.

Reg had completely forgotten. "Dammit," he said. "Put them chips back in the oven a minute, Ivy. Come on, come on. Get back out the front door or we'll never have our supper. Go on dog, you go first."

The family were grouping themselves together on the front step ready for a photo when Bella Delgado hailed them. Bella had dropped by to see her aunt after a cold jog along by the river and back. She grinned at Pat.

"Hello! Are you moving in at last? Oh, Auntie will be so pleased. It's been ages since, well since Miss Birch was living here. Are you taking a photograph to commemorate the occasion Mr Green?"

"Yerse. Tryin', but I'm all thumbs. It's cold out 'ere."

"Look, let me. You go and stand by Ivy. That's it, scoot in behind your daughter. OK Phil, come in a bit. There! That's one. Another? Alright, Stringer, you jump up into Pat's arms and I'll come in a little closer. There, that's two. Oh hello, Aunt Eliza. Look, Pat and Phil are moving in today."

Miss Muggeridge smiled, happy at the prospect of finally having some pleasant next-door neighbours.

"Oh, well, isn't that nice?" she said. "All your furniture in and everything, is it?"

"Not quite. We've a bed and a kitchen table and four deck chairs but it's a start. There's a carpet and some bits coming from the auctioneers in Paisley Road tomorrow, but we can't wait any longer, so here we are!"

Ivy smiled at Pat's excitement. "Finally growin' up, Miss Muggeridge, so they are. Wedding' bells next Easter, you know. Movin' in together is a bit previous in my view, but it's the modern way. They can save up a bit. I'm sure they're off to a good start here in Wag Lane."

Miss Muggeridge had decided views on people needing to be married before they moved in together, but she said nothing. Everyone was so very excited – even Reg. She put the key in her own front door and ushered her niece inside.

"Well I hope you'll be very happy," she said. "Don't forget, if you need a cup of sugar or some vinegar for those fish and chips I can smell, just knock and ask. Come on Bella. Let's put the light on and see about our supper too, shall we?"

Phil closed his very own front door and switched on his very own porch light, feeling like a king. Honestly, he thought. If you'd have told me a year ago I was going to have a home of my own, a gorgeous fiancée and be next-door neighbour to old Eliza Muggeridge I wouldn't have believed you. Yet here I am, and here I'm staying.

"Oy! Have we even got any vinegar for our chips, missis?" he called. "And how about a pickled gherkin and a slice of bread and butter?"

* * *

10.

Ash tree

Sketches

The younger Juniors' annual visit to the town castle fell on a freezing cold February afternoon. Huge billowing grey clouds filled the sky to the north lending a dramatic aspect to the monotone scene of shadowy ruins and jagged masonry as the group crossed over Stokes' Steps. The river was the natural northern boundary of their mundane little school world – the town representing something far more worldly and exciting, with its thrilling cocktail of ancient history and modern life. Between them, like a ribbon, the Wain ran dark and sullen, matching the ominous sky. The Steps were a border crossing from one world to the next.

Forms three and four chattered loudly as they clattered along.

"We done the castle last year too. It's brilliant," said Rebecca Rockwell. She was clutching the new sketchbook Mr Paton had recently issued, and feeling very motivated to start using it. The lowly third formers only had a simple questionnaire sheet to fill in for their castle assignment. A sketchbook, thought Rebecca, was far more sophisticated and creative. Rebecca liked drawing well-enough, but she preferred writing about things – after all she had won the essay prize last Founder's Day. She was eager to begin work on the castle. "Sir, can I write things next to my drawings? Like even imaginary things?"

"Why not?" answered Mr Paton, wishing he had put on stouter shoes. "Your sketch book will reflect all your own ideas about it, Rebecca. A source book and also a record."

She knew what he meant. It would be a really useful thing, he had explained to the class, to learn to take notes and make sketches from their own observations. There was no better way of reminding themselves about what they had seen and *felt* at a particular time on a particular day, he said. He hoped they would continue using a sketchbook throughout their lives. The notion had come to Mike when he saw Jimmy Birch drawing and scribbling away in his tatty old exercise book every time he stayed with them at Caster Cottage. This was what explorers did long ago, thought Mike. Adventurers, plant hunters, *plein air* artists. Why shouldn't everybody take one everywhere?

He and Charlie Tuttle marched along together, proud of the school's neat turnout. The kids all looked organised and happily expectant, reasonably intelligent. Duffle coats, macs, scarves, caps, hats, gloves and stout shoes were the orders of the day. It really was bitterly cold.

"How's the baby doing?" asked Mike, politely.

"Oh, Gwennie's a marvel. Been perfect from the moment she was born, that one," Charlie informed him happily. Little Gwennie was the apple of his eye. "She's two months old and it's like she's always been here, you know. Marvellous thing, human development. She smiles and sings away! Nothing she likes better than her brother counting her little toes for her." He sighed, missing his baby daughter.

There never was a human baby as accomplished as this one, thought Mike indulgently. He wondered what it would have been like to be a father. Then he remembered Jimmy Birch and decided he and Ernest were as near having Jim as a son as either of them actually wanted. They could enjoy the lad's company for the day and hand him back when day was done. An ideal arrangement.

The visit went smoothly and the day was growing dark by the time they were all trooping home across the Steps once more. Sleet stung the back of the children's knees and made the path even more slippery. As they turned in at the school gate it began to snow big proper flakes. The old building had never looked as welcoming as it did now. The windows glowed. Mr Green had switched the porch light on to welcome them home.

Rebecca clutched her sketchbook to her chest, already planning tomorrow's improvements and eye-catching presentation. She had views and close-up studies and quite a few notes jotted down. It had been harder and more tiring than she thought to select her points of interest and concentrate her imagination, but over all it had been huge fun. She would have to check some of the technical words for spelling errors and tidy up some scrappy sections as she wanted this book to be pretty-well perfect. There might be a display, after all. Possibly a prize. The castle was wonderful and the museum a revelation, as always. She would do it all to perfection. Just like Mr Tuttle, she couldn't envisage her most treasured accomplishment to be found wanting.

Parking stalemate

"That little car park is perfectly ridiculous. We all have cars now. Well, most of us do," grumbled Toby at one of the staff meetings. It was a theme he returned to about once a month. "Honestly, who agrees with me? Something must be done."

"Done? Like what?" Mrs Clark was at a loss to provide a sensible answer. They'd been over this a thousand times.

"Well, a larger space made."

"How? There's no room either side. You've the kindergarten here, and Reg's house there. What do you propose, a multi-storey?" Peggy was as exasperated with him as Skip was.

"Well, obviously not. Can't we pinch a bit of Reg's veg patch or something? He won't mind."

There was uproar.

"Not if you want to live," muttered Jean. She glanced at May Fisher, who was busy knitting.

"Something has to be done – an overflow somewhere. I can't keep scraping my car doors and waiting for Charlie to come out and shift his jalopy every evening so I can get out. It's ridiculous. And what's going to happen when we have our arts centre, I'd like to know? Where are *they* all going to park?"

"They'll walk."

"Park in the street."

"They jolly well won't. The new farm shop complex is building a large place for cars. Why can't we? We have enough land."

"Oh Toby. It will cost a fortune."

"No it won't. Just a field or something. Rope off some of the Donkey Field.

"No!"

Doomed, thought Toby. I'm doomed. They're blocking this just so as I end up walking to school and getting fit. He folded his arms and shut up.

"Toby has as many plans for this place as you have," chuckled Charlie, nudging Skip. "Look at him. Dreaming away about rows and rows of cars all neatly parked."

Mrs Clark nodded. "And he's probably collecting the parking fees in his head too, Charlie. Or planning to hold car boot sales there on Saturday mornings. I'm not giving in to him."

Cold comfort

The caretaker left the man to it. He had shoved him inside, locked the door and disappeared. There was a meal of cold meat, bread and pickled onions on a plate in the little kitchen halfway down a corridor, and a mattress in one of the other rooms. A hurricane lamp hissed and shed a dim glow as it stood on the table. Shutters had been closed across the only window. The fellow could rest here, locked in for his own safety.

He sat down and tried to stop shaking. Even without taking his filthy mittens off he devoured half the meal. He was famished. He twisted the knob on the lamp and a slightly brighter glow lit up the area. There was an apple and a half-bottle of whisky on the dresser. Ignoring a perfectly good mug he swigged several mouthfuls straight from the bottle and finally began to feel better.

This place and its welcome were basic, but then he could not complain as he had not exactly been expected. Not this year anyway. Only a series of coincidences had eventually enabled his arrival at all. They had planned for his defection six months ago.

The journey had been terrifying. Leaving his city and walking, walking, over the mountains in the dead of winter without food or shelter ought to have killed him, yet here he was. Here he *was*! That was something to celebrate. It did not matter now how deeply suspicious they had been at the border, nor how he had had to virtually force the contacts to accept him as genuine, with priceless information to impart. It had been rough.

Where was he? A little further along his trail, in a cold derelict house eating basic rations. Soon, maybe tomorrow after they had questioned him, he would qualify for something better. Maybe in London, or even Canada. He didn't care very much where he ended up, as long as it was somewhere he was genuinely free and genuinely safe.

The man took the lamp and the food to the room with the mattress and lay down. Shivering, he pulled a rug across himself and closed his eyes. This was not like the movies of life in the West he had seen. MI5 would be back for him tomorrow. The caretaker had used that word in his own language several times, so he understood perfectly. Maybe tomorrow would bring more walking. Maybe a car ride. A bus? How far was London? Would they take him to some prison to debrief him? It seemed most likely. Behind the scenes they must be running around like headless chickens, now he had surfaced. It was almost amusing to think of himself being the centre of attention when he had spent so long trying not to be noticed. All those years – all those years. He would be treated better once they knew what he had to divulge. He would be a hero, like John Wayne.

Unable to settle, he sat up and finished off the food and whisky.

He would feel safer if he could be sure nobody had been sent after him, to rub him out. Execute him before he could spill the beans. That was what the KGB was rumoured to do – send assassins after defectors and simply wipe them out. They could not afford secrets getting out, and he really did know a few very, very important secrets.

The fellow pulled his odd little cap down over his ears and went stealthily through the entire house, attic to basement. There was nobody there. The house was huge and empty. There was nothing but the sound of snow hitting the windows as it was flung by the wind. He returned to his mattress and fell asleep.

Buffeted by the wind and blanketed by falling snow, a strange shape drifted down out of a black cloud. Down and down it came, rocking, drifting off-course, hanging, tipping, tumbling over the Eastern Levels. It disappeared abruptly, leaving Mr Wichelow, the curate of St Andrew's church, to wonder briefly what it might have been.

Theo had been sitting up with a sick parishioner well into the small hours, and was doing his best to reach home in one piece through adverse weather conditions. He rode a motor scooter, quite new and rather noisy, along East Church Road from the outlying cottage where he had spent the evening, and was now wondering whether he ought to stop to answer a call of nature, or press on home to the vicarage and his cosy quarters. Mrs Williams would have left the light on for him, he knew, and some supper on a tray to fill his growling stomach. She was a kind soul.

He glanced briefly upwards as the oddly drifting shape caught his eye, then rapidly returned his concentration to the dangerous pot-holes in the roadway. His headlight wavered and juddered as he negotiated every yard. Best get home, he thought.

It was probably only a trick of the moonlight anyway. A lost migratory bird or a piece of plastic come loose. Although it *had* looked a little like a descending parachute. He grinned to himself. Nobody would ever dream of parachuting on such a night as this in the bleak midwinter, or in such a deserted place.

Theo dismissed the incident and pressed on.

A fearful chase begins

The following night the weather worsened. Not only were snowflakes falling like volcanic ash, they were being tossed up, down and sideways by a capricious gale, and sticking to everything they encountered. They were splattered against every tree-trunk, every wall, every roof, every dead leaf and stick. Every pile of tangled weed, every thick briar patch, every ancient shrub and stump stood heaped to double its size. In the short moments between day and night the familiar became incomprehensible and grotesque, covered by a thick shroud sent directly from arctic hell.

A stealthy figure emerged from the kitchen window of Longmont Lodge. It was dressed in dark clothes – a donkey jacket, an oddly stiff little cap and a pair of tall foreign-looking boots. The man slithered and slipped across the yard, clinging hard to some iron railings until his bare hands burned. He groped his way around the building to the front, only to return a few moments later, panting hard.

The roadway would not do. Better find another route.

His mind raced in panic. His host had told him to lie low today, and wait for them to move him when the weather cleared, but he could not shake this terrible rising fear in his stomach. He knew – he just *knew* – he had been discovered. The more he worried about being shot dead, the worse his fear grew, so he decided to escape. It was his only chance. He would find his own way to London and stay out of sight until it was safe to declare himself once again.

The fellow stared into the snowy maelstrom, trying to judge his orientation. He plunged roughly westwards down a sketchy track into the dense cover. All too soon he became hopelessly lost.

A second man, who had waited long patient hours for his prey to break cover, pricked up his head in the shadows of the lodge's front gate. He sniffed, catching a fleeting impression of someone disappearing. This watcher settled his light-weight sniper's rifle across his shoulder, squinted into the chaotic vegetation, and stepped after the first, as silent as a snow leopard.

The wind howled overhead among the chimney stacks and trees where all was thrashing movement and fury. Down below in the choking netherworld, lay an immense labyrinthine underchamber, cloaked and perilous.

The hunter was glad he had cut the local telephone lines while he waited for his man to break cover. They would blame the weather for that. It was a pity no message had reached him about where to find a key to the building. His handler usually provided that information early on in a mission, only this time there were three possible places to cover and no details had come. Something must have gone amiss. However, luck was with him and his quarry had broken cover even as he lay in wait. It would take a clever shot in these conditions, but the assassin *was* clever. He stepped confidently forward, as cautious as a cat, peering this way and that for footprints in the snow.

Unaware he had already been spotted, the first man's spirits lifted when he emerged from the scrub on a small rise topped with swaying pine trees. So far so good. He pulled his coat clear of some wrenching thorns and squinted into the night. Maybe from here he could make better speed. It wasn't late, but it was already as black as midnight.

If only there were some kind of glow coming from the town he knew to be nearby, but there was none. There were no stars, no moon. He leaned against a tree and tried to sense the best way forward, but it was impossible. He pulled his cap closer over his ears and ploughed back into the wilderness forest.

When the hunter arrived at the same spot a few minutes later, he too paused. He flipped his rifle round to his chest and squinted through the night-sight. Maybe – there. What was that? He squeezed the hair trigger. Noting only a brief spurt of snow where his silent bullet fell, he stepped forward to investigate.

Nothing. A miss. The gunman scowled, hoping he had not spooked his quarry. No matter, he thought. I can take my time.

Snowdrop

Jimmy Birch had been so miserable and mixed up he hadn't had the will to go home after school, so he climbed into his favourite wilderness tree where he felt safe, and perched where he could see his own front door.

He knew Auntie May was at home, but he simply didn't feel up to talking with her. His head was full of his dead mother, and remembering how it had felt long ago, on freezing nights like this, to curl up against her bony back. Such un-comforting and uncomfortable touching confused him now as much as it had then. So he sat gripping the familiar ash bough as the gale swayed it this way and that, and watched the turmoil of snow in the faint glow from the road, wishing he could somehow turn himself into the great grey-skinned, multi-limbed tree.

Then the feeble street-lamps flickered and went out.

Jimmy sobbed silently into his sleeve, eventually drifting into a frosted stasis where only the life within the tree kept him connected to the world. His mind and body faded. All he sensed was the bulk of the ash, the sap alive deep within it, and anchoring roots twisting and diving down and down through the snow far into the chilled earth. The boy fell asleep.

He did not hear the approach of a man in tall boots and a peaked cap threading his way heavily towards him down the rudimentary pathway, working laboriously around blanketed swathes of ancient shrubbery and over giant wreathes of ripping briars. Neither did he see the man's pursuer, two hundred yards further off in the night, as he hauled himself up onto the slippery remains of a huge fallen oak and brace himself against its jutting root structure. This man scanned forwards through his rifle's telescope sight, his finger on the trigger.

The hunter had tracked his man by noting the occasional un-filled footprints and broken branches. He sensed he was getting closer. He could almost make out a shadowy figure plunging ahead. He squinted hard through the night scope and was rewarded with a brief glimpse of his quarry pausing for breath beneath a large ash tree.

The assassin fired – at the exact second Jimmy Birch fell out of the tree onto the head of the man below.

The fellow shouted and scrambled out from under this sudden zinging avalanche. With a tremendous effort he plunged onwards into the forest and disappeared.

The huntsman hissed through his teeth in frustration, incensed at having been thwarted a second time. He was not used to misjudging a shot. He sent another bullet zapping after the man in his fury, but the fellow was gone. He made his way to the tree to discover what had fallen out of it.

The hunter kicked at the hump of snow and that lay inert at his feet. What was this? A dislodged bundle of snowy rubbish? A dead animal? A nest? No – by god, it was a child. How could a child be there?

And there was blood in the snow.

Cursing, the man grabbed a handful of the child's clothing and jerked him over. An urchin of some sort. He ran his hand over the spindly limbs and found an obviously broken leg and a nasty long gash clearly made by his bullet in the flesh of the thigh.

He scanned the ground and pushed his finger into the wound searching for his bullet, but could find nothing. His shot must have clipped the kid as he fell, taking a chunk of flesh with it. The fall had caused the leg to fracture.

The gunman peered around, trying to tell if there was any likelihood of other boys dropping down unexpectedly from above. No. Nothing but the wind searing through the snowy woods and his quarry gaining ground, getting away. The world was icing up.

He packed snow roughly into the boy's wound and pulled him to a slightly more open area where he left him. The incident had been a shock, a tiresome setback, but was not his current concern. Someone would come looking for the kid, no doubt. Better to press on while he still could.

Panic-stricken by the falling object and thwack of a passing bullet, the man up ahead ploughed further and further into the unknown – into the awful, unchartered, black, grey, white dangerous chaos. He was in a terrible nightmare race for his life. Each breath was like a razorblade in his chest as he dragged his shaking limbs through the hostile wasteland. The blanketed undergrowth clawed at him, denying him passage. Time and again he balked at the sheer volume of it and ended up squeezing like a snake underneath a log, or forcing his way backwards through a wall of brambles. When he could neither squeeze nor crawl he climbed, swaying perilously before jumping down into the blackness. He tried always to stay low, knowing a bullet between the shoulder blades was a real possibility. But it was so difficult! If the assassin did not get him, this hellish forest would.

After a while the wind began to die down slightly, which allowed the clotting snow to fall more intensely. This shut out the howling trees and shrank his world into a grey claustrophobic tunnel. Flakes cloaked his shoulders and head and weighed like lead on his back. The carpet of snow hid ankle-breaking dips and perilous rocks and jagged stumps. Distance, direction – time itself – had no meaning. All that mattered was getting away. The sniper grew enormous in his imagination.

Quite unexpectedly, the man suddenly fetched up at a perfectly normal brick wall. The surprise brought him to his senses. He pulled himself up to look over it. Beyond the wall and a sturdy wooden fence he could see a quaint square structure. An old well-housing? Beyond that was a gap in the blackness that might be the roadway he had been hoping for. He paused and drew breath. He must finally have reached civilization again. A mere hour, maybe a little more, had passed since the avalanche. He shook his head and drew breath.

The defector clambered around and over and under and through, not caring what tracks he made. He pressed himself back against the wall for a moment trying hard to recall a once-glimpsed map of the area. Surely there was a town and a river somewhere near? If only there were street lights! Perhaps the storm had taken them out as they often did at home. He put his scratched and dirty hands in his pockets and decided to continue as quickly as he could. His pursuer would also make rapid progress once he too reached this road. The race to escape was nowhere near over with.

He edged across the space and found a black river winding below a snowy bank. Good. He would turn left and keep this river on his right. There was bound to be a bridge somewhere soon.

Freshly hopeful, the man in the cap plugged on.

May's worst night

Miss Fisher was beside herself with worry. Since coming home from school she had been peering out of the window, wringing her hands. She finally buttoned her coat back on, closed her front door and trod cautiously back down the darkened lane towards Mayflower. It was later than suppertime, and now that the electricity and telephone had stopped working, she simply *had* to go out searching for her little boy herself. Something must have happened to him – he had never stayed out so late before. She would begin at the school.

It was tough going for the old lady in that snowy gale. Even crossing the road was hazardous, although there was no wheeled traffic nor any pedestrian to be seen. May planted her stout zip-up boots precisely, hating the feel of the snow as it slipped wetly inside her socks and wishing her torch had stronger batteries. Half-way along the road came an even more hazardous road, Mellow Lane, with its icy muddy potholes lying in wait beneath a thick white carpet. Gingerly, arms outstretched like a tight-rope-walker, Miss Fisher edged her way forward.

Knocking loudly on Reg and Ivy Green's front door, she was relieved to hear the door-curtain pulled back and see Ivy's kindly face peering out.

"Oh, my lor', Miss, whatever's the matter?" Ivy dragged her inside as the dog Stringer jumped and fussed a welcome.

"It's Jimmy, Ivy. I can't find him anywhere." May's face looked grey with worry. They went to the warm kitchen where Reg was covering a plate of stew ready to take over to his bed-and-breakfast guest at the lodge. Realising this would have to wait, he thrust it back into the Aga's bottom warming oven.

"What's going on? Is your Jim out in all this? Little perisher. No, don't worry, Miss, we'll find 'im. Just wait till I get me cap tied down. Stop fussing Ivy, do. Now where's that…" he felt in his pocket. "Wait, what? Phone's not working, you say?" He picked up their receiver. No dial tone. No electricity. "She's right, Ivy. Look stay here while I just…"

Reg took a small wind-up radio transceiver out of one of the scullery cupboards and set it on the worktop. An unusual item, but there could be trouble about and he might need to make a call.

Ivy nodded, knowingly. This was serious. Reg privately checked he had his clasp-knife, a reliable torch and a whistle as well as a loaded pistol in his roomy overcoat pocket. He did not let the ladies see the gun. He pulled on his boots.

"I'm coming too, Reg," stated May Fisher. Her tone brooked no argument.

Reg unbolted and shoved open the back door that gave onto the school playground. Stringer shot past him until the snowdrifts brought him up short. He stood waiting, then suddenly cocked his head and stiffened, listening. He tilted his head from side to side trying to isolate the sound he had heard beyond the snow, beyond the gusting wind.

"What is it? What you heard, Stringer? Is it Jimmy? Go seek Jim – but go careful."

Reg and May scrunched after the little dog, across the smooth whiteness that came up to their knees, to the iron gate that led into the wilderness. It was difficult to unlock, but eventually Reg managed to heave it open. Stringer leapt onwards into the tangled masses of vegetation, pausing every now and then to check the two were still following. He whined anxiously. He clearly disliked the ponderous pace of their progress.

What minimal path there was required single file progress. Reg followed the jumping dog with his torch, and May did her utmost to step into the deep foot-holes Reg's boots made. Every plant seemed bent on pulling them back or catching their coats, forbidding their passage. Once they had to make a wide detour around what appeared to be a huge herd of elephants cowering together under the snow, but the little terrier ploughed courageously forward and never faltered. He finally stopped at a mound of snow and gave a single bark. The mound stirred. Reg shone the torch over it.

"Jimmy Birch, is that you?"

"Ow! Oh!" whispered the boy.

"Jimmy, oh Jimmy!" cried May falling down beside the child and brushing away the snow. "Darling, are you hurt? What's happened?"

In the torchlight the pinched little face was bloody and torn. Ice caked the boy's lashes and brows, his hair, his ears, his blue lips. He lay with one foot at a nasty angle. He had lost his school cap and both wellington boots. Reg nudged May aside and ran an expert hand over the lad's limbs to see what was amiss.

"What was you doing, little-un? Tree climbing I'll be bound. Never mind, you tell me where it hurts. It's alright, son, we'll tek you 'ome in a jiffy and warm you up. Stringer, stop lickin' his face a minute. May, gimme that scarf of yours. Kid's fell out some tree and broke a leg by the look of it, and I think he's cut 'is leg pretty badly on a branch on the way down. Must've fallen over 'ere and couldn't go no further. There's a real nasty gash in his thigh, though I can't see it properly. Snow's froze in it a fair bit, thank god. Yes, good dog, good dog. Did you 'ear him cry out? I bet you did, you got good ear'oles. No, I'll use my tie as a tourniquet at the top of 'is leg and then we'll rope 'em together with our scarves. Good job he's passed out cold again, May. This part is going to hurt, poor kid."

Reg bound the unconscious child up like a parcel, hoisted him over his shoulder, and with May shining the torch and Stringer bounding ahead, they retraced their gruelling steps to Reg's warm kitchen.

"Oh my god, Jimmy Birch!" cried Ivy. "Oh, poor little beggar. How did it…? Why was he…?"

They lay Jimmy on the sitting room sofa where Reg finally got a better look at the boy's wounds. May and Ivy covered him in rugs and sponged his face clean while he was out cold. Ivy poured water, found bandages and poked up the fire before filling two large hot water bottles from the kettle she kept permanently on the Aga.

Reg took himself into the scullery and turned knobs on the radio set. He kicked the door shut as he did not want the women to hear his conversation. It took a while before Sir Hugo answered.

"Bosun?"

"Problem sir." Reg explained about the child's accident. "Dunno why he would be out there, but the kid's got a broken leg and what might be a sideswipe wound on his thigh from a high velocity bullet."

"A bullet wound? Are you sure? How the blazes... Wait." Hugo had a rapid think.

Reg Green would not be using this radio unless it was a genuine emergency. They were in the middle of a sensitive defector situation, the weather had closed in and normal communications were down. And in the middle of all this it appeared a schoolchild had been hurt. Hurt badly too, from what Reg was saying. Deliberately? Unlikely. If the kid had been shot it was most probably from an enemy assassin sent to dispose of their valuable defector. This had happened before, right under their noses. Hugo ground his teeth. He had given his word nothing would ever happen to put Mayflower's children in danger. Now this. Damn and blast, he fumed. More complications.

"Alright, Reg. I will get through to London somehow. Emergency channels. They'll be able to send a local ambulance to you. And I will physically go and check our latest guest at the lodge. See if he is still where we hope he is. Give me twenty minutes. Out."

In less than fifteen minutes Hugo was standing in the freezing cold hall of Longmont Lodge, back on his radio.

"Bosun, our guest has disappeared, which most likely means he's been spooked and on the run. There's no tracks that I can see, thanks to this damn blizzard, but no signs of violence either. I'm alerting Tremayne, and sending him up to the railway station as he's closest. That's the fellow's most likely route out of town on a night like this. HQ has radioed our local hospital. They are sending an ambulance over to your place. That's if they can get across the river. You stick with the boy for now. Over."

"Aye-aye sir," acknowledged Reg. "Not sure an ambulance will make it to my front door, though. Over."

"Very good. Do what you must and let me know your position. Try and keep your head down, I don't want any more casualties. Over and out."

* * *

11.

Mill

Bick joins in

Mrs Bicknell was doing her best to make headway through snow that was already a foot deep, even in town. She had been to the Church Institute in Castle Square to hear a talk on Spring bulbs given by the chairman of the local Allotments Association and was beginning to wish she had not left it so late to walk home. Nobody seemed to be going her way, so she plodded alone through the swirling blizzard, past the castle wall with its gaping ancient entranceway, and down the incline to Stokes' Steps, which was her shortest route across the river. There were no street lights, only a weird ambient glow emanating from somewhere. Maybe the moon was behind the clouds. It seemed much later than it was. The river sluiced silently along, black and evil-looking, unstoppable even in these freezing conditions. Bick put her head down against the wind, feeling sorry for any creatures that dwelt below the stone arches.

The cobblestones of the Steps were treacherous. Bick kept her gloved hand firmly on the parapet until she made it safely to the far side. Here the wind suddenly dropped, leaving the snow to pelt down on her furry hat like a billion sticky soapflakes. She had to stop and fish around for her hanky, take off her spectacles and wipe them clear. Turning back the way she had come she noticed an ambulance with its headlights on parked near the castle wall. A policeman in an old-fashioned cape was talking urgently with the driver and pointing in her direction.

As she turned back, the figure of a man in a cap and long boots slithered past behind her, possibly on his way down the road to the station. He grunted at Bick's distracted 'good-evening' and pulled his funny foreign cap lower. Bick stood and waited while the ambulance men struggled across the Steps carrying an empty stretcher and two medical bags between them. The caped policeman accompanied them.

"Evenin' Constable," called Bick, wildly interested. "Someone took ill?"

PC Pink huffed and puffed, giving the men a steadying hand where he could.

"That you, Mrs Bick? Can't see a blessed thing tonight. You shouldn't be out in all this, it's getting real bad. Yes, we had an urgent call come in. The boys here was luckily only having a game of cards, so I told 'em to meet me by the castle, toot sweet."

"What's happened?"

Just then, stomping gingerly up Fen Lane – his arms apparently full of blankets – came Reg Green. Miss Fisher was hurrying along beside him, holding an awkwardly large golfing umbrella over the blanket bundle.

PC Pink called out, "Lay yer stretcher down there, boys. Gawd, Reg, whatever's bin goin' on?"

The two ambulance men took the unconscious child from Reg and placed him softly on the stretcher while the other four shrugged together beneath the umbrella. Reg Green filled them in on what he knew of Jimmy's accident, only leaving out any reference to possible gunshot wounds. They peered down at the little body being strapped securely onto the stretcher. A cover was pulled up over his head by one ambulance man, while the other checked the patient's vital signs.

Meanwhile, across the road, the sniper emerge from well corner and, seeing them blocking his path, turned north over Stokes' Steps. Leaving the trail of footprints, he slipped past the preoccupied group like a shadow. He spared them a swift glance, concluding the boy's body must have been discovered and was the focus of this little scene. It was annoying they was blocking his way, but he could work round the problem. He pulled his hood tighter about his face, hitched the rifle round under his arm, and strode as quickly as possible across the slippery stone causeway and up towards the town.

Bick looked up and caught a glimpse of the man's shape receding into the night.

"No, I'm not leaving Jimmy," Miss Fisher was saying. She handed the brick-like radio handset to Reg. "You lead on, Mr Pink. I'll follow alright, don't you worry about me." Her tone was firm. "Thank you Reg. I'll be at the hospital with my boy."

"Alright then, Miss. Give us your house keys and leave everythink else to me and Ivy. Phone when you can."

The stretcher bearers, May and the policeman shuffled gingerly back over the steps, carrying their tiny patient beneath his pile of rugs. Pink shone a torch ahead, but crane her neck as she might, Bick could spot no further sign of the shadowy figure that had crossed only a few moments before.

She rapped Reg's arm smartly to gain his full attention, and – forgetting the earlier pedestrian – told him about the furtive stranger with the gun over his shoulder that she had seen, guessing it was most likely something Mr Green would want to know about.

He whistled. "Just now? Why didn't you say? No, well, alright. Wait a minute while I 'ave a think."

The dog was at home in the warm with Ivy, which was good. Reg did not want Stringer to be shot at by any foreign marksman. It was also bad, as the dog was an excellent tracker even in conditions this atrocious.

Just then the radio crackled, making them both jump. Wide-eyed and shivering, Bick held the big umbrella and watched as Reg twiddled knobs and listened as he answered. Eventually switching it off, he filled her in a little.

"So, here's what's 'appenin'. Mr Tremayne's gorn up the station," Reg explained. "Trains is all held up, according to London. He'll rope that young porter Kevin Smith in to search the place and nab anyone trying to travel out of town that way. Sir Hugo believes there's definitely two foreigners on the loose somewhere. One we was aiming to take down to Lambeth for interrogation, but there's also this other bloke, who's no doubt been sent to pop him orf before he can tell us anything useful. He's the gunman you must've seen crossing the bridge. If that swine's as good as they say he is, he's probably not far behind the first, providing he's not lorst him in this ruddy weather."

Reg glanced around. "This is a right mess. Why our man couldn't just stay put I dunno. Well, as there's nobody else available, Ada, I'll have to follow 'em misself. See if I can't stop one bugger murderin' the other bugger. Yes, don't you worry about me. Look, will you take this radio back to Ivy for me? I'll contact 'er soon as ever I can. It's too much to carry if I'm to follow and ketch this bloke. It's heavy and awkward. You go and fill Ivy in so's she can update Sir Hugo on it. Ivy knows all about everythin'."

Bick stared at him. "Yes, o'course, Mr Green. And I'll stay with her in case Sir Hugo needs anything else doing. And I'll keep me eyes peeled too, like always. Please, *please* – do be careful! This is all so… Gor, what a carry-on." So saying, she took the radio in a shaky hand and disappeared into the dark, her little torchlight wobbling madly as she tried to hurry.

A welcome recruit

Reg Green gritted his teeth. This horrible evening wasn't over yet. He ducked his head and stepped forward as fast as he could in the rapidly disappearing wake of the ambulance men.

"That you, Reg?" called a cheery voice, just as he reached the central span of the Steps across Latimer Island. He looked up to see Ben Nesbit grinning through the murk. "Not much of a night to be out."

"That it ent," grumbled Reg. He ran his eyes over his friend. "Where's your Land Rover?"

"Laid up. I'm heading home on shanks's pony, more's the pity. Took my shotgun into the gunsmith's just before it closed, only now the blasted buses aren't running, and all the street lights have gone out. Where are you off to?"

This could be a piece of real luck – not something that happened very often in Reg's secret service experience. His mind raced back and forth over the current situation. Without the radio he could not request direct orders, but that could be dealt with later. Here was Ben Nesbit, a wholly reliable fellow, a friend, a gamekeeper used to tracking things on foot. He was an unarmed civilian but that didn't matter. Reg took an executive decision and rapidly explained to Ben the unlikely pursuit he was engaged upon.

"You know how to follow tracks, Ben, better than me. This fellow I'm after is a real public danger and well-armed. It may not come to shooting 'im, but I could seriously use your help to follow the murderous bastard and lock 'im up somewhere safe.

You're a professional. You been in the army, right? This assassin's out to kill our latest iron curtain defector, and *he* might be only a little way ahead of this armed sniper in the middle of the town."

Ben stared at Reg in disbelief. Was he pulling his leg? No, he looked deadly serious, and Reg wasn't one to lie. "I… " he began.

"I'll square dragooning you later with Sir Hugo, I promise. This is honestly a matter of national security, I swear," added Reg, fervently. "Only, come on mate if you're coming. It's urgent and it's top secret. I don't think they can be that far ahead." He resumed his progress towards the town, where the castle walls loomed black against the indefinable light.

Ben pulled himself together. "OK, Reg. Count me in. Betty won't be worrying where I am just yet, I suppose. How far ahead is this – this gunman, do you think? I wish the damn snow would stop. Do we know what either man is wearing? Are they *both* dangerous? Where are they most likely to be making for, do you think?"

Relieved, but wishing his friend would shut up, Reg beat his hands together and nodded towards the town. "No idea. But thanks, Nesbit. Best we get moving – and stay very, very quiet. There's no reason this bloke won't just turn round and shoot us too, if he gets the chance. Come on."

The assassin paused on his slippery climb onto one of the high ramparts of the castle walls. He wanted to see if he could spot his quarry from the highest vantage point available, but it was proving a more challenging ascent than he expected. He cursed the ridiculous weather and the unexpectedly awkward terrain with its multiple entanglements. Who would have thought silly little England could be so hostile? It had all looked dull and simple on the map. He raised his night scope and swept a slow full circle.

He hurriedly ducked down as he glimpsed two figures dimly silhouetted in the castle gateway. One, he realised with irritation, was the school's caretaker – a stout old warhorse he knew to be an MI6 agent. The other was the tall fellow he had passed on the bridge. They were clearly out searching for their missing defector. Him too, most likely. Definitely. The caretaker had carried the boy to the medics, so he was probably not dead. The sniper was mildly relieved about this. Now the second fellow was pointing down at the snow around the gate of the bailey yard. He must be some sort of tracker. That old lady must have spotted him, and told the caretaker. They were on his tail. And he had lost his own target somewhere!

Damn! The sniper slithered silently back down into the darkest part of the yard, while his mind re-calibrated the situation.

These two sleuths were an unexpected nuisance, but if he could manage to pick up his target's trail and eliminate the rat swiftly, his mission might still be salvaged. All he had to do was stay ahead of Holmes and Watson, eliminate his quarry, and disappear. All was not lost. If they got in his way he would silence them too. Serve them right. The moonless night and this foul weather might just work to his advantage. He would edge along beside this river, then at the next crossing, if he had not found his man by then, he would return to the well-house and start over. They should not be hard to shake off.

He smiled inside his masked hood.

The long, cold trail

Ben and Reg hunted for tracks slowly, methodically and warily. Ben went first while Reg plodded awkwardly behind. They finally picked them up where their man had clearly spent some time scaling the castle ramparts.

"He'll have sought a high vantage point, I think," whispered Ben. "See here? This is where he's dropped back down. Probably taking a shufti for his target. Maybe he's even spotted us. He's not that far ahead."

The inner bailey was black as pitch although somewhere up above a nebulous moonglow was beginning to backlight the falling flakes. They slithered on, up and down and around various hidden lumps of masonry, until they came to the low-linteled sally port on the western side. It was the only gateway on that side of the castle, and opened onto Market Street. Nowadays it was not so much a gate as a narrow crooked tunnel. Inside its tumbled stonework a man could shelter quite easily. Maybe, if he clambered over the fallen sections into the roofless chambers beyond, a person might even dwell undetected inside for a few days. The frozen earth floor was bare inside the sally port tunnel and Ben's torch picked out the fresh imprint of their quarry's boots ahead of them.

They emerged into Market Street and peered left, then right. The softly falling snow was easing, only to be replaced by tiny pellets of biting ice which the suddenly re-born wind whirled viciously into their sensitive faces.

"Damn it's turned cold again," complained Reg, beating his arms. He wished he had proper snow gear on, not this overcoat and a pair of old wellington boots.

"This way," murmured Ben, switching his flashlight off.

Their target had turned sharp left outside the castle, and over a set of spiked iron railings to the steep riverside below the curtain wall. His footmarks were unmistakable. Reg risked shining a torch briefly around on the snow-covered weeds and reeds of the slanting bank in case of ambush. The edge of the heavy black river water was rimmed with ice. Nobody, not even a rat, was to be seen. The two struggled over the boundary railings, hanging on for dear life to the roots of shrubby willows and rank elder that grew down there. It was perilous work, edging forwards, especially when they were only too aware the nice safe level road was only a few feet above them.

After a hazardous scramble of several hundred yards, the bank widened slightly, permitting them to proceed more normally across rough snow-shrouded grass. Ben whispered he had picked up the track again and pointed to a low-lying, faintly defined path. Reg could make nothing out but had long ago decided Ben knew what he was doing.

He grunted, "Go on," and resumed his wading progress behind the younger man.

To their left lay the river, to their right Market Street curved in a wide arc on its way to the distant village of Ironwell. This coarse piece of riverside scrub spread out and merged into the lower portion of Banford Heath with its acres and acres of boggy marsh and tussocky grass, impenetrable mats of reeds and sharply spiked thorn bushes. Walking here was ankle-breaking even on a fine Summer's day, never mind a black and freezing Winter's night. However, the snow out in the open reflected a little more light and they could begin to discern a little of the terrain, its shrouded lumps and bumps, hazards, holes and hollows.

"How's the leg holding up," whispered Ben as they stopped briefly to reconnoitre.

Reg had no trouble with his new hip bone, replaced a year ago. His only concern right now was finding their two men. He made no comment, merely took his pistol out of his pocket and checked it.

"What the hell?" Ben hissed, shocked.

"There's no chance I'm letting our bloke get snuffed out by that fuckin' bastard with his fancy silencer. Not on my watch. He ent gettin' past me," growled Reg. There was no need to explain further. He would tell Ben about little Jimmy Birch later if he had to. Best keep the troops focused.

"Come on." He shoved his friend and they set off, Ben rapidly re-calibrating the seriousness of the danger he might have let himself get into. Had Reg *really* mentioned the British Secret Intelligence Service? And foreign assassins sent to kill their own countrymen? It sounded like a Le Carré novel, and Ben didn't like it one bit. Pistols in overcoat pockets – rifles with silencers? He might seriously have to interfere if Reg looked like killing anyone, even if it was all for Queen and country. He kept chewing on the danger as he read the tracks and led his friend slowly but surely across the darkened heath.

Like a couple of stealthy Inuits, the two worked their way doggedly forward, keeping low. Every so often they caught a brief glimpse of their target's shadow moving in the gloom, but mostly they were relying on his snowy trail. The fellow was making surprisingly rapid progress in a very definite direction, which led Reg and Ben to believe he must possess night-glasses or some other device to assist his choice of route. It was far more difficult for the two of them, and they were ill-prepared for such a polar trek. The snow shrouded the lumpy tussocks of the treacherous terrain and they often found themselves floundering into the deceptive dips between the huge mountains of grass. Sour-smelling wet mud lay sticky beneath the icy carapace and pulled at their boots, while the sullen river sluiced past somewhere to their left waiting for them to slip and fall in.

Reg felt each step crack and water come bubbling up over his frozen feet in their thin rubber Wellingtons. Both men's faces began to rime over as they forced their way against the reborn wind. It was agonisingly freezing and slow going. Their legs were soon as heavy as iron and their ears became deafened and sore from the battering blasts. The darkness deepened, walling them into a world that consisted only of immense physical effort. They were pressed down, squeezed tight, and forced to fight every small step of the way.

We must have crossed over Latimer Street crossing already, Reg thought suddenly, pulling his brain sharply out of a reverie of fatigue. Their quarry had not turned down it to cross the river as expected. This concerned Reg. Why not? It was the first turning out of this hellish heathland. It would be the obvious choice and the perfect way to lose them. He concluded the fellow had most likely simply missed the turning – as he had himself. It would be completely covered in snow, it was night, the area was unfamiliar, and it was unlit. All of which boiled down to the fact that the three of them were in for an even longer and more brutal hike, probably all the way to Ironwell and the next bridge.

Why was their quarry sticking so close to the river? Was the sniper choosing this route on purpose? Had he abandoned his mission or simply lost his target? He was certainly leading them a dance. A perfectly good bridle-path ran parallel to the river some distance to their right across the slightly higher ground, but the sniper seemed hell-bent on leading them through the boggiest, most exhausting areas. It's deliberate, thought Reg. He knows we're here and he wants us to break our bloody legs. He's forcing us to slow right down and be wary of every step. He'll turn round and pick us off as soon as ever he gets a chance.

The crazy wind suddenly dipped, dropped and died and an icy moon slid through a slit in the clouds to ride high above. Its chalky face gazed down on their slogging drama like a horrified spectator. The pursuers halted, catching their breath. Reg rested his hands on his knees and Ben clambered up onto his back and knelt there, scanning the land ahead.

"I think I see him about half a mile away," he whispered as they resumed their gallumphing walk. "He's further off than he was at the castle and making better speed than we are. I can't tell for sure whether anyone's ahead of him, but I don't think so. If he gets to Ironwell, Reg, he could go either north or south over the bridge. If he makes it as far as Weston Forest we'll lose him for sure. The railway line passes right through there and he could just hop on."

Reg had thought of that. "If he's bent on escaping us, he could. But if he still means to finish off 'is man he'll likely circle back around, pot him in the railway station where he's most likely lying safe and warm waitin' for the morning milk train, then hop aboard 'imself and Bob's yer uncle. He'll be over the sea to Skye. And if 'e gets a chance 'e'll turn and pot us for sure. Then it's Goodnight Vienna. I just 'ope Mr Tremayne's already somehow managed to run that silly little rabbit to ground, I really do."

Ben blew out his cheeks. "This whole adventure is very nasty. We really ought to try to capture this sniper, not shoot him."

Reg grunted, wishing he'd kept his radio with him. "Nasty is right. Best get a move on and pick the bloke up quick, Ben. I don't like our odds after Ironwell. Come on."

The assassin was livid to note he was still being followed. No matter how he darted from thorn clump to bramble thicket, these two bumbling pests still stumbled and staggered relentlessly after him. They were not professionals, anyone could see that, but neither were they unskilled. Luck was certainly with them, not him. His own trail had gone cold while theirs roared like a furnace. Did they not realise he might stop and shoot at any minute? He wiped his sleeve across his ice-stung eyes. Only he couldn't – not yet. He needed a better vantage point, higher than this swampy desert. There had to be some tree or building he could scale to get an advantage, surely. Killing these two would be a pleasure.

He scanned ahead through his scope as the pellets of snow eased off.

A large old building, possibly a disused factory or mill, stood like a medieval cathedral against the moonlit sky with its racing ragged clouds.

The assassin ploughed on and eventually came close to the place. Panting and leaning against a gatepost he peered up at the brickwork with its ancient weather-board cladding. A vast circular wooden structure clung like a carbuncle to the side of one wall. It was a watermill.

Nothing moved, there were no lights. The huge old wheel was chained.

He sniffed. It did not feel or smell entirely uninhabited. Maybe there were animals penned somewhere within. Maybe a family of millers lay snug in their beds upstairs. He studied the enormous ancient waterwheel tethered by heavy iron links above the clotted surface of a deep narrow pit. Scanning higher he noticed a timber stairway that zig-zagged forty-five feet or so directly up the same wall. It climbed to a small platform and granary door situated directly under the gable. As a vantage point the platform could not be more perfect.

He fought his way onwards through clumps of arching ice-sheathed brambles to the base of the wooden staircase. It was far less robust than it had first appeared and pieces fell off when touched it. There were whole sections of steps missing at the lower end and part of the handrail near the top leaned unhelpfully outwards, pointing downwards like a dreadful finger. It had been alternately soaked and frozen for decades, chewed by beetles and covered with green mosses and lichen, and so infiltrated by slime and rot it could hold no more – just like the wheel itself. Icicles dangled. Nothing had been made to bear weight or shift round in fifty years. It was as dangerous as ever a structure could be, but it was all he had.

The assassin began climbing the wooden steps. It was tough going in the dark shadow, even for an expert, but at least the flesh-stripping snow had stopped. He clawed his way slowly up, testing each step with his boot, lunging across gaps. Chunks of rotten timber occasionally broke off and fell noisily down into the chasm below, some hitting the old paddles before disappearing into the disused millpool, cracking its thin ice and sinking like pieces of scrap iron. He was making a dreadful noise, but it could not be helped. Speed was everything. He clung to a swaying strut halfway up and paused briefly to look back across the expanse of snow-carpeted heath.

The two hunters were still plodding nearer, one behind the other.

Finally reaching the platform, the gasping climber edged gingerly over to the rickety handrail. He set up his rifle, bracing it as best he could while the wind gusted and tugged at him. Now was his best chance, when they were still coming on. He moved himself into position and squinted through the scope. He tried not to shift his weight more than was necessary as each movement caused the stairs to groan and rock alarmingly.

He saw his pursuers. Like Wenceslas and his page the tall man led the shorter, weaving laboriously across the uneven snowfield.

The shooter relaxed and breathed out. As the moon slipped behind a hurrying cloud he squeezed the trigger.

Ben and Reg both heard the zip of the bullet not a foot away and jumped for the nearest mass of snowy thorn bushes.

"Git down," hissed Reg. Horrified, Ben obeyed. Reg parted a few twigs to peer at the building.

"He's up the mill." Reg took out his pistol again and forced a round into the chamber. "Somewhere up that wooden scaffold. I'll have to get nearer."

Ben barely registered the weapon or the remark. He was almost too scared to think.

They stared into the darkness, trying to make out exactly where their foe was. The wind hurled the clouds across the moon in fits and starts but by looking slightly to one side they thought they could just make a shape out, hunched at the very top by the granary door. It was a perilous position, made doubly so by the weather conditions. How the fellow had climbed that high so rapidly was astonishing. It must have been like climbing the frozen rigging of an ancient sailing ship. The watchers crouched panting, waiting for another shot to come.

Yet even as they craned forward, the unexpected happened. There was a slight tremor, a shivering jolt like another shadow flickering against the mill's wall. Then came a terrible, tearing, creaking groan. Horrified, Reg and Ben stood up and watched as the entire wooden staircase with its platform suddenly yawed out from the wall, twisting and shuddering as bits dropped off like broken teeth. They gasped as the rifleman at the top dropped twenty feet and lodged, trapped with his legs either side of a wooden beam. They heard him scream and watched him struggle. Then came another even more awful sound as the entire rotten staircase bucked and collapsed, taking the man down with it into the darkness.

Ben and Reg broke cover and ran as fast they could. They scaled a fence, and laboured across the snowy yard to the side of the mill, just as a dim light came on somewhere indoors. They shone their torches around, looking up, looking down into the millpool and over the broken snow.

The dead man was not difficult to locate. Falling from such a height, he had crashed through four decayed waterwheel paddles and spokes as if they were made of wet cardboard. His specialised rifle, still clipped to his body harness, was now wedged between one of the gudgeons and part of the massive timber shaft of the broken millwheel. Its owner hung from it, quite dead. His body swayed suspended like a wartime parachutist caught in a tree, twisting slightly. One toe almost touched the water. His head was whipped backwards at an ugly angle, his chest arched out towards the sky.

"Good god, Reg! Look!"

They stepped forward, unsure of how to get to the body, how to pluck it down. Reg reached out – then stopped, feeling Ben's hand holding him back. The wind gusted. The dangling body jerked, as the rifle slipped a little. The wind blew again, sending spinning pellets of snow up into their faces. Before they could make another move the assassin and his horrible weapon suddenly and silently slipped vertically into the deep, deep waters beneath the wheel-pit and completely disappeared.

The huge wheel's ancient anchor chain, thus briefly released, clanked loudly and the whole arcane mechanism moved ponderously for half a turn before catching again.

At their feet the scumbled surface of the water-pit closed back over its foul black contents.

"Oh my god! Can we get him?" cried Ben urgently.

"Not a hope in 'ell," answered Reg grimly, pocketing his revolver. "Bastard's gone. If that fall didn't break his back its certain-sure he's drowned dead be-now. That wheel pulled his body right under. It's going to take a grapplin' 'ook to get 'im out, even if we can find 'im. Oy, shape up, look lively."

Ben dragged his gaze away from the horrible wheel and the evil slimy waters to see Faye Winstanley clumping bravely round the corner of her home in cowboy boots, nightie, overcoat and woolly hat. She held an old fashioned hurricane lamp in one hand and was brandishing a golf club in the other.

"I say," she shrieked through the wind. "Who is it? Are you burglars? I heard the most awful din. I'm not without defences, you know."

"It's alright, Miss," Reg hollered back. "It's only Mr Green from the school and Mr Nesbit. Would it be alright if we came inside? I think there's something we ought to tell you."

* * *

12.

Stringer

At the railway station

Toby heard his emergency radio handset buzzing and listened anxiously to what Sir Hugo had to say. He went straight down to the old lady's bedroom and checked that Gibb was out for the count. Having to leave her alone on such a wild night did not bother him one iota. He hurriedly put on his overcoat, boots and hat, grabbed the radio and went out into the snow.

It was hard going. All he had to illuminate the way was an old bicycle lamp he had found in the kitchen drawer. He slipped and slid down to the main road then forged his way up towards the station. Well House, where the Tuttles lived, was completely dark – its garden blanketed in thick virgin snow dunes, drifts blown high against the walls and hedges. The house on the next corner was the same. Tremayne slithered across the level crossing and finally made it into the station building.

Inside he discovered Kevin Smith and Mr Coker the station master in an urgent discussion about the state of the final section of line from Weston to Banford.

"But the rill that flows *this* side of the Eye is still ice-free, Mr Coker. I seen it. It's running through Mint Pool as far as Cat Island. I tell you, we're more sheltered this side of Latimer."

Mr Coker shook his grizzled head and blew on his fingers. "I dunno, Kevin. It don't mean the milk's getting through."

They looked up in amazement as Toby shoved his way in and stamped his feet on the mat. He pulled the door shut behind him.

"Good evening, Mr Tremayne, Sir. Nasty night to be out. Sorry, but I don't think you're going to be catching a train anywhere tonight. The last one should have left Ledgely forty minutes ago but there's no sign of it yet. Probably snowed in t'other side of Weston is my guess. Phone lines is out too."

"Oh, that's not why I'm here. Mr Coker," Toby assured him. He knew all about the phones.

"We still have our old telegraph system in place," interrupted Kevin proudly. "It come in right useful tonight."

"It would do, yes." That was a valuable piece of news. "No, look, can I have a word with you gentlemen somewhere a bit warmer?"

Mystified, the two railwaymen took him into the cosy ticket office where a bright little fire crackled in the grate. Toby closed the door and leaned against it while he explained the urgent need to apprehend any foreign traveller, should one materialise at the station this evening.

"He's an escaped what?" asked Mr Coker, bewildered.

"Defector. He's escaped from behind the Iron Curtain – so rather valuable to our side, don't you see. He's not been – he's not had time to tell us his important information yet, though, and now we think there may also be a marksman after him."

"What, someone wants to bump him off, like? For coming over here and telling us Russian secrets?"

"Yes. So we simply must pick him up as soon as we can and keep him safe. Until Sir Hugo and I can move him down to London."

Kevin whistled. This was like a story on telly. "How can we help?"

"Well, I'm told he's likely to be heading this way, to catch a train or board one secretly. There's no buses or other traffic so this is his most likely route out. Don't think he has any money, so he could be waiting nearby ready to jump on one of your puffing billies down to London or somewhere, to get away from this shooter, don't you see? He's not running from us, but he's bound to be terrified. As far as we know he doesn't speak English. He's mid-height, wearing leather boots and has a sort of Dutch-style cap on. Small beard. Looks like Lenin. Have you any passengers who might be him?"

Coker shook his head and looked at Kevin. "We ent, have we Kevin?"

Kevin stared at Mr Tremayne, his mind racing. "We've no passengers at all, sir. And no trains neither. I ent seen anyone wanting to travel since the four o'clock left. But we ought to take a proper look around."

"I was hoping you'd help me with that."

Mr Coker had an awful thought. "Here, the other feller – the one with a gun you say is after him. Could he come walking into my station too?"

Toby held up his hands. "Look, I honestly don't know. It's best Kevin and I make a thorough search though, right now. You stay in here, Coker, near your telegraph machine while we have a scout around outside," ordered Toby. "If you're up for it of course, Kevin. I know I am asking a lot, but there's no alternative. I must impress upon you that this is all very top secret and hush-hush."

The railwaymen stared at each other.

"No need to worry, Sir. Job's gotta be done," said Kevin stoutly. He'd seen loads of films like this.

The two left the dumbfounded Mr Coker to sit down and have a confused think about the last ten minutes. He locked the door after them and put a kettle on to boil.

The station's booking hall was deserted. It was not a large building, but there were various little rooms, the coal area, the outside lavatories, a ladies' waiting room, to search. Kevin shone a bright flashlight into every nook and cranny and cupboard, but they found no one hiding, nor any hopeful traveller anywhere on the premises. No footprints on the snowy platform either, and none on the rails. They moved into the car park, where Toby pulled a business-like pistol from his pocket and held it at his side.

My god, thought Kevin. He really is 007.

They unlocked and searched the various sheds and buildings as best they could, but there was no sign of anyone. They slithered the short distance down to the crossing gates.

"Trains have to crawl across 'ere," Kevin called into Toby's ear above the whistling wind. "Easy enough to jump aboard."

Toby nodded. They poked the drifts and piles of snow-shrouded sleepers and lengths of iron rails stacked amid stone chippings, old cans and old crates. Then Kevin wrenched back the corner of a heavy tarpaulin.

And there, crouching – shielding his eyes from the torch's glare – was a terrified man in an odd-looking cap. He raised his bare hands immediately in surrender.

"Thank god," said Toby Tremayne, waving the pistol. "Come on, comrade. This way. There's a nice warm ladies' waiting room indoors, and a cup of tea with your name on it." He waved his gun again and the man nodded, relieved to have been found by the British and not his murderous countryman.

"There's a lock on that waiting room door, right, Mr Smith?" asked Tremayne quietly, putting the gun back in his pocket and feeling for his radio.

"Oh yes, sir. Nice and strong. And I'm not going to let this bloke out of my sight until your men come to take him away," answered Kevin with a grin. "I'll guard him with my life."

"Excellent, Mr Smith. You'd make a good special agent, you know."

What happened to Jimmy

May Fisher, PC Pink and the ambulance crew slithered and staggered over Stokes' Steps to the wharf-side where the ambulance was parked. Although little Jim Birch had been strapped firmly down he weighed so little the wind tried to tug the stretcher out of the men's grip all the way across. May did her best to steady it, hanging on to the policeman with her other hand but it was rough going. They both climbed determinedly into the vehicle as the crew slid the stretcher into its slot and finally closed the doors. There was no point ringing the emergency bell, no other vehicle was out that night.

It was a slow and slippery ride. May and Pink braced themselves as the vehicle swayed and skidded across icy stretches as the tyres tried to maintain traction. They were glad not to be able to see out, although by the time they reached their destination both felt decidedly queasy.

The duty surgeon had set plenty of bones, but had not seen a rip in a thigh as straight as a sabre cut before. He guessed a broken branch had caused it even though there were no splinters or other residue in the wound, only a few threads from the boy's torn shorts. A few centimetres either way and Jimmy might not have been so lucky. Had an artery been ripped he would have bled out. As it was, the surgeon guessed that the cold, the thick snow pack he had landed in, the wad of snow in the wound itself, and the tourniquet had saved the child's life. He stitched Jimmy up while his colleague dealt with the fractured ankle. The boy was out of the theatre in an hour and into a side room on the children's ward, linked up to various machines and slowly warming up.

Pink had returned to the Police Station by the time the doctor came to talk to Miss Fisher.

"Well," he assured her with a tired smile. "Your lad's going to be just fine. We'll keep him a couple of days, just to be sure. Are you his granny?"

"I'm his foster mother."

"Oh, I beg your pardon. Does he have a social worker we should call?"

"Yes. I will phone her as soon as ever I can."

They sat and discussed Jimmy's injuries, his past health and his immediate needs. Then May Fisher bedded herself down in a plastic-covered armchair, as best she could, right beside her boy. There was no question of her leaving his side for an instant. Once alone, she found herself shaking. Tears cascaded down her cheeks like a silent waterfall as she watched over his bandaged little body. How could it have come to this, she cried in her heart.

After a while, a thoughtful nurse brought her a cup of tea and a biscuit.

"There now," said the nurse kindly. "You've had a nasty shock, me duck. He'll be OK, you see. Boys are tough little chaps. He'll be alright now he's defrosting. That leg will mend. Don't you worry, me darling. And it's such a terrible night, isn't it? We've no electric except for the generator, so I'll bring you an extra blanket."

Jimmy stirred. He coughed and opened his eyes. He took a chestful of air and opened his mouth. "Mum!" he croaked.

"I'm here, darling. I'm here. It's Auntie May. You're alright. You've had a little bit of a bump, but don't worry, you're going to be just fine. I'm here. I'm right here." She stroked his poor grazed head and he closed his eyes. "Shhh, shhh now, darling. Go back to sleep." She kissed his pale cheek as he drifted off again.

May's world shrank to the four walls of the little side room, the boy in the bed, and all the machines that dripped and ticked and dosed his battered body. And she thanked her god for all the good, gentle and clever people who tonight were caring for them both.

In the morning

The next day the world outside was as white and crisp as a wedding cake. It shimmered with azure shadows beneath a bright shining sky devoid of clouds. Children played snowy games. Thoughtful neighbours swept each other's pathways. Workmen, shoppers and dog-walkers emerged to enjoy the morning.

May Fisher was still beside the bed when Jimmy woke properly. She was dozing, her head on her arm as it lay on his mattress. He smiled on seeing her open her blue eyes.

"You're not knitting," he whispered, trying to pat her white hair.

Tears slid down her face, much to her irritation. "No," she answered, brushing her cheek and putting on her glasses. "How do you feel?"

"Sleepy. And my leg hurts. My head hurts. What did I do?"

"Fell out of a tree into the snow. Stringer found you. You've a nasty cut under this big bandage and your ankle is broken."

"Broken? Like Jumbo?"

May Fisher nodded. Jumbo Ellis had been an accident-prone Mayflower boy. "Yes, like Jumbo. Jimbo."

Jimmy smiled too. He squeezed her hand and gave her a look of such love she would have burst out crying again had not a nurse breezed in at that moment. It was Elaine Granger, a firm favourite on the children's ward, the wife of Joe Granger.

"Oh good morning, Jimmy. I see you're awake. I expect you're thirsty. Now then, Miss Fisher, how's our boy doing?" She smiled her wide smile at the little shrimp in the big bed surrounded by snowy pillows. My word, he could do with fattening up a bit, she thought. She read over his notes, took his temperature and checked his dressings while May went off to find a lavatory and spruce herself up.

On her return she discovered Sir Hugo and Mrs Clark in the waiting area. They were sitting silently and it looked as if they had had a disagreement. Mrs Clark jumped up and ran to May.

"How is he, May? Poor little Jimmy! Is he very bad?"

Miss Fisher gripped her outstretched hands. "No, he's going to be fine. He's a tough little fellow."

"Oh thank god," gulped Skipper. She turned to Hugo, who was waiting his turn.

"That's wonderful news, May," he said, genuinely relieved the lad was not likely to die. Skipper darted a look full of venom at him.

"Yes, well," she hissed.

Hugo ignored her. "How can we help? Would you like us to go and fetch anything for you, or take you somewhere? I have the car. The roads are just about passable in town."

"No, no thank you. Tell me, how is Mr Green? He was wonderful last night, Mrs Clark. He carried Jimmy all that way to the ambulance. You know, if it hadn't been for Stringer and Reg I don't know… I don't think… We might not have found him in time."

"Ah, the dog," said Hugo. "He has a good nose."

"Can Jimmy come home?" Skipper asked. She flicked another look at Hugo. He had come clean and told her about Reg's suspicion there had been a gunman in the wilderness last night whose shot had clipped the lad's leg as he fell. To say she was incandescent was an understatement.

"Not for a few days. He has a broken ankle and a chunk out of his thigh where he caught it on some branch or something. He lost quite a lot of blood, but the cold helped save him. The doctors wants to keep an eye on him for a while"

"I see. Oh poor little chap! Well, you'll need a few bits and bobs from home. I expect Hugo could run me back to get some things for you. I'll feed Marigold."

"Yes, well thank you. I'm sure Jean will see the cat doesn't go hungry. I suppose I could do with a few things. Oh, here's Ernest."

Ernest Chivers and Mike Paton hurried in, stamping snow off their boots.

"How is he? What on earth was he doing out there, May?" they asked anxiously. Percy Watson, the local postman they had stopped and had a word with as he was struggling in to work, had told them about the accident. Ernest was clutching two picture books and a bag of sweets, Mike a small potted plant. "How's Jimmy doing?"

One by one, visitors came and went bringing little gifts or peeping round the door to see how the lad was. May was relieved when the telephone lines were fixed and she could ring Jean to ask her to put the word round that she and Jimmy would be coming home the following day.

Mrs Harris, Jimmy's social worker, called by late in the afternoon after everyone else had gone, to see how her charge was faring and ask what in heaven's name he had been doing up a tree alone at night in a snowstorm. May did her best to explain, then left the two together while she went for a cup of tea in the little bar near the front door. She never discovered exactly what they spoke about, but afterwards Mrs Harris found her and gave her an enormous hug.

She told her she also had some news. Miss Fisher sat quite still, fearing more trouble, but she could not have been more wrong. Mrs Harris informed her Jimmy's case had been expedited and was ready to put before the adoption panel. Which meant, if there were no objections, May would be Jimmy's legal guardian by the Summer. She said she had told the boy already.

Mrs Harris stopped and let this sink in.

"Jimmy is very sorry he worried you so much last night," said Mrs Harris as they stood near the front door. "He says his head was very muddled and he couldn't find the right words to talk to you, so he went up the tree for a think. He says he'll talk about it soon. And he will. And I'll make sure I'm available too. He has had a lot to deal with, but he'll get there I'm sure, with your love and patience. It wasn't anything you did, Miss Fisher, or didn't do."

She patted May's arm. "There really wasn't anything else you ought to have done, you know. You found him – you and Mr Green, and that marvellous little dog. That's what matters. You brought him to safety and to medical help as fast as anyone could. No parent could have done more."

Mrs Harris tied her headscarf firmly under her chin. "By the way, Jimmy also tells me he would like to be called Jim Fisher after he's formally adopted," she smiled.

May stood and stared. "That's… that's… " she stammered. It was all too much.

"I know," Mrs Harris answered with a smile. "Now please stop worrying and get back to his bedside. He needs you."

May Fisher returned to her sleeping boy, her head spinning with tiredness and relief. What a wondrous life this is, she mused, misquoting Marvell. After losing my boy, finding him, then him almost dying and ending up here, a wonderful ripe apple suddenly drops from nowhere into my lap. Jim Fisher, indeed.

May picked up the knitting bag Jean had brought her that afternoon and took out the piece she was working on. She pulled out a few rows and began again.

This will make a nice warm cardigan for Mrs Harris, she thought.

Aftermath

Miss Winstanley's mill was descended upon, twenty-four hours later, by a discreet squad of Toby's specialist clean-up agents. While Fay accompanied Reg Green to Alf Rose's cottage in the village to discuss the possibility of Horace joining Persephone in her field next Summer, Toby and Sir Hugo stood a grim watch over the retrieval of the sniper's body.

A beefy, rubber-suited diver managed to free the drowned corpse of the assassin and his mangled weapon after a difficult half-hour, and brought them to the surface. There followed an awkward slippery struggle in the cold mud to pull him out. Task done, the men zipped up the body-bag, stacked a few of the more dangerous pieces of fallen frozen timber onto the bank and departed as anonymously as they had arrived.

Fay returned home, pleased with her visit. A letter on the kitchen table from Sir Hugo Chivers suggested that, come the better weather, she might apply for a grant towards rebuilding the damaged wheel and the dangerous staircase. He would see it reached the right people. As it was, Mr Tremayne and his volunteers had cleared away some of the fallen timber and tidied up a little for her while she was out. Her home was safe now. He liked to be a good neighbour.

Miss Winstanley was surprised and delighted at such kindness. She had been told only that Mr Green and his friend had been chasing a burglar when they saw the wind and heavy snow take her woodwork down. The burglar had, alas, escaped into the night – but Reg was sure the police would catch the villain. It had been very kind of Mr Green to take her to meet Alf Rose while Toby's helpers cleaned up for her. She was a little overcome by the generosity of her friends.

She discussed the day with Persephone as she fed and brushed her.

"You're getting a boyfriend next Summer, old girl. Horace is to be put out to grass in your field. Mr Rose will have a nice, new, nippy little electric milk float, he tells me, and he wants Horace to join you here in the lap of luxury. Won't that be fun? He'll pay me a little too, of course. It would be far too expensive stabling him at the Mint if he's no longer working. So there you are! A new playmate. I wonder what Alf's doing with the old milk cart. Or does it belong to the dairy, do you suppose? I should think an electric float would be much more trouble than a horse, especially in this weather. This mill will be like a palace after we rebuild that wheel, you know. Maybe I can open it to the public and you and Horace can give rides round the paddock."

Persephone blinked sleepily as her felt bonnet slipped down, as it always did, over one eye. There was always something to look forward to.

On the train

Toby and Hugo spoke to Kevin Smith and Mr Coker again a couple of days after the terrible snowstorm. The pair were still slightly rattled after all the drama, although neither divulged details to their nearest and dearest. Kevin had told Iris he had helped apprehend a wanted fugitive from Ledgely Prison – which was as near the truth as he would go. Mr Coker had said equally little to Mrs Coker. In fact he remained so quiet all the following week his wife assumed he was going down with a cold.

"So is there likely to be any more of these defectors, Mr Tremayne?" asked Kevin.

"No," Toby said firmly There was no point in saying that there might be. "All finished and closed down, Mr Smith."

"Mr Coker," interjected Sir Hugo. "I want to thank you for keeping this away from the general public. No point upsetting folks, is there?"

Coker shook his head. "No sir, there ent. Business as usual. Smith and me, we know how to keep mum when it's a matter of national security. Don't we Kevin?"

"Yes sir. No worries on that score." He wasn't going to let the side down.

"Jolly good show," said Toby. "Well then, we'll be toddling off. Thank you both again. You really have been most helpful."

The two gentlemen left to board the train for Ledgely. They relaxed in the first class carriage of a three-car train, which was surprisingly busy today.

The new diesel engine chuntered as it slid slowly along beside the thawing river and ground into Weston Halt. Several more people boarded the other two carriages, bound for the London sales Toby judged from the look of their large handbags. Hugo stretched his legs and lit a cigar. They had their compartment to themselves.

"Green did a good job."

"He certainly did," agreed Toby. He unbuttoned his coat as the place was warming up nicely. "Considering."

"The boy's going to pull through, the doctor told me. Damnedest thing, him being up that tree."

"He's a funny kid. Still, as you say, damnedest thing. I suppose the head's still not speaking to you?"

"No. I don't altogether blame her attitude, mind you. I swore the schoolchildren would not come to harm when she first discovered what we were up to, so one almost getting killed by a bloody sniper isn't putting her in the best of moods. I'm rather glad to be off, truth me told." Hugo frowned. "What do you think we should do about the Nesbit fellow?"

Toby pulled a thoughtful face. "Some kind of nice little reward? I hear he's looking for a new job."

"Gamekeeper isn't he?"

"Yes. Not much of that in Banford though these days. The shooting is all further north on Lord Kenner's estate I hear."

Hugo nodded. He could put the word out at his club, he said. Maybe something else would crop up that they could help Ben with. Hugo was going there today, and to this law office, and to the estate agent about the Church Road properties.

"The Nesbits are currently in a tied cottage. They have to move out in March," Toby continued.

"Do they indeed?" said Sir Hugo. "Now there's a thought. Maybe something could be managed by then."

Toby agreed. "That would be wonderful. Ben needs some employment too, though."

"Does he care what he does?"

"Don't know. Don't think so."

"You might keep him on the books and maybe find a few small areas he could help with, couldn't you? Part-time? He's a sound enough chap, I think. Didn't panic when Reg co-opted him. You wouldn't have to tell him much."

"I think I could. He's a useful sort, as you say. I could train him up. Yes, I think I could certainly find a use for him."

"Alright then, I'll mention it today and let you know as soon as I can, though you know how slow such clearances can be."

"You back off to Europe tomorrow?" Toby asked.

Hugo smiled. "Yes." That was quite enough discussion of his movements.

The two opened their newspapers and sat in convivial silence, one doing the Guardian crossword, one the Times.

Grey hairs

Mrs Clark was surprised her hair was not greyer than it actually was, after all the recent happenings. She gazed at herself in the staffroom mirror and tucked in a wayward strand.

Reg wandered in with a bucket.

"Sorry. Thought this was empty," he muttered. He had been trying to avoid her since the fateful weekend.

"No, no, it's alright. Come on in. Perhaps we can have a little chat while its quiet, Reg."

Reg's heart sank. He knew how mad she was with Sir Hugo. Him and Mr Tremayne too, by extension. He clanked the bucket down and stood waiting.

"I just wanted to say… Well, I wanted to thank you."

"What for exactly?"

"Well saving Jimmy, of course.

"Oh." That, he thought. Alright, he could accept that. "It were Stringer really."

Mrs Clark became animated. "No, not just the dog, though of course you couldn't have done it without him. No, for performing that first aid and carrying Jimmy all through that awful weather to the ambulance. Heaven knows how he would have reached the hospital without you."

Reg shifted his weight. "Kid's alright now. Home and safe."

"Yes, and a good deal happier in his mind, so I believe. May's had an especially long talk with him. Mrs Harris too. And I'm going to."

"I thought he were actin' a bit upset," said Reg. "He 'ad a little cry with me the other day. Missing his mum or summat."

"Yes," answered Skipper, perching on the arm of one of the chairs. "But it's more than that. He's apparently sad that Janey missed out on the type of life that he's having now. He didn't really know her very well, I think. Never had the chance, poor lamb. Do you know anything about her upbringing?"

"Nope. Never come across the gal much, except as a cleaner and barmaid. She weren't too bright, I don't think. Never said much to 'er, nor she to me. Poor old Jimbo."

"Yes. It's all very sad. But thanks to your efforts her lad will be fine."

Reg was still angry and disgusted at what had happened to the boy, but he did not know whether the headmistress was aware of the full picture.

She studied his face. "I do know he was probably shot, Reg. Hugo told me."

He breathed out. "Yerse, well. And I'm mortal sorry for that, Miss. Mortal sorry. I done my best, me and Ben, to find the swine what done it and take 'im out. He's beyond doin' anyone any harm now, though, so you can rest easy."

Skipper had been informed the shooter had met with an accident later that night, and was now dead. She half-believed in the accident but was also worried in case Reg and Ben had actually killed him.

"But there's only we four who know Jimmy was accidentally shot, isn't there? You, me, Sir Hugo, and Mr Tremayne?"

"Yes. Ben don't know. May Fisher don't know, even."

"Right. And Jimmy himself does not know. He thinks a tree took a chunk out of him, right? That's what I thought." Skip wanted to be clear. "Ben's now recruited into the service is he?"

"Yes."

"What else ought I to know about?"

Reg didn't have clearance to tell her about the observer corps or Mrs Bick, or the way in which the assassin had met his end, or where their troublesome defector was now, so he shook his head. "Nothin' Miss. Nothing I know of."

"Alright. If you're sure. Well, I'll let you get on. I just hope all this horror is finally over now, Reg. I cannot and will not have my children put in harm's way, whether it's accidental or not. Sir Hugo and his confounded secret operations are not going to hide behind our school any longer. I simply won't have it."

She stalked past him and went back to her office.

Reg picked up his bucket and eased himself down onto the floor to get at the trap under the sink.

He was heartily glad to be unclogging pipes once again. Angry headmistresses were a whole lot easier to handle than rescuing half-frozen children and pursuing dangerous gunmen across the frozen wastes in a blizzard only to watch them die.

* * *

13.

Jimmy starts to recover

Life had settled down again by the last week of February. Jimmy rested at home with Auntie May while Miss White, a large, elderly lady from the Dane Street side of town, came and taught Form 2. Miss Fisher was personally glad of the break as she found that Jimmy's recent adventure had been almost too much for her. So she slept while Jimmy slept, pottered round the house performing domestic chores, and was surprised at how the simple everyday tasks soon helped her regain her familiar equilibrium.

Jimmy himself was both contrite at all the bother he had caused, and relieved he had not been told off too badly. He was no delicate flower, but this brush with death had been very frightening. It was not only himself he felt upset about, though. He never – never, ever – wanted to see that look in his angel's eye again when she had found him bleeding in the snow. He could not bear Auntie May to ever have to shed another tear because of his silly behaviour. Therefore, even though he experienced a good deal of pain, Jimmy never complained about the exercises he had to do, or additional medicine he had to swallow. He knuckled down to the homework Mr Tuttle sent round every day and did his best to make amends.

Everybody dropped by to see him and encourage his speedy return to school. Dean brought him a library book, Joey some photos of his allotment patch, even though there was not much to see. He told him the snowdrops were coming out, and Jim sighed wishing he could be there to see them. Mr Tuttle brought the baby and stayed for a long cup of tea with May in the kitchen while Gwennie lay in Jimmy's arms watching television. Fiona and Tim brought him some packets of seeds and a small bag of compost. Grandma Dora was there every day, listening to him read his book and playing garden layouts with his favourite toy. Mr Chivers and Mr Paton did the household shopping and Auntie Jean brought Sweep to see him every evening. Even Mr Tremayne and Mrs Clark came by, asking how he was. It was a little overwhelming, as Auntie May well knew.

"Is that tight enough?" she asked one evening as she was helping him tie a plastic bag over his plaster cast before getting into the bath.

"Yes, but now the stool's fallen over," he said. She propped the thing back up so he could rest his foot on it while sitting in the water. It was all rather awkward and took ages. He was not a particularly modest child, for which May was glad, as otherwise this activity would have been virtually impossible. It would have been a 'lick and a promise', as her mother had called it, and not a proper wash.

"What are you making for Mr Green?" she asked, shampooing his hair and rubbing hard.

"A card. You said do a card with thank you in it. So I am." Jimmy was glad when the shampoo was over and the shower attachment that looked like a telephone handset squirted into life and swooshed all the bubbles off his head. That bit was fun. "I'm putting a snowdrop on the front."

May laughed. "Well that's appropriate!" she said. "You were a snowdrop yourself. Mr Green will see that joke. What about Mrs Green?"

"I'm making her twelve labels for next year's jam. And please would you buy me some glue out of my pocket money to go with them? A little bottle."

May nodded. "I will. That's a very good idea. She will like that. She was very kind to you."

Jimmy shoved one of his boats under the legs of the stool, imagining it was coming in to harbour. He wished they could stop talking about his accident. The subject came up every day and, though he tried not to sound ungrateful, it was embarrassing.

Auntie May lifted him out and dried him with a large white towel.

"There. Fresh as a daisy!"

He kissed her cheek. "You always say that."

"Well I might not get my kiss if I don't," she answered.

Tucked up in bed, he eased himself over onto the side that didn't hurt and drowsily studied his room.

It was as small as the one in Wag Lane had been, only nicer. He had a blue cupboard called a tall-boy, and a box called an ottoman for his toys. There was a chair on which his clothes lay ready for the morning. He had a pillow and a soft eiderdown all to himself. The carpet was red, the curtains had printed images of trees and flowers. Jimmy struggled out of bed and hobbled across to the window to pull back the curtains. That was the only thing, the curtains. He hated not seeing out at night time. He hated not seeing the sky full of stars and the moon when it peeped in. He loved the rain that fell against the glass because then knew he was safe at home. Auntie May wouldn't understand.

But she did. She understood perfectly about how anxieties became programmed into the human mind at an early age. So she always closed the curtains when Jimmy went to bed, and knew that before she herself turned in, he would get up and pull them wide open again. It was all about taking control.

Jim Fisher nodded and climbed back into his warm bed. Tomorrow would be one day nearer Spring. One day nearer going back to school. One more day he could spend with his angel.

Bill is encouraged

Jean and Toby were going over the Summer sporting fixtures in the staffroom, even though they were still a long way off. It was Jean's free period – a short weekly break each member of staff enjoyed that Chloe and Skip had rather grandiosely introduced when they first joined Mayflower. She was not best pleased at having her hour hijacked by Toby.

"So, invite Sorburn for a tennis match? Will they be able to rustle up two competent players? They're only a tiny little village school. They don't even have a proper court. They just knock about on the field with a couple of rackets."

"Well, we can but ask. They might surprise us with a Wimbledon champ. And how about a staff match?" Toby had a look in his eye Jean had previously only seen in the headmistress's.

"Oh come on! Bella might be up to it, but who else?"

"Mike? You? You're sporty."

"Have you seen my waistline lately? No Sir, not in a month of Sundays."

"What about extending it to the PTA?" Toby wasn't about to give up.

"Well, why not just have a PTA versus Dane Street's PTA then," squawked Jean.

Toby grinned. "Alright. I'll give them a call."

"You do that. Now if you *don't* mind, I have some marking to finish and there's only twenty minutes of my free period left. Go on, off you trot. Go and annoy somebody else."

Toby bumped into the vicar coming down the stairs. He had been taking Form 6 for what he called his weekly philosophy class. Others called it Divinity. Toby had previously thought of it as RI until he had been put right by Guy Denny who told him Bill covered a far wider range of human thinking than mere Christianity. After that Toby revised his opinion of Rev Bill.

"Morning!" he cried. "Glad I've bumped into you, old man. I wanted to ask how your land yacht is coming along?"

Rev Bill was delighted someone had remembered his little project. "Oh, quite well, thank you for asking. Rather nicely, actually. I'm laying out some of the actual timbers in the garage at the moment. Keeping it out of June's way, you know. I can't say she's that impressed with it yet, but it's early days. I spent most of Christmas drawing various designs. And I've spent a while in the public library too. Not that there's much there, you understand. I think it will be mostly up to me and what I remember of aerodynamics from the RAF to get this right."

"Did you know the Americans down at the airbase in Fenchester built one during the war? While they were waiting to be parachuted behind enemy lines? I suppose it helped pass the time."

"Yes, I'd heard about that. I saw a photo on one of the books I borrowed. Super little thing. Well, not so little. I think they used some spare aeroplane wheels to give it a bit of extra weight."

Toby laughed. "What happened to it?"

"Capsized and broke into a thousand pieces, I believe. I expect our east winds were a little too much for it."

Toby held his coat for him by the front door. The silver cabinet was there with every cup and award polished to perfection by Pru Davidson and labelled by Mrs Clark.

"Well I hope you get it flying along the turf safely and don't end up upside-down in the wilderness," chuckled Toby. "Let me know when it is ready to sail. We could try it out on our sports field."

Bill looked really pleased about this. "Alright," he said. "I will. You're on. Never mind June and her 'where am I going to put the spare jumble sale boxes now the garage is out of bounds?'. I'll go and buy myself a new screwdriver and get busy."

Case conference

"Well, *I* think she's had another little stroke," sighed Dr Legg, who was discussing Lady Longmont with her colleague.

"Probably had several," Dr Granger agreed. He had seen the old lady last week and had not liked the look of her. She was definitely going downhill. "Is she being nursed properly, do you think? Taking her medicine regularly? Who looks after her general welfare?"

"Mr Tremayne is her lodger, so he's in charge. I believe he was a friend of hers years ago, from what I can understand. And Mrs Bicknell goes in to prepare a meal and clean around the place. Not every day, but you know."

"Should we get Meals-on-Wheels to call do you think? Can she eat?"

"Oh yes, a bit. Not sure about Meals-on-Wheels though. She's mostly preferrin' soup or porridge or mashed potato an' gravy from what Bick says."

"Alright then. Shall I ask Hilary to drop by? Take a look at her?" Granger opened his diary.

"Good idea. That Miss Muggeridge has also been in. She's a kind soul, though a bit forbiddin'. Cycles about the place on that old bike about two miles an hour. Looks like she's somethin' out the nineteen-thirties. She says she's sat with the old lady a time or two."

"And there's one of the Mayflower kids visits too, I believe."

"Yes, Kay Fordam her name is. I met her. Lives in Weston. Grumpy little party, but the old lady seems not to mind her. I can't understand what the child gets out of it."

"Probably doing it because her dad asked her."

"Maybe," said Dr Legg.

Granger looked at his watch and picked up his bag, "I must be off. I've a case of pneumonia in Trafalgar Road, a dementia in Portland Street, and little Jimmy Birch's leg to see to. I think, if there's time, I will drop by Dora York's on the way back. Will you cover Lady Longmont?"

"I will. Go on, off you go. And watch out for the floods down by Ironwell mill. They're thinkin' of plantin' those boggy places up with rice next year. Like paddy fields they are."

"Oh right," smiled the doctor. "That will please Lady Longmont. Bick says she likes a nice rice pudding."

Comfortable words

Once again, after last year's budget constraints, Mayflower could afford the Animal Man's visit. He arrived with a car full of grey wooden carry-boxes containing a selection of live creatures with which to delight and educate the schoolchildren. Everyone was pleased he had been able to come.

"Hooray!" yelled Mungo as he flung himself through the classroom door and knocked over the nature table. It was the second time this had happened and Miss Delgado was not as forgiving this time as she had been before. Mungo worked the dustpan and brush so perfunctorily in his clean-up today that Kelly Pearce grabbed it off him in disgust and finished the job herself. Her desk was right next to the nature table and she was fed up with it being splattered with acorns and crumbling leaves and old conkers. Mungo needed a proper telling off in her opinion.

"D'you think he's brought snakes? Or a leech? Or a baby octopus this time?" Mungo was desperate to see an octopus and kept drawing multi-tentacled versions all over his rough book.

"More likely a guinea pig or a pair of budgerigars," commented his teacher as she dragged the nature table to the other side of the room. Kelly hung the dustpan back on its hook and helped rearrange the remaining display, smugly delighted that now the table had been moved she was unlikely to be inconvenienced again.

"The children wasn't allowed to say nothing last time," Steven informed Miss Delgado. "They just had to all sit and be silent. For *ages*." He was used to assemblies being short and musical rather than zoological. The longest ones were on Tuesdays when the Vicar came and there was a twenty minute hymn practice tagged onto the end. Tuesday mornings made Steven fidgety.

"There weren't no money for the Animal Man last year," Kelly enlightened her teacher. "But he come every year before that. Even when we was only at playgroup. Which was before we ever even *come* to this school. My sister said."

Miss Delgado clapped her hands and sat them down after this garbled explanation. The register was called and the children sent off two by two to the lavatory ahead of Visitor's Assembly. The last pair returned just as the bell rang. They all lined up ready for the descent to the hall.

"And remember – no clapping, no ooing and ahing. No *noise*, Mungo. Just sit still and watch. The animals are not tame pets, they are wild and will be scared. Do as you're asked and try to learn lots. I will take my notebook and a pencil so we can remember all the creatures we saw when we get back."

The exciting morning kept everyone thoroughly enthralled. Dr Giles stood on the stage and one by one opened a box and removed the creature it contained. He explained its life cycle and habits to the hushed audience before inviting questions.

He was a curious figure – almost as curious as the creatures he brought. He must have been about sixty although it was hard to tell. He was short and stout, spoke in a crisp Oxford accent and knew exactly the right amount of information to impart to his youthful audience. Today he showed them a mole, a parrot, a toad and – most glorious of all – a barn owl. Dr Giles selected four lucky children to come up on the stage and hold each animal for a short time before returning it to its box. Ronnie, from Miss Fisher's form cupped the mole carefully in his inky fingers. Although his teacher was still at home caring for Jimmy Birch, Miss White was proud of his gentle handling of the little creature.

"Make sure you wash your hands for *ten minutes* before lunch" she whispered loudly to the ecstatic Ronnie who resumed his place next to her after the mole had been returned to its box. "With soap, and properly."

Ronnie nodded, barely hearing. He was watching the next fascinating box being opened. It was a bird.

The parrot was a big hit, especially with Mungo who instead of sitting cross-legged, raised himself to his knees in an effort to catch the beady eye of the loquacious doctor.

"Sit down," hissed Miss Delgado. "Mungo!"

Mungo feigned not to hear. He wriggled and hoped he was noticeable. Dr Giles did spot the boy with the halo of mousy hair and the evident desperation to be chosen to hold the bird. The doctor took four questions from the audience, then beckoned Mungo up, warning him to be calm, slow and gentle. The boy pulled on the thick leather glove and the bird stepped carefully onto his fist. Bella thought Mungo was going to burst with happiness.

"You stink," said the parrot quite clearly, and squawked. The audience gave a quickly suppressed hoot of laughter. Mungo looked astonished, then ashamed and finally defiant. The parrot said it again and again, much to Dr Giles' irritation. He had warned them the bird might speak a word or two it had learned, although usually it remained silent during school visits.

"This bird's rude," Mungo told the doctor. Everyone wanted to laugh again, but did not.

"He has no concept of manners, my child," stated Dr Giles loftily. "He merely echoes what has been said to him."

Bella Delgado was not so sure. Mungo could indeed smell a little ripe some days. Maybe the bird was being mischievous, maybe it was simply telling the truth. She assumed parrots had a good sense of smell.

Mungo stroked the bird's chest feathers, eyeballing it suspiciously. It repeated its previous message, which sent another suppressed wave of mirth round the hall. Dr Giles took back the bird and motioned the boy away in annoyance. The parrot screeched as it was returned to its box and the door firmly re-latched.

Miss Delgado's sympathy was all for her humiliated lad. He sat down at the end of the class line and put his head down on his knees. Jason, a kindly classmate, scooted over to Mungo's side and put his arm round his shoulders.

"Sorl right, mate," she heard Jason whisper. "Somebody had to teach him how to say that. It was prollerby that old man. When we have to draw the stupid parrot after break, you can make it all the wrong colours. That'll learn it to be rude."

Mungo nodded and grinned at his friend. "Yeah," he whispered with a giggle. "It won't even know."

Miss Delgado sat mystified, distracted by the idea that what Rev Bill might call 'comfortable words' were often not what she would have chosen at all.

Twenty-one

Bella's twenty-first birthday also fell on the day of the Animal Man's visit. Ivy Green had baked a special cake and set it on the table in the staffroom after the children had gone home, for a little tea party. It was a beautiful blue and had 21 in white icing on top. When Bella came in, everyone clapped and wished her a happy birthday. She was overwhelmed and delighted.

"Oh, thank you!" she cried. "What a wonderful surprise. I didn't think anybody knew it was my birthday."

"Haha! That's all Peggy's doing. She plots everybody's lives, don't you Peg?" said Toby.

"I do, and don't you forget it," said Peggy. "I hand out your wage packets too."

"Come on, Bella. Cut this cake or we'll all starve to death," urged Ernest. He handed her the bread knife and they sang Happy Birthday. Bella handed round platefuls of fruit cake while Cathy poured tea for everyone.

There was a present to be unwrapped next to the cake on the table. The staff sat round and watched as Bella undid the ribbon and discovered a box containing a single string of pearls, and some lovely drop-earrings to match. She was thrilled, and held an earring up against her dark hair.

"Oh they're lovely! Thank you all so much. I love them."

"Everyone chipped in," smiled Skipper, pleased her choice was so well-received. She had spent a long time at the jewellers in town trying to select something special and had a feeling some timeless, elegant pearls might be the right answer.

Reg and Pru shuffled in. They had broken off their after-school cleaning to come and wish Bella well. The girl's heart was brimming over with gratitude that life had brought her to this school and to this staffroom.

"Your back wheel's lookin' like it's got a puncture," Reg told her.

That deflated her. "Oh no," she cried. "Not another one. That's three since Christmas. What on earth am I riding over, I wonder?"

Mike slipped some of the cake's fancy icing off his plate onto hers. "Maybe just the cold," he suggested. "You'll have to trade your bike in for a little mini, like Cathy."

"I haven't got rid of my bike," said Cathy indignantly. "It's in the shed until the weather improves. I shall ride it again, you see."

"Look at this lovely necklace, Reg," said Bella.

"Very nice I'm sure," he said, sipping tea. "Proper lady you'll look now. All la-di-da."

The next day, Bella wore her new finery to school. Her hair was up in its usual bun and the earrings looked beautiful hanging down against her polo-necked jumper. She felt gorgeous. Even the children commented.

"I like your necklace Miss."

"Are them new earrings, Miss?

"Miss, did you get them jewels for your birthday?"

Michelle Oswald had an idea during art that afternoon. "Miss, can we – like – all paint a portrait of you? With your jewels on?"

Bella laughed. "Really? Who wants to do that? Oh, everyone. Right – I see. Then that's what you can do. And – just before you all go mad getting out the paints – how about we ask every form to paint a portrait of *their* teacher? And if anyone wants, they could try the other members of staff, like Mrs Clark or Mr Tremayne too."

"Or Mrs Bailey or Dr Legg?"

"Or Mr Green or the *dentist* even?"

"Yes. Someone on Mayflower's staff. The grown ups."

"What about Stringer?"

"And Nicky?"

Bella could see the idea had caught on. "Yes, them too. But *only* when the classroom teachers have been painted properly. And they have to be *good* paintings that cover *all* the paper. Not just splodges and scribbles. Careful studies *with details*."

The children nodded sagely. Miss Delgado was big on taking your time and doing things thoroughly. She didn't mind if it took a little longer for you to learn to read or write or draw or finish your maths. It wasn't all a big rush with her.

Michelle sighed with happiness. "Shall I take a note round, Miss? Tell everybody to start painting?"

Her teacher grinned. "Yes, if you like. Vicky can go with you, and don't be too long. Jolly good idea, Michelle."

Reg changes horses

"I don't know yet," said Sir Hugo. "It's still being discussed."

"Well how long do they have to discuss it for?" asked Toby. He was irritated it was taking so long for Ben Nesbit to receive a formal thank you and some recognition from the powers in London. "I've sent in my report, Reg has done his, and we've produced the very dead body of a KGB assassin. What more do they want?"

Hugo raised an eyebrow. "Now don't get melodramatic. It's because we are up here, out in the exotic wilds of Fenshire rather than somewhere normal like the Pripet Marshes or the Gobi Desert. You know what they're like."

"Yes, well, I think Nesbit is a very decent sort. He'll be an excellent asset. I could use him."

"May I remind you that this operation of mine that we are winding down, Toby, has to be properly decommissioned. It all takes time. I grant Nesbit's proved himself sound but how exactly will you use him in the future? Tracking Lady Longmont to church and back every Sunday? Seeing Mrs York doesn't start lending aid and succour to every passing Russian circus?"

Toby puffed deeply at the rather good cigar he had been given. The two men were sitting in the Yeoman while Reg was at the bar ordering beer. There was no one else in the snug at present. Reg came back with three tankards of ale.

"Mrs Bicknell's over in the Public Bar nursing a Guinness. That Miss Muggeridge is with 'er," he informed them.

"Well don't let on we're in here," murmured Toby. "Leave them be."

Hugo nodded.

"What would you say to Ben Nesbit doing a little extra work for us, Reg?" asked Hugo.

Reg sucked the froth off his moustache and wiped the back of his hand over it. "Ben turned out alright. Didn't balk at trouble when it come out of the blue that night – nor at the weapons, nor nothin'. Not really. Took it well, considerin' how dangerous it turned out. He knows 'ow to track too, and keep his mouth shut. When we was at the mill, he never said a dickie-bird to the donkey-woman. He ent said anythin' to anyone since, neither. Just at present he could use some more work, not to mention a roof over his 'ead." He took another pull at his beer. "I'd say keep 'im on probation for a bit – stick to watching, reporting and such like. Like the kids and Mrs Bick done. See how 'e goes."

"Send him for a few weeks down to Portsmouth first?" Portsmouth was where agents were currently being given some basic training.

"Nah. It might spook him. Bed him in 'ere first and see how 'e does. I'll keep watch if you like."

"And you're alright switching over to the Home Guard then Reg?" Hugo meant working for MI5 rather than his own MI6.

Reg was glad this had come up. "Yes. Quite content, Sir. You see, Ivy and me – we like Banford. We'd like to retire round here one day, seeing as our Pat's just settled down and is getting married, and our Terry is doing so well as a gardening handyman. We got roots here now."

"I see." Hugo was slightly miffed that Reg was transferring ships so happily. "Right then. You'd better carry on."

"Right you are, Sir."

"Excellent," said Toby. "Glad to have you on board, Mr Bosun."

Hugo set his tankard down. It was not a type of drinking vessel he appreciated. "Very well, if you're both happy, I'll put a rocket up HQ and see if they can't expedite matters. They'll let you have all the paperwork, Toby."

"And you'll see what can be done for Nesbit's lodgings at the same time?" persisted Toby. He drained his beer to the last drop.

Hugo nodded. "I will. That's in hand. Now then, how about a fresh glass and a little chaser?"

* * *

14.

Allotments

St David

"It's a daffodil," stated Rebecca Rockwell.

"No it's a leek. Mrs Clark said so."

"Daffodil!"

"Leek!" shrieked Vicky Ryan.

"Hey what's going on, you two?" asked Mrs Raina, who was on playground duty. "There's no need for arguing."

"She said the sign for St David was a leek. That's an onion-thing. Who the heck has an onion-thing as a sign?"

"St Onion, that's who," chirped Katy Jackson, butting in.

"Manners, girls!" cried Mrs Raina sharply. The girls stood in rebellious silence. Mrs Raina was very gentle and kind but when she was cross you had to look out or there would be certain-sure trouble. Several children nearby were edging closer in the hope of overhearing a drama.

"You could ask Mr Tuttle," suggested John Mason, a placid child. "He's Welsh."

Mr Tuttle strolled over, mug of coffee in hand and a whistle round his neck.

"Did I hear someone mention St David?" he asked mildly. Mrs Raina left him to it.

"Please Sir, is it leeks or daffodils for St David?" persisted Rebecca, who liked things clear-cut.

"Well his story is a little lost in the mists of time, but the leek is generally reckoned to be his emblem. I dunno why. Maybe people thought as you do, that it was a bit lowly for such a famous bishop – even in the sixth century." Charlie thought Rebecca might have a point. Daffodils were prettier.

John butted in again. "And daffodils would be flowering about now. There's lots down the side of our road as you come to school."

"Right. See girls?" said Mr Tuttle. "They are both very recognisable emblems. St David most likely enjoyed both." He grinned at John gratefully, who nodded.

John wandered off, wondering whether he might try and grow some leeks in his school allotment plot this year. He already had daffodils.

Rebecca and Vicky also left Mr Tuttle to drink his coffee in peace. They headed away, deep in discussion with Katy Jackson about what frocks bishops might have worn in the sixth century.

Charlie stood by the cricket pavilion, sipping his coffee peacefully, wondering whether St David might have welcomed a little caffeine with his morning breaktime leek-flavoured biscuits.

Fizzing kettles

The clock at the back of the room was ticking – the only sound in the place. It was as if the entire school was listening to it.

Form 6 was doing its best to concentrate on completing the Eleven Plus examination, which would decide which secondary school each child would attend the following September. If they passed they would go to the Grammar School in Fenchester. If they failed, they went to Portland Secondary Modern. Mrs Clark knew which one she preferred for her boys and girls, though she said nothing.

Nicky the cat stretched and trotted out into the empty playground, glad of the peace. Now the weather had become warmer he made for the wilderness where the freshly sprouting undergrowth offered him two main advantages. It was cool, and the deep shadows rendered him almost undetectable to the mouse and bird populations. He hopped and skipped over fallen logs and soaring brambles to perch on a log seat that might once have been in a small clearing made by the PTA, but was now rapidly being overtaken by weeds. Most of the spaces so diligently cleared last year were now, like this one, completely swamped. Clouds of smoke-like pollen rose from the yew trees into the warm air, making the cat sneeze. Everywhere was stretching out and upwards into the Spring.

The children felt like stretching too, after sitting and concentrating for so long. The lengthy tests went on for two mornings with a make-up day on Wednesday. When the torment was eventually over, and the clock told them it was time, the top class burst out of their confinement and hurtled round the playground like demented chickens. Mrs Clark came outside and told them it was dry enough to allow them on the Donkey Field, which sent them whooping and hurtling off in that direction.

"They're like fizzing kettles!" laughed Skipper.

"Do kettles fizz? I suppose they might," answered Toby. "Anyway, I know what you mean."

"Have the decorators finished in the lodge yet?" she asked, as they sauntered down Apple Alley.

"Nope. Some issue with – what was it? – soak-aways. That means drains. Terry's on it."

"He's a really good bloke to have around isn't he? I wonder if he would like to job-share with his Olly Hobbs once Reg decides to retire," mused Mrs Clark.

"Job-share? What an odd concept. But actually quite a good one, now I think of it. Share the job out between them, you mean? Well, if we don't have to fork out for two lots of wages and national insurance and pensions I suppose it might work. One Green is merely a younger version of the other anyway."

Skipper laughed.

"It's Mothering Sunday at the weekend."

"I have no mother, alas."

"I know that, but you can share mine. Are you coming round for lunch on Sunday after church with Mike and Ernest? You know how Mum loves a full house."

"That would be lovely. Thank you. Yes please."

Skip kicked at a stone. "Is Hugo still around?"

"No. Gawn awf. Pastures new and all that. He told you he was leaving."

"Yes – I suppose. Will he ever come back, do you think?"

Toby felt like shaking her he was so exasperated. For a teacher she was a jolly slow learner. Did she still not understand what sort of man Hugo was?

"Not sure. Look, there's the kid Latimer fighting again! I swear that boy's going to be the death of me this year. Hey, Latimer! Cease and desist child, or you'll be indoors and in my room for the rest of the day."

Captain Noah

The school choir looked as smart as could be. Thirty children, the maximum allowed, marched two by two over Stokes' Steps and up into town like a small green army.

"Now whatever you do, visit the lavatory before we start," said Miss Delgado, nervously. "Got that? Yes, I'm looking at you Sylvia. You can't put your hand up half-way through Noah's flood."

The modern biblical piece they were singing was Captain Noah and his Floating Zoo, and it constituted the entire second half of the morning's singing. The first was taken up with a variety of songs chosen by the individual schools taking part. Each of the four schools had chosen two favourites to perform, then they would all come together to perform Noah. Everyone had loved rehearsing the piece and sang with gusto. It was a good deal more fun than the traditional airs they were usually given.

"Lady Longmont won't be there. It's such a shame. She used to be quite a champion of this little shindig," commented Charlie.

Mrs Clark nodded. The headmistress had come along to help organise the children this morning, and to enjoy her school's performance. "I know. She's gone downhill a lot recently. I honestly ought to go and see her more than I do, but…" Skipper tailed off, realising guiltily that she had not been anywhere near the invalid since January. She changed the subject. "I'm rather glad this singing thing only happens every other year. Last time it was awfully competitive. I must say I approve the committee's decision to hold it more as a show than a competition. I don't like pitting one school against the other."

"What about football? What about netball?" asked Charlie.

"Oh well, they're OK. Sports you know."

"Eleven plus?" Charlie persisted, knowing she hated the exams.

"You know what I mean. It's creating artificial animosities which can drive children to resent each other later. It's the foundations of the class system in this country."

Charlie ignored that, but was slightly intrigued. "Is that the reason you went to work abroad?"

"Partly. Partly, I suppose. It was complicated." It had not been complicated at all. A very simple decision.

The Wool Hall looked, for once, as if it were wide awake and ready to host a horde of noisy schoolchildren. Usually it was a sleepy, dowdy old place frequented only by elderly visitors listening to speakers holding forth on the Wars of the Roses or gardening. Its main advantage was that the seating in its auditorium was comfortably raked, and the gangways conveniently wide. When Mayflower arrived and shuffled its way into their reserved seats in the stalls, a little orchestra had already assembled and was tuning up.

"We never had an orchestra before, Mr Tuttle," whispered Jago Lawrence in awe. "I thought you were playing for us?"

"I am. I told you there would be a few more musicians, remember?" Charlie shrugged his coat off and hurried down to take his place at the grand piano. Mrs Clark and Miss Delgado could deal with the kids from now on.

Dane Street Primary kicked off with David of the White Rock, followed by The Vicar of Bray. Sorburn C of E sang two jolly songs from the BBC school's music series. The local prep school sang one song in French and one in Latin. Then Mayflower shuffled into place and gave the audience their renditions of Widdecombe Fair, and (Charlie's personal favourite) Men of Harlech. It was a rousing finish to the first half.

"Girls! Follow me if you want the toilet. Boys, go with Mr Tuttle. Mrs Clark is staying here with those who don't need to pay a visit," called Miss Delgado. Skipper was impressed. The young teacher was right at home in this chaos and had everything nicely in hand. She must remember to compliment her.

After the break every choir was packed onto the stage to belt out Captain Noah. The drums rolled, the cymbals crashed and the saga began. The boy who was singing the part of God was one of Dane Street's most experienced choristers.

"I wish our Red Martinez could have sung this for Mayflower's glory," sighed Skipper to Bella.

"Good at singing, was he?" she asked.

"Brilliant. He went down to London and sang on TV."

"Oh wow. That's impressive." Bella listened to the performance with its catchy tunes, entranced. "You know, we could put this on ourselves, with the little ones acting it out in front of the choir. I'm sure someone could play the drums and bash a cymbal. They could have cardboard animal heads on old rulers or stuck on sticks. I could make a flat sort of ark that the children could sail away in."

"What about the rain?"

"Dunno. Ribbons? How about old tape from a tape-recorder fluttering out of cardboard clouds?"

"Sh! Please!" admonished a woman from behind.

"Sorry," muttered Skipper, with a wink at Bella. They subsided into silence to enjoy the music, while both their imaginations raced with dramatic possibilities.

After the rainbow had appeared and the final applause had died down, the mayor rose and thanked everybody, Mayflower joined in the last madness – elbowing their way out again. It was a long, loud and irksome shuffle back to the outside world and to gather everyone safely on the pavement in Market Street. Mrs Clark resorted to blowing her whistle rather sharply. Several passers-by smiled in amusement.

"Now into your twos, please. *Twos*, Stanley. Well who was your partner? Has anyone seen Mr Tuttle at all?"

"He's coming down the steps now, Mrs Clark," called Bella. "Over here, Mr Tuttle!"

"Alright everyone. Are we all here? Yes, I've counted them twice, Mr Tuttle." Mrs Clark turned, feeling more than a little sympathy with Noah and his wayward passengers. She raised her arm. "Right then, keep your wits about you. Watch the traffic, please, and stay together. Now then, off we go – two-by-two-by-two-by-two-by-two!"

Kay gives a present

It wasn't much, but Kay had tried to create a page of old photos from the ones Lady Longmont had handed to her. She had carefully cut out one side of a packet of cornflakes and pasted all the photos that were in a decent condition onto it, transcribing the words on the back to little labels underneath. She was rather pleased with the result, and took it round to see the old lady the afternoon of her birthday.

Miss Muggeridge let her in, quietly glad to see the child. The cranky old lady she watched over was a real trial these days, and if it hadn't have been for the little tambour of embroidery Miss Muggeridge usually brought with her, she would have been very bored indeed. The old lady spent each day lying on the sofa, saying little and drifting in and out of sleep.

"Come in, duckie. She's in the sitting room on the sofa. I'll be in the kitchen listening to the radio. Would you like a cup of tea?" Miss Muggeridge asked. "Oh, have you brought something you've made? Well, isn't that nice of you."

"Oh, no tea thank you," replied Kay, startled at such consideration. "Thanks, I'm fine."

She pushed open the door and went in.

The invalid lay with her eyes half-open against some cushions. She did not look very comfortable. The room was chilly.

"Oh, it's you," Gibb croaked.

"Happy birthday" Kay wished her, thinking there wouldn't be any more birthdays for this old person.

"What is this?" Lady Longmont did her best to pull herself up a little against the cushions. "What's all that rubbish?"

Miffed, Kay stood her display on the coffee table against a stack of books. "Well, if you think it's rubbish... " she said, turning on the light.

Lady Longmont peered at the photos. To her each one seemed to be at the end of a long dark tunnel. She squinted right and left, feeling some remark was expected.

"Who are these people?" she asked.

"You. And your parents. And your husband. And maybe some friends. I thought you'd like it," said Kay.

"Hmph," commented Gibb. She tried again to focus and remember while Kay waited. "That looks like my brother Erskine, the scrubby little quagger." She tapped a photo with a long-nailed finger. "That one. He's the one. Never very bright. He gave away ... " She stopped, aware she was thinking out loud.

"What? Gave away what?"

"The crown jewels of old England," muttered Lady Longmont with a smirk. "You won't catch him now. I closed his curtains for good, so I did. You won't catch me either."

She lay back, exhausted.

Kay was disappointed her friend was not more thrilled by her gift. It had taken quite a while to make. "Shall I put it in your bedroom for you?"

"No. Don't want it. Put it in the dustbin. Don't want to see those people."

Kay folded her arms and scowled. "Well that's not a very nice thing to say to someone who brought you a present."

"Isn't it?" Gibb was drifting again. She closed her dry eyes and let her heart thump in her chest – lup-dup it went. Lup-dup.

Kay picked up her gift and shoved it back in its plastic bag. She would take it to school for their Victorian history table. Maybe Mrs Hewitt or Mr Tremayne would appreciate it.

Bill offers some counselling

"I don't want all that, do I?"

Cake very often featured in the staffroom at a Mayflower morning breaktime. Today it was Guy's birthday and Cathy had just handed him the most enormous slice of chocolate sponge.

"I think you do," she said with a smile.

"Oh well, if it's compulsory." He grinned back, and took it happily. "Any more news about Ben's job search?"

Cathy sighed. "No, I don't think anything's come up. My husband can't take him on, I'm sorry to say. I believe he's going to work with Terry Green if he can't find anything permanent."

"Oh dear. And Lady Day's only a week away. Have they somewhere to move to?"

"Yes, I believe there's a little two-up two-down near the Market Square that's empty and affordable. I do wish they'd had more luck in all this." Cathy and everyone else had tried so hard to help the Nesbits find a new home, and Ben a new job, but everything had fallen through.

"How's Beth? Oh, and how's Debbie doing now?"

Guy licked the icing off his fingers. "Beth's fine thanks and very happy at the Fenchester clinic. Deb is still pretty low, although the doctor says she's over the worst of it. Glandular fever is a horrible thing."

"It certainly is. Well give them my love, and I hope Debbie is feeling perkier soon, and can get back to uni. Gosh, isn't this cake delish? I think it came from Mrs Lara's shop."

"Oh well, that accounts for it. Her stuff is always super-good. I don't know how she does it."

Rev Bill breezed in. "Ooh, I say, good-oh! Someone's birthday?"

"Guy's," said Bella. She was stacking some squares of Binca on which her class had been practising their sewing skills. Some were acceptable, others less so. Mungo's was by far the grubbiest. She took it over to the ironing board where she was trying to sponge and flatten them out ready for mounting on card.

Rev Bill accepted some cake and sat down beside May on the old sofa.

"How is Jimmy now?" he asked quietly.

"He's coming along fine, thank you. The plaster comes off in the Easter holidays. He's scooting around on those crutches pretty well and everybody is very kind in school." She nodded at Charlie Tuttle. "Charlie has been wonderful about bringing him up to speed on some of his schoolwork."

"Only needed a little extra encouragement, did he?"

"A bit more than that," admitted May. "But he is trying very hard. I help of course, but I want home to be home, not more school."

"Quite right too," said Bill. "Has Mrs Harris found him anyone to talk to? I mean, *really* talk to – about his mother and so on. And what happened to her."

"Yes, but he's not at all keen on telling strangers what is hurting him." May glanced hopefully at Bill, who took the hint.

"Oh? Yes, sure, I could have a word if you like. If you think he'd let me. He knows me well enough, so perhaps he'd be able to spit out if there's something still worrying him. He talks to you?"

"Yes he does. But I'm the one who's there everyday, and Jimmy is very good at covering things up, saying what gets him through the moment and not what is really at the heart of the matter."

Bill nodded. He had met a few people like that in his life, especially children. "They can sidestep, or lead you off-track quite cleverly. Often they don't even have words to describe their emotions, do they? I suppose if you're brought up with abuse or negativity or melodrama it would be normal to you, right? It's understandable. Look, I'll make sure I have a quiet chat with the lad before that plaster comes off, shall I? Pastoral care and all that?"

"Would you, Mr Williams? I'd be so grateful. Mrs Harris will be too. I think opening up to a man, not someone in school or someone close to his usual domestic world might be a real help. Thank you very much indeed."

"You bet. Now, then, may I cut you a slice of that amazing cake? If I don't act fast it will disappear like dew in the morn."

Something blue

"Dad. Dad!" cried Pat.

"Gawd, what now?"

"Where's my something blue?"

"You what?"

"Something blue! Dad, I can't get married 'less I have something blue. I've got me borrowed, me new, and me old, but I ent got nothing blue. *Dad!*"

Reg did his best to focus. He had been at Phil's little bedsit pouring a stiffener into them both, which had rather blurred the edges of the wedding morning's panic-stations.

"You look lovely," he said, admiringly. "My little gal."

"Dad! I need something *blue*. I was going to have that ribbon Viv gave me, but I can't find it anywhere. What you got that's blue? Lor, how many have you had? I can't find anything suitable in this drawer and the car's just turned up."

Reg was never one to fail a damsel in distress. He was good at emergencies – Sir Hugo had told him so. He scratched his head.

"Got a duster. That's blue with little chequered squares. That do?" He pulled one out of the pocket of his caretaker's twill coat that was hanging on the back of the kitchen door. "It's clean."

"Oh my good godfathers! Alright, give it here. No turn round I'm going to stuff it up the leg of me… there that's done. Does it look lumpy?"

"Lumpy? No, I told yer. You look lovely." Reg beamed at his daughter.

"Stand still while I do yer tie better. What on earth have you done with your hair? There, that's it. Now, are you ready?" She patted and tweaked him until she was happy with his appearance.

Reg was growing maudlin. "I'm ready. Don't want to let you go, my little lambkin, but if you're sure?"

"I'm sure, Dad. Phil's a good bloke."

"He's a Price, Most of them Prices are in prison." It was true.

"Yes they are, but Phil ent like them. You know that. Now come on, it's time to go. You gotta give me away and I need you ship-shape and Bristol-fashion, like Mum said."

"I know, I know. Come on then, my darling little girl. Hang on to yer old dad's arm one last time. Yes I've got me ruddy keys. You're going to nag poor Phil to death. There now, let me open the car door and tuck you inside. All aboard the Skylark. Up anchor, and take us to the church, my man."

Wildlife watch

"Eugh! Look at that," cried Mick McDonald. "Is that them?"

"Yes," answered Nurse Presley with a great sense of satisfaction. "Nits."

"Jonah's got nits! Jonah's got nits!" screeched Olive Thorn dramatically.

"That'll be quite enough of that!" cried the nurse firmly. "You're next to be checked, Olive, so stand still. Jonah, you're to go home. Collect a bottle of special shampoo from Mrs Bailey when your mother comes for you. Makes sure she follows the instructions in the wee pamphlet. You may return to school in two days. Off you go down to the office."

Poor Jonah left the classroom, collected his satchel and blazer from his peg, and clomped down the Iron Duke staircase to the office. His mother wouldn't come home from work just for this, he thought. He was doomed to sit in isolation in the medical room all day.

"Did I get them from the animals at Mr Quincy's?" he asked Cathy Duke mournfully.

"No, love. Nits like clean heads. Maybe they found you on the bus or somewhere. Don't worry, you'll soon be back to school."

Not soon enough in Jonah's view. He liked school and didn't want to miss any of this year. It was his last at Mayflower and already they were half-way through March. Secondary school loomed and he definitely did not welcome that prospect. He knew he was never likely to pass for the grammar school – which was fine. Portland would suit him better. It had a rural science department and a model farm with actual sheep and real pigs. His weekend job with Mr Quincy at the veterinary clinic brought him in contact with quite a few farm creatures. Pigs were Jonah's favourite. That was something to look forward to, he supposed.

Mrs Duke studied the lanky lad. She knew his mother would be loth to stop what she was doing this morning to come and get him. She would take her own sweet time. Neither could Cathy be sure she would follow the stated procedure Jonah's hair required, so she explained the shampoo's dousing requirements to the boy himself. He was far more sensible.

"How about you help me with this bird table outside the window while you wait?" she asked. "I could do with some expert advice. I can leave the dinner money for a bit."

Jonah perked up. He knew the office ladies fed the birds on a little table that Mr Green had hung in the bushes by their back door. The medical office window looked out that way, and Mrs Duke could watch them feeding from her desk through the glass of the outside door. It was an awkward spot but she had made the best of it, hanging coconut halves and peanuts on strings. Jonah was only too pleased to be asked to help.

"What needs doing?"

"Well, I think a squirrel must have been practising its circus skills on the table yesterday as the string is broken and all the bits have fallen into the water dish. Could you help me clean it up?"

Jonah soon had the little bird table suspended from its branch again. He and Mrs Duke swept up the mess and put out some fresh seed from a bag she had brought.

"Apparently I should be giving them this stuff instead of the usual crusts and biscuit crumbs. The pet shop man said it was better for them," sighed Mrs Duke. "But I think it will just attract rats."

Jonah nodded. "It might," he said. "Rats will eat anything. Please may I wash my hands?"

Just then Mrs Webb turned up to collect him. As predicted, she was not best pleased at having to come into school from work for something as embarrassing as nits, but at least she had come. Cathy thought Mrs Webb would probably have preferred her lad to be sent home for having double pneumonia rather than lice, she was so embarrassed. Mrs Duke had little sympathy for her. Over the years Mrs Webb had been a very rough-and-ready mother, often sending Jonah to school without his dinner money, PE kit, swimming gear, homework, permission slips and all sorts. She remembered the year the Webb's cat had produced kittens and how upset the boy had been that his father was going to drown them. Mayflower School only had its beloved Nicky because Jonah had explained it all to Mrs Clark who had stepped in and saved them.

After the Webbs had gone, Mrs Duke returned to counting the dinner money and bagging it up ready to take to the bank. It was rather pleasant having the office to herself this morning. Peggy was having a dental check-up and the nurse had said she preferred to inspect heads in the individual classrooms rather than the medical room. Cathy finished what she was doing and peeped out at her refreshed bird table. Surely a few cheeky sparrows would have found the seeds by now.

As it was, the only creature to be seen was the school's black cat trotting stealthily up the path to the side gate, with a robin hanging from his mouth. He slipped nimbly between the bars and scuttled across the road to his own garden and disappeared.

"Nicky! You little…!" cried Cathy.

So much for encouraging the birds, she thought angrily. Wildlife was alright when it was decoratively charming, but not when it was red in tooth and claw.

Or clinging to one's hair, she admitted, with a quick little scratch behind her ear.

* * *

15.

The sardine can

The Nosh Club's Easter Cake Sale preparations weren't the same without Jimmy. Dora ran the little club after school on a Tuesday for an hour, and she missed his little face and ever-hungry enthusiasm. Although he was back at school he tired easily, and went home promptly at the end of each day.

"Granny," he said to her one day while he was visiting. "What was it like in the olden days?"

She was interested that he seemed to have discovered history. Up to now he had given every indication of only living in the present moment. Perhaps his mind was developing, she thought.

"When do you mean? Back when I was a little girl?"

"Yes – then." Jimmy guessed that his young mother and Grandma Dora must have lived at about the same time. Just after dinosaurs.

Dora sighed. She usually tried not to dwell on her early days, but this afternoon she did not want to disappoint, so she focused on the facts, not the feelings.

"Well, my mother died of a very bad cough called TB when I was two. I was living in London then with my father. I was sent to my grandmother's at Whitstable by the sea, where I slept in a little loft you could only get to by climbing up a ladder. Granny worked in the oyster business. When I finally came home, my father had married his cousin Minnie. It was quite a shock to meet my new mother."

Jimmy was astonished. "I have a new mother," he said, as if she had no idea. This shared experience drew him closer to Dora. "But I always knew mine."

"I'm afraid mine wasn't as nice as yours. I was glad to go to school every day."

"But you had a daddy?"

"Yes, but he was always working. He was a postman. We had to go to bed early because he had to get up at four o'clock in the morning."

"Did you have a nice bedroom like me?"

"No. I didn't even have a proper bed. I slept on the sofa in the front room. It was cold."

Jimmy thought about that. This was similar to his early days.

"Then my brother Clive was born. He was a lovely baby. I loved Clive. We used to put on plays in our front room when we were children. And concerts. He would dress up and I would recite the poetry I learned at school. I won a scholarship to the girls' grammar school when I was twelve, but I couldn't go because we didn't have enough money for the uniform."

"What did you do?"

"I went out to work when I was thirteen. I sorted newspapers. They make your hands very dirty and sore."

Jimmy laid his warm hand on hers and she smiled.

"Then I trained as a telephonist. A telephone operator, the person who connects calls between people," she explained. "It was a much better job than the newspapers. And I joined a tennis club at the weekends, which was great fun. I adored playing tennis. I met some very good friends there. Ethel and Jay, and my friend Lonny and her brother Charles. I married Charles."

"Do you go and see your friends still?"

"No. They are all dead and gone, darling. And my poor brother. Now I live here and I have you."

Jimmy stretched up and hugged her. He could tell she had not told him everything but he was glad he knew enough. "Weren't you happy when you were a little girl?" he whispered.

"No, not really. I missed my mum. Like you do, I know. But I never really knew her properly, you see. I was too young. All I can remember is her long hair spread on the pillow. She had beautiful fair hair. It has been much nicer for me to be a grown up."

The next afternoon Jim took himself over the road to St Andrew's church, where, as luck would have it, Rev Bill was tidying up after the flower ladies. Jimmy sat quietly in a pew, having a think. His brain felt a little like a sardine tin whose key had gone missing. He did not know how to open it.

"Hello, Jim. How's the leg?" asked the Vicar. They had enjoyed a few games of gin rummy together in recent weeks but the ideal moment had not arisen in which to have much of a heart to heart. Until now.

"Fine, thank you," said Jim, automatically. He liked that the Vicar called him Jim. It made him feel grown-up. "Are you putting those bits in your compost heap?"

"Yes, in a minute." Bill came and sat beside the lad, who looked tiny in the immense church. The ancient clock at the back ticked heavily as if it were drawing attention to itself.

"It's nice in here – a good place to have a little peace. Better than a scratchy old tree anyway." Bill nudged him, indicating this was a joke. "Thinking about anything special?"

"Well," began Jimmy. The sardine tin lid uncurled a bit. "I bin thinking. About my mum. And feeling sorry about her, how she lived. You know, before she knew me. Before I was born." He paused and moved his aching leg a little. "I can't find anybody who can tell me much what she did. Except she worked in the pub. And, see, I don't think she can have had a very nice life when she was a child. I think if she'd of had a better time with her own mum and dad it might of been different. Then it wouldn't of been like it was after I come along." There. He had explained that part.

"I see."

"Now she's dead and in your churchyard and I – I can't really remember her. Her face nor anything. I have no idea what she was really like. I never asked what she wanted to be one day, or what she liked. I dunno if she liked dancing, or painting, or cooking or nothing. It's as if she's in a story but I've lost the book. I do have a photo of her on my wall. Auntie May put it there to remind me, but it doesn't. Not really … "

"You don't recognise her?"

"I know it's her, cos I've been told. But it's like she's just some girl by a river. So I have a question."

"A question? For me?"

"Well…" The lid was rolled right back on Jimmy's sardine can now.. "Is it… do you think it would it be alright if I sometimes make up a pretend about her?"

Bill sat listening.

"Not a proper black evil lie, just a pretend. Like if I pretended the photo was taken on my birthday when we were together, having a picnic by the river or something. Not a lie that would hurt her."

"Did you never have a picnic with her?"

"I don't think so."

Bill stood up and walked about a bit, wondering what King Solomon would have answered. He returned to his pew.

"Jimmy, you know it is wrong to lie and how lies can hurt. But honestly? I don't think exercising your imagination occasionally about your mum's life is going to hurt anyone very much."

Jimmy's eyes were dark with concentration.

"It wouldn't hurt Auntie May?" He never, ever wanted to hurt his angel, especially by becoming a liar.

"I see your point. I think it depends how much of your 'pretend' you share with her. She would probably be hurt if you started crowing, like Peter Pan, about how wonderful things used to be, when she's here trying so hard to make you happy. Auntie May has changed her life completely to bring you safety and love and a happy home, so try not to overdo it. That's all I'm saying. I suggest you let yourself dream about your mum and the life she might have had, but also take a few photos of your Auntie May, and Grandma Dora and your school friends. Build some real, lasting memories *now*. Start a collection, or a scrapbook or a memory book. I'm sure Mrs Williams can find you a camera in her jumble sale box."

Jimmy's face cleared as if the wind had blown a cloud away. He nodded and the Vicar could see the child relax. They smiled at each other.

"Alright now?"

"Yes. I think so. Thank you. You have good ideas." Jimmy had plenty to focus on now his sardine can had finally been opened up.

"You are very welcome. Now then, if you feel up to it, come and show me where you think I ought to build our new compost heap. We're getting so many hedge trimmings and lawn mowings the old one is overflowing."

Good news at last

Ben and Betty Nesbit moved into a tiny terraced rental property while Ben split his workdays between Terry Green's handyman business and the gunsmith's shop in town. Coming from one of the manor's spacious lodges, the Nesbits had to put most of their furniture in storage. The new place was dreadfully cramped.

Toby walked round and hoped he was bringing welcome news, even if the timing of it had been unavoidably delayed.

"Knock-knock! May I come in?" he called through the open front door.

Ben emerged, wiping his hands on a tea towel.

"Oh hello, Mr Tremayne. Come on in. Nothing to do? Like a coffee? It's only instant, I'm afraid." He led the way down a step to the back room – the front being piled with boxes of belongings. "No, leave the door open. I find I'm a bit claustrophobic these days, being cooped up in this place after so much fresh air at home. Not used to life in a town yet."

"Hardly surprising, old man, hardly surprising. Employed though, I hear? That's good." Toby tried to sound encouraging.

Ben nodded, ruefully. "After a style. Guns are something I know about, so the gunsmith's is simple. But I admit I miss the outdoors. I know I mustn't look gift horses in the mouth, and working with Terry on this and that is alright. I'm lucky to have work – there's plenty that don't. Trouble is I'm a bit long in the tooth to retrain or take up an apprenticeship. I'm heading for retirement with unwanted, outdated skills."

He made the coffee and they took their mugs out into the backyard. It contained a rotary washing line, a dustbin, some old pram wheels, and a wooden orange-box.

"Young Jimmy's coming round later with a plant in a pot for me, he says. It will improve the yard, apparently. I'm going to make him some kind of contraption with those pram wheels and that old box that he can push round the place. Take a bit of the strain off his weaker leg, you know, but still allow him plenty of exercise."

Toby was impressed. "He does like to walk, doesn't he? But he seems stronger each day, even though the doctor seems to think he will always walk with a limp. It was that – that gash from the tree that took such a lump out of his thigh, they say. It was a very nasty incident. My guess is the snow and the cold stopped him bleeding to death. It really was a terrible night. Hugo and I were most awfully glad you were around to help out like you did. Reg couldn't have tracked that blaggard without you."

Toby offered Ben a cheroot and they leant against the coal bunker, puffing smoke into the breeze and sipping their instant coffee.

"So," began Toby, getting down to the point of his visit. "You'll no doubt be wondering why I'm here. Truth is, I've come to offer you two things. You can say no to both, of course, and proceed upon your merry way as before, but I hope you don't. I'm truly sorry it has taken so long to arrange. Hugo and I have tried to expedite matters, but this has never been entirely up to us. We had to gain various clearances. It's only now I'm at liberty to approach you."

Ben was intrigued. What on earth?

"First thing I've come to offer on behalf of HMG is – some proper employment, which may be a little more to your liking than the gunsmith's dingy old backroom, and fixing leaky bathrooms with young Terry Green."

"Employment? You want me to work for the government?"

Toby ploughed on. "Part-time. Part-time undercover surveillance work for MI5. For me, in fact. I would want you to monitor this whole area for anything un-toward. Act as a watchdog, if you like. You'd work alongside Reg Green and answer to me, not Hugo Chivers. The two of you ought to be able to watch well enough without us having to resort to little old ladies and small children as we have in the past. This would be a much more professional and methodical business. You would be expected to hike the fields and heaths and riverbanks regularly, from – say – the northern outskirts of Banford down as far as the race course, then take in Weston Forest out to the eastern levels and Greyfriars. It's a lot of territory and you may think it too much. And in all weathers, of course."

Ben's smoke was forgotten in this unexpected vision of a future which made his head spin.

Toby pressed on. "The other part of the employment, the non-secret public 'cover' for you, would be to take over the management of the new shopping complex at Abbey Farm. Maybe even set up and run one of the units as a little garden centre type of place one day. Nothing too onerous. You'd have the right staff helping you, of course. That would be your cover. What do you say?"

Ben was gaping like a codfish, his face quite red. "Are you serious?" he said.

"Well, I can see you'd want to think about it a bit. The two jobs might not be all that appealing at first, but… "

Ben stood up and walked rapidly round and round the little yard. "Oh my god, oh my god," he breathed. "Of course I'll take it. Both, naturally. If you think… If you think I can do all of – what you describe." He paused. "Just as long as I don't have to actually shoot anyone or go fishing dead foreign bodies out of millponds."

Toby shook his head. "No, no. No more of that. Hugo's safe house operation's closed down and there'll be no more defectors coming this way, as far as I know. But we do need to set a roving watch. That's something of a priority." He was pleased Ben was looking at the offer so eagerly. "Oh – there's another thing I forgot to mention."

Ben stopped and waited for the catch.

"The other thing is, this little cocktail comes with the offer of a house."

"A house?"

"Yes. If you want it. Hugo wondered whether you might like to move into Chloe Shaw's old place in Church Lane. Rent free of course, as Hugo owns it. His place is next door. You'd have to keep a weather eye on his property too, which is currently empty. He'd like someone around that he trusts. Chloe's place has three beds and quite a large garden of its own. But if you'd rather stay on here… "

Toby did not get to the end of that thought as Ben let out a whoop of delight.

"Oh my *god*," he kept repeating. "Toby, I'd – we'd – Betty and me – we'd be delighted. Yes, Yes, thank you. Thank you *very* much!"

Pleased, Toby chucked away his cigar stub and shook Ben's hand.

"Jolly good, then. Tell the memsahib when she gets back from the hairdresser's or whatever. And again, I'm sorry it took this long for us to finalise the package for you. You can see it was a trifle complicated. The house in Church Road is empty and ready when you are. Have you taken this little palace on for a lengthy rental?"

"No, no," said Ben, distractedly. "A month only. I didn't want it to seem too permanent somehow. Toby are you sure about all this?"

"Completely. Can't think of a better man for the job. You'll be doing HMG an enormous service, old man. Well, that's all I wanted to say. Have fun making that contraption with young Jim this afternoon. See you around."

And with that, he pottered off to the post office while Ben Nesbit sat down on the back doorstep and sobbed with relief.

Contraption

Ben felt much more composed by the time Jimmy knocked on the front door. The boy was without his crutches and carefully carrying a geranium in a pot.

"Hey, come on in," called Ben.

"Do you live here now?" asked Jim, looking around.

"Not for long. We're moving to Church Road, Mrs Nesbit and me. Mrs Shaw's old house. And I'll have my dogs back soon too." Ben was so infectiously happy Jimmy started grinning.

"That's nice for you. That house is opposite the church and the river. Here, I brung you a blue geranium. Auntie May says it's a tough old boot." He handed it over. "It's for helping to save me when I fell out of the tree."

Ben chuckled. "Why thank you. It is a bit like you then – a tough old boot. I didn't do much, not really. I was mostly helping Mr Green. He and Stringer did all the real saving. Can I keep it to plant in my new garden?"

Jimmy nodded happily. He followed Ben out to the little back yard and saw at once that it really wouldn't be the right home for either the potted geranium or the Nesbits. "I'll help you plant it when you have moved in," he offered.

"Thanks. I'll take you up on that. Now have a look at this. I found these old wheels when I was turning out the shed when we moved house, and this wooden crate. I don't know what I was keeping them for but they were just too good to throw out. So, well, I thought I'd make you a contraption."

"A what?"

"Contraption. It's what I'm calling it. A box on wheels, so you can trundle all kinds of stuff around and strengthen that leg at the same time. You'll push it. Or pull it, it doesn't matter. Or tie it on the back of a bike and drag it along."

"Like a barrow with four wheels?" asked Jim excitedly.

"Exactly. Or I could make it into a go-kart, of course, for you to ride in. But I thought… "

"No thank you. A push-thing would work best for me. I could stand plants in it to take to my friends. Or carry my gardening tools round to Grandma's." Jim's eyes sparkled. Maybe he would be allowed to take Gwennie for a ride in it. It was as if he had been offered a Rolls Royce.

"Right then. A contraption it is. Here, you can help me with it this afternoon if you're not otherwise engaged." Jim shook his head. "OK then, sit on that plastic chair and pour us some of that orange squash while I'll get my tape measure."

The afternoon was magical for both of them. Ben was still on cloud nine from his conversation with Toby and could not wait to tell Betty about everything when she returned on the six o'clock bus from Fenchester where she had been meeting up with two of their daughters for a shoe-shopping spree.

Jimmy was completely enthralled with the whole idea of having his own boy-powered vehicle. A set of wheels was exactly what he needed. He already owned a little plastic barrow, but this 'contraption' would be far bigger and more useful. If he ever grew to be a good enough gardener to take on one of the town's allotments he could trundle his stuff back and forth like a grown-up in it. Or help Auntie May with the grocery shopping. Or deliver some puppies to Jonah at the vets. Jimmy had a thousand uses for it mapped out in his head by the time he left to go home at five o'clock.

As he limped slowly home, he looked around with fresh eyes at the familiar landmarks. Longmont Lodge on the corner seemed a little sunnier, now someone had cut back much of the undergrowth on its north side and the wilderness fence was being replaced with a fine brick wall. He ran a hand along the old railings and was glad of the leafy shade under the trees. There was the old well with its funny little square house and bramble-covered palings. Turning down Fen Lane at last, he waved to Mrs Hewitt in her front bedroom as she polished her windows. By the time he reached his own house, Auntie May was on the step looking out for him expectantly.

She was relieved these days when he returned home after any walk, never quite trusting that he had come to no harm. But she made no obvious fuss about it. No song and dance. It wouldn't do to show her anxiety.

"A letter came for us today," she informed him after he had told her all about the contraption.

"A letter?" Jim could not imagine who might be writing to them.

"From Mrs Harris."

"Is she sending me away?"

"No, darling. You're staying right here. But we have another date to see the judge. We will all go to meet her together."

Jimmy, wide-eyed, tried to understand. He smiled his tiny smile, the one he used when he was unsure.

"What would you do if they took me away?" he whispered.

Auntie May put down the potato masher and folded her strong arms. "I'd knit them all jumpers with no head-holes, that's what. And no arm-holes either. See how they like that!"

Hot work

Dean and Kay were larking around on the war memorial steps in Ironwell. This stone cross stood on the centre of the village in an open area known as the Platt. To one side lay the village green where an ice cream van was tempting them to spend their pocket money.

Kevin Smith came round the corner, pushing a motor bike.

"Hello, you two," he called, stopping and wiping his brow. "Phew. This is harder than it looks."

Dean bounced over, closely followed by Kay.

"Hi Kevin. You bought a bike then?"

"Nah. It's just a lend off a bloke I work with down Fox's. See if I like it."

"See if Iris likes it, you mean," laughed Dean.

Kevin grinned back. "You're right. Your sister might not approve of me doing a ton-up on the Fenchester Road now we're expecting. Gawd, I can't wait for this baby to arrive. She driving me bonkers, she is."

Dean nodded in a man-of-the-world way. "Girls get cranky," he said.

Kay walloped him with the carrier bag she was holding. "Oy, you. Less of it," she cried. Dean and Kevin grinned conspiratorially.

"Nice bike though," said Dean. "You could put one of those side-cars on it, like Miss Winstanley has, to carry Iris and the baby around."

"Do I hear my name being bandied about?" asked Miss Winstanley herself, popping out of the shadows of the oak trees nearby. "Oh I say, Kevin. Lovely velocipede."

Kevin assumed she meant the motorbike. "Yeah, thanks. Something the matter with it at the moment but I'll fix her up alright. Now my Auntie's moved out and we've got the run of our place, I can have the garage to myself. That's what Iris says anyway."

"A sort of gentleman's retreat?" grinned Fay.

"Exactly," said Kevin. "I shall need it too. The house is already full of baby clothes and cots and baths and stair-gates and what-not. I'll need a hideaway if I want to keep sane."

"I'll help, if you like," said Miss Winstanley, unexpectedly. "With the bike, I mean. I'm quite a dab hand at engines."

Kevin nodded. "Alright, you're on. Thank you Miss. I might take you up on that." He turned back to the Mayflower children. "So what are you lot up to? No good, I bet."

Kay said, "We're going to go and buy a lolly at the van."

"Ninety-nine," Dean contradicted her.

"Orange Maid!" Kay was thirsty.

"Alright, bossy, two orange lollies it is." Dean gave in gracefully. Perhaps his mum would buy him a ninety-nine later if the van was still there. "Come on, 'fore he goes."

They waved good bye and ran away across the grass.

"Nice to be young and out of school," said Miss Winstanley. She rather missed her old teaching days, although her other two enterprises were keeping her more than busy this year. The textile gallery was growing in popularity, and she was considering adding a small cafe to her attractions. And the pasture beside the watermill now housed not only Persephone and Horace, but also two new donkeys rescued from a closed-down petting zoo beyond Ledgely. Their names were Bobby and Tulip – not exactly classical names, but memorable enough. They were a stubborn pair, not as placid as the original two.

"Yes. Well, I'd better keep pushing this bike if I want to reach home before suppertime," sighed Kevin. " 'Though I'm hotter 'n the hinges of hell right now, as Mr Green would say. Maybe I could buy you a lolly, Miss? To give me a bit of encouragement, like?"

Fay laughed again. "That's funny," she said. "I was just about to ask you the same thing!"

* * *

16.

Abbey Farm

Problem solved

Toby and Reg went to take a look at the new Abbey Farm shops. It was Sunday and there was little traffic on the main road. The air was chilly although the sun shone in a blue sky, so they stepped out at a fair pace.

"Did you know your old home finally fell down last week?" asked Reg.

"I did. Ben told me." There was not much that escaped Toby's new roving informer.

The Holt had been bequeathed to him by an uncle, but it had burned down soon after Toby arrived in Banford. Since then he had moved in with Lady Longmont at Banford Place. He did not care a fig about the Holt. It held nothing of any value to him.

Or so he imagined. Had he known what lay rotting in the disused well in the back yard under a ton of rubble and ash he might have thought otherwise.

"Alright if Terry and me salvages a few timbers or stones here and there from time to time?" asked Mr Green.

"Yes, no problem. Take all you like. You'd be doing me a service. Maybe you can make us a bird table or something for school."

"Aye-aye, Sir," said Reg amicably.

Stringer, who was bounding ahead, turned off down the lane to the farm and the men followed. It was rutted and muddy from the comings and goings of the builders' trucks.

The rambling old farmhouse, parts of which pre-dated the destruction of the abbey for which it was named, looked very forlorn. Its yard was no longer filled with wandering chickens and pieces of discarded machinery but with stacks of modern building supplies, a foreman's caravan and some heavy digging equipment. Toby and Reg followed the dog a little further down the hill to the site of old pigsties.

"They've made a good start," commented Toby surveying the levelled area.

Reg stood and lit his pipe, deep in thought. "Don't look like they found nothin'," he said.

Toby nodded. "No. No it doesn't, thank god. And they won't, now they've concreted the whole lot over."

The two stood remembering that, in all probability, the body of a man lay entombed there.

Stringer snooped around, cocking his leg on a few bushes.

"I think it works very well as a car park, don't you?" asked Toby.

"Yerse," answered Reg. "So long as no one ever spots a ghost covered in pig muck."

Morning routine

Jimmy always went out into the back garden when giving his nose a good blow. Auntie May was absolutely fine about dealing with a range of disagreeableness when it came to children, but when it came to Nose she was adamant. If you sneezed you left her classroom, closed the door, and blew you nose and cleaned up outside. Jimmy had learned that lesson early on when she had been his teacher, so now he made sure that one of his first tasks each day was a jolly good blow outside in the back garden, while she was still in bed asleep. On rising at dawn, he dressed and tiptoed downstairs. He put the kettle on to boil, used the outside lavatory, and blew his nose.

Depositing the handkerchief in the special hanky saucepan, he washed his hands and went back to the yard while the kettle came to the boil. It was wonderful out there with the birds and the awakening trees. At the bottom of their long thin garden were an apple tree and a pear tree, and over the back fence a field with some bullocks. Up in the sky the last star was fading and sunlight was beginning to catch the dewy leaves, making them sparkle. He looked around at the field and the garden and the little house he was so happy living in. This was home. All he needed now was more space to grow things. The allotment association was wanting to buy the field at the bottom to extend its holding, and Jimmy hoped they were successful. He would love to be able to climb the fence and step down onto his own allotment one day. There would be vegetables for everyone. He would deliver them from his contraption.

The kettle boiled, so he made a half-mug of tea and took it carefully upstairs to Auntie May. He set the mug down and cuddled in beside her.

"Ooh, thank you. How are our carrots coming along? Did you move Hannibal?" she asked.

"The carrots need a little longer. Hannibal no, not yet." he said. "Auntie May… "

"Mmm?"

"Can I go and help Mrs Hewitt this afternoon?"

"Do what?"

"Mow her lawn. And Auntie May… "

"Mmm?"

"Can I go for a walk with Granny tomorrow?"

"Of course. Just don't get too tired. Or let *her* get too tired either. She's an old lady. No pushing her on the swings or paddling that canoe up and down the river."

Jim looked so scornful May almost spilled her tea.

Marigold sauntered in, meowing politely and sharpening her claws on the carpet, only to be yelled at in unison.

"How does bacon and egg sound?" asked Auntie May.

"Both together? Lovely!" cried Jim. Usually it was one or the other. "And can I have a tomato? And a potato cake too? Please, oh please, oh please?"

"Good heavens, you're turning into a gannet! Or a gobbling turkey. Or a bottomless pit. No, Marigold, stop that. Now go and give her some Kittipix, please, before she shreds this carpet. I want to get up, and I don't need an audience."

Gwennie goes to school

The Tuttle's baby continued to be completely delightful.

Cathy and Peggy were cooing over Gwennie as she lay in her carrycot waving her arms one afternoon, and discussed her progress. Charlie had had to bring her to work that day as Fiona had been called in to the hospital – some muddle over shift allocations she said. The baby was currently chewing happily on her bare toes.

"Crumbs, I wish I could still do that," commented Peggy, who had frequent pain in her left knee.

"That would entertain the governors," stated Cathy, as she squinted over the first aid box she was replenishing. "Have we any more of those square plasters? The big ones?"

"Look in the medical cupboard. I think I stuck one on Yulissa's arm when she had that sting."

Mr Tuttle breezed in. "Hullo," he smiled. "And how're my favourite three witches?" He scooped his daughter into his arms and nuzzled her soft little cheeks.

"Here, don't you go calling them witches, you Welsh Merlin," cried Toby, also clattering in with an armful of French exercise books, which he promptly dropped. "We'll never get anything but frogs and evil smelling liquids out of them if you do."

"Gwennie's cornered the market on evil smelling liquids already," said Charlie as he handed the baby to Peg and helped Toby retrieve the books.

He returned to class with Gwennie in the carrycot, for the final hour of school. His form had begged to be allowed to watch over her while they finished off their history projects and he read them a little more of their serial story. They promised to be extra quiet and good.

The novelty of having a baby in the classroom was thrilling. Rick and Carl had devised a paper and string mobile to hang over the carrycot, and Poppy had used her last clean hanky to knot into a rudimentary dolly. Even dour Gloria Mason smiled when the baby gripped her finger. Normally, as Gloria told tales to the teachers on all of them the children disliked her, which caused Gloria to become resentful and mean. But to have the wonderful baby obviously select her for a finger-gripping suddenly made Gloria overwhelmingly happy.

"She likes you, Glor," commented Sylvia, kindly. Gloria smiled back, and her entire day changed for the better.

"Can we pick her up, Sir? *Please!*" wheedled Poppy. "We won't drop her. Promise."

Charlie had to give in. Gwennie loved being passed around like a parcel while the children told each other to mind her head, watch how she could nearly stand up, and demonstrate how much she liked to give each of them a dribbly kiss. If their teacher had not insisted he keep Gwennie on his own knee while he read a scant fifteen minutes of the serial, the children would have gone home and told their parents they had spent the entire day carrying Baby Tuttle around.

Jimmy stayed behind after the rest of the class had gone home and gave the baby her mid-afternoon bottle. She gave a wheezy grunt with each swallow and gazed adoringly into his face.

"You're a real squeaky gate. Yes you are! I'll have to get some of that grease Mr Green uses on the playground gate," Jimmy murmured to her. He sat her up for a burp, then she snuggled down against him and fell asleep. Jimmy sat comfortably in the story chair, happy to be resting while beautiful Gwennie dozed.

Charlie glanced at them. "You're like the faithful Prince, waiting for Sleeping Beauty to wake up," he said.

Jimmy grinned. "She's so pretty," he said, not for the first time. His heart swelled with love for the baby. "She's going to have lots of boyfriends. But I'll be her first."

"That you will, my lad, that you will. She's a very lucky little lady. Now then, I've finished doing these books, so how about you ride home with me and you can keep playing with Gwennie while I make tea for you and Tim? We can tell Auntie May on our way out the door."

Jimmy was torn, but he had already made a promise. "No, I'm very sorry, but I can't. I have to go and help someone with their garden." He really wished he could go, but a promise was a promise and a garden was a garden. He stuffed his homework books into his satchel and bade his teacher farewell.

Downstairs, Mrs Nesbit was closing her classroom door.

"Are there you are. I thought you might have forgotten me," she smiled.

Jim shook his head. He would never forget a promise to help with a garden. It wasn't possible. "Nope," he said.

They walked slowly out of school and across the road to the Nesbit's new home in Church Road.

It was a pretty place. Betty had decided to call it 'Turners' as it represented a real upturn in their fortune. There it stood, all pretty tile and brick, diamond leaded panes and solid oaken woodwork, a graceful Edwardian dwelling currently being brought into the modern world by their arrival. The garden covered about an acre but had been left to fend for itself far too long. The edges of the borders and lawns had been trimmed back a little and Terry Green had had a go at the hedges, but the rest was a shaggy mess.

Jim had come along to suggest the optimum planting positions for Betty's new dahlias and skimmias, penstemons and salvias. He had already spent hours studying the garden's various sections – where the sun was in the mornings, when the east wind caught that line of blackcurrant bushes, which part was dampest. The old pond he would renovate, and give Mrs Shaw's little frogs a chance to thrive. He had discovered a slow worm in a neglected compost area, and some ancient nest-boxes nailed in a pear tree. Mr Nesbit was going to fix those.

Mrs Nesbit was genuinely thrilled Jimmy was helping them. No one knew how to design a garden like young Jim Fisher. He might be only eight, but he already possesses more practical knowledge than many an eighty year old, Betty thought, as she watched the lad sigh with pleasure at the work before him. She handed him some apple slices and a dish of peanut butter.

"Thank you," he said. He took out his old exercise book and showed her the plans he had drawn as they sat at the patio table together.

Life couldn't get any better than this.

Being perfect

Kay's mother repeatedly asked why she had no *girl* playmates.

"There are plenty of nice girls in your school. What about that Angela Johnson from Holly Lane? Why do you always go trailing around after the boys? That ragamuffin Dean Underwood and that rough Joey Whatsisname? You should invite Angela round here to play with your doll's house or the nice puppet theatre we gave you last Christmas. Go on, go and ask her to tea. Take your bike," she ordered, exasperated.

Kay threw down her pencils and washed her paintbrush as slowly as she could get away with. It was no good. Some days you could slam around yelling No, but today wasn't one of them. She zipped up her windcheater and pulled on (what she liked to call) her cowboy boots. Walking to Angela's and back would take a good long hour. There was no way Kay was taking her bike.

Angela Johnson. Nice enough. Liked music, played the trumpet. Was good at French. It could be worse. Hopefully she would be out. She was just so *girly*.

Everywhere today seemed blue and gold, to Kay's eyes. The distant hills, the wetlands north of the Heath, the diesel train as it slid towards Banford on the far side of St Mary's cemetery. Crossing the road and gaining height as the lane passed through Oxthorpe, her legs began to tire and she slowed to a pleasant ambling pace. She looked up towards the green slopes of Holly Hill ahead of her, some wooded, some neat with fresh grass and wildflowers. A few puffy clouds graced the skies and everywhere birds darted and chirruped. She had been this way many-a-time, but it was never the same twice, and it never disappointed. Kay took a deep lungful of cold air and vowed one day to live here so she could see this magical blue hill every morning when she woke up.

Far away down the end of one grassy track, lay the burned out cottage known as the Holt. Maybe she would buy that and renovate it when she grew up. Perhaps she would become a painter or a writer and live there until she was ninety. Or possibly own race horses and win tons of money up at the racetrack. Part of this area was named Nag's Common after all.

By the time Kay had dawdled her way out of the wild parts and back into the suburban housing development where Angela lived, she was in a much more mellow mood. Angela was, unfortunately, in.

"Would you like to come to mine for tea? You don't have to, but my mother *said*. She thinks you'd like to play dolls or puppets." Kay scowled again when she remembered that part. "Do you?"

Angela – tidy and neat in a short kilt and an oatmeal jumper – shook her head, much to Kay's relief.

"No thank you," said Angela. "But I would like to come out. For a walk maybe. Thanks. It's nice of you to ask. The other kids round here are all a bit young for me," she explained, as she dextrously scraped her blonde hair back into a pony tail and kicked off her slippers. "Mum! I'm going round Kay's for tea!"

"Back by seven, then, please!" called her mother from the kitchen. "Mind how you go. Have a nice time."

"Gosh, is that all the bossing your mum does? Mine's a nightmare," grinned Kay as they clanged the gate shut after them and trotted back up the lane to Holly Hill and its muddy trackways.

Angela laughed. "She can be too, sometimes. But I've done my violin practice already and finished my homework so… ." She shrugged and jumped across one of the many deep ruts in the path. "So I can just play. Thanks for coming for me. I'd have to get out my stupid dolls or do some cooking or something otherwise. I'd much rather be outside."

Kay was astonished. Who would have thought Angela Johnson would prefer a muddy walk to staying in and practising being a perfect girl? It just showed you.

"Let's climb right up to the top, shall we? Then go to mine down Nag's Hill. It's the long way, but by the time we're home tea will be ready. I'll show you my writing studio if you like." Kay was feeling magnanimous. She rarely invited anyone into her old shed. "I paint in there too, sometimes, but it isn't terribly clean. The spiders make a lot of cobwebs."

"Golly, you *paint* too? I knew you were good at drawing. I'd like to see your studio, though. Maybe we could fix it up? Kick out the spiders?"

Angela was full of surprises. Not a squeal about the nasty creepy-crawlies, plus an unsolicited personal compliment and an offer of help. She was rapidly becoming Kay's best friend.

The girls walked and clambered up and up, to the very top of the hill where they could gaze on the distant counties and delight in all the colours and possibilities which the afternoon – and their lives – had to offer.

Boys, Kay decided as they strolled on, were alright, but they were limited. They had different dreams, and they always had to *tell* you stuff. They never asked what *you* thought, what *you* dreamed about. Girls, it seemed, were less self-centred. At least Angela was, and many of her ideas coincided with Kay's. It was quite a revelation. Angela liked freedom and possibilities and music and art and being outdoors, and adventures, just as Kay did. It was strange, hearing Angela talk, and it was deeply comforting to know Kay was not the only one who had ever had such thoughts. Maybe girls weren't so bad after all.

Philosophy

May and Reg Green were sharing a quiet moment together in the staffroom after school. Reg had the plug off the urn and was re-wiring it, while May was turning out a box of old cups and saucers from one of the cupboards. She had the muckier job.

"I dunno why you think anyone would want to drink out of any of those," grunted Reg. "People prefer mugs, these days. No one wants a fiddly little saucer."

"Miss Broadstock liked to use them. For governors' meetings and so on. Visiting parents. The vicar. The Bishop of Fenchester came for lunch once."

"I know. I had to crank that car engine of his when it wouldn't start. Hillman Minx, it were. Blue."

May smiled. "These have a pretty design. Not today's fashion though, I suspect. Mrs Clark said to put them out for the vicar's jumble sale."

Reg took the box and stacked it with some others containing withdrawn library books beside the french window while May washed her hands. "How's little-un's leg doing?"

May sat down at the table with a sigh, and began playing with the sugar in the bowl, spooning it into heaps and pathways. "Alright, I think, Reg. He never complains."

"I know that," nodded Reg.

"But, well, I still blame myself for him being out there in such a night. Why couldn't he come and talk to me when he was so miserable? He would at least have been safe at home, not falling out of flesh-ripping trees."

Reg sat down too and patted her fidgety hand. She brushed her cheek with an impatient gesture.

"Oh I know. The doctors have reassured me. The vicar. So has Sir Hugo. So have you. So has Mrs Clark. Everyone. But I still blame myself. Jimmy shouldn't have been out so late in all that weather, Reg. I ought to have gone to find him earlier. If it hadn't been for you and Stringer… ."

Reg stood up again. This wouldn't do.

"No good goin' on like that, Miss. Fact is, you, me and the dog *did* find 'im. Jim's safe and sound now and doing fine in every way. He's a different lad now the vicar's had a word with him. He knows he's going to be properly adopted too. You and him, you'll be alright." He leaned against the sink, studying his friend. "You're fretting too much."

She turned haunted eyes on him. Good lord, how this old lady did suffer, he thought. She puts up a good front, though. It was all about appearances with May Fisher's generation. Don't let on, keep mum, stiff upper lip, even though the bombs are raining down and we might be blown to smithereens.

Reg chewed his moustache as he reflected on the irony of his own life. He put up a good front too. There was nobody with more to keep secret than bosun Reg Green.

"Look, he's growing up, your boy. He loves 'is Auntie. 'E won't do nothing to up-skittle you again, you mark my words." Reg poured her a mug of water. "His leg's really improving."

May nodded. "I've put him in those old fashioned long sort of shorts to cover that nasty scar. The skimpy little ones most boys wear these days simply won't do. If he had a little more meat on him it might not look so bad."

Reg smiled. "Very sensible too. Them corduroys will serve well, 'im likin' the gardening life the way he does. I remember flannel suits, you know. Terry used to wear one when he went to school." He was trying to lighten the mood. "Your Jim's still a great one for walkin', isn't he? That should exercise and strengthen him. His rattly old contraption should help. It were nice of Ben to make that for 'im. I should take a leaf out of Jim's book and stop worrying, if I were you. Put yer best foot forward, so to speak."

May Fisher nodded and stood up. He was right and she knew it. Look ahead, not astern, if you wish to see the future, she remembered her mother saying. A sound philosophy.

"I will, Reg. I really will try. It's Jimmy who keeps me going, you know. All his little routines and pleasures. I can't remember what I did before he arrived."

"Ha! That's kids for yer. Ivy says if it weren't the washin' and ironin' it were the cookin' and cleanin' kept her busy when our two was little. She's right too. She'd be sittin' around twiddlin' 'er thumbs now our Pat's moved out, only Terry's worth five all by 'imself. Mind you, he's talking about moving in with that Vivienne of 'is one of these fine days. They're lookin' at one of them run down places in Ironwell, opposite the old forge. Used to be a pub. The company that's developin' the Abbey Shops has bought several old empty cottages from his lordship's estate sale, and that's one of them. So if he managed to buy one they'd live right opposite a pub."

May laughed. "Well that would suit him. You too, I should think!"

They took the box of teacups and books out to the front door from where the curate had said he would collect them. May pulled on her coat as Jimmy came out of the library where he and a few other children had been doing their homework with Mr Chivers. May knew better than to hug him or call him darling in public. Reg was relieved the old lady was back on form.

"All done?" asked Miss Fisher. "Good boy. Now then, it's macaroni cheese tonight, isn't it? That won't take two shakes of a donkey's left leg to prepare, so how about we walk over the Steps and buy an ice cream at the new corner shop before we head home? You can play on the swings for a bit in the park if you like, while I read the paper. How does that sound?"

It sounded tickety-boo to Jim.

Off they went, the oddly assorted pair, one limping like an old man, the other a brisk and sprightly old lady.

Reg shook his white head and filled his pipe for a pleasant smoke. "Bein' in love is funny thing," he told the dog who came to sit by his foot. "Find the other 'alf of yerself and all's well. Fix on the wrong 'alf, 'owever, and yer life's goin' ter be cockeyed for ever."

Stringer tilted his head at these words of wisdom, and settled down with a philosophical sigh.

Supper time had to come eventually, he supposed.

Donkeys

Horace, Persephone, and the two new donkeys were standing in their field munching mouthfuls of sweet tender grass. Persephone licked at a flower that had become wedged in her teeth and eyed the young woman who was leaning over the fence and clicking her tongue encouragingly.

Fay Winstanley loped across from weeding her veg patch and greeted the newcomer.

"Hello there! Admiring my donks?"

"Pardon?"

"The big donkey! Her name's Persephone. Other one's Horace. Not a donk, obviously, but I think of them as such. Then that's Tulip and that one in the corner is Bobby. Got another one arriving next Tuesday. Retired from the seaside, if you can believe that. Used to give rides to kiddies."

Bella Delgado laughed. "I thought people retired *to* the seaside, not from it," she said. "How-do-you-do. I'm Bella from Mayflower School. Do you remember me?"

"Of course," beamed Fay, showing quite a few of her own horsey teeth. "Nice to see you again. Are you on a bike ride?" She had spotted Bella's bike lying beside the roadway.

"Yes, I try to spend an hour biking about each day. Keeps me fit. Sometimes I walk." said Bella.

"I was just about to have a cuppa. Would you like to join me?" asked Fay.

Bella climbed over the fence and they patted and fussed the animals before strolling over to the house. Bella was admiring the little painted caravan in the yard when a car drew up and the driver wound down the window. It was Dr Granger.

"Afternoon," he called. "I say, I wonder if you can help me?"

The two women went over. He was brown and handsome and had his sleeves rolled up today as it was warm. He grinned boyishly.

"I'm looking for Iris Cottage. I know it's here somewhere, but for the life of me I can't remember where exactly. A Mrs Smith."

Fay hopped up and down. "Oh golly, well, there's Lily and Rose and Iris and May Cottages so I'm not surprised. Quite a *posy* of flowers. I think they were all once owned by a Mr Lavender, hence his liking all things floral. Go up here and turn left and I think Iris is opposite the Old Forge."

"What, the place that used to be a pub?

"Yes, after it closed as a blacksmiths, of course. Couldn't really have both together could you? Although I suppose the Mint has its stables so running two businesses in one is not unheard of around here." Fay was grinning like a hyena and gabbling while Bella stood smiling serenely.

"Well, thank you," said the doctor. "And what's your name, may I ask?" he said staring in admiration at Bella's dark and graceful beauty.

"This is Bella Delgado, from Mayflower School. A new teacher this academic year," Fay informed him. "We're just about to have a cup of tea. Would you like to join us? Come on! The more the merrier, Doctor."

Bella remembered who this man was now. Newly married, she thought, catching sight of a wedding ring on his left hand. And still flirting.

"Ah, very tempting, dear lady, very tempting. But no, I can't, alas. I have to finish my afternoon rounds. It's hard to resist two such delightful damsels – but no. Resist I must. Iris Cottage awaits. Onwards and leftwards."

He let in the clutch and drove away, waving.

Fay and Bella had a cup of tea together, then Fay showed her around the little gallery of textiles and other local artwork. As Bella rode away on her bike she brooded about charming Dr Joe Granger. He was certainly a memorable medico. She would have to watch out for him.

* * *

17.

May Queen

A bubble bursts

Hugo Chivers phoned Skip one evening. She had not been expecting a call so she was not prepared for the sudden eruption of emotions this communication caused her.

"Hello? Hugo! Oh, I'm alright, thank you. Yes, Mum too. Where are you?"

"London still. Fly back tomorrow morning."

"Europe?"

"Yes, that's right. Look, I just wanted to say… "

There was a pause.

"What?"

"I know you're still angry, and I'm not blaming you. No one meant to endanger your schoolchildren. I certainly never did. How's the boy doing?"

"Much better, thanks to all of us rallying round. And no one knows how he came by his accident except you, Toby, me and Reg, if that's what you're worried about."

That was satisfactory. Hugo nodded to himself as he sat in his London club, a brandy at hand.

"Good. And the Nesbit couple?"

"Living in Chloe's old home, like you wanted. Ben seems very happy. He's managing the new local shopping place but seems to spend a lot of his free time out walking the fields with his dogs, just as before. Betty's much happier now they are settled."

"Good. The Buntings are doing well in retirement. And is the old lady still hanging on?"

"Lady Longmont? Yes. Toby tells us she's pretty out of it most of the time, though. Mrs Bicknell and her friend do most of the caring. I really ought to go down and see her again."

Skipper had been twice but had not found the old lady in any condition to receive visitors. She privately thought she should be in a home, she was so frail. But Toby said no, and he had the last word, so there the woman stayed, mouldering away.

"I'd leave her be if I were you," advised Hugo.

"Why do you say that? She can't do any more harm can she?"

"Maybe not. How's Ernest and that fellow he lives with?"

"They're fine."

"Well, I just wanted to let you know I'll be getting married in a couple of months."

There was a long pause while Skipper reeled from this blow.

"Pardon?" she breathed.

"I said I'm getting married. Adele is a translator. We have a very nice apartment in Brussels. Toby will look after any future questions you may have about…and, well, anything else really."

Adele. A vision of an elegant, cosmopolitan female swam before Mrs Clark's eyes.

"Congratulations. How lovely."

"Oh, yes, thank you. Yes, I think it will work rather well." Hugo checked his watch. "Look, I'd better go. There's someone just turned up with a message. Cheerio, Skip. No hard feelings. All the best."

The line went dead. And with it the mirage that had previously danced so captivatingly for so long in Mrs Clark's imagination popped, like a soap bubble.

She went upstairs to her room and closed the door.

Pips

Ernest was embarrassed by his father's departure. Especially as this time, he was informed, it was absolutely one-hundred percent final. As usual, there were odds and ends left for his son to tidy up.

He received a note from Brussels instructing him to either keep the garaged car himself or hand it over to Mrs Clark, her own motor being little better than a rust-bucket. She would no doubt appreciate the gift. Skipper did eventually accept it, mainly because Ernest loathed it so much. She was determined to wrench something worthwhile from the ruins of her relationship with Hugo. She drove it straight down to Fox's garage and traded it in for a nice new Vauxhall. Ernest understood and approved. The Vauxhall was poetic compensation.

"Parents are a right pain in the neck," he observed to Toby one morning as they were shepherding children into school. "Mine's getting married to some thirty-seven year old in Europe."

Toby nodded. "I heard. I'm sorry. Well, you know what I mean. Have you met her yet?"

"Nope. Don't especially want to, although I'm sure I shall have to. Like I say, a pain in the neck," he repeated.

"It's old people. They go mad sometimes."

Ernest smiled. "And how is your landlady?"

"Still barking. Doesn't say much anymore, or get out of bed now. Just glares at me and gnashes her dentures. Growls a bit, with a carnivorous red glint in her eye."

He blew his whistle and the lines of children trooped into school. Ernest hurried off to the library to prepare for the first group of the morning, while Toby stood looking at the sycamore trees blowing in the wind on the far side of the road. How pleasant it was to have such a lovely view from the school gates. He could see right across Hendy's Fields to Roffett's Wood and distant Holly Hill.

Joey Latimer ran round the corner.

"Late, Latimer!" cried the teacher.

"Sorry, Sir. Mum forgot to put my lunch money in so I had to go back."

"Don't blame your poor mother. Never mind, Joe. Come and see me at break time, would you please? And bring Dean and Jimmy Birch with you."

"Yes Sir. You got a new job for us?" Joe was quite excited.

"No. Not this time. The opposite in fact." Toby sighed and walked into school through the front door with the lad. "No more Observer Corps required from now on. Thanks Joe."

Toby paused a while on the main staircase, looking up at the tall stained-glass windows. Oranges and pomegranates, apples, pears, cherries, lemons cascaded amid a mass of stylised leaves and dominated the design. Highly appropriate emblems for a school whose ethos was one of dealing with various pips, he thought. Some small and tender, some a whole lot larger and tougher.

May day

The children were performing their May Morning mummers play. St George slew his dragon deftly, the May Queen was crowned ceremonially, and the be-ribboned maypole was danced around charmingly. The parents clapped and stamped their feet like proper pagans, even though the vicar had blessed all proceedings in a suitably Christian manner. As always, everyone loved it.

"Miss, Miss! That dragon blowed fire on me! It did!"

"And you're not burned? Well, I never!" said an astonished Mrs Nesbit as she and Mrs Moore stood with her class of five-year-olds, watching the performance.

"Brandon stuck his tongue out at it," another round-eyed kindergartener informed her.

"Oh dear me," commented Mrs Moore gravely. "That won't do at all. I hope you would never do such a rude thing, Matthew."

Matthew, who had been known to lapse once or twice in the matter of good manners, was well-aware there were usually consequences following poor standards of behaviour in school. He shook his head. "No, Miss," he said, puffing out his cheeks while he thought about this.

Mrs Clark – also an actress worthy of Shakespeare – laughed and joked with everybody, pointing out the usual collection buckets and reminding the audience that the cake and handiwork stalls would be open in the school hall until ten minutes to twelve. "Don't miss the children's exhibition of pet and other animal portraits on the walls while you're there," she called, as the rush began.

Toby and Skipper mingled as the sale of goods proceeded. Playtime had been extended so that the children could guide their parents around and encourage them to fork-out on soft drinks and biscuits, a sausage pie for supper, and a second-hand book or two.

"Have you any books left in your library at all?" Toby asked Ernest. They had retreated behind the piano together to watch while Mrs Clark roamed the entrance hall.

"I do. It's amazing how many are actually donated by parents throughout the year, you know. I keep several boxes of these in a cupboard especially for these jumble sales. Duplicates and suchlike. We never seem to run out."

"For god's sake don't call it a jumble sale. Skip will have your guts for garters."

Ernest laughed. "Yes, alright. May Day Sale, then. Art Show. Cake Sale. Not many of those left unfortunately."

"No. Popular items, cakes. Is that Julia Scott looking at the paintings? I haven't seen her for a while."

"Yes. Lord, she's carrying that awful poodle of hers." Ernest was not a fan of Pongo.

"It almost makes one wish there really were a fire-breathing dragon somewhere about, doesn't it?" laughed Toby. "St George and his Barbecuing Dragon would make a good essay competition title."

He hurried off to see if a miracle had happened and there were one or two cakes left to buy.

Rock and roll

Banford town dozed pleasantly in the afternoon sun. Its ancient streets marked the lines originally defined by the leather-shod incomers from the nearby continent – the hunters, herdsmen, fishers, farmers, weavers, woodsmen, holy fathers, merry wives, soldiers, sailors, tillers and tradesmen whose feet beat the muddy tracks into usable paths and whose stubby hands set the very first cobbles and tiles.

The outlines and angles of its miscellaneous roads and buildings were roughly sketched, the in-filled colours harmoniously blended. It was a tumble of a town, solid and warm, nothing shiny or geometrical about it except for the sudden glint of light on a river-water ripple, or the flash of green glass as someone opened a window. Its surfaces were mostly dull and warm to the touch. Trees blossomed and fluttered in its squares and open spaces. Hand-bent railings topped the fat limestone walls. Oaken gates, clap-boarding, pantiles (with thumbprints of the makers still visible) and flagstones were everywhere.

A jigsaw of a place, was Banford. Towers, spires, turrets, mansards, gambrels, dormers were all there – somewhere. The buildings shrugged against each other like groups of drunken chums. Some were thick and coarse, others delicate and sophisticated. They were linked by a network of mossy walkways and flagged steps that sprouted ribs of bent and twisted iron in the form of gates and railings. It held tight to its base, resembling a coral reef crusted over with barnacles that sprouted from living rock in order to shelter generation after generation of citizens from the tide of dangers the world constantly shoved towards it. Secretly, within each mortared stone, lay the imprints of slow-grown shells and tiny sea-monsters. The town was solid – as much a feature of the landscape as the river that ran beneath its castle walls. It harboured and nurtured all who dwelt within, and had done so for almost two thousand years. Banford town lived its own, slow, crusty life beside the rippling water – tucked securely, contentedly, in place by the soft fields and gentle hedgerows, come rain or shine, feast or famine. It barely grew. It hardly breathed. Its jigsaw shape was fixed.

The school bus pulled into the central square. The majority of its teenage passengers alighted, chattering and larking about like birds on a lawn. Most headed for the corner shops to buy sweets or crisps, while others dutifully set off for home, drifting away up the streets and avenues. The old red bus puffed a cloud of hot blue exhaust fumes, ground its gears and was gone.

A tall schoolboy and a gangly girl strolled off together in the general direction of Mayflower School, where they had both once been educated. Reaching the river, they felt the pressure of secondary school life ease and the rosy memories of junior school bob back up.

"We used to come up here to Woolies after school sometimes," said Ryan, remembering. "But you was mostly always stuck indoors doing your homework, wasn't you?"

Shelley nodded. Her mum was the school's cleaner and Shelley had usually to wait at school until her mother was ready to go home each day, which often meant remaining for a couple of hours after the other children left. Her mum still cleaned the place, but now Shelley was permitted far more freedom. She liked walking home with Ryan Hale. He was a gentle giant of a boy, not too bright, not too handsome, and Shelley adored him.

A stalled car was blocking the narrowest part of Wharf Gate just where they wanted to step onto the river's footbridge. A man was angrily cussing as he flung open the bonnet. Ryan and Shelley were obliged to stop and watch the drama.

The man took his jacket off and undid the cufflinks on his shirt prior to rolling up his sleeves. He was clearly furious, as was the driver behind him who could neither pass nor reverse. The line of cars began to grow. Someone hooted. One bright cufflink fell on the cobbles just as a lady stepped out of the bookshop. She noticed it and quickly retrieved it.

"Hello again," said Bella. "Is this yours?"

Joe Granger straightened up and bashed his head on the bonnet cover. "Ow! Oh, er yes. Yes. Thank you. Miss Delgado isn't it?"

"You're holding up the street, Dr Granger!" yelled a delivery man.

The doctor turned back to the interior workings of his car and stared at it, hoping this would somehow reveal the problem. "It was alright this morning. It just conked out and now won't even make the right noise when I turn the key. Bloody thing."

Bella and he peered together into the dark unknown.

Ryan gave his satchel to Shelley to hold and crossed over the road. He tapped the doctor on the arm. Granger only just remembered the bonnet lid in time.

"Excuse me," said Ryan.

"Not now, son."

"No, but excuse me. I can fix your car."

Granger looked doubtfully at the lad. He looked like a halfwit in those round spectacles and that too-tight Portland Secondary School uniform.

"No – he can," called Shelley supportively from the side lines. She had no idea if Ryan was any good at motors, but had immense faith.

"Alright then, genius, what do you suppose it is?" growled the doctor. Someone was already walking belligerently towards them from one of the stationary cars.

Ryan started rocking the car vigorously from side to side. "Jammed starter motor, I think," he puffed. "It's steep here."

Joe Granger joined in the rocking while Bella and Shelley stood watching, wide-eyed.

"There, now try that," said Ryan slamming down the lid. Joe climbed in and the engine started up straight away. The drivers in the line behind cheered.

"Fantastic!" laughed Joe Granger. "Thanks, lad! What's your name?"

"Ryan Hale, Sir. You'll be alright now."

"Well thanks, Ryan. I won't forget to sing your praises when I take the car in to get it serviced next week. Very many thanks indeed. Alright, alright, I'm going," he cried to the line behind and leaned out of the window to wave. "Catch you another day, Miss Delgado," he added with a boyish grin.

Bella placed the cufflink in his hand. "Maybe," she smiled.

Shelley was as full of happiness as could be. Her hero had saved the day. Why on earth the beautiful stranger had not kept the cufflink to use as an excuse to meet the handsome doctor again, she could not say. It was what she would have done. It was the type of thing that happened all the time in the slushy romantic novels her mother brought home from the library, and that she too secretly devoured. Shelley would have handed the cufflink back to him on a moonlit night in a secluded glade. Their lips would have met. There were many moonlit glades and lips meeting in her mum's books. Shelley sighed with rapture.

"Nice, Ryan. Where'd you learn that trick?" she asked, handing him his things.

He shrugged. "Dunno. Dad, I think. And telly. You just got to free up the jammed starter mechanism. I'm going in the army when I'm older," he added, for the umpteenth time. He took out a grubby hanky and wiped his hands. "I'll prob'ly work on servicing tanks."

"It was a lucky thing we was passing by," Shelley said. "The whole town might've ground to a standstill without you helping."

"Come on, then, old lady," said Ryan. "Let's get going. My belly thinks me throat's been cut."

Shelley trotted quickly along beside him, astonished at all the wonderful things life brought your way when you weren't actually looking. Even in an ancient town like this, romance was simply everywhere.

Domestic goddesses

"Please, Mrs Green, may we help with the dishes?" asked Tania. She loved every part of the Nosh Club, from writing down the recipe to the washing up.

Ivy Green nodded her head. The little group was finishing for the day and ready for home. "Yes, duckie. You carry that pot of spoons, I'll bring the bowls, and Jim'll wipe the tables, won't you Jim?"

"Yes, Mrs Green," piped Jimmy Birch. Or Jim Fisher as he now liked to think of himself. "And I'll bring the cloth and close the door." Set him a routine and he was as reliable as clockwork.

The children and Mrs Green clattered off down the stairs while Jim finished his table-wiping. He glanced out of the window over the tops of the trees towards Longmont Lodge. It was a fine view from up here. The sunlight fell on the many windows making the tall old property look more like a glittering palace than a lodge. Jimmy wondered whether there had ever been an even larger house standing in the wilderness once, near where the Mayflower children dug their neat little allotment squares. Or a giant's castle. What was left of the grounds was mostly impenetrable jungle this Summer, throttled with vines and nettles and lethal with spiky briars. Nothing anyone did made much of an impact on its nature. The grown-ups had tried various ways to tame it, but it had just come roaring back again. Children only played around its edges, leaving the animal life the pleasure of the vast fairytale depths. The kids enjoyed digging in the earth, finding plants and climbing the trees. Jim still adored climbing trees, despite his accident. He was good at it too. There was nothing better than being high up in a sturdy swaying tree. Balancing and meeting each bend and twist was like riding a huge magic horse. You could be a sailor adjusting the rigging and listening to the sea-wind as it sang in the spars. Or an acrobat. Up near the wild sky Jim found life.

The boy stopped daydreaming and took the cloth downstairs to Mrs Green in the staffroom. She was wiping the tray and standing it up against the cupboard.

"Oh there you are! I thought I'd lost you. Tania and the others have just gone home. Here's your pot of soup, my dear. Yes I know it's called chowder, but it's still soup. Wasn't it kind of Mrs Owen to send us that recipe?"

"Mrs Shaw," corrected Jimmy. "Does she like it in her new school, do you think? I miss her."

"We all miss her. But yes, I think she's happy now. No more wet old English weather."

"No more crying over Mr Shaw being dead."

"That too." Ivy looked hard at Jimmy, but her voice was gentle. "You missin' your mum still, eh?"

Jimmy nodded. He was used to being asked this by now. It didn't bother him anymore,

"I got my Auntie May. She's my angel," he reminded Mrs Green.

Ivy smiled. "Yes I know, lovey. She'll enjoy this soup you've made, now won't she? There's your tub of it. Give me that cloth back, and off you pop. Go straight home, mind, and give it to Auntie May to warm up in a saucepan for yer tea. She'll be 'ome by now. And don't you worry, my little duckie. Mrs Shaw's 'appy now in America, and your Auntie May'll be 'appy with that chowder. It'll warm the cockles of her 'eart."

"Alright," echoed Jimmy. He thanked Mrs Green – the woman who had always made sure he had food on his plate, no matter what. The one who had warmed him up that snowy night.

He went home as fast as he dared to Fen Lane, clasping the tub in the manner of a wise man bringing a votive offering to a goddess, while overhead the trees bowed in the wind and the birds sang and sang their hopeful songs.

The soup would definitely warm Miss Fisher's heart cockles. Jim would make sure of that.

Preparing for the future

The renovations to the interior of Longmont Lodge were, like the farm shop complex, coming along well. Jamal Raina had looked into the school's finances and made some adjustments, so that from now on the lodge could be considered another educational, rather than mothballed residential, establishment. The money this released was spent on ensuring all the utilities were up to modern specifications and that the whole place was freshly decorated, warm and dry. The costs were considerably less than Mrs Clark had feared, which cheered her and Peggy's spirits considerably.

Life itself continued, and she pasted on a brave face. Hugo might be gone, Max dead, Joe Granger married, but good old Toby Tremayne was still there, out of all her menfolk. She was relieved she had no romantic feelings about Toby. He and Reg Green were proving far more worthy than the others, so she made up her mind to relax and just enjoy them. Forget soppy love and silly dreams. Solid reliability, truthfulness and practical help was the order of the day. Of course these two continued their connections with the secret intelligence service, but if their activities no longer impacted her precious school, she could forgive them. She wanted nothing more to do with secrets.

Skip, Reg and Toby were sitting together looking through a carpet sample book one morning in the staffroom. A representative from a local flooring company had left some cumbersome great books on the table and they were trying to select the colour and style for the main corridors in the Arts Centre.

"You won't have to vacuum every day," Mrs Clark was pointing out.

"I ruddy well will. Or Pru will," retorted Reg. "Or someone will. You gotter have summat over them floorboards, stands to reason, but plain cream Axminster ent it."

Toby flipped one of the pages of the sample book. "Patterned?" he asked. This was all rather tedious. Pick one, he urged them in his mind. Then we can all get on with our day.

Peggy Bailey entered with the day's fresh milk supply and put the bottles in the fridge. "What's all that? Oh, carpet. For the Lodge?"

"What about this for the corridors?" Mrs Clark asked her.

Peggy snorted. "Too light. Show every mark."

"Thank you. It's what I said," muttered Reg.

Toby got up and filled the kettle ready for breaktime. Surely on such a beautiful morning they would all be better off outdoors in the sunshine?

"The blue carpet squares it is then. Or are the green ones more appropriate?" Mrs Clark persisted.

"I'd go with that sap green colour. More relaxing. They're the same price?" Peggy's prime concern was always cost.

"Yes. We're only doing the first and second floors for now. You happy with green Reg?"

"Green it is. Gotter be, seeing as I'm Green meself." Reg was as irritated at being asked to choose as Toby, but he did not want the headmistress to pick something wildly impractical. You had to watch her. He rose, goal achieved.

"Now then, how about we wander over to the field and take a look at that wicket, Mr Tremayne? I mowed it yesterday but it might need another goin' over."

The two men escaped the world of carpets with relief. Outdoors everywhere was full of dappled light and sun. Apple Alley had plenty of fruit coming along, and the children's allotments were already colourful and trim.

"Has Ben reported this week? Is he settling in?" asked Toby as they strolled along.

"To the work, or the house?"

"Both."

"Tramps for miles, just like he used to. Says 'e takes in the farm shop building work on the way 'ome most days. He hasn't come to me with anythink out the ordinary he's spotted. Nor's Bick."

"Me either," confirmed Toby. That was good. No news was good news.

"Nothing much to manage down the farm shop place yet, neither. Site manager says all the units are spoken for. That'll take more of Ben's time come Summer, I should think," Reg went on.

"Mmm. That will be alright. By then we'll know we're not under any more scrutiny. How do they like the house?"

"Good. Bigger than they've been used to, of course and there's only the two of 'em rattlin' around in it, but if the wife's 'appy he's 'appy. And it *is* a very nice house."

"Where will you retire to, do you think? One day?" Toby asked Reg.

"Oh, probably go to one of them little renovated terraced places in Wag Lane near Pat and Phil. It's what Ivy'd like, though I've a fancy for Weston meself, near where Terry wants to be. Nice down there. The village 'as trains and a corner shop. A little bit of fishin', a decent veg garden and the woods to walk in would suit me. We're not heading that way yet, though, me and Ivy. Not for a good few years. You'll stay round Banford, will you Sir?

"Oh yes. I'm still acting the jailer to her ladyship for the moment, don't forget. However, she's signed the property over to me, you know."

"I didn't. That's a stroke of luck." Reg was surprised.

"Luck be damned. The old bitch owes this country something, and she can bloody well pay some of it off by providing me with a roof over my head in my dotage." Toby scowled at the thought of the frustrating old woman and her closely guarded secrets. London still had not unearthed the full extent of her working practices even now, and Gibb wasn't talking. "I might ask the headmistress to share the place with me, once she retires. What do you think? Would it raise eyebrows?"

Reg thought about that for a few puffs of his pipe. "No, I don't think so. Like – married?"

"No fear. No, she could live in the west wing and I could have the east wing. Meet up in the evening for supper, type of arrangement. Trim the hedges together, plant bulbs, go on hols, that sort of thing. I'd still be busy with London from time to time, as you know."

Reg nodded. "Die in harness we both will, Sir, you're correct there. Yes, I should think your idea would work. The old lady can't live much longer can she?"

"No. The doctor doesn't think she'll last a month. But she's proving dreadfully tough. She could out-manoeuvre us all yet."

Reg nodded. "Now then, Sir. This 'ere cricket pitch. To mow or not to mow – that is the question."

* * *

18.

Randel Bay

May's birthday

May Fisher was sitting alone in her classroom at the end of another afternoon, sorting out the needlework box. It had been a good day. The children had worked hard and enjoyed digging in their school allotments during the morning. Ronnie Tolland had suffered a bad nettle sting, but that had been the worst disaster. Zoe handed him a dock leaf which soon had him smiling again. May nodded. They were a nice class this year. Kind. Some of them could even sew quite well. They did not appear to have suffered too much from their rocky start in kindergarten during the Molly Parrott / Jo Winton episode. May frowned to herself. That had been an upsetting business which escalated out of all proportion. Mrs Clark had been a real star during those nasty weeks. She and Mrs Owen both.

There was a knock and Dr Legg put her head round the door.

"Afternoon, Miss Fisher!" she called cheerily. "Would you mind if we came in?"

May smiled in surprise. "No, not at all, it's lovely to see you Dr Legg. Oh, Mrs Harris!"

"Hello there!" Mrs Harris, Jimmy's social worker greeted her. "How are you? Enjoying this super weather?"

"Have you come by to see me about something special, or is this just a drop-in? I can get my coat and be ready for home in a jiffy. Jimmy's downstairs in the library with Ernest, doing his homework."

May was in a dither. Never had the doctor and the social worker arrived together since she had started fostering Jimmy last year. She could not decide what their joint appearance signified. However, they were grinning – so maybe that was something positive. Whatever could it be?

"No no. We're not here for an inspection. We've just dropped by with some more good news."

May's heart skipped a beat. Surely not… It was too soon, wasn't it? She gripped the arms of her chair and opened her mouth a little. Oxygen seemed to elude her.

Dr Legg rested her bag on the desk as it was awkward and heavy. Mrs Harris rummaged in hers and brought out a sheaf of papers.

"It's about the adoption."

I knew it, thought May.

"We know how anxious you are about it, so when Mrs Harris called round to tell me I jumped straight in the car with her," laughed Dr Legg. "Her front seat will never be the same again! Oh no."

Mrs Harris laughed too. "Here," she said, coming round and turning to one particular page in the packet of official documents. "Look. It's official. The court has expedited your adopting Jimmy. You only have to sign this paperwork and attend one more time in Fenchester and you are officially his mum."

Miss Fisher stared harder. Her heart beat so fast she felt she could jump through the window and run all the way to the town and back. She grasped the papers in a shaky hand and tried to make out the words, but they danced and blurred. She felt for a handkerchief up her sleeve.

"Really? Really and *truly*? It's so quick. Oh my goodness." May could not stem the flood and burst out crying. "Oh thank you! *Thank* you, Mrs Harris! I'm so sorry, I just… "

"It's alright. We both understand. I knew you'd want to have the news as soon as possible. There, now. Shall we go and find Jimmy?" Mrs Harris was walking on air. A sad and difficult case had reached an excellent conclusion in record time. Some days she really loved her job.

"Yes, dry those eyes now, Miss Fisher," ordered the doctor. "I want to see your Jimmy's reaction. Or Jim as I think he likes to be called now. So grown up, who'd-a thought it? Let's go and find your boy and make his day too."

Overcome, May Fisher left her desk, her chair, the needlework box, her classroom world, and descended to the library to give her son the news they had been waiting for. As they hurried down the front stairs she told the other two women, "It was my birthday the other day. I don't think anyone has ever given me a more momentous gift. It's like my life is starting fresh, from this very moment. I cannot thank you enough. No, I really cannot thank you enough."

Dr Legg and Mrs Harris glanced at each other again. It was always gratifying to be the bearer of good tidings, but it was truly wonderful to have worked hard and managed to fix a tiny piece of a broken world.

"Well, at the risk of sounding a little indelicate, that was the easiest birth of a son I have ever attended," chortled the doctor, looking at the new mother.

If May Fisher flushed with embarrassment at this remark, it was difficult to tell.

Bob-a-job

Theo Wichelow, the curate, gathered the Cubs and Scouts around him in the church hall. It was Bob-a-Job week, an event which required a few words of caution.

"Now then, lads," he began. "You all need to stay safe this week. You know the kind of jobs you might be asked to do, so please remember not to take on anything that your parents or I, or you yourself, might consider dangerous or too much for you. Alright Joey?" He gave Joe Latimer a particularly hard stare as the lad was more than a little reckless these days.

Everyone nodded dutifully.

"What if no one wants us?" asked Billy.

Theo sighed. "Then you move on, don't you? Remember to have the customer sign your cards when you've done the job to their satisfaction, and bring the money back here to me by five each day. Now, are there any more questions?"

There were not. The lads knew the drill. They looked very smart in their uniforms – a good, presentable bunch. Mr Wichelow dismissed them and went to spend an hour with his beehives in the wilderness.

Dean and Joey cycled down Market Street to Ironwell, knowing the rest of the troop would be heading the other way, down Merland Way or up into the town. The two had decided they would be more likely to be paid extra if they aimed for places which rarely received a visit from the Cubs.

Miss Winstanley at the mill was second on their list.

Fay was adjusting Persephone's new poke bonnet when they hailed her from the road. The donkey gave the boys a long-suffering look and butted Joey in the chest. Horace, the milkman's aged nag, stood chewing thoughtfully in the shade of a chestnut tree next to three donkeys and a mule.

"Morning, you two. What's the lark today then?" grinned Fay, grinning toothily.

"Bob-a-job, Miss," Dean informed her. "Need anything doing?"

"Well, as a matter of fact I do. You any good at working a broom? Got a new donk arriving this afternoon from the seaside somewhere, and I need to keep it inside for a bit, so the stable could do with a sweep out. That of any interest?"

"Oh yes, we can do that," they cried. Just the thing. A nice indoor task out of the hot sun. It shouldn't take too long.

The undercroft of the mill where the animals were stabled was indeed cool and dim. The sound of the millrace echoed loudly as the water poured over the little weir beyond the mossy brickwork making them wonder how anything could possibly manage to sleep in there. It was a huge undercroft, and a little grim. It was not as empty as the boys had expected. Part of the space had a brick floor and had been boxed into stalls a hundred years or so ago, while the rest was beaten dirt and a few dead weeds. Pieces of harness hung on wooden pegs and there was a green painted two-wheeled pony trap resting on its shafts at the far side. Nettles and ferns grew from the floor at the damper margins where bands of light filtered through the broken timber walls.

"Wow, this is spooky," said Dean.

"I s'pose it is a bit," agreed Miss Winstanley. "Now then, this stall is where I think I'll put him. See those rings in the wall? I can snub him to those if he's a nibbler."

"A nibbler?" asked Joey.

"Likely to nibble my bottom when I feed him. I don't want a chunk taken out of me, do I? It'll take a while for him to get used to us, it always does. They soon come around of course. Tulip and Horace and the others will help."

"You'll soon have a proper donkey sanctuary," said Dean, passing Joe a broom. "Do you rescue them from a fate worse than death, Miss? Or *death*?" he added, as he and Joe tied their scarves around their faces to prevent breathing in the dust.

Fay laughed. "Yes, I suppose. The knackers yard, if you know what that is. I've always got along with the rejects in life. Can't take them all in though, more's the pity. They usually arrive with a few health problems – like this one – and vets cost money, alas."

"One of our mates at school works at the vet's in town," said Joe, pushing a shovel vigorously at the heaps of muck.

"Oh? Mr Quincy?"

"Yes. Jonah works there whenever he can. He's good at animals."

"And birds. I helped him rescue a swan once."

"Goodness, that must have been dangerous."

"Yes, I suppose it was. You should make friends with Jonah. He'd look after your donkeys for you. Free probably."

Dean was not sure about that statement. Offering veterinary care gratis was not really in the Cubs' remit. "We could maybe come by again one day, if you like," he said, frowning at Joe. "Bring Jonah along too. He knows a lot of health stuff."

"About our four-legged friends?" asked Fay. "Well, thank you. Very kind. Boys often drop by here. Or paddle up in canoes and suchlike. I shall look forward to meeting him." She doubted this lad could be of any practical use but she felt this was a day to Encourage The Young.

Dean and Joey eventually finished their floor-sweeping, shovelled the pile of muck into a heap by the field gate, and stuffed a feed-net with fresh hay so the new arrival would have something to munch on. Joey managed to soak his shoes when filling the water trough from a zinc can, and Dean had a coughing fit. Miss Winstanley was all smiles at the end of their hour and not only signed their cards and handed over some money, but also provided sandwiches, crisps and a bottle of Lucozade each.

The boys ate their snacks on the steps of the war memorial, thinking how pleasant it was to be almost grown up and working for actual money in the real world.

"I wonder what she'll call that new donkey," mused Dean.

"Luke. Get it? Luke O'Zade," laughed Joey. "Ha! It'd be good that would. We could hitch him up to that little wagon thing and take him down the shops."

"Yeah! Doing people's shopping. That's gotta make us a bit more than a bob-a-job," said Dean, ever the entrepreneur.

Nurse Presley receives a shock

"What do you mean, they're out?" cried Nurse Presley as she stood on Miss Fisher's doorstep.

"Miss Fisher's at the seaside and Jim's gone round his granny's," Rick Hodges from next door informed her calmly. "It's the little ones' school outing. They're at Randel Bay."

"Well *when*, pray tell, might they be expected home again?"

Rick shrugged his shoulders in a manner that irritated Hilary Presley beyond words. He let himself in though his own front door and was gone. Hilary stood and fumed a while longer, then took a determined step towards the front gate.

The nurse screamed loudly and jumped back in fright as a small animated rock appeared to roll rapidly through the bed of irises and Solomon's Seal. It crashed into the front wall with a terrifying thwack and stopped, as if stunned. Hilary clutched her bag.

The curate happened to be passing and saw her alarm.

"Oh, Nurse," he cried, "Whatever is it?"

"There's a… It's a… " stammered Hilary, pointing.

Mr Wichelow leaned over the wall and stared at the offending object with her. He stretched out his arm and picked the rock up. Some scaly legs emerged and waved around, affronted at being held upside down.

'Oh!" grinned the curate. "It's only a tortoise! Poor thing's rather dazed I should imagine. Look, it has this address painted on its shell. What a hoot."

"A hoot is it? A tortoise you say? I never did see such a thing. It fairly scared the wits out of me. Why would it be hurling itself at yon wall, d'ye think?"

"Probably trying to escape. The vicar told me this one is particularly adventurous. They found him fallen down the well on the corner once. I expect it's looking for a mate somewhere." Theo stroked the tortoise's shell. Hannibal's head emerged. He started snapping his mouth and looking as cross as any tortoise could.

"There there, old boy. No good trying to leap over the garden wall to find a girlfriend, you know. You'll give yourself a horrible headache. I doubt you'll find another tortoise around here to set your cap at anyway."

Hilary Presley, fully restored to complete self-control and natural huffiness, lost patience with this whimsical smut.

"I have no doubt you're well-able to discover where this wee dinosaur should be penned, Reverend," she cried, "So if you'll excuse me, I'll be about my business."

She closed the gate behind her and drove off.

Theo stood stroking the struggling tortoise for a while longer, then gently put him back by the irises. It was a good thing Miss Fisher had painted her address on the animal's shell. Maybe a tether would also work well these warm afternoons when reptilian thoughts lightly turned to hopes of romance.

Jim appeared, limping along in his own dreamworld of plants, plants and more plants. He greeted the curate and closed the gate behind him while Theo explained why he was standing there. Jim smiled and picked up the escapologist. Hannibal put his head out to be stroked. Jim's was a touch he knew well.

"He must've dug his way out again. We keep him in the back in a sort of pen on the grass. But he likes adventures, don't you boy?"

Jimmy pulled his latchkey out from the neck of his shirt and unlocked the front door, still clutching the tortoise. Mr Wichelow waved them adieu, thinking what a pleasant little story he had witnessed – the happy orphaned child and his wandering tortoise, taken in and adopted by a lonesome old lady. He sighed. His own childhood had been rather sparse too. It was only now Theo was discovering the joys of being part of a friendly community. In Banford, at St Andrew's, and as part of the Williams' chaotic household he was finding his feet. He had his bees too – an added bonus. Bees were like family to Rev Wichelow.

And the Cubs and Scouts, he remembered. One must remember the lads.

The curate sauntered down the lane, doing his best to whistle through his teeth like the milkman. One day he'd manage it. One had to have a bash at things in this life. Have a go, Joe, and not give up, was going to be his motto. Hannibal's adventurous attitude was setting them all an example.

Coming home

Bella had really enjoyed the school outing to Randel Bay. She sat with her children on the bus, feeling very windswept and a little sunburnt. Her shoulders tingled and there was sand under her fingernails.

She glanced at Brian Dunwoody, sitting next to her. He wasn't the most popular boy in the class so had found it hard to partner-up with anyone. She guessed most teachers were stuck with sitting next to the odd-kid-out on trips such as this. Still, Brian looked as though he had had a nice time. He was fast asleep against the window, his hair stiff with salt and his hands sandy and grubby. He appeared to have lost a sock. He was clutching a bucket containing a piece of seaweed and a little empty crab shell. The close atmosphere in the bus was making the bucket decidedly smelly.

Bella stood up and wrestled with the overhead skylight, finally forcing it upwards with a jerk. A waft of cool air blew down on everyone. Miss Fisher sleepily congratulated her. She was looking quite flushed and had actually removed her cardigan, an occurrence Bella had never before witnessed. Miss Fisher today also sported a floral skirt and open-toed sandals.

"Did you enjoy today?" May whispered to her.

Bella nodded enthusiastically. "Oh I did. I think everyone did, don't you? I'm already looking forward to next year."

"It's a pity that beachside toilet block isn't a little larger," said May, remembering. "It's a long wait for all the girls to go through." The teachers wisely insisted everybody make themselves comfortable for the return journey and also wash the day's grime off their hands. The driver did not deserve too much sandy mud or any unpleasant accidents on his nice flocked seats.

Bella chuckled. "Yes. Maybe next year there will be a few more. I'm surprised there were so few holiday-makers around. It's such a lovely place."

"A little early in the year, possibly," agreed May. "Yes, it is lovely. Quite wild except for those pretty houses set back behind the dunes. Now then, how have you taken to Mayflower do you think? Does it suit you? You certainly suit *us* very well."

"Oh thank you," answered Bella, very touched by the veteran teacher's unsolicited approbation. "I actually love it. It fits in with everything I have always loved about school – the family feeling of support, the sensible pace of the infants' curriculum, the use of the outdoors to show the children what's truly valuable in life."

May nodded. Mayflower certainly included all that. "And the buildings? Surely you would have liked a little more up-to-date equipment and some draught-free classrooms?"

Bella shook her head. "I don't think those things really matter. There's loads of extra equipment anyway in the attic isn't there? Like that old projector. That little storage room is a real Aladdin's cave. Our school has a splendid working library – not many primary schools have those any more, let alone a librarian. And Mr Green and Terry can build anything, I should think. They made me such a neat little hamster house, you know. I think Hammy Two's delighted with it."

May laughed. The new pet house was indeed a thing of beauty. "So you're going to stay?"

"Oh yes," Bella assured her happily. "Maybe one day I'll even be lucky enough to become headmistress myself and continue to run the school the way I like. Which is to say exactly as Mrs Clark does now."

May studied the girl's face. She certainly looked content. Mrs Clark could do a lot worse than hand it all over to Bella Delgado one day.

The old coach bumped and rattled along the country lanes, following the sunset towards home. The driver squinted his eyes and kept adjusting his sun visor, superficially irritated and yet inwardly content that another successful Mayflower School outing was ending happily. No one had gone missing and no one had thrown up or asked him to stop the bus. Not yet. He tugged down the peak of his cap and pulled the knob that squirted the windscreen with water to wipe away the build-up of dead insects. Yes, another good day, he thought. Be home in time for supper.

The parents collected their tired darlings from the school gate and it was not long before Miss Fisher herself was opening her own front door, hoping Jim had the kettle on.

He stood at the sink, a colander full of freshly shucked peas in his hand. She kissed his forehead and sat down in her favourite chair.

"I brought some more shells for you to edge that garden path with," she informed him. She pushed her picnic bag towards him.

"Oh, what can that be?" he asked, spotting a feathery plant sticking out of the top. It must have had a very long journey.

May's eye's twinkled. "Ah, now that's your *real* present," she said. "Part of the edge of the car park by the beach has crumbled away since we were last there. It was probably that nasty storm last month that did it. Anyway, this tamarisk was on the brink with half its roots hanging out, so I rescued it. I thought if anyone can give it a home and make it grow, you can."

Jim picked it up gently. It definitely looked peaky but was not yet entirely dead. Miss Fisher had tied her hanky round the little root ball and pulled a plastic bag over that. It might just survive. He grinned and came over to hug her. "It's brilliant," he said. "Thank you. Can I go and dig it in? It will be thirsty."

So am I, thought May. She waved him out into the garden while she filled her own mug with tea. If there was a plant that needed some digging in, she knew she must take a back seat.

There he was, her boy, crouching by the lavender bush, making room for the scraggy old plant, finding it a stick and tying it up as tenderly as if he were putting Gwennie's booties on her delicate little feet. Giving it a drink of rainwater, creating a shelter. She sipped her brew and watched.

My lad is going to be quite tall when he's older, she thought.

Jim Fisher finally seemed to be growing normally. His limbs were stronger, his waistline slimmer. His skin was a nice golden brown, his hair was thick, and his mind was brimming with botany and horticulture. What more could a mother want? She stared up at the evening sky and watched a flock of birds dipping and darting over the meadows.

What more indeed?

Only to take these blessed sandals off and have an early night, she decided.

New Mexico

"Yes, well, it's all desert I suppose," said Mr Chivers, vaguely.

"Desert? Like sand dunes?"

"No. More sort of gritty, I think. With some sage and creosote bushes. Windy, too, going by what Joe Granger said." Ernest was trying to imagine what New Mexico was like. He was basing most of his ideas on old cowboy films, which even he knew were mostly filmed in southern California or Spain. "Why do you ask?"

"I wanted to send Mrs Shaw a picture of us on a bus all coming to see her. It would be Mr Fox's red bus and it would be arriving at the front gate of her school. And she would be standing there looking surprised," Mungo informed him.

"You don't remember Mrs Shaw do you?" asked Ernest as he hunted along the library shelf for a suitably helpful book.

"No, but we send letters to her American school, and her Grade 1 children write back. It's pen-pals. Mine's called – what's he called? – Dennis. That's right. He's a boy. He has two sisters and two puppies. His real name at home is Husky something. It means he is an actual Indian warrior who doesn't give up. But at school they call him Dennis." Mungo was full of information today.

They sat looking at a book on New Mexico for a while, then Mungo's time was up and he went back to class, taking several books with him. He drew a picture of himself and Dennis riding a horse across the desert on the reverse of the letter he had composed that morning. Unfortunately he ran out of yellow crayon, so the gritty ground was rather more brown than he would have liked. However, Miss Delgado said it was excellent and that Dennis was sure to like it.

"The horses' legs were hard," added Mungo, doubtfully.

"But the hooves are a really good shape. I like the trail of hoof-marks too."

"I seen those in the mud at the donkey field," Mungo told her.

"Our donkey field?"

"No, the one with real donkeys in. In Ironwell," he said.

"Oh yes, I know it," nodded his teacher. "Now then, go and tidy up and then we will be ready for some more Olga da Polga."

Mungo hopped off and was soon back with the others, sitting cross-legged at the teacher's feet, listening rapt to their favourite tale. Bella could not help wondering, as she ended the chapter and closed the book, what the children in New Mexico listened to. Maybe she should write to Mrs Shaw herself and find out.

Although she drew the line at adding a colourful drawing on the back of her letter. Her ability to render horses' legs accurately was only about half as good as Mungo's.

After school

Sandi and Bella often finished their schoolday with a game of tennis on the grass court. Terry Green had mown it, redrawn the tramlines and put up the net for them. He had even oiled the metal gate. It was fun having a knock-about after school in the late afternoon sunshine when the only other sounds were the calling birds and the wind through the trees. The women biffed the ball back and forth in complete contentment.

"Oh game, set and match!" cried Sandi as the final shot whizzed past her. "Well done."

Bella, pleased she had won today's game, threw her racket in the air and shouted hooray. She knew she ought not to crow with delight but Sandi would take her exuberance in good part. They gathered up their things, let the net down a little, and wandered back through the lodge's stable yard to the old terrace around the back of the building.

It was looking far less weedy than usual. A large stack of new timber stood to one side, waiting to be used in the renovations inside.

"Gosh, will they be using all that, do you suppose?" asked Sandi.

"I guess so. It seems rather a lot doesn't it? Mr Tremayne says they need to create better workspaces out of some of the rooms with partitions, so perhaps that's what it's for. I say, here comes one of yours." Bella sipped fizzy orange from her can and nodded towards the path beside the ancient shrubbery where a figure was slowly ambling towards them. "Hello, Jimmy!"

He looked up from his handful of leaves and smiled. "Hello Miss Delgado. Hello, Mrs Raina." He came over and sat beside them on the step, resting his satchel on his knees. "Was that you playing tennis? I could hear."

"Yes. Miss Delgado won. She is a very good player," Mrs Raina informed him. "Do you still play in the wilderness after school?" In her opinion no one should be allowed to wander in the jungle unsupervised after school hours, but she knew this was probably unenforceable. Certainly not children who climbed and then fell out of trees and broke their legs.

"Auntie May knows I'm here," said Jim, reassuringly. He showed her a little red Snoopy wristwatch. "We found this in a junk shop so I can tell the time." He was proud of this new accomplishment. "I'm to be home by five. It's macaroni cheese for supper. I like that."

Bella laughed. "You like everything," she said, remembering how he relished Ivy Green's dinners. "No wonder your Auntie May says you're growing like a weed. Do you have fertiliser in your sandals?"

Jim burst out laughing. That was a grand joke. He wished he had thought of it. "No," he cried, "But I can get some!"

"How's the leg these days?" asked Mrs Raina.

"It's all mended, thank you very much," he said. "My scar pulls a bit where the tree bit me, and I can't kick so well as I yuster. But it's OK." He always had his answers ready now. "I could bring you some fertiliser for your children's allotments, Miss. I load it in the box on my contraption. I get it down Mint Farm Stables."

"Do you? That's very enterprising of you. How much does a load cost?" Bella was impressed.

"Nothing, for our school," he informed her. "The man lets me have it free. I get a load and take it to anyone who wants it. It's good stuff. Old, not new. New wouldn't be good."

"Really? Why not?"

"It's poster rot down first so it's not too strong. I got a book with it in."

"That's what it's *supposed* to do, is it?" corrected Sandi, automatically. "Well, who knew?"

Jim grinned at her. She was always nice to him. He loved his extra time with her in the little quiet room at the top of the building. It was like being in a bird's nest, close up under the old eaves near the sky. You could ask Mrs Raina to explain anything, and she always would. It wasn't often he could tell her something in return. "Do you have a garden at your house, Mrs Raina?"

"Yes, but it isn't really big enough for vegetables. Mr Raina doesn't like gardening very much anyway. We buy our produce from the greengrocer."

"There might be a greengrocer's in the new shops down at Abbey Lodge, mightn't there?" asked Bella. "They say it's going to sell only local farm produce. Maybe our students could flog their excess lettuces there in the Summer. It would be a very convenient place to shop on your way home."

Sandi laughed. "It would indeed. I've been lucky enough to be given quite a lot of veg from these allotments. We do like fresh vegetables in our house. Especially Raja and Nanda when they are home from school." Her two children were at boarding school all term and she missed them very much. "Nanda makes a very good vegetable curry."

"Oooh, I like that," said Jim. "You gave Auntie May the recipe didn't you?"

"I did. I'm glad you like it. It's very healthy."

Jim left them at the gate. They turned and waved to him as they crossed the road together on their walk into town past the new zebra crossing.

He decided to use the crossing and was soon in St Andrew's churchyard, kicking through the grass and looking for his mother's name on the memorial plates at the far end. Nowadays, he was much less worried about visiting her than he had been. Now it was a place of life, rather than death. In fact, he enjoyed coming here and tending her little plot. It drew him closer to her.

He soon found the place and cleared the weeds around it a little. Last week he had planted a tiny rose there. He gave the plant a little water from the heavy old watering can Rev Bill kept by the outside tap. It looked to be doing well.

"There you are, Mum," he whispered. "Nice and tidy. I'm off home now 'cos Snoopy says it's time for macaroni cheese. See you next week."

Toby Tremayne bumped into him as he walked back over the zebra crossing.

"What ho, Jim me-lad. What news from the rialto?"

Jim frowned. "I didn't come that way, Sir," he said. "But it's time for tea so I'm going home."

"Excellent. Jolly good. I'm off for a walk to the pub. Have you seen Mr Green anywhere?"

"No, Sir. But I can hear Stringer coming. I 'spect Mr Green won't be far behind. Bye."

"Adios, child. Ah there you are, Mr Green. Ready for our game of darts? Yes, good dog, Stringer, get down. Right off we trot."

* * *

19.

Racing

Skip and Toby go racing

The MG slewed to its usual rattling halt outside White Cottage. Toby hooted the horn and leaned over to open the passenger door. He and Skip were off to the races.

"Come on, hop in!" he cried.

Skipper trotted down the path trying to do up her handbag, and hopped in. "Morning!" she gasped.

They accelerated away and hurtled dramatically round the corner onto the Fenchester road, Toby accentuating the fun with wild elbow movements and cries of "Nyaaar!"

"I hope you have your lucky shoes on," Toby called against the gale of wind. "I want to win a few bucks today."

"I'll need them if you're going to drive like Jehu son of Nimshi all the way," Skip replied tartly, as she clutched at her hat with one hand and the dashboard with the other. "It's a good job we've not far to go."

The local racetrack was out on the downland beyond the town's southern limit. Today it lay like a shining swathe of gorgeous green silk thrown across the patchwork of dull agricultural fields. It boasted a modest grandstand, a collection of paddocks, a car park, some stabling and very little else. It was far from posh, but was popular with the county's racegoers nevertheless.

They parked in a dusty field and made their way to the entrance, where they were surprised to encounter Mr Berry, the PTA secretary, looking very sharp in a shiny blue suit and a similar hat to Toby's.

"Good morning," he greeted them, peering through his rather thick-lensed glasses. He was so like his son Bill in Form 4, it was uncanny. He had a racing paper tucked under his arm. "Nice day for it."

"It is indeed. Have you any hot tips for a couple of beginners?" asked Toby, wondering whether Mr Berry was a bookie.

Mr Berry grinned, showing a collection of mis-aligned teeth. "No, not really. Except maybe Avalanche in the twelve o-clock. I know a bloke who knows the trainer. Might be worth a flutter. I'm thinking of possibly buying a leg one day."

"Are you? Then I hope someone else buys the other three. Thanks, Mr Berry. We'll certainly follow Avalanche with keen interest. You heading this way? No? Well, we'll bid you adieu."

Toby hustled Skipper this way and that like an expert, causing her to wonder whether he was not as unfamiliar with this type of venue as he made out. After all he had mentioned time spent at Longchamp and Monte Carlo before now. It may not all have been sight-seeing. Today Tremayne was sporting his brown Italian trilby which made him look slightly less like a gentleman and more like a tout in her view. She was not a fan of this hat. Another thing she noted was that he had a wad of cash in his inside pocket, as opposed to her few modest pounds pocket money which were carefully zipped inside a purse within a secure handbag pressed firmly against her side.

They gingerly put a little money on several horses chosen at random, and surprised themselves by breaking even by coffee time. Avalanche finished second in the twelve o-clock, which was additional encouragement. After these heady thrills they shouldered their way into the little restaurant where Skip was convinced she saw Toby bribing the head waiter to find them a good table by the window. It was very pleasant sitting there with him, watching the racegoers in all their finery. The waitress bustled over and Mrs Clark looked up.

"What can I get you?"

"Good afternoon," said Skip in an icy tone. The waitress glanced sharply at her and Skip was gratified to see the woman wilt.

"Oh. Mrs Clark," said Jo Winton jerkily through clenched teeth. "Well, what can I get you?"

Toby glanced up from the menu. "Two beers and a chicken sandwich each," he stated. He could see Skipper's lips pursed shut as if by glue, so knew something was up.

The waitress disappeared.

"Friend of yours?" he enquired mildly.

Skip filled him in. Toby listened, nodding wisely. The look on his companion's face told him how unsettled the encounter had left her. It was energising her in a way no amount of horse-racing ever could. He poured her a hefty glass of red wine and let her disjointed rant fizzle out.

"Well, that seems to have been a very nasty business, but you dealt with it pretty successfully. May must have been terribly hurt, especially as the Parrott woman left too. There's no age-limit on name-calling is there? Unnecessary at any age if you ask me. It left a bad taste all round, I dare say."

Skipper nodded. She had not thought about Jo Winton for ages, but found that she still disliked the woman intensely. She ought to forgive and forget – rise above it, being a supposedly Christian soul. But somehow, where Jo was concerned, it was proving a tough ask. The woman had crossed the boundaries of decent behaviour and couldn't care less.

"I know. I shouldn't let her get me down. I think it was just the surprise at seeing her again – here, of all unexpected places."

"Quite. Now then, forget her. Put the business behind you. No beastly waitress is going to spoil my day out with you. Scoot round this side of the table a bit, and look at the runners in the two-thirty. See anything you fancy?" Toby was determined not to let a passing raincloud mar his enjoyment.

They picked a couple for the three o'clock. One was named Dora's Boy and another Western Pilgrim. They agreed the names were hopeful omens. Dead certs, probably.

A different waitress finally brought their lunch and they resumed their enjoyment of a pleasant day out. There was no need, Skipper decided, to taint a lovely afternoon with ancient misery. Toby was right.

The tired couple eventually drove home fifty-two pounds up, which thrilled them both. Skip's feet were throbbing and she was more than a little windblown by the time they turned into the drive at White Cottage. Dora had some supper ready despite having spent the day in the garden. Toby gave her a bearhug as he was starving.

"You are the best of us, you know that?" he informed her. "Now where's your cooking sherry?"

Dora laughed and sat down. She'd had fun herself in the long herbaceous border, tweaking out stray weeds and tidying up the various plant clumps. Her floral colour scheme of all-white at one end leading through a gradual drift of sunset shades to dark, almost black, flowers at the other was coming along nicely. She was writing down the name of everything she had planted in a little book, including the range of insects and birds that preferred the different areas. She intended keeping this record throughout the years from now on.

"When I'm gone I expect you to weed that border," she informed them both.

Skipper chuckled. "You're not going anywhere yet," she said. "Oh Mum, I forgot! We saw Jo Winton today."

Dora had to think for a moment. "That dreadful person who made May's life such a misery?"

"Yup. She was waiting tables up at the racetrack restaurant."

"Well, she *has* come down in the world, and no mistake," said Dora, thoughtfully. "I wonder who she'll upset there. Did you speak to her?"

"No, not as such. She pushed off pretty much as soon as she recognised me."

"Hmph. Waitressing eh? I thought she worked at that nursery in town?"

"So did I."

"This pie is delicious, Dora," interjected Toby. "And I don't like pie."

"Oh, yes you do," the two ladies laughed in unison.

His remark had the desired effect of ending the tedious conversation about Mrs Jo Winton, and led to a long discussion on the various types of pie in the world, both savoury and sweet, and the different merits of each. As usual, Toby and his gift of the gab brought a degree of level-headed good humour back into Skipper's life. It was quite a talent.

All-change at the lodge

Reg stood peering up at the front of Longmont Lodge, checking the newly painted window-frames. The place looked wide awake and almost habitable since it had started to receive a face lift. Ivy stood beside him in a smart new zip-up jacket and striped skirt. She pointed towards the roof.

"They going to replace that new dormer roofing Mrs Clark had to 'ave done?"

"No. No need," her husband replied. "Good for ten years yet. Mr Tremayne says it's all surprisingly sound inside too, 'cept for that bit by the window on that corner yonder where the rain's rotted out the sills. Gotter replace the whole lower window frame."

"That'll cost a bob or two. They keeping all them nice stained glass bits?"

"Yerse. They finished the pointin' and the brickwork last week. Cleaned it all down, like. Mort o' spiders, Terry said there was."

Their son was helping Paul Moore and his crew with some of the work. Terry had never been keen on spiders ever since his sister had once dangled a plastic one over the banisters as he was going up to bed. Reg and Ivy chuckled at the memory.

"They gonner paint all that Tudory woodwork black again?"

"Yerse. Sharpen it up, that will. Look nice against the white. You comin' inside?" asked Reg.

"Well just for a bit. I said I'd go round the vicarage later and price up them cakes. Mrs Bick's helping too, and 'Liza Muggeridge. And her niece, that Miss Delgado. She's got a right fancy name and no mistake," said Ivy, puffing up the steps to the front door after Reg.

Stringer shot past their legs and galloped along the bottom corridor to where he knew Terry had been working all week. He trotted gloomily back when he found Terry was no longer there.

"This the only kitchen?" asked Ivy, sniffing at the small room Reg had hitherto used as something of a hideout. "If upstairs is all going to be made into classrooms they'll want somewhere bigger and brighter for a cuppa tea."

"They're talkin' about convertin' the main dinin' room for that. Refectory Common Room, they're going to call it. Have one of them self service counters and things in packets."

"Packets? Lor, people won't want to turn up and eat packets. Plus they'll need 'elpers for that. Packets don't materialise out of thin air. Soulless things, packets is. Cups don't wash themselves up, neither. You go out in the evening for a nice little course on something arty, you don't want to be makin' new friends over a packet and a paper cup. Will the tea come from a vending machine?" Ivy was scornful.

"No. Boiling water out of a kettle, 'e says, and proper cups. Tremayne said they might get one or two servers in. Part time, like. Serve sandwiches, tea and coffee and whatnot. Tidy up after folks. Come and look down the end here."

They walked further down the corridor to the main entrance hall, a vision of past grandeur, all solid oak, fancy plasterwork and tile. It was looking much brighter than Ivy remembered. A dust sheet lay on the wide old stairs and someone had been up a tall stepladder and started cleaning the enormously fancy window.

"Sir Garnet loved this 'ouse," said Reg, folding his arms. "I'm glad it's going to be used again."

"All for education, Sir Garnet were," agreed Ivy. "Funny old boy, but a good heart."

"Bit like this place," agreed Reg. "Good hearted. Like you too, sometimes, old lady."

Ivy cuffed him and pottered back outside. Time for some light relief at the vicarage with her own friends. She couldn't be doing with husbands going all sentimental over a building renovation.

Friends

Kay was following Stringer and Nicky who were trotting side by side along Mayflower Road on the Thursday afternoon of half-term, bent on exploration. It was funny how those two stayed friends, the child thought. They were so different.

She kicked along, scuffing her new sandals as much as she could because their polished perfection annoyed her. She had pushed her bicycle (which had a slow puncture) all the way from town where she had gone to purchase some sunglasses with her pocket money, and was coming back this way in the hope that she might bump into Jimmy or Dean or Angela or maybe even crosspatch Joe. But her friends were nowhere to be found. Only furry pals seemed to be out this hot afternoon.

"Stringer! Here," she called to the dog. He wagged his tail and licked her hand as she stopped to pet him. Nicky the black cat rubbed around her legs. She found a peppermint in her pocket and offered it, but neither animal was impressed. She sighed and put it in her own mouth. The two animals skipped off and turned down the lane to the railway station, where Kevin Smith and Mr Coker were about to enjoy a cup of tea and a slice of seed cake in the quiet coolness of the waiting room.

Kay pushed on the way she was going, thinking about her Mayflower chums.

Angela was out playing with Linda Wright who lived in the next road. Angela was alright most of the time, but had not turned out to be quite as adventurous as Kay would have liked. She wasn't one for getting muddy in the fields or soaked looking for minnows in the shallows of the river. Not for long, anyway.

Dean Underwood would be Kay's preferred playmate out of all of them, but he was apparently in Ledgely with his mother buying something or other. School shirts, that was it. Kay liked Dean because he was always cheerful. He was nice-looking too.

All the girls wanted Dean to like them, so it was gratifying he included Kay amongst his genuine friends. He was reliable too. He was kind. He might still be besotted with little Zoe Smith the redhead from Form 2, but she was just a baby and he'd surely get over her one day. The thing about Dean that nobody but Kay apparently noticed was that he kept his real nature hidden. Like she did herself. Dean yearned to be a dancer, but his mother discouraged it, his sister laughed at it, and no one (apart from school) genuinely thought it was a proper activity for a boy of ten. So Kay felt deep sympathy for Dean. After all, she reasoned, he was old enough to know his own mind, wasn't he? Shouldn't he be encouraged to fulfil his dream? Ten years old was when you were a completely formed human being, in Kay's view. You knew what you liked and who you were at ten. Kay vowed to always remember how it felt to be ten. She recognised Dean's frustrated hopes. She knew that when she was old enough to be free of her parents she would become a writer of some kind. They wouldn't stop her doing what she wanted, no sir. But she would only become an author when she had lived a full life and had something serious to write about. She wondered whether Dean would one day fulfil his ambition of becoming a professional dancer. Probably not. Unlike her, he never complained or whined about the thwarting of his innermost desires. He didn't have Kay's stubborn streak. He simply shut up and tried his best to fit in with other people's plans. He was too nice. No doubt he would end up as a plumber or something normal. What a waste. He would be such a great dancer. Kay reckoned Dean dealt with life's setbacks differently to her and Joey. It was a shame.

Joe Latimer used to be a good playmate. She and he had become friends when she first arrived at Mayflower, tracking through the wilderness with her, ranging over the fields and buying sweets at the newsagent's after school. He had been up for anything then, even rescuing swans with Jonah. Joe had been fun, and easy to get along with. He would let Kay join in the kick-about on the field with the lads if she wanted. He would even go to the cinema with her, and stand up for her when anyone picked on her. But gradually he had become rougher and more disagreeable. More unpredictable. She didn't altogether like Joey Latimer any more. Plus, he idolised Dean Underwood to the point of obsession. It was silly. He didn't seem to care for the company of tomboy girls any longer.

Then, last but not least, there was little Jim Fisher. He might be a strange duck, but Kay saw herself and Jim as two odd-ones-out. Fish out of water. She knew what it was like to be alone – standing off to the side, looking on. Jim did too, only he handled it better than she did. Despite everything that had happened to him, he was completely sure of himself and comfortable about life. He accepted what ever came his way with a kind of grace. He didn't care tuppence what anyone else thought about him. Not that Jim was a wimp, for all his weedy pixie looks. He could stand up for himself, and for what mattered to him. He possessed a very hard right fist when pushed beyond his limit. No one took him for a fool any more either, even though his schoolwork was not the greatest. He knew plenty of important stuff. He understood everything about growing plants, about nature and the countryside. Everybody knew that. He was impressive and pretty brainy in Kay's view. And Jim always managed to be friendly, and let you share his world. He didn't insist you liked it, he just showed it to you. You had to make the first friendly approach, but once he took to you he was very loyal. Jim judged nobody, even if they were as different from him as could be. If you were interested in what he was interested in, there was no better companion. If you weren't, he ignored you. He was his own man already, Kay decided. As set in his ways as, well, Father Christmas. He would be the same at eighty as he was now at eight, she guessed. He had been through a lot, as Kay felt she had. Only Jimmy had figured out his own salvation.

Kay did not think there was similar hope for her. She would probably be wandering and searching and making mistakes all her life.

So there you were. That was it. Friends. Funny how people were so different.

Kay crunched up the tiniest remains of her peppermint and looked about through her new sunglasses. Over the wall in the field opposite the Mint Public House she could see Mrs Tuttle trying to groom her rotund pony Twitch, who kept trying to bite her backside. Kay lay her bicycle down in the undergrowth and went over.

"Hello, Mrs Tuttle!" she called. "Would you like me to hold her head for you?"

Fiona turned round grinning. "Oh! Kay, how wonderful! Would you? Do you have time? She keeps nibbling the back pocket of my jeans and she's had all the carrots I brought. Honestly, if I'm ever going to get someone to buy her she has to look better than she does this afternoon. I've never seen so many burrs in her coat, and its full of dirt."

Kay grasped Twitch's halter firmly and stood while Fiona brushed and plucked at the pony's coat.

"Were you out for a bike ride?" puffed Fiona.

"Puncture, worse luck. I was walking home. No one's around to play with."

"Hmm. It's hot too. Tim and Mr Tuttle are in the back garden trying to get the baby to paddle in the blow-up paddling pool they bought her. I took the chance to come and do this."

"You're selling Twitch?"

"Trying to. She won't make a very good pony for Gwennie, she's too cranky. Maybe we'll buy a gentler one when she's a little older and if she actually wants a pony. Do you ride?"

Kay did. She had lessons with Captain Henderson on a Monday after school. She loved it, imagining she was out on the wild prairies chasing bandits instead of trotting obediently along sedate English bridle paths. The riders all had to wear hard hats and string gloves and jodhpurs, which was a bore. Kay would rather have ridden a Spanish saddle with long stirrups, and sported a bright check shirt and Stetson. Fiona laughed in agreement when she told her.

"I'll ask my Mum if my little sister wants a pony if you like. My step-dad will buy her anything she asks for."

Kay thought the spiteful little pony would be about the right temperament for Cynthia – mean.

"Who's your step-dad?"

"Nigel Armitage," glowered Kay.

"Don't you like him?" asked Fiona. The girl looked like a thundercloud.

"Not much," Kay admitted.

Fiona delved no further. It did not take a psychologist to understand resentful children. "Can you bring her round a bit? I can't get to that other leg. There, that's it. All done, now, Twitch. Off you go and don't end up in that bramble patch again or you'll be the death of me. Come on Kay. The least I can do is offer you a glass of squash and a biscuit as a thank you. Maybe Tim could fix that tyre for you – save having to ask your step-dad. Golly, this stile is a bit rickety. Now then, pick up your bike and let's go find the others round the back shall we? Thank you so much for your help. I couldn't have managed half so well without you."

Kay smiled and went happily with Mrs Tuttle. Her other friends might be elsewhere having fun, but she was open to making new ones this afternoon. You just had to make a start.

Rev Bill goes visiting

Rev Bill went to the Cottage Hospital for his usual Wednesday afternoon visits. He had a few parish magazine's left in his plastic carrier when he was finished, and thought he would leave them at the little shop by the cafe in the front entry on his way out.

He checked in on Mrs Money and her tiny new baby that he privately thought ought to be christened 'Penny'.

He sat beside Mr Blenkinsop for a while, even though the poor man was still comatose.

He talked to the ward sister regarding old Miss Hartigan, whom he considered ought to be moved into a side room in order to give the rest of the ward a rest from her endless shrieking. The sister explained that side rooms were all in use and the elderly demented lady would just have to be sedated. Bill was upset about this, knowing how shy and reserved poor Miss Hartigan had always been in years past, and how much she would not have wanted to upset anybody or be a nuisance in her final days.

It had been a much more cheerful experience to chat with a lad called Tyson who was having his leg put into a plaster cast. He was one of Mayflower's ex-students by only a year or two, but looked large enough to be in the sixth form at secondary school. Tyson lived opposite St Andrew's on the corner of Church Road, so Bill knew him quite well. He had broken his leg playing cricket, he told the vicar. Tripped over his own feet. The boy chattered happily away about school life for a while, and really perked Bill out of his gloomy mood.

As he arranged the magazines on the counter, Bill mused on life – its moods and seasons. Then the doors swooshed open and in came Mike Paton.

"Oh good afternoon, Vicar. Coming in or going out?"

"On my way home," answered Bill. "Can't say I'm a fan of hospitals, though don't tell the man upstairs." Bill imagined Quakers most likely had a more frequently-used communication line to the Almighty than some folk. They possibly used it more assiduously than knee-benders like himself. "You visiting someone?"

"No no. Just delivering some withdrawn library books. Ernest's outside parked by the kerb with the engine running so I've got to be quick. I thought I'd run in and see if there was anyone to help carry the boxes up to the children's wing. A porter or something." Mike gazed around hopefully.

"Lucky I was here then," said Bill. "Come on, I'll give you a hand. How many boxes are there? Do we need to throw a patient off a trolley?"

They found Ernest waiting anxiously beside a grass verge and retrieved two awkward boxes of books. He drove off to wait somewhere less likely to cause a traffic jam while Mike and Bill lugged the boxes back indoors. They were heavier than they looked, but it did not take long to deposit them with the children's ward sister. She was delighted with the donation, but said she would have someone wipe a little disinfectant over each before allowing them onto the bookshelves. You never knew.

As the two men were returning down the corridor they overtook a woman who was struggling along and apparently fighting with a pair of crutches.

"Drat the things!" she cried, trying to swivel the arm pieces and catching Mike smartly on the shin.

"Having trouble?" asked Rev Bill. "Ah! Hello, Miss Winstanley. I see you're battling a pair of recalcitrant sticks. Looks like they're alive. Can we help at all?"

Mike adjusted the things while Fay hung onto the vicar's arm. One of her ankles was expertly bandaged and she clutched a large cloth bag. Bill relieved her of it before she dropped it all over the floor.

"There," said Mike. "They should feel more comfortable now. What have you done to your poor foot?"

"Ankle. Sprained the dratted thing when I fell off the step getting the critters' breakfasts. Slippery. God's way of telling me to buy a pair of wellingtons that fit, really. Long story short, ended up here. Discharged now. Trying to find my way out. Why do they make it so bally difficult? Heading for the bus stop."

Mike had never thought the cottage hospital was big enough to become lost in, but he sympathised. When you were in pain you probably weren't that focused on way-finding.

"I'm sure we can give you a ride home," he offered.

"No I'll take her," said Bill. "You're all the way out on Caster Street. I'll run her back to the mill. I ought to call in to St Mary's anyway. The vestry has a mouse problem."

"Are they nibbling your nice clean surplices?" grinned Mike.

"Hassocks. The mice are making a right old mess. It's as if someone originally stuffed the kneelers with straw or cheese or something and now the varmints have discovered it. Holes everywhere, the churchwarden tells me. There now, Miss Winstanley. Here we are, back out in the fresh air."

Fay smiled her toothy smile. People were so splendid. Her irritation subsided and her all enthusiasm for life brimmed up again like a never-ending well of joy. "A lift would be very kind indeed, Vicar. Thank you, I won't say no. I'll lend you Persephone at Christmas for your manger scene if you like. Tit for tat. One good deed and all that."

Bill laughed. "I might pass on that offer. Though I may come begging a home for a few *surplus* mice in the very near future. Ha ha! I'm sure they'd be happier in your mill than in a village church."

Mike helped Bill settle Fay into his massive old Humber Hawk car. She virtually disappeared behind the dashboard, but felt very grand and safe in its leathery embrace.

"I say, this is posh. Feel like her majesty," she chirruped.

Mike said goodbye, and Bill clambered in beside his passenger.

"Now then, clunk-click. Alright, your ladyship? Let's get you home. Need any shopping on the way? No? Well, that's good. We can enjoy the ride across the heath together on this lovely Summer's day. I'll tell you all about the mice, and you can update me on your donkey sanctuary."

In a cloud of heavy blue smoke, and making a sound like a hippopotamus waltzing on the gravel, the car slowly rolled away.

* * *

20.

The Well

Moving on

A skinny woman hurried along the pavement with her head down. She did not usually come this way – there were too many awkward memories this side of town – but she had missed her bus and so was having to walk. This was a short-cut. However, she was not especially keen on being seen by people she once knew. The last time she had spent any time in this neighbourhood was when she was indulging in a brief extra-marital encounter with a man who rented one of Hall Manor's lodges. But soon after she met him he had left town abruptly, leaving no forwarding address, which she considered very rude behaviour. This whole corner of Banford was poorly behaved, in Jo Winton's opinion. You came here looking to help their backward little school out, willing to lower your standards and fit in. You were very good at the job too – better than they appreciated – but where did it get you? Hounded out of a job, was where, following completely fabricated accusations of harassment. Jo glared at the ground as she scurried along, as if it were also passing judgement.

"Hullo," piped a voice breaking her reverie.

Mrs Winton looked up. A small boy in a check shirt and old fashioned khaki shorts was pushing a box on wheels towards her on the pavement. He didn't look all there, somehow. Mentally impaired, Jo swiftly concluded. Physically too, judging by his odd gait. She had read an article about it. She was just about to stand aside and let him pass when she realised who he was.

"Oh, hello, Jimmy. How are you doing these days?" Mrs Winton tilted her head in a gesture that sought to convey both attentiveness and professional understanding. It was what such a poor little handicapped mite deserved.

Jo racked her brain to remember the lad's circumstances. She prided herself on her encyclopedic knowledge of every child she had ever come in contact with, although this one had only been an Infant when she worked at Mayflower School, not a Junior. Mrs Winton, being obviously intellectually more capable, had worked more closely with the older children than lowly Carol Moore who was far more suited to wiping bottoms and cutting dinosaurs out of sugar paper. A strange little worm of a boy, was this Jimmy-lad, who could have done with fewer allowances being made for him in Mrs Winton's view. Firm discipline and plenty of copying up nice easy work that she drafted out for him were how Jo would have managed Jimmy Birch. Instead he had been molly-coddled by all and sundry since the day he arrived.

"I'm very well, thank you." Jimmy knew he ought to remember this lady's name, but he was struggling. "My leg's still a bit sore sometimes, but this contraption helps."

Mrs Winton had no idea what the child was talking about, but there might be information – some gossip – to be gleaned.

"Oh deary me. Did you fall over? I could look at it if you like. I have some first aid cream in my bag." She undid the clasp and started ferreting around.

"No thank you," cried Jimmy in alarm. "I fell out of a tree by mistake and broke my ankle. But it was weeks ago and it's mended now. In February, in that snowstorm. The tree took a big lump out, but no one can see it because of these shorts. Auntie May says it prolly won't get much more better, but I can still walk around OK. Didn't you used to work at Mayflower school?"

"I did," said Mrs Winton, shutting her bag again with a crisp snap. "Who's Auntie May?"

"Miss May Fisher. She's a teacher. I live with her now."

That was a golden nugget of news that had not come her way before. "Really? How nice. Why is that?"

"My mum got knocked down and died, so I live with Auntie May now."

"In Fen Lane?"

"Yes. Do you want to come and say hello?"

"Oh no thank you. She and I... No thank you. And do you like it there?"

"Yes. I think it's very nice. I have a whole family now."

"What do you mean?"

"Uncles and stuff. I got a nice bedroom, and some pets and medicine."

This was all very interesting. So – feeble old Miss Fisher had taken in a malformed stray, had she? Perhaps she wasn't past being useful after all. Jo Winton shook her head. No, that crabby old hag with her eagle-eye and fussy old fashioned ways represented everything Jo despised. She ruffled little Jimmy's fluffy brown curls.

Jimmy ducked. "Hey!"

"It was very silly to be up a tree in the snow, you know."

Jim scowled.

Mrs Winton smiled and nodded understandingly. "I'm sure you'll soon get over all that nasty bed-wetting you used to do. And one day you might even learn to read," she assured him confidentially. "I would have taught you by now, if I had stayed at Mayflower, but it's not the place it used to be."

No, thought Jim, it isn't. It doesn't have you in it. School was brilliant and he loved it. He decided he did not care for Mrs Winton very much. "Well goodbye," he said abruptly.

Mrs Winton hurried on her way without bothering to respond. He was only a kid after all.

So, she thought, I was right. Mayflower School and all its silly little fuddy-duddy misfits are still stuck in their old-fashioned rut. I wouldn't be surprised if it wasn't closed down by the government soon. She despised the place and every school like it.

If Jo had her way education would be drastically different in the future. People should come to think more like her, and want their children to be up-to-date, learn how to make a ton of money and *have* things like televisions and those new computers she'd read about. They wouldn't be wanting all that digging around in allotments and times tables and teaching them to read fairy tales. They would want much more non-fiction, science and maths. Less history, less singing and silly art. Certainly less French. They'd want television, not old-fashioned steam radio. They would want games and competitions and prizes. There would be rewards and proper incentives. There would be no place in tomorrow's world for sitting in lines and learning your ABC. No place for holding hands and walking in a crocodile or singing nursery rhymes. Jo had read many an article about what the brave new world needed.

She beetled past Mrs Hewitt's house and crossed the road to Stokes' Steps, even happier than before to be leaving the antiquated neighbourhood behind.

Jim Fisher, meanwhile, trotted along and forgot all about her.

Intelligence

A few days later, Jimmy came across Kay sitting on a stile opposite Banford Place, by the boggy piece of land known as Cannon's Level. It was opposite Mint Farm Stables where he was hoping to collect some rotted horse manure for his vegetable patch in his contraption. Kay did not greet him, but he sat down on the lower step of her stile anyway.

"Why are you sitting here?" he asked, flipping on the contraption's brake.

"I'm cross." Kay glowered down at him, wishing he would disappear. She did not want to see school friends today.

"Why?" he asked.

"Why not?"

He couldn't answer that question, but he ploughed on anyway. "Did somebody make you cross?"

'Yes."

"Who?"

"My family."

"Why? What did they do?"

"They just *are*. They're all – you know – boring." It was hard to explain how dreadfully pedestrian the rest of her family was, in her mind. Kay's brain flitted and jumped like an energetic acrobat from one thing to another, while her mother, in particular, seemed to be only able to understand things one at a time and at a walking pace. Like a baby. One – slow – topic – at – a – time. It was very frustrating. Boring.

"They didn't do nothing?"

"Nothing. They just wear me out."

"But you've got loads of toys and a nice big house," persisted Jimmy. "And a bike."

Kay scowled harder. Adults told her she was spoiled, but she didn't *feel* spoiled. She wasn't a brat, was she? "Why do you stay with that old Fisher? She's not your real mum. You could go anywhere you like."

Jimmy looked at her and shrugged. "But I don't want to go anywhere. I *like* my new family. It's only small. It's always been small, I s'pose, but it used to be really *hard* when it was just my old mum and me. I never seen her much. We never... But now I'm at Miss Fisher's its better. I got a bedroom and toys and a grandma and uncles. And a cat. I'm adopted."

"But they're not your real uncles, are they? You've only got a pick–n–mix family. Mine's real, worse luck, only my dad isn't my real dad."

"I don't think it matters if they're real or not. My real Auntie – the one in Ledgely – she don't want me, but my new family does. I think it's nice for *them* all too, because it was like they were just waiting around for me to arrive to make them into a proper group." This was another difficult concept to describe, but Jim felt he had made a fair go of it.

Kay stood up and picked a long stem of grass to suck. Jimmy Birch's opinion did not count for much, she thought dismissively. However, she felt slightly less cross because she now had a new idea to think about. Maybe there was something in what he said. Every family was made up of a different mixture. Pick–n–mix could possibly work alright, even if it wasn't always your own pick.

"See yer," she said.

"See yer," he echoed.

Kay wandered up the lane to Hendy's field, while Jim sat happily for another hour, drawing various grasses in the old exercise book he kept in his battered satchel. His thoughts did not end just because Kay had gone. He was beginning to discover that thinking things over could be done calmly after all, once you found some useful words, and once you had teased the ideas into separate strands. Then you could consider them one at a time, for as long as it took. Drawing helped him think and keep track.

Kay was also having a good long think as she mooched through the fields and footpaths. Jim made a kind of sense, she supposed grudgingly. Families could be, and often were, whoever you happened to have around. After all, people didn't chose who their *actual* relatives were, did they? Kay reckoned it was simply luck if you happened to like them, or had anything in common with any of them.

Only very rarely was anyone (such as, astonishingly, quiet old straight-laced Miss Fisher) ever handed a genuine chance to *choose* a relative off the shelf. And *she* might not have offered to take Jim in if he had been just any old kid. Jimmy Birch had always been special to her. Everyone knew it. Fisher always liked the oddest children in her class, giving them special attention and encouragement. Kay began to see the old lady in a new light. Maybe a fairy godmother watched over people like Miss Fisher and handed out extra pieces of good fortune when they needed it most. Maybe Miss Fisher was herself a fairy godmother.

I could do what she does. Maybe I'll grow up to be like her, Kay thought. Choose my own family and write books. Then I'd be lucky.

Having finally calmed down, Kay turned and went home to see if any of the old photos and notebooks Lady Longmont had given her remained in the jumble under her bed. Most of it she had chucked away, but she did discover a few small black and white photos and some scraps of paper caught under the folds at the bottom of the original cardboard box.

She took them down the garden to the room in the old brick building she was allowed to use as a play-space. Some of its walls must have been part of the medieval priory after which her house was named, as they were built of semi-dressed limestone blocks and odd pieces of ancient arch-work. It was where the family left her completely alone, and she liked it very much for that reason. She was less keen on the spiders and other creatures that obviously enjoyed the peace and quiet too, but once she had set up her old table and put a fresh cushion on top of an orange box for a seat, she was content enough. She left the door open in order to gain a little extra light and hear her mother if she called.

Kay studied the three remaining snaps more closely. One was of a grand house with boys in Eton collars playing croquet. One was of a horse. The last was a studio portrait in a paper frame showing Edwardia Longmont at about twelve years old, sitting bolt upright at an open window. The intelligent face appealed to Kay, so she wedged it into one of the cobwebby corners nearby.

"Knock-knock!" called a voice. Dean came in just as rain began to spit. "Hey! Your mum said you were down here somewhere. Nice hideout."

"Hi Dean. What you doing here?" Kay kicked another orange box over to him and he sat down.

"Nothin'. Came to see if you wanted to come and play over the woods. We've set the parachute up again after we stashed it away last Winter. Me and Joey. He's just buying some sweets at the shop."

"Yeah, alright. I'll ask my mum for some drinks, shall I? I think it's cherryade. Here, can you put this empty box in that corner? Thanks."

Dean chucked it. "What was in it?"

"Just some of Lady Longmont's old rubbish. She's gone dotty. She gave me a huge bag of photos and little books full of numbers she found under the stairs once, but I already binned all those."

Dean wondered whether Mr Tremayne would have liked to see them, bearing in mind where they had come from. The observers might be disbanded but it was the sort of thing he might still be interested in. Maybe there'd be extra pocket money in it.

"Where's the parachute exactly? Over the forest? How did you get it? It must make a great tent." Kay was ready to go. They bolted the door, took some drink from the kitchen fridge without asking, wrote a note, and went looking for Joey.

"Yeah, the parachute is brilliant," said Dean. "It's a bit torn though now, so we might have to chuck it if it rips any more. It's a shame, cos it's been good fun."

Dean and Kay waved as they saw Joey coming up the road towards them with a carrier bag swinging from his fist. "Hey Joe! Kay's coming too. And her mum's given us cherryade."

The afternoon perked up considerably after that. It was fun playing in the trees, ambushing each other and hunting for polar bears despite the odd shower of English rain.

Dean went into school the following Monday, and told Mr Tremayne about the photos and the fate of the little books with numbers in them. Mr Tremayne seemed mildly interested.

Nits

"No, well, it's not the best shampoo I must say. But until they bring out something more effective we're stuck with it I'm afraid, Mrs Bailey," said Nurse Presley, primly. "It's all there is."

Peggy Bailey glowered afresh at the nurse. She put the shampoo sachets in her desk's third drawer and promised herself a good going over with one tonight.

"Now then, who else have I to see? I've finished with Jimmy Fisher, and Brian Dunwoody. That Karen Hunter's hair really needs a proper cut. It's aye like a great bush. Dirt is hard to wash out when it's like that. No wonder she has livestock." The nurse sniffed.

"I thought you said nits preferred clean heads," growled Peggy. She had bushy red hair herself, and today it was definitely itchy. "I've never seen Karen with greasy hair. Her mother keeps her spotless."

"Och, well, there you are then," stated Nurse Presley. With that baffling remark, she picked up her bag and waltzed out, leaving Peggy frowning.

Cathy came in and read the signs. "Nurse gone, has she?" Cathy filled the kettle and flipped the switch down.

"That woman. I wish they'd pension her off."

"Well at least Karen is the only kid in the school with nits this time. Did she check your head too?"

"She did, the old bizzom. She'd just love it if I had some. I believe I'm allergic to her, never mind anything else. Argh, she makes me itch!" Peggy handed over her mug for a rinse. Cathy smiled as she washed up at the little sink in the nurse's room.

Toby Tremayne waltzed in. The ladies saw less of him these mornings now his office had its own direct outside phone line, much to Peggy's relief. She could get on in peace while he gabbed to his newspaper editor or whoever else urgently needed him.

"Morning, beautiful ladies," he greeted them. "Nitty Norah gone? Good. Speaking of nits, might I enquire who the nit-wit was that cut back the rose from over the front porch? It's the most beautiful yellow thing and was going to be glorious in a few weeks." He looked quite peeved.

Cathy sat still and quietly sipped her drink.

Peggy bridled. This morning wasn't improving. "I did," she stated, indicating a couple of buds stuck in a jam-jar on her desk. They looked far too immature to ever blossom.

"No, not just a few buds. There's a whole section been hacked back."

"Couldn't say then," said Peggy curtly. "Mr Green probably. Go and call him a nit-wit." She was still scratching her head as he left the room.

"Did you ask Reg to cut that yellow rose back?" Toby asked Skipper who was bowling down the corridor on her way to take the fourth form for an hour.

"Yes. Has he done it? Oh good," she hurried up the sunlit front stairs, wishing there was a rule that allowed adults to take them two at a time.

Toby frowned again. He strode down the bottom corridor to Reg's boiler room and knocked.

"Yerse?"

Toby popped his head round.

"Morning, Mr Green. That yellow rose has had a bit of a trim."

"Covered in greenfly. Comin' away from the wall. Didn't get cut back last Autumn for some reason. I was told to trim it this mornin' by madame." Reg turned his screwdriver tighter on the piece of electrical pump mechanism he was fixing, puffing a cloud of fragrant tobacco smoke from his pipe.

"A little drastic, wasn't it?"

"Maybe. But drenching greenfly in soapy water does no good. Not for long anyway. Hadn't been tied up prop'ly neither. My fault, I suppose. Most things are around 'ere. So I took me hedge-cutters to it. It'll come back, alright." Reg raised his eyes to his visitor. "Why? Was you attached to it?"

"No, no. It just seemed a shame, is all. I agree greenfly have to be dealt with. But cutting it back so hard seems a terrible shame when it has just started flowering. Ruins the aesthetic of the porch too. Those yellow roses always lend the front a sort of comforting, welcoming look. Very English. Softens the aspect, so to speak."

"Well, there's plenty of that ruddy wisteria left. That lends a somewhat soft aspect to the place. I believe there's a mains water leak somewhere under that front bed, that's why the damn things grow so well." Reg was uninterested in this conversation. What was done was done, what was clipped was clipped. "Anythink else?"

"No, no." Toby hesitated. It was quiet here at the moment. "Do you think the headmistress will pursue anything further following the incident last February, Reg?"

Reg shook his head. "Nope. Why? Are you worried she will, Sir? You know 'er better'n me, but I don't believe she'll say nothing more now it's over and done with. It's the kids' safety she cares about, which is only right and proper, you ask me, seeing as how she's in loco whatsit. Jim's pulled through alright, and the whole thing is fading into the background now our operation is all wound up." Reg flipped his whiskers with an oily finger. "There's no reason for her to get angry no more is there? She's over it, you mark my words. With Sir Hugo gorn, school's back to normal. Did they find any more of that treasure the girl threw out?"

"No. Nothing more, alas, alas, alas. Bloody kid says she only kept a few bits. Chucked the rest in the dustbin weeks ago. What I'd have given to have seen that boxful! What little we *did* manage to salvage was worth it, though. Yes, those few bits were definitely worth it."

Reg looked at Toby and put his screwdriver down. "Right then, if there's nothin' else, I'd best get on, Sir."

Toby backed out. "Yes, OK, thanks Reg," he said.

Greenfly on roses, spies, assassins, red tape, stroppy officials or head lice. No matter what, all infestations had to be dealt with one way or another. But so far, little Mayflower School had proved slightly more successful at coping with its troubles than the combined British Secret Services, thought Toby ruefully. Compared to this resilient little place HMG is always running a day late and a dollar short.

Dr Legg's morning walk

Joe Latimer was doing well in his martial arts class on a Saturday morning. It was held at the Lido's Function Hall, a rather stark room at the back of the ticket desk. This year the Lido was trying to update its image and increase revenue by holding a few ballet, gymnastic and Judo classes for local children. Joey attended with several other Mayflower boys, and found that directing his restlessness into controlled precise movements helped calm his bouts of anger to the point where he could get through several days at school without knocking someone's block off. His mother was glad to part with her hard-earned cash for the class each weekend as it saved her having to be called into Mrs Clark's office so often. She hated the idea of her sweet little boy growing up into a thug. It was probably just puberty kicking in, her neighbours told her, but she was not so sure. She'd been with several men who treated women badly. Some only hit you with nasty words, but plenty more preferred their fists. She hoped it *was* only hormones with Joe, and that he would soon grow out of it.

"You off then?" she called one morning as she heard him open the front door.

"Yeah. See yer," cried Joey and slammed the front gate.

He liked walking up to the Lido wearing his karate kit. It made him feel like a warrior. He practised a few kicks and hand-chops at bushes and branches along the way. It was a grand Summer morning, dewy in the hedges but dry underfoot, and the air smelled of hot grass.

At the corner, Dr Legg emerged from her front gate. She had promised herself some early walks when the weather permitted, and today was set to be fair. Exercise might reduce her waistline a little, she hoped. As always she was colourfully dressed, although today she wore flapping trousers instead of her usual bright skirt. To Joey she looked a little like an exotic ship whose sails were being adjusted to catch the morning breeze.

"Hallo!" he called. He liked Dr Legg.

"Oh good mornin'. Joey, isn't it? And how are you this wonderful day?" They fell in together along the lane, the doctor trying to recall why Mayflower was worried about this lad.

"I'm off to judo," Joey informed her, in case she had not guessed from his outfit.

That's right. Mrs Clark had said he was becoming belligerent. Dr Legg glanced sideways at him, summing up his energy and constant movements in one go. "Why do you like martial arts then?" she asked.

Joey shrugged. "I'm joining the army when I grow up. You have to fight if you're in the army."

Dr Legg digested that as the birds sang all around her in the hedgerows and the blue sky arched up and up into the peaceful heavens above their heads. Her trainers were already covered with the chalky trail dust the boy's fancy footwork was scuffing up.

"So you'll be ready for anythin'," she nodded. "I see. Judo would be good preparation for that. Do they teach you how to stay calm and in control in your class too? Or is it hit first and think later?"

Joey was silent for a moment. He hadn't really thought about staying calm or being in control in judo. "I just like the kicking," he said.

Most likely some army man would provide the orders once he made it to a regiment. He wouldn't have to be in control or stay calm.

"My brother learned a little boxin' at school when he was young. He enjoyed it too." Dr Legg rambled on. "He told me the very best fighters were the ones who did the most thinkin' first. Not only *what* to do and how, but also *why* they were doing it. Not just about themselves either. He told me you had to know what motivated your opponent. Really motivated him. Once you knew that, my brother said it was simple enough to figure out the most effective method to neutralise him with as little damage to either of you as possible."

That sounded far too complicated to Joe. He preferred to kick first and think later.

"Most people just wanna punch you and touch you and maybe kill you," Joe explained. "You should be able to stand up for yourself. I'm not letting people ever mess about with *me*. I'm not a weak little kid who doesn't know what's what. I'm strong. I'm not going to be pushed around." He jabbed and slashed angrily with his hands and danced about like a boxer. Why bother thinking about it?

"I see. And who did that to you? Who touched you?" Perhaps the beautiful morning air was making her brain work more intuitively than usual. Not 'does', but 'did'.

Joey stopped and looked her fiercely in the eye. "No one," he lied, pulling his belt tight around him. "I better get on, I'm late. Bye." He ran off down the last few yards to the main road, and crossed over to the Lido.

Dr Legg called a goodbye, but Joe was gone. She stopped where a well-worn track led across Hendy's Fields.

Right on the money, she told herself. Past tense. She would call in at White Cottage and see whether the headmistress was at home. Maybe she could beg a restorative cup of coffee while she told her of her suspicions. It had been an interesting start to the doctor's fitness regime, but that could be resumed tomorrow.

Dr Legg wiped her hot brow, and clambered ponderously over the stile.

A new arrival

A knock came at the Nesbit's back door. Terry Green and the dogs were out of earshot at the bottom of the garden, and Reg was talking to Ben in the hall, so Betty wiped her floury hands and opened the door herself to discover Jonah Webb, the vet's volunteer apprentice, standing there with a small cardboard box. He looked up at her, shyly.

"Mr Quincy sent me with this," he explained, holding up the box. "We hope you like it."

"Oh, why thank you, Jonah," answered Mrs Nesbit. "Come in, come in. Do you want a biscuit?"

Ben and Reg obviously heard the word 'biscuit' and joined them. Ben opened the packet of custard creams, offering the first to Jonah. "What you got there then?" he asked.

Jonah placed his box on the table and accepted a biscuit. He grinned – a rare event that made his serious face light up. "It's a surprise. For your new house. From Mr Quincy. Take a look."

Betty and Ben and Reg peered into the box to discover a black and white kitten curled up on some newspaper.

"Oh! How lovely. Jonah, thank you."

"We had two of 'em come into the surgery. Donated. The other one's gone to some people in Holly Hill Drive. Mr Quincy thought as how you might like this one, seeing as your old cat Binky was killed, like. You might have mice here in this new house, or spiders even. Kittens are good at spiders." Jonah looked up at the ceiling as if expecting to see it festooned with cobwebs. "Do you want it?"

"How much? Does he want a donation or something?"

"No, it's a present," explained Jonah again. "House-warming."

"Well, in that case, yes please. Oh hello – aren't you lovely?" Ben scooped the kitten into his large hand. The kitten had four feet and a bib of pure white. Her large eyes shone like lamps.

"Looks like 'e's wearin' socks," commented Reg. He tickled the kitten's ear and it began to purr.

"Room for another?" Terry Green poked his head round the door. "Ooh, a kitten. Isn't he sweet?" He levered his boots off and sidled in next to his dad.

"Socks is our new kitten," said Betty, happily. "Is she a girl, Jonah?"

"We think so. Mr Quincy says bring her in to be spayed in a few weeks' time." Jonah nibbled a biscuit and spoke with professional authority. "Keep her indoors till then."

"So then, how-do Socks," smiled Ben. "I hope you turn out to be a good mouser. And I hope you don't mind a few lumbering great dribbly dogs either."

The kitten snuggled inside his jacket and went back to sleep. Dogs could wait.

A good day

Charlie's children were all happily working in their school allotments – digging, watering, trimming, weeding. Mrs Clark went outside to see how they were getting on.

It was June, and the fine sky was clear and high. A daytime nightingale's song rippled far away, and a breeze shivered the full green leaves of the wilderness's odd collection of specimen trees standing like sentinels above the scrubbier, lower growth. Here a splendid redwood, there a ginko, a blue cedar, a Japanese maple, a mighty yew, a fig, a sweet chestnut, a majestic copper beech. Below them, like some lowlier stratum of creation, common birds fluttered and sang in the wide untidy willow and lilac, dogwood, elder and blackthorn. Mrs Clark inhaled the magic atmosphere and felt like singing too.

"Mrs Clark," called Gloria Mason importantly. "Your Nicky's up that tree."

The headmistress peered through the needles of a cedar in the direction indicated. Nicky was indeed worming his way along a whippy bough of dubious strength. He was a good size but convinced in his own mind that he remained kitten-like and lightweight. The humans stared up at him as he performed his tight-rope act.

"Come down, mate," cried Carl Goodman, holding out his arms. "We'll catch yer."

Jim Fisher whistled his toothy whistle. Nicky recognised the sound and wobbled.

"I wonder what he's after," said Mrs Clark.

"Prolly a bird," Gloria informed her. "Cats eat birds."

The other children glanced at her scornfully. Was she trying to educate the head teacher about cats eating birds? Really? Gloria had the grace to blush.

"He'll be alright," stated Jimmy quietly. "Leave him be." He finished weeding his square, then moved on to help Sarah who was daydreaming and did not like getting her hands too dirty.

"He's rather wobbly," commented Mrs Clark, nervous at Nicky's tightrope walking. "I don't think he can turn round. Oh, he nearly fell! Nicky!"

The cat meowed and froze on his slender branch. There was an ominous cracking sound, and everyone gasped. The children all began offering advice and foreseeing a terrible disaster. Mr Tuttle came over and scratched his head in concern.

"Oh, is that Nick? What's he… Should I go and get a ladder do you think?"

"Oh, he will be alright, I'm sure," ventured the headmistress. "He's just…Oh dear! Stay still, Nicky! Well maybe a ladder wouldn't be such a bad idea, Mr Tuttle. Peter, go and help Mr Tuttle."

Charlie and Peter hurried off to the storage room where the caretaker kept his ladders. It wasn't long before they returned carrying one between them.

"He's still up there," Carl told him. The cat was mewing piteously and clinging like mad to the branch. Once he appeared to try to turn around but all the onlookers began yelling at him, so he remained glued to his spot.

Gillian Davy began to cry, which set several others off. They sobbed histrionically and begged Mrs Clark to call the fire brigade. She was almost of a mind to do so, only perhaps, she said, they had better try to reach him themselves first.

Mr Tuttle climbed shakily up the tall stepladder. One of its feet suddenly sank into the soft ground causing him to leap off just before he fell. Carl caught the ladder and they tried again, but with the same result.

"Gillian, dear, do stop that awful sniffing. Have you no handkerchief?" asked Mrs Clark testily.

"Doh. Sorry Bissis Clark. I fick it's bleedi'g."

This new drama required everyone to focus on poor Gillian, offering advice and multiple tissues from various pockets. They tipped her forwards, they tipped her backwards, pinched the bridge of her nose, sat her down, hunted for a key to put down the back of her collar, and generally tried to stave off the blood with plenty of old wives remedies and hankies.

By the time Gillian's nose had stopped bleeding and everyone remembered Nicky on his branch, the cat had disappeared.

Jim looked up from his work on Sarah's square with a little smile. "Nick came down head-first about five minutes ago," he said. "He's quite alright."

"Well!" cried Mr Tuttle, collecting the stepladder and heading back to the lodge to put it away. "He may have to be in the next Christmas panto if he's going to be such a melodramatic actor."

Gillian's eyes grew round and she did her best to smile. "Oh good," she said. "Puss in Boots."

* * *

21.

Tennis

A moment for peaceful thought

All was quiet. Skipper roved silently around her domain, loving the atmosphere of the building when the children were working hard and the sun was burning into the old stone and brick and wood. She tapped on Toby's study door and found him in his armchair working on compiling a crossword.

"May I come in?"

"Mmm. Just finishing this off… There. Done." He threw his scribble pad on the desk. "What can I do for you?"

"Nothing, really. Just noodling about thinking how lovely it is when everyone else is working and I'm not."

"Well now you have the PTA solving most of our knottier school problems, and me for everything else, I think you're probably OK to retire to Bexhill and run the place from there."

"It's Cathy and Peggy that shoulder the bulk, I know that. All I have to do is flit about," smiled Skipper. Then she had a thought. "I don't want to think about retirement yet. I want to die in harness, like old Miss Broadstock. Are you're trying to pension me off? Where could Mum and I go? My house comes with the headship." Skipper began to look anxious as her thoughts accelerated.

"You'll come and live in Banford Place with me. You and Dora can have the west wing and I'll have the east wing. I was talking to Reg Green about it. We'll rechristen it 'Las Vegas' and tell everyone we're running a casino. You can potter in the garden while I'll mix dry martinis."

Mrs Clark laughed. "Alright, you're on. Mum will love that. How is your landlady today, though? I ought to have asked." She felt guilty again. "I ought to have visited."

"Oh, still lying in bed looking daggers at me. Bick gets a little nourishment down her each day in the form of broth or milk or something, but the doc says it really can't be long now. I arrive home every afternoon every day expecting her to have pegged out."

Skipper really did not like his tone when he spoke about poor old Lady Longmont. She knew the woman had been a foreign spy until very recently, and ought by rights to be chained up in the Tower of London or deported or something, but she still had a soft spot for her. Until recently Gibb had loved being part of Mayflower's governing body and anyone who loved Mrs Clark's little school couldn't be entirely beyond redemption. But Toby and Hugo were bound to be unforgiving when it came to traitors.

"I really ought to walk down and see her," said Skip. "Maybe at the weekend."

Toby sniffed. "Alright. But don't expect too much. She isn't entirely *compos mentis*, even on a good day."

Personally, he could not wait for the old woman to pop her clogs and for the whole sorry saga to be over. Hugo and he had managed to get the powers-that-be to agree not to lock her up, but that meant Toby and his crew taking on these irksome round-the-clock monitoring duties. They dared not foist her off on anyone else. Lady Longmont was far too slippery, too old, and still retained far too many important and sensitive details of her ages-long undercover operation to be exchanged for anyone who currently mattered to western intelligence services. Despite the code books and photos they had managed to retrieve they still only knew part of her network. She should be locked up and the key thrown into the Thames, in Toby's opinion. But she was far too frail even to be housed in a British high security prison hospital. So she stayed in her own home under house-arrest, and here they all stayed too. Stalemate.

"Are you going to buy the house after she dies, then?" asked Mrs Clark, sitting down at Toby's desk and helping herself to a toffee from a blue dish. 'Banford Place' always sounded like a special sort of fish to her.

"Done. In fact she's left it to me in her will," he replied.

"No! Seriously? How did you wangle that?"

"No wangling involved. Gadzooks, the very idea, woman. All legal and above board I assure you. I'm an old friend of the family, don't forget, so nothing simpler. She has no living relatives. Her solicitor came down from London six weeks back and finalised the papers."

Well blow me down, thought Mrs Clark. You sly old snake. When were you going to tell me that? Out loud she nodded and said, "I see. You really do fall on your feet don't you?"

Toby inclined his head. "I try. Born agile I suppose. Cat-like qualities. But I'll happily take you in when you're free to join me."

Skipper sucked her toffee and studied the man before her. Another pleasant-looking, slick-tongued dissembler. They were everywhere. So when would Mr Tobias Pelham Tremayne let her down, she wondered. What else was he hiding? There was bound to be something nasty left in that particular woodshed. She needed to listen more closely and not be beguiled by the looks at these charmers, she thought. Ears before eyes.

"What on earth are you thinking about?" asked Toby, amused by her expression. "You have a face like a squished tomato."

"Ears," she replied. "I'm going listen more and look less."

"Well, mind you don't break your ankle," grinned Toby. Women were completely dotty sometimes, this one included. "*I* might have nine lives but I'm not so sure about you. And don't look at my ears, I know they're like jug handles. Come on. Let's see if the urn's boiling and take our cuppa out to the field. Be ready for breaktime."

"We could take another look inside the Lodge too," said Skipper. "See how the builders have left it."

The last of the decorators was preparing to leave as Toby and Skipper arrived at the lodge's backdoor. Ted Jolly was alone, washing paintbrushes in the kitchen sink. He was a famously slow worker but did a thorough job. He had been the bane of Peggy Bailey's existence when redecorating the school's interior last Summer. Skip noted he was a messy brush-washer, and edged a can of Vim closer to his elbow.

"Everything's very bright and beautiful now, Mr Jolly," Toby complimented him.

"Ah," said Ted. "Needed doing."

"Has the paintwork been finished upstairs now?"

"In that new – whaddyer call it – refectory, you mean?"

"Yes, in there."

"Ah. 'Tis all done. Looks alright too, though I says it as shouldn't." He bade them good morning and left.

Toby and Skipper went up to inspect his handiwork. It had formerly been Sir Garnet's opulent drawing room, but was now furnished with informal groups of comfy chairs, a few tables, and a little kitchen alcove. It was rather like the school's staffroom, comfortable and welcoming, only larger. The walls were creamy white and the new, tough carpeting squares were alternately green and beige. The faded old flowery curtains had been laundered and re-hung to good effect.

"Doesn't it look grand?" beamed Skipper.

"Very nice," said Toby. He checked in a few cupboards. Jars of instant coffee, sugar, a big box of teabags, two kettles, mugs, tea-towels. "Is this going to be enough?"

"Well, there's only the Art Club signed up so far," answered Mrs Clark. "Early days."

Toby's vision was for the whole building to be seething with happy, industrious people. Language learners, pottery groups, local history enthusiasts. Clog dancers on the patio if necessary. Currently, the only affordable alternative venue that many groups had at their disposal was the Lido's back room.

"Let's take a gander at the bogs," he said.

"Honestly! You're worse than the children," Skip answered.

They both approved of the hygienic new toilet cubicles on the first and second floors. The third floor would be reserved for storage, the ground floor for offices and three practice rooms where some second-hand pianos now stood waiting for the piano tuner.

There came the familiar sound of a dog's scrabbling feet in the corridor and Stringer burst upon them, wagging his tail furiously.

"What ho, Stringer old boy. Ahoy there, Mr Green. We're just taking a quick look-see."

"Mornin' Sir, Mrs Clark." Reg hove in view in his venerable brown overall coat, and looking slightly sunburnt. He had been mowing the cricket pitch but needed a breather somewhere cool. "You admirin' the lads' handiwork?"

"Yes. Cathy says there's several groups enquiring about availability next September."

"That's a good sign. She in charge of runnin' it?" Reg took out his pipe and filled it while Stringer found a comfy chair and settled down with a deep sigh.

"For now. If it's popular, we may have to instal someone in that little office by the front door of a morning. Take bookings, give directions and so on," said Toby. "Who do we know might like a little morning job?"

"Not Ben Nesbit. He's fully booked," said Skipper.

"How about that Mrs Lewis who did supply teaching with us once? Nice woman, very organised. Arty," suggested Toby.

"Rosy? Yes, she'd be rather good. I could give her a call. Ring a Rosy," chuckled Mrs Clark.

"Very amusing. Come on Reg, show me the patio. Terry says he's been hacking the immediate jungle back a little more," said Toby.

They opened the french windows and stepped down onto the rather grand terrace. Reg puffed his pipe contentedly in the shade as the other two looked around.

"Well this is a huge improvement," cried Skipper delightedly. "Those tubs of geraniums look very bright and jolly."

"These tables and chairs will be pleasant on a sunny afternoon," agreed Toby. "People could sit here and eat their sandwiches."

"Like ruddy Kew Gardens, so it is," commented Reg, guessing their next waste of money would be a couple of huge sun umbrellas.

Stringer had a cursory sniff round, hoping for something a little more exciting than emulsion paint. He cocked his head on hearing the distant sound of children let loose from school. Several were heading this way. He trotted off to meet them at the allotments and help with their summertime harvesting, or weeding, or mud-pie building. Stringer wasn't fussy. Anywhere the children were was more fun than sitting about listening to people discuss umbrellas.

Reg watched him go.

"That dog shoulda been a schoolteacher," he said wisely, puffing clouds of aromatic smoke into the air. "Put a whistle round 'is neck, ask 'im nicely, and 'e'd do playground duty for yer."

Infestation

Yulissa Fielding, from Form 6, watched a honey bee amble along a sunny windowsill beside her in the library. It was late afternoon, and a few children were finishing off their homework before leaving for the day. It was peaceful and pleasant in there. The afternoon sunlight reached inside the tall room through the stained glass of its window and shimmered on the book jackets.

"Mr Chivers," she whispered loudly. The librarian came over to her. "There's a bee flown in. Someone might be allergic." She had been stung once and did not want it to happen again.

Ernest realised what the girl meant even if she did not express herself particularly clearly.

"I'll see if I can persuade it to leave, shall I?" He slid a library card under the insect and managed to flip it out of the head-height casement.

"Sir! This chimney's buzzing." Wendy Clarke and Trevor Black were at the opposite end of the long room, near the fireplace. Everyone stopped work and started giving advice.

"It's raining soot! It's an earthquake coming!" cried Chrissie Hart, who was prone to slight exaggerations.

"No it isn't," Rick Hodges assured her. "It's probably just a bee got stuck."

"A bee or three, oh dearie me!" sang Billy Hill brilliantly. "Mr Chivers, shall I move the rug out a bit? And this chair? For some extra air?"

Rick and Billy tugged the items away from the hearth, while Mr Chivers clutched the dustpan and brush distractedly. This fireplace caused a great deal of trouble one way and another. As they looked, a few bees and a clot of soot rained down into the empty grate. Everyone jumped back.

Ernest pulled himself together and told the children to go home at once while he dealt with the problem. It was no good everybody standing there waiting to be stung by a swarm of sooty bees. He closed and locked the library and went to telephone from the office. Peggy was on the point of departing for home, pulling her cardigan on and locking the filing cabinet. She raised her eyebrows on hearing Ernest's latest tale of library woe and offered to ring the curate, Mr Wichelow. Or would he prefer Mr Bracegirdle the sweep? Ernest ran his hands through his hair causing it to stand on end.

Mike Paton came in, having tried the library door and found it locked.

"Oh, here you are. What's up?"

Ernest rang the curate who sounded thrilled at the prospect of a new swarm. "Have you looked to see how far up the chimney it is?" he squeaked.

Ernest began to lose patience. "I'm calling Bracegirdle too. He must have dealt with this issue before, surely."

Peggy left them to it.

Once Mike and Ernest had braved a return to the library and taped a large piece of cardboard over the fireplace opening, the curate appeared. He lay on his back, undid the cardboard, and did his best to see exactly where the bees were, but it was no good.

"Black as the inside of a tram-driver's glove," he commented, coughing a little. "I can't get at it. Let me know when the sweep arrives, though, would you? I'm sure between us we can rescue them without destroying them."

Mike and Ernest sealed the hole back up and retreated. They called in at White Cottage before driving home, to tell Mrs Clark.

"Bees?" said Dora. "Skip, there's bees in the library."

"Better than bookworms, I suppose," quipped Mike. Ernest sighed.

Mrs Clark decided there was nothing extra to be done since they had alerted the only two people she imagined could help. She went over to take a look for herself, and found Pru Davidson huffing and puffing in the entrance hall.

"Can't get into the libr'y, Mrs Clark. Mr Chivers 'as locked the dern door on me. Stuck that there sign on it, Do Not Enter. Can't clean when I can't get in."

Skipper was explaining the situation to her when Reg Green arrived carrying a mop and bucket.

"Bees is it?" he said, grumpy that he had not been the first to know. "Had 'em before, we'll get 'em again, no doubt. Bracegirdle knows what to do. Or I could get an exterminating sanit'ry bomb."

Mrs Clark was aghast at such a thought and said so. If the curate could rescue the creatures there was no need to annihilate them was there?

"Just as you like, Miss. Make a ruddy mess though, bees do. Get into the brickwork too, sometimes. Probably move on in time without too much 'elp from us, if yer let 'em." He raised a hairy eyebrow at Mrs Clark. "You ask me, it'd be best to concrete the whole chimberly up and put in a nice electric heater."

That was never going to happen, the headmistress informed him. Pru and Reg exchanged glances. Here she goes again, they thought.

It took the best part of a week before Mr Wichelow and Mr Bracegirdle were confident the infestation had been fully cleared.

Ernest kept the library closed until it was safe for visitors again. While the bees were still there he took boxes of carefully chosen books outside to the shadiest part of the playground, and let the children select one each. Then he would read stories to them on the grassy bank under the horse chestnut trees on the field. The children lay and listened avidly.

"You do read stories nicely," Yulissa complimented him, flicking her hair behind her shoulder and gazing into his eyes. He had just finished one of the Mr Twink tales and she loved it.

"Thank you. I can't go wrong when I have such brilliant tales to read though, can I?" he smiled at her.

"And when we have our own Mr Twink right here," she said. "Look, there's Nicky. He's Mayflower's very own detective cat isn't he?"

"Yes, he is," answered Ernest. "Now then, what shall we have as our next story? Oh, I know the very thing. There's a super story called A Swarm in May. How about that?"

Yulissa gave him a very old fashioned look on hearing that title.

"Must we?" she said. "Because honestly, Mr Chivers, I've had quite enough of bees for one term. Can't we just have another Mr Twink?"

Dogs and ducks

Cassius, the lurcher, lay beside the baby's pram as Gwennie slept out in the garden. Above them, the apple tree cast a dappled blue light upon the bright green leaves. Cass was neither asleep nor awake, but lay on guard listening to the sounds of the distant river, the breeze in the reeds, and the occasional distant tumbling song of a skylark.

The baby stirred and made some gurgling sounds. Cassie roused himself and stood on his hind legs to look into the pram. Gwennie had kicked off her soft rug and was waggling her hands the way she did when she would soon require picking up. In a few minutes she would start crying. Cassie whined and pulled at her rug, licked her funny little hand. He sped off to the kitchen where the family was washing up the dinner things, and barked for attention.

"What's up, Cass?" asked Tim, wiping his hands on a tea-towel, glad of an excuse to abandon the drying-up. "Gwennie yelling is she?"

Tim and Cassie ran quickly down to the pram and were surprised to find a female mallard duck squatting on the end of it at Gwennie's feet. The duck was obviously inspecting the interior's suitability as a potential nest for her eggs.

"Hi! Get off!" shouted Tim.

Cassie barked in glee. Here was a game at last!

The duck regarded them with disdain, flapped her wings a little, and refused to budge. Tim and Cassius stopped, astonished.

Just then Sweep, Mrs Hewitt's springer spaniel, hurtled past. He had spotted the flapping of the duck from the open gate as he was being taken for a walk down the road, and yanked the lead out of Dean Underwood's hand and raced up the drive.

"Hey!" shouted Dean, running after the spaniel.

"Whoa!" cried Tim as Sweep tripped him over and he went sprawling.

Cass leapt around in joy and joined Sweep in a good loud shout at the duck, who squawked and finally withdrew to a safe distance beyond the garden hedge where she did some angry tail waggling.

The two dogs wagged their tails too, and kept jumping about eager for their prowess as chasers-away of dangerous ducks to be recognised by the slow-brained humans. Tim managed to regain his feet and picked up the baby who was crowing with delight at all the hullabaloo. Dean eventually snaffled Sweep and grabbed the lead firmly.

"Yes, good boy, good dog! Hello Tim, yes, there you are Cassie, you're a good dog too. Wow, sorry about that, Tim. Is the baby alright?"

"Gwennie's fine, aren't you little sis? Yes, you're both very good dogs, but get down now. Blimey, what a cheeky duck! It's a good thing Cass and Sweep were on the case though, wasn't it? She could have been smothered by feathers! Though I have to say, not much in the way of wildlife bothers her. My sister could be raised by wolves, you know, and still be laughing her head off. She's always happy."

Dean saw what he meant. "Not a bit scared was she? She's like Mowgli in the Jungle Book."

"Just as long as she doesn't start swinging through the trees like Tarzan," laughed Tim. "Come on in for a bit, Dean. Milk and biscuits are calling us from the kitchen. Yes, *biscuits,* Sweep! Come on Cass. Let's tell Mum about the Dastardly Duck and the Daring Doggie Duo, shall we? Make a good composition to write up in school."

"Yeah," said Dean. "Until someone tops it with the tale of 'Baby Gwennie and Three Wild Bears go on a Picnic!'"

Farm shops

The little collection of five recently opened retail businesses and the café at Abbey Farm were proving very popular with local people. Each unit was spoken-for and several were up and running by mid-June. There was a saddlery, a greengrocery, a bread and cake shop, a butchers, and a gift shop.

The saddler – a Mr George Hayward – sat and worked at his leather-work in full view of all the passers-by. Fascinated shoppers stopped to watch him create belts and pieces of horse tack in between selling items such as wallets, gloves and hand-stitched bags. Mr Hayward could turn his hand to fixing almost anything, as long as it involved leather.

The butcher's shop was a branch of Hearn's in the town. Mr Hearn's twin sons, David and Donald, had followed their father into the business and now enjoyed running their own establishment, dealing directly with the local abattoir in Ironwell. There was a queue every Saturday morning for their weekend specials.

The green-grocery owners specialised in locally produced fruit and veg from the various allotment associations. It was all seasonal fare so far, although they intended to extend the range of stock later in the year to include Christmas trees and potted plants. Shoppers were happy to see bananas and oranges too, but mostly it was potatoes, cabbages and raspberries. Mrs Norah Jacob and her son Steve, who ran it, were especially proud of their large refrigerator with its sliding glass door that housed all the fresh dairy produce, and Simon Dawkins' twelve rare breed pigs were more than content to dispose of the shop's leafy wastage every day.

The gift store had been established as a small cooperative. It brought in many an inquisitive shopper looking for a birthday present or a special card. It was run by Mr and Mrs McNeal, a Scottish couple who, alongside the usual items, displayed as much locally made craftwork, such as paintings, hand-made sun-hats and hand-thrown pottery, as they could. Miss Winstanley had had several of her woven hangings and tie-dyed tee shirts accepted and was eagerly awaiting her first share of the profits.

The bread and cake shop was a branch of Mrs Lara's thriving business in town. She now employed two pastry chefs in her main kitchens, and supplied various cafés and restaurants in Banford with daily delicacies. Miss Muggeridge and her friend Miss Sheldon had signed up to be the saleswomen at the Abbey Farm outlet. Every morning they busily sold bread and pastries, but had no hand in the running of the small café that had been built a little further down the hillside overlooking a lovely view of Hall Manor and its lake, despite it also stocking Mrs Lara's wares. The café was managed by Orlando and Lucia Bruno, an Italian couple recently moved up-country from Devon. It also encouraged local artists to exhibit (though not sell) their work on its walls, which created a huge amount of interest and delight in the neighbourhood. The place immediately became known as 'The Gallery'. Miss Winstanley had several items on display here, and a poster advertising her own Mill Gallery in Ironwell. It was all very arty.

The Abbey Farm Shops started off busy and continued that way. Cars came and went. Vans made deliveries, pedestrians walked, some pushing children in prams, some helping elderly neighbours, some wheeling shopping bags laden with groceries. If anyone remembered farmer Len Kirk, his pigsties, and that smelly old slurry pit, they soon forgot. Everywhere flowers grew and blossomed in the rich soil. Through the stately trees there was a splendid view past the manor and the distant agricultural fields to the eastern river levels. One day the shopkeepers thought they might possibly even add a children's playground to their site's amenities. The little complex never looked back.

The Arts Centre

The first group to use the new Longmont Arts Centre was a sketching club. For two years its members had foregathered every week at each other's homes, but now they felt so confident in their abilities they wanted to branch out. The four elderly ladies and two retired gentlemen who constituted the club, were delighted to set up their easels in one of the Lodge's newly renovated upstairs rooms. It had a sink, a set of tables and views across the wilderness to the heath and distant Ironwell village. They threw the windows up to let the breeze in, and pronounced it perfect – especially as it was so inexpensive. The group spent half their first morning sketching outside in the shadiest area of the garden, then came indoors for elevenses in the refectory.

Dora York was one of the artists, and it was she who had suggested the venue to the others. Dora specialised in detailed botanical watercolours, another interest she and her 'grandson' Jim Fisher had in common. They often compared drawings over supper after spending a happy afternoon together.

"Anyone take sugar? I can never remember," Dora cried. She had taken it upon herself to make the coffee today but quickly decided they should have a proper rota, starting next week. She wasn't prepared to take on the role of organiser.

"Isn't this a splendid facility?" said Douglas, looking all round. His wife, Dulcie, agreed.

"Douglas, don't put your feet on that chair, dear. I wonder how many classes will sign up."

Dora thought it was going to be quite popular. "Well, I've heard there's two more groups starting this week. Some beginners are learning French with a Mam'sel Dubois who's retired from the Grammar School in Fenchester, and a needlework club on Friday mornings. Not sure who's running that."

"Isn't it that Miss Winstanley? The donkey woman at the old Mill?"

"Oh, is she doing it? She's very arty. Knows her stuff too, from what I hear," commented Harold Khan, the other male in their group. "Doesn't she go around lecturing in schools, Phyllis?"

Phyllis Clare said she did. Her granddaughter was studying collage and printing at Portland Tech and had enjoyed Miss Winstanley's lectures last term very much indeed.

Dora, Muriel and Dulcie washed up the cups and put them away while the others disappeared off to the loos and back upstairs to their art room.

"This is really so lovely and quiet," smiled Muriel, as they walked down an airy corridor. "But it must be a beast to keep clean. This carpet along here is original, you know, and hardly worn. I believe it was made specially for the place back in the twenties."

Dulcie was suitably impressed. "Golly. I hope none of us drops ink or paint or anything on it. I'd have done it out with those carpet tiles if I'd have been in charge. We'd better check everyone's shoes for mud too, as we've been out in the garden. I bet old Sir Garnet's housekeeper made him change into slippers before coming up here."

Dora laughed. "She probably did. I daresay who ever is in charge of cleaning all this will have a hoover stashed somewhere nearby. I don't believe Pru Davidson is taking it on, or Reg Green, though."

"I heard that nice Mr and Mrs Snell were to do it. He's been wanting to start up a little cleaning service for a while now. They only live in Ash Lane and have bought one of those ex-GPO vans that he's kitted out. This place should be a good start for them," said Douglas, who had caught them up. He heard a fair amount of local gossip when he went down to the pub in the evening.

He hung his jacket on the back of his chair and sat down. "Very nice it all is, Dora. I'm going to enjoy working up my sketch from this morning into something I might sell down at that new gallery café. Yes, I would say this new Arts Centre is going to do our group just fine."

Kay turns a corner

A couple of Mayflower dads had come into school one Saturday morning to help Reg mend the cricket sightscreen. There had been an unexpectedly brisk wind one night and the thing had blown over, cracking a couple of the wooden boards and causing a wheel to fall off. Edwin Jefferson's dad Bob, and Kay Fordam's stepfather, Nigel Armitage, were both keen cricketers who had offered their services. Reg greeted them with genuine gratitude.

"Me lad Terry's off on 'oliday this week, or I wouldn't 'ave 'ad to ask yer," he explained. Terry and his girlfriend Vivienne were currently sunning themselves in Spain. "Very good of you, I'm sure."

"No trouble at all, Mr Green. I've brought a bag of tools," said Bob.

Nigel smiled blithely. He was willing, but rather clueless when it came to DIY he said.

Reg possessed quite enough tools for an army, but he said nothing. All he needed was manpower to steady the cumbersome sightscreen while he hammered and screwed it back together. However, Bob Jefferson enjoyed constructing things and turned out to be a real help. After an hour's hard labour the three finally managed to fix the splintered woodwork and set about re-attaching the wheel. As the axle it sat on had bent, it took a little doing. The three men were hot and sweaty after manhandling the awkward piece of equipment back upright.

Kay Fordam stopped her bike by the playing field's fence in the cool shade of the horse chestnuts to watch the final manoeuvring. Bob and her stepfather were lifting one end of the heavy brute and pushing, while Mr Green slapped some thick oil onto the wheel's axle.

"There – there – drop the bugger down there. That'll do it," grunted Reg, finally satisfied.

Bob and Nigel duly dropped it where it might be edged left or right, depending on the time of day the next cricket match took place and where the sun was likely to be.

"Gawd! What's it made of? Mahogany?" puffed Bob. He was hefty, but the old piece of equipment had taxed even him.

Nigel lay on his back staring up at the leaves on the trees, unaware Kay was nearby, watching and listening.

"You know," he said, "I'm trying to encourage my girl Kay to play more cricket. She's developing a really good eye for a ball and might make a decent spin bowler one day, I think. I'm really proud of how she sticks at things. Games like cricket aren't every girl's cup of tea."

"No, they ent," agreed Reg. "Your Kay's got a mighty sharp temper on 'er, I'll say that for 'er. I wouldn't like to craws her path too orfen." He had seen kids take Kay on when she was in a bad mood, and was in no doubt about her ability to stand up for herself.

Nigel laughed. "You're right! She can be a handful, but I wouldn't want her any other way. She's got grit, that one. She doesn't like me much at all."

Bob took a swig from his thermos of cold tea. "Why's that then?" He couldn't imagine his boy not liking him.

"I suppose because I'm not her real dad," sighed Nigel. "She misses him, even though he left her and her mother with nothing and disappeared back to his original family once the money was all gone."

"Bastard," commented Reg.

"Indeed. Maybe she thinks I'm going to abandon them too, I don't know. I've tried telling her I never will. I never would. I couldn't. But she keeps on punishing the rest of us and trying to push us to the limit. It's pretty exhausting." Nigel hadn't put any of this into words before, but now he had started he couldn't stop. "I really like Kay, but she doesn't yield an inch. I *know* I'm not her dad, but I would like to be friends," he sighed. "Maybe one day."

"Well, good luck, old man," said Bob. "Girls aren't the easiest are they?"

"It ent just girls," said Reg, knowledgeably. "It's kids. They got – whajamacallems these days? Hang-ups. That's right. They got hang-ups. Too much disruption in their lives, not enough stability if you ask me. I could name a few in this school."

The men sat there, rambling on – discussing children, the joy of cricket, and the vagaries of modern life, while Kay slipped away and cycled slowly home, having a jolly good think about Nigel Armitage.

So he *did* think about her. He *did* want to be friends. He wasn't going to up-sticks and leave them no matter how abysmally she behaved. That was interesting. Maybe he wasn't quite such a wet weekend as she had assumed – after all he liked cricket enough to volunteer to help fix the stupid sightscreen. Kay liked cricket too. Very much, in fact, and not just because Miss Delgado did. She scoured her brain but could find no memory of her real father ever playing a ball game with her, but Nigel was *always* suggesting they go and have a little practice on the smooth lawn out the back of their house. Nigel had bought her this bike too. He gave her pocket money each week. He was the one who had suggested she have the little playroom in the outbuilding all to herself. And he paid for her riding lessons. Mum seemed to like him.

Maybe Nigel wasn't so bad. He'd said he was proud of her. That counted for something.

Maybe – just possibly – she might say yes this evening, if he asked her to bowl a cricket ball again. She grinned to herself. That would surprise him.

"Perhaps I *will* grow up to be a demon spin bowler. If I do, it'll be my step-dad that taught me all I know."

* * *

22.

Land yacht

Quavers

"Well I don't think its decent, two men sharing a house. Glenda Paton would be spinning in her grave," stated Mrs Mason, who was having a chat with her friend Mrs Wilson outside the new Arts Centre.

"You don't think there's any funny business about it. Is there?"

"Maybe not. But I still don't think its decent. It don't *look* very nice. Maybe alright in the city, I suppose. I daresay those kinds of men are two a penny in Fenchester, but not round Banford. Plenty here says the same."

"Oh, who?"

"Never you mind."

"Well I don't see it matters much any more. We've all been liberated these days you know."

"Who has?"

"Women's lib. That's why we had the Beatles."

"They ent women."

"I know, but one for all, and live and let live…" Mrs Wilson persevered.

"Well, I don't hold with it. T'ent decent."

"Well they ent bothering you, are they? Live and let live, I say."

"You're a very forgiving sort of body."

"I try."

"That's them now. There they go look, in that funny French car. Happy as Larry ent they?"

"They are. Good luck to 'em I say."

"Hmmph. That Mr Paton taught our John," Mrs Mason said.

"And?"

"Well, nothing. No funny business, but I weren't happy about it."

"I can't see what you're making a fuss about it for. Mr Paton's a very good teacher."

"Mmm. I grant you that. Knows his maths and science."

"Well then."

"Quaker too. So they say."

"What's that got to do with anything?"

"Nothing. Funny though." In Mrs Mason's book every slight difference added to her general distrust. It all added weight to her theory.

"I think you ought to let two very nice men be, and not go speculating on what you don't know. Mr Chivers is a lovely man. Been there years too, both of them. Right well, I'm off to the bakers. Do you want anything?"

"No thanks, I'm alright."

"Right then. Cheerio."

"Cheerio, me-duck."

Joe Latimer had been listening to this conversation with flickering interest as he lay on his back on one of the old tombstones in St Andrew's churchyard in the sun, waiting for Jim Fisher to unload his latest jumble sale contributions from his contraption at the Church Hall. The two local women had stopped for a gossip in the shade, right near the part of the churchyard where Joe was waiting. When Jim finally returned, Joe and he walked up the road together, pushing the rattling contraption between them.

"Some people don't think two blokes ought to live together," Joe informed his buddy.

"Why not?" asked Jim.

"Dunno. Or be Quavers. Mr Paton's a Quaver."

Jim sighed. Sometimes Joe didn't make a lot of sense. "Why can't he be a packet of crisps? That can't be right."

Joe nodded. Jim was right. It made no sense.

"So why shouldn't they live together, then?" persisted Jimmy.

"It ent decent, apparently. I heard two ladies saying it were funny – like peculiar," said Joe. "I think it would be good, two friends living in the same house."

"Married people do," commented Jim. "I live with Auntie May. I can't see what the fuss is about. Lots of people live with lots of other people. It's nice, living together."

"Some people live on their own though. My Uncle Len does. He lives up in Manchester."

"Where's that?"

"North. Long way," the knowledgable Joe told him. "Miles. You gotta go on a train all day."

That was impressive.

"You'd have plenty of room to stay, then, if you were to visit. He'd have a spare room."

"Yea, I suppose. Anyway, them two old ladies were potty. Wanna go down Ironwell tomorrow and get some crisps in the corner shop?" Joe had exhausted the topic of teachers and their living arrangements. He was far more interested in buying a packet of Quavers.

"OK. Meet you at the gate after school."

"OK."

Jim turned for home up the quiet lane, while Joe increased his pace and waved goodbye. The contraption rattled and jolted and jangled as Jim pushed it along, announcing to all and sundry he was on his way. Auntie May would have the kettle on for their lunchtime cup of tea and a sandwich. He was looking forward to the sandwich. It was to be sardine. On the doctor's advice he was trying to eat a little ordinary bread each day and waiting to see if it still interfered with his tummy. So far the trial had been going a week with no unpleasant side effects. Jimmy was thrilled.

"I like sardines," he told Marigold who came to meet him at the back gate. "And I'll save you a little tiny bit."

Marigold purred and rubbed round his skinny legs. She knew when things were going well.

Goblins

Mungo was kicking a tennis ball along the pavement and thinking about colours. He had recently been told he was quite artistic, which pleased him even though he wasn't sure whether it might eventually lead to something he could make money at. Maybe if he become a portrait painter, or a sign-writer, or a man who designed wallpaper he could make a profit. He liked the wallpaper in his bedroom which was green and swirly and had little cars on it. It was better than his sister's which was just white dots on pink. Anyone could have designed that, but not everyone could draw little cars. If Mungo drew some cars, he would paint them yellow or red or blue or purple. Most real cars were boring colours like black or white. Why couldn't you get cars like patchwork quilts or rainbows? Designing them like that might make him some money.

The tennis ball decided to sail over a wall, through some railings and into a vast array of nettles.

"Nuts," said Mungo.

He clambered after it as best he could. The nettles stung his bare knees and brambles clawed at his shirt but he wanted that ball back. It was shadowy over here at the furthest corner of the school's wilderness, cold and a little bit scary. His ball was a dirty white colour and hard to see, but he pressed on. It was quite an adventure for a six year-old.

Mungo wormed his way into the thicket, hoping to see his ball somewhere obvious. Nobody, he thought, had come in here for a very long time. It was dark from the overhanging trees despite it being early afternoon. There! Was that his ball? No, it was only a stone. He came to a large cage made of wooden bars that had once obviously been painted white. Several of the wooden slats looked wonky so he wiggled them and they pulled out quite easily, allowing enough room for him to squeeze inside the dry little area. The bars all around made a sort of house, in the centre of which was a circular brick wall a few inches high. This looked old, weedy and crumbly. The rank smell of fox, or it might have been cat, caused him to wrinkle his nose. Beside the wall, ferns sprouted and moss grew. It was all very dark and echoey. Mungo suddenly felt nervous.

"Oy," he said, trying to shout bravely. "Any goblins down there?"

No goblins replied, so he lay down and edged forward to look over the little parapet into the gaping hole at the centre of the space. It was no good being scared of goblins. You had to face them head-on.

Nothing. Just a waft of damp vegetation and a feeling of feathers in his tummy. It was like staring over the rim of the world. His stayed quite still until his eyes adjusted to the blackness. Little by little he began to make out faint, slow, shifting circles as drips landed on some kind of oily surface twenty feet down. A treacle well? No, it didn't smell right. Was this a hole down to the river? No. Why would anyone make such a thing and build a little house over it when you could just cross the road and find fresh water flowing under the town's bridge? Was it a fishing place? A secret dungeon? It was a mystery to the child. He flipped a small stone over and saw more ripples.

Mungo could now make out a soft shape, like a bag, on a ledge in the wall, but it was out of his reach. Anyway, it looked moist and nasty. Maybe a goblin's sack full of beetles, although probably it was just a dead frog, or a fat toad. Mungo squiggled backwards the way he had come.

His tennis ball appeared at his elbow.

"How did you get there?" he asked.

Back beyond the outer cage he wedged the pales in as best he could and clambered out the way he had come until he was once more safe on the public footpath. He was brushing himself down, hoping his mother wouldn't ask too many questions, when Mrs Hewitt and Sweep came by.

"Hello, Mungo!"

"Hello, Mrs Hewitt. Hi Sweepy. There's a good dog."

"You look as if you've had an adventure," said the teacher.

"I have," replied Mungo. "Can Sweep play with my tennis ball?"

"Not on the road, but he may when we've crossed over. On that grassy piece by the river. Now then, are you going to tell me about your adventure?"

Mungo grinned a gap-toothed smile and handed Sweep the tennis ball to carry.

"Well, one suppolla time," he started in the correct manner. "When I was hunting goblins, I saw a toad in a hole."

The passing of an era

"Nope, no response." Toby was on the phone to Dr Legg. He had looked round Lady Longmont's bedroom door and been alarmed when she had not glared and hissed at him to piss off as usual. The glassy eyes were moving in the bony skull, but that was all. Gibb hadn't shifted position since being put to bed last night. Her two hands lay on the sheet like pterodactyl claws. He picked one up and let it fall. There was no resistance.

Let her lie, he thought, and closed the door. Then he phoned the doctor.

Toby was just putting the receiver down on the second of two further phone calls when Dr Legg herself knocked on the back door and clattered in. As it was early morning, she had not left for the surgery yet. Lady Longmont was not only her landlady but also a neighbour, so she had hurried over at once.

Afra Legg examined Lady Longmont carefully, kindly. There was nothing to be done except warm the bedroom a little more, give her sips of water and let nature do the rest, she said.

"It won't be very long now Mr Tremayne," she told Toby. "You'd better call school and say you won't be in today. Is Miss Muggeridge coming by?"

"No, it's one of Mrs Bicknell's days. I'd rather it was her, truth be told. Oh dear. I suppose I'd better go and sit with the old duck, see if she has any pearls of wisdom for me before she passes through the pearly gates. Thanks so much for dropping by, Doc. I really appreciate it."

"I'll be back this evenin', if she's still with us." Dr Legg was again slightly affronted at Mr Tremayne's off-hand manner. Did he not care about this grand old lady's passing? "It's very sad, but we're all called in God's good time. I have no doubt milady has led a very interestin' life."

Toby nodded cordially. "I'm sure you're right. Well, thank you again, Doctor."

Mrs Bicknell arrived at nine and nodded her head with understanding and considerable relief. "It'll be a blessing for us all, Sir, and no mistake. You'll be in your study, will you? I'll sit and do me knittin', like I said, and come and get you if she speaks, or if there's any change. You want me to turn her over every half hour? No? Just leave her be. Right then. I'll bring you a cuppa coffee later on."

Mrs Clark drove down at break time and found Toby out in the garden smoking a cigar. It was a still, muggy day and the smoke hung about for several minutes before dispersing.

"You alright, old thing?"

"Me? I'm fine, thanks. You going in to see her?" Toby kissed Skip on the cheek.

"If that's OK with you. You've been so good, keeping her going so long. It must be hard to know this is her last day, even after all the trouble she's caused." She was convinced Toby had a soft heart somewhere behind his façade.

Toby nodded as if she were correct. "Yes, it will be the passing of an era. Oh, here's Bick. Everything steady as we go Mrs B?"

"No Sir, I'm afraid she's gorn. Passed away a few minutes ago. Never uttered another mortal word. Her old 'eart just stopped tickin', like a clock what's wound down." Mrs Bicknell wiped her eye. She had told herself she did not care about the traitor's passing, but in fact she found she did. Another old woman had gone to meet her maker, and Bick herself therefore stepped forward a pace towards the finish line. "Comes to us all, Sir."

"Oh Mrs Bick, don't upset yourself," cried Skipper, putting her arm round her. "Come on, let's go in and tidy her up while Mr Tremayne rings the undertaker. Or is it the ambulance?"

The three went indoors and took one last look at the shell of the old woman as she lay like a stone-carved medieval queen in her bed. Edwardia Longmont's body had become so spare it barely caused the bedclothes to rise. Her face was a bony mask, revealing nothing of the wealth of ideas and memories that had so recently fizzed within her.

"She's like a doll," whispered Skip, a tear falling from her eye. "A sad wax doll."

"Yes, m'," agreed Bick. They stood and stared.

Toby calmly organised everything, and by midnight was once more standing in the garden smoking a cigar. Since the undertakers left he had once again been through every room of the house, walked over each creaking floorboard, stood and stared through every grimy window pane. Banford Place felt empty and forlorn tonight, but it also seemed to be more than prepared for its next incarnation. Intrigue had departed. The house champed at the bit awaiting a better, happier life.

Mr Tremayne flicked his cigar up towards the moon. The stub rose into the luminous aqua light, then fell into a dark, dark flowerbed where it glowed a while, then finally faded to nothing.

"Good riddance," said Toby out loud. "Never mind the rest of it. Time to move on."

Skippering

Skipper Clark sat on a log seat in the wilderness with a mug of tea. She had spent the morning shuffling numbers around with Peggy and would spend the afternoon writing up the school's record-book. It was lovely to recharge one's batteries out here, away from it all.

She looked up at the lofty redwoods and the shimmering, billowing willows.

We should all live one day at a time, she told herself, as if it were an original thought. Follow little Jim Fisher's example. That lad had taught her a great deal about life, and dealing with ups and downs.

Her log seat was not far from where Jimmy had dropped into the snowdrift and hurt his leg so badly. Poor child, she thought. He will never be free of the consequences of that fall. It was very fortunate Stringer had found the boy so quickly, and that Reg had been able to carry him all that way to the ambulance. Very fortunate. She could imagine the scene – the blood in the snow, the falling flakes slowly covering him until he froze. Her anger still rose at the thought of how close Jimmy had come to being killed.

She was glad Hugo was gone. Her school was uncompromised now, safe and sound. No more lies and cover-ups. No more secret goings-on. No spies and deadly assassins. Life would be lovely and normal now he had vanished. Murder would not lurk in these magnificent trees.

Skip leaned down and picked up a glittering silver tube from a weed beside the path. Not a pebble. No, a – a *bullet case*? Her heart skipped a beat. No, it couldn't be. Surely not. Wait, was this the casing from the bullet that had nearly killed their little Jim? She hurled the thing as far into the bushes as she could, and stood up, shaking.

At that moment, Dean Underwood called a hello and came gambolling up the path.

"Hi Dean," Mrs Clark had never been so glad to see anybody. "What's up?"

"Mr Paton says would you like to come and see the vicar's land yacht taking its first run across the Donkey Field?"

"Oh yes, I would," she answered with relief. "I didn't know it was finally finished."

"Yep," affirmed Dean. "It's really good. They found three matching wheels down the quarry where someone had dumped them, and the boards from some of the builders' left-overs in one of Mr Green's sheds."

"What about the sail though? I thought that was a bit of a problem."

"Yeah, but no. I think they nailed a bunch of sheets together." Dean wasn't quite sure. "Look, there it is Miss."

They were back at the field where half the school was standing around, waiting excitedly for Mr Paton and Mr Chivers to release the newly constructed land yacht ready for its first run across the cricket field. It was a windy day and the sail cloths were flapping madly in the breeze like so much laundry on a line. The vicar was climbing onboard.

"Miss Clark, Miss Clark!" screeched Crystal Peters, bobbing up and down like a jack-in-the-box. "The vicar's going to sail his boat!"

"So I see, Crystal," laughed Mrs Clark. How she wished Chloe were still around to see this latest fun. They probably didn't build many yachts in New Mexico. She would tell her all about it this Summer when she and Dora took their first trip to Taos.

"Hold it steady, you boys," ordered Rev Bill. He was business-like in shirt-sleeves and had tied a baseball cap on his head with a length of ribbon.

Four of the biggest boys in the school hung onto the back of the wooden platform as the wind tried to tug the cart out of their hands. Mr Paton lent his weight too, while the vicar settled himself onto the cushion he had strapped on as a seat. Ernest Chivers was pushing from the front to stop the thing taking off.

"I wish you'd included a handbrake," he grunted.

"Where are the Cubs? Oh, they're all down at the far end like I suggested. Good. Don't worry, they'll stop it if it looks like zooming into the cricket pavilion," said the vicar. "What do you mean, no brake? I've a perfectly good set of brakes. This stick on a pivot and my two feet. What can possibly go wrong?"

His wife June stood with the children. "Oh, do be careful, Bill," she called.

Crystal, a motherly sort of girl, squeezed her hand comfortingly. "Don't worry, Miss. Them Boy Scouts will catch him if he blows away."

The vicar eventually let go and careered madly across the field while everyone yelled encouragement. The yacht scooped and hopped left and right like a live thing all the way to where the Cubs stood, and almost upended itself in front of them. The children grabbed at the deck and lunged at the sails and soon had Rev Bill back on his feet, none the worse for wear.

Mrs Clark came up as he was straightening his dog collar and trying to look as composed as a vicar should.

"Well, Bill, and how was that?"

"Exactly like surfing, dear lady," he grinned. "Like flying once again. Like being alive!" He gave her a massive hug and swung her round and round, much to the children's amusement.

June was affronted at this behaviour. "Bill! William!" she cried.

The boys towed the land yacht back to the far side of the pitch again. "Who's going next, Sir? Can I have a go?"

Mike Paton sat on the yacht next and navigated it with much greater skill sedately around the perimeter of the field, only stopping when he came up against some particularly large molehills. Mr Green happened to be nearby and placed an anchoring hand on the mast.

"You putting out to sea then?" he enquired.

"Maybe. Have you any binder-twine or strong string I could use to hold that section of sail down, Reg?" Mike grabbed the yacht while Reg rummaged in the pocket of his brown overall coat. He brought out a piece of knotted twine. He always had a length or two to hand.

"How's this? I were going to use it for me clematis up against that back wall, but you can 'ave it. Only cost yer fourpence."

"Deal. Thanks," smiled Mike. The children were crowding round again. "OK you lot, hang on to the back while I tie this a bit tighter."

The wind tugged and the children laughed, and eventually the yacht was trimmed to Mr Paton's satisfaction. Mike navigated without further upset to the Cubs and clambered out. The children pushed and towed it back to the start again.

"Coming for a ride, Mrs Clark?" yelled Joey.

"Come on, Miss," the rest shouted. "It's easy. We'll keep you safe."

Mrs Clark shook her head but, swept up in the fun and energy of the moment, she allowed herself to be led firmly to the yacht and helped onto the makeshift seat. Mr Paton ran over and climbed back in beside her, as he doubted she was strong enough to yank the various ropes around by herself. Rev Bill and the boys steadied the wheels, wondering whether it would move at all with two adults on board.

Mr Simms, the local photographer suddenly popped up at the far end of the field, camera in hand. He waved cheerily just as Skipper was reiterating her decision to disembark. The boys let go and the whole contraption hiccupped and jerked forwards once again, veering this way and that as Mike Paton grew even more dextrous at controlling it. They sailed majestically to the cricket pavilion, around the sightscreen and back along the front fence. They then swerved in an elegant semi-circle and drew to a stop exactly where they had started. A huge cheer went up from the children and Rev Bill threw his cap in the air.

Mr Simms came hurrying over, a broad grin on his face.

"I got all of that run," he panted. "New movie camera! Absolutely first rate, Mrs Clark. A complete circuit. First rate! I can show you the footage on the screen in the hall once I've processed the film."

Mrs Clark laughed and said she had had quite enough excitement for one day. "I'm glad you're happy," she said. "But before you sell this one to MGM I want to review it, and see if I match up to Julie Christie."

"Oh you do, Miss," cried Joey, who was clueless when it came to movie-stars.

Skipper laughed. "And Mr Paton is Steve McQueen is he?"

"He's brilliant," shouted Joey. "Everybody is brilliant! This is the best school with the best teachers and the best land yacht in the entire world!"

Mike looked at Skip.

"Well you can't get a better recommendation than that," he said with a wink.

Concert

The final concert of the school year kicked off the end of term festivities in traditional fashion. As usual Charlie had spent hours and hours deliberating on which songs would best show off the musical talents of his singers and players. He also wanted to include a couple of theatrical items if he could, as many children enjoyed dancing and performing. They saw new ideas on TV every day, which prompted some to dream about a future career in show biz.

Dean Underwood was such a one, although Charlie noticed the boy was speaking less frequently these days about becoming the next Fred Astaire. Dean attended gymnastics instead of a dancing class, which must be a disappointment. It was also disappointing to Mr Tuttle who considered the boy had real talent. However, gym was a more suitably boyish activity according to his mother, so to gym he went. Charlie Tuttle sighed and hoped that one day attitudes might change. It was a funny thing, dancing. Country dancing was perfectly acceptable, with its sticks and bells and silly ribbons. Even ballroom, at a push. But ballet or tap or any type of modernistic Isadora-Duncan-style expressive dance was completely out of the question for a lad. If Dean had been born into a different culture in a different part of the world, he might have been a maestro.

"Never mind, Gwennie," said Charlie, as he held her on his knee and showed her the piano keys. "We'll give him a major part in our concert. And you, young lady, may grow up to be a bricklayer or whatever you want."

The hall was a-buzz with expectation when the afternoon of the concert came. The orchestra (still fondly nicknamed the Scrape Bang and Blow Brigade) settled themselves down in the front of the stage. The six recorders, three violins, and eight percussion players fidgeted nervously as the choir filed in behind. Zoe Smith, back by popular demand, featured in the singing once again, her missing two front teeth barely hindering her delivery. Last year, Lizzie Timms had been the female star of the show, but now it was Zoe's turn to shine. It felt wonderful to be leading the singing and grinning at the audience. Zoe had no trace of nerves in her stout little body.

The programme galloped gaily along from the very start. Mr Tuttle showed off the talents of each individual class with carefully selected items, ranging from the babies singing Old MacDonald Had a Farm, to Mr Paton's litter-pickers belting out the theme song from The Wombles. After that there was a section from one of the BBC school's broadcasts which involved three children performing a mime to the catchy tunes that went with the theme. Next, Dean stood next to Zoe and tap-danced while she led the choir and audience in several numbers from the Sound of Music. For the grand finale Dean brought the house down as Joseph in an amazing technicoloured dream-coat, which had been created for the occasion by Sandi Raina out of pieces of glittering fabric she found in the attic's costume boxes. The audience stood and applauded while Charlie, with Bella who had helped him, took bow after bow.

"Well," cried Dora to Miss Muggeridge. "Another Mayflower triumph!"

"Highlight of my summer, is this concert," stated that lady, pulling on her crocheted gloves and buttoning her jacket. "I can't think what we did for entertainment before your daughter started all this. Cinema ent nothing like a good live show, is it?"

"That it ent," agreed Bick, as she scooted her green chair over towards the wall ready to be stacked back in a pile by the team of boys who stood ready to spring into action.

Dora smiled and went to relate their remarks to her daughter who was standing outside in the sunshine and bidding everyone farewell.

The children cleared the stage and soon the hall was empty enough for Pru Davidson to start pushing a dry mop back and forth over the yellow parquet. She looked up in surprise as a shadow loomed over her, and she almost curtsied when she saw who it belonged to.

"Oh, Sir Hugo," she cried, unable to find anything else to say.

"I seem to have missed all the fun. Would Mrs Clark be anywhere around, d'you know?" Hugo asked.

'Out them doors, Sir," she answered.

"And my son?"

"Dunno, Sir."

"Right. Ah, Toby! There you are, old man. How did the end of term concert go?" Sir Hugo turned to find Toby Tremayne advancing on him down the hall steps. "I seem to be too late."

"Good to see you, Hugo. Skipper's out this way, bidding the hordes farewell. The concert was a tremendous success, as always."

"Shame I missed it. Ernest around?"

"He and Mike are in the car park trying to the untangle the bumpers of those audience members who came by car, I think. Honestly, we'll have to extend that little space if more and more people go on buying motors. Gone are the days of children walking ten miles to school and back every day." Toby grinned as he ushered MI6 out of the french doors again and down the side path past the boiler room. "You staying a while? How's married life?"

Hugo raised an eyebrow. "As you'd expect," he said rather coldly. There was no need for Toby to be asking about life in Brussels. Nor, really, did he need to know how long he would be staying. It wasn't any of MI5's business. "I'll stay a couple of nights," he conceded. "Putting up at the Yeoman."

"Right. You received our report regarding the outcome of the hunt we had for those old code books of Lady L's? Rather a good catch, I thought, on the boy Underwood's part. It took a bit of time, but the local coppers helped. I don't think the council was best pleased having its rubbish tip raked over for a week, but needs must. And those notebooks we did manage to retrieve have filled in several gaps for us. We've a far better understanding the old witch's most recent operational methods. Closed down all we can. You saw all that?"

Hugo nodded. Old news.

"You've come for the funeral?" Toby went on.

Hugo nodded again. "Of course. Why else?"

Why indeed. Lady Longmont's funeral was to be held the following day. Both intelligence officers wanted to make sure they saw the old woman well and truly planted six feet under. It wouldn't hurt to have a quiet word with her solicitor about the will either.

This gave Hugo a thought about his closed-up home, Garratt's Hall. "I think I'll have a word with that Jamal Raina fellow. He may have someone in mind – some company he knows of – that might want to take out tenancy of the Hall while I'm not there. Ernest doesn't want it. You don't need it. It may suit some local law firm. What do you think?"

"Good idea. Though would you want it turned into an office?"

"I'm not fussy. Maybe. I won't be needing it again, will I? Anyway, I'll take a stroll over there tomorrow, and see what he says. Ah, now here's Ernest. You're looking a little hot and bothered, dear boy. Car park attendant's career rather tougher than you're used to I suspect?" He grinned, boyishly.

Ernest controlled his temper. Trust his father to turn up late and start belittling things. He muttered a greeting and barged past. The staffroom was hopefully out of bounds to Hugo now he was no longer one of the Mayflower team. There would be tea and orange squash and celebrations in there.

Toby and Hugo strolled on, eventually emerging at the gate onto Bridge Road without having seen Mrs Clark or anyone other than homeward bound schoolchildren and their parents. Hugo was nettled. It felt as if he was being seen off the premises when Toby closed the gate and shot the bolt firmly home.

"Bye then, old man. Safe travels. Let us know how you get on in Europe," called Toby.

Hugo raised his hat and turned sharply away. He walked off down the road towards the town, his expensive heels tapping crisply as he went.

I shall do no such thing, he thought, crossly. Let Toby Tremayne know my movements? The very idea. It's none of his – or anyone else's – business.

* * *

23.

Kay and Nigel finally hit it off

"That's it! Now steady as you go, love," called Nigel, the team coach. He was watching Kay pitch in the annual staff-kids baseball game. She was concentrating on aiming an under-arm ball straight through the centre of Mr Denny's stomach. "Easy!"

Wham! Mr Denny swung and missed, but he had to run. Joey Latimer, the catcher, caught the ball and flung it straight to first base.

"Owzat?" screamed Colin Wright, temporarily mixing up his cricket and baseball yells.

Mr Denny walked back to the pavilion, crestfallen. Bowled out by a little girl! He would never live it down. He had considered himself the great hope of the staff team, but now it was all over. Kay and her dad were dancing around like mad things. He took off his cap and wiped his brow.

"Sorry, team," Guy sighed. "She's a demon pitcher, that one. I should have known, after all I was the one who put her in the first cricket eleven." He accepted a consolatory glass of lemon squash and dropped his bat back in the bin.

"Never mind, old boy. Better luck next year eh?" laughed Toby.

Bella handed him a digestive biscuit. "Her dad's been coaching her. Honestly, she sent that ball off like a meteor. I say we give the little monsters a taste of their own medicine when we're in the field. No making allowances for their only being children. Don't yield an inch."

They were grand rallying words, but they did not produce a result. The children's team won by a wide margin and gathered round Nigel Armitage when it was all over with whoops of joy.

"You're a crackin' bowler, Kay," grinned Colin. "Best we've ever had."

"And hitter," said Freddy. "She slogged that ball of Miss Delgado's so hard it nearly broke the staffroom windows."

Kay slapped him on the back. "You're not so bad yourself, Freddy me laddo. I'm glad we did it again though. I like our mix of rounders and softball. It's a good game."

"Edgar Briggs's mum said Dane Street is going to get a team up to play us next year," said Colin.

"Woah! They have twice as many kids in their school as us. More to choose from. We'll have to make sure we get a load of practice in next Summer." Kay would by then be in Form 6, while Colin and Freddy would be at secondary school. They were browned off at that thought.

"You and Eddie and the rest had better be *really* prepared. Can't have Dane Street beating Mayflower," Freddy said. "Maybe I'll come back and help Mr Armitage coach you on Saturdays."

They sat under the trees to cool down beside Kay's stepfather. He raised his glass of squash to the team. "Well done, guys," he said.

"Couldn't have done it without you, Sir," said Edgar. "We needed a good trainer. Someone who's, like, just on *our* side. The teachers get all cocky thinking they're obviously going to win, and it can put us off a bit. Psychological warfare, that's what it is."

Nigel laughed. "Well they're not so cocky now, are they? They might be taller and stronger than you but you lot are much quicker and have had far more practice. Plus you can run faster – and have this demon lady bowler."

"Pitcher," said Kay. "If you mean me."

"I do. Yes, pitcher. It's not easy, bowling underarm when you're used to cricket. Are you all playing the staff at a cricket friendly this year?"

"Only if there's time on the last day, Mrs Clark said. I hope we do, only *some* people are going away on holiday so they won't be around." Colin was annoyed at the thought. He took his cricket very seriously. "Our team might be short of a few good players."

"Don't worry," suggested Mr Armitage. "Let's wait and see what happens."

Colin nodded. "Just don't go taking Kay away on holiday yet," he said. "Please."

Photorama

Mr Simms had finished the last of the indoor photographs, and was setting his old-fashioned panoramic camera up for the whole-school shot outside. It was another lovely morning and the tarmac of the little playground was already hot, even though the shadow of the school building covered half of it. He had the boys set out benches along the back fence and some chairs for the staff in the front row. Behind would be a tasteful background of Summer foliage where the overgrown wilderness area met civilisation.

The various classes trooped out and lined up where he directed them. The boys had been told to put their blazers on but to remove their ties. The girls looked fresh and cool in their pale green cotton dresses with neat white piquet collars. No one wore a cardigan. Mr Simms hoped the staff looked as tidy as the children. Patiently, he arranged them all to his satisfaction – changing one or two tall ones for little shrimps who upset the symmetry of his composition. Eventually even Nicky and Stringer managed to stay still long enough for the photographer to judge the scene perfect.

Simms disappeared under his black sheet and peered through the viewfinder.

Mick McDonald and Ivan Amos from Form 6 looked at each other. They waited for the camera to begin its mechanical sweep of the long lines, then jumped down from their bench and ran to the far end before it finished, so as to be in the photo twice.

"Done!" called Mr Simms. "I'd like another though, just for luck."

"Alright. Stay still everyone, please. One more," shouted Mr Tremayne.

The boys scampered back to their original places and repeated their prank.

As everyone was heading back indoors afterwards to wash their hands and get ready for lunch, Mr Green nabbed Ivan and Mick by the collar.

"The old tricks ent always the best ones you know," he said, amicably. "You wanna be smart and be seen twice? Well, I got two sets of buckets and mops waitin' for yer, and a mucky bottom corridor what wants a good goin' over. It'll tek the two of yer. And for a second job, the front flower beds want weeding. Mr Denny is perfectly fine with you missin' a couple of breaktimes, 'cos I asked 'im. So you better report to me this afternoon, you young scoundrels. I'll be waitin'. And don't make me send the dog out to find you, or I'll double the jobs."

Ivan looked at Mick as they plodded gloomily back upstairs to their classroom. The Iron Duke rang with the sound of their feet in a doom-laden clanging.

"Some people have no sense of comedy, mate," puffed Mick. "They don't see the bigger picture. They just ent got no sense of comedy whatsoever."

Expectations

"Yes, well I wish I wasn't going," Mrs Clark told Jim Fisher. "I'm not fond of the dentist."

They were sitting in the garden of White Cottage after school one day watching Dora tie up some trailing clematis fronds against the wall. Jimmy had not been well, having eaten one too many sandwiches, the doctor said. For the immediate future Jim would have to go back to steering clear of bread products again. It was a bore, but necessary if he was not to repeat the digestive misery he had experienced in recent days. He had spent yesterday lying on the sofa at home, but was now strong enough to be with Grandma, lying on a sunbed in the garden. Simply being out of doors cheered him immensely. He patted Mrs Clark's hand comfortingly.

"Mr Andrewartha is very nice," he assured her. "He counted my teeth and said the new ones are much better than the old baby teeth. He gives you a sticker for your shirt. Have you still got your baby teeth?"

"No. But I've had these ones a long time now, so they may have a few cavities in them. Anyway, it isn't Mr Andrewartha, it's a Mr Chris Fraser. He's Australian. Apparently Mr Andrewartha needs an extra helper this year as he is so busy, so he took this new Australian man on."

The temporary dentist's origins meant little to Jim. He assumed people in Australia had similar teeth to people in Banford.

"Oh. Well I expect he will be nice too. Maybe he'll have a kangaroo with him. Or a wombat. That would be fun to have in a dentist's room."

Mrs Clark smiled indulgently at such infant fancies. "Maybe. In any case, I had better get going. I don't want to be late." She ruffled his hair and waved to her mother, then went indoors to clean her teeth one last time.

Jim lay on his sun-lounger and played with the figures and plants in his toy garden layout until Grandma Dora joined him for a cool drink.

"Grandma."

"Yes, Jim?"

"Do you get any more teeth?"

"How d'you mean?"

"Well, after your baby teeth fall out you get grown-up teeth. Do you get any more after that?"

"Only plastic ones." She sat down and pulled the rug round him.

"Plastic?"

"If you need them. When you get old, like me. Sometimes teeth wear down, so the dentist takes the old ones out, and makes you a plastic set that fits in the gaps. If you want."

That was a thought.

"I'm glad I'm not old," he said. "I don't want plastic teeth yet."

"Alright then. Just remember that sugary food is what makes teeth decay. But if you brush your teeth properly and pick them clean each night yours should last a lifetime."

A lifetime. That was good to know and quite easy to comply with, especially as he was not that keen on sugary food.

"Is orange squash sugary?" he asked.

"Oh yes. And lots of things, so make sure you slosh water round your mouth and keep it fresh whenever you can."

That was all very interesting. Jim decided water would do him as a cool drink from now on.

"Is milk alright? And tea?"

"Yes. Now, how about I find some cards and we have a game of Beat Your Neighbour Out of Doors? Or would you prefer Rummy? Move your garden over a bit, we'll need a bit more space on that table."

As the two settled down to a game of Rummy, Mrs Clark hopped in the car and drove through town to the Paisley Road surgery where she read through Lady Longmont's obituary in the local paper and two magazine articles about home-made Christmas decorations before Mr Fraser's secretary called her into his dental surgery. The first thing she noted on entering was a poster showing Bondi Beach. The second was a line of stuffed soft toys – a kangaroo, a wombat and a duck-billed platypus.

"Mrs Clark? How do you do? I'm Chris Fraser. Sorry to keep you waiting. That's it, sit there and hold still while I put this round your neck. Now then, if you're a really good girl you might get a sticker today. Open wide, please."

Mrs Clark lay back while the dentist seemed to be counting her teeth, secretly wishing she could hold the cuddly kangaroo and the wombat for a little comfort.

The duck-billed platypus she could live without.

Sports Day

"Why is it so blessed-well *hot* every Sport's Day?" moaned Toby as he and Jean set up the judges' table with the scoring sheets and freshly buffed-up Inter-House Sports trophy. The children were bringing their chairs out of the building to the classes' designated viewing areas. Mr Green had marked squares on the grass for them to remain in when not running or jumping or throwing various objects, although he had little hope this would keep the children penned back from the live activity areas. Reg usually spent Sport's Day yelling.

"It's July, my dear. You ought to be used to the heat, though. Don't tell me Italy wasn't hot." Jean fanned herself with one of the clipboards. Toby did not talk much about his time abroad, preferring to divert such conversations on to something else whenever it arose.

"It was. But this is pretty steamy, today. I wonder if it will thunder?"

"As long as it holds off this morning, I'll be content. I don't want anyone collapsing with a fit of the vapours." Jean bustled off to supervise her class who were emerging at that moment.

A bee buzzed round Toby's panama hat as he set up two large sun umbrellas, and pulled four chairs around the table. There. Now they were set.

Ernest, meanwhile, was plugging in the outdoor loudspeaker, hoping he had carpeted the long cable to the announcement table sufficiently with old mats so that no one tripped over it. It was quite a stretch from the pavilion's only socket and it would not do for anyone to break an ankle. He went to check if everything was working.

"Testing, testing," he said, tapping the microphone. There was a loud whine, but the thing appeared to be adjusted properly. Ernest breathed a sigh of relief. That would prove to Mike that he could be practical with electrical equipment too. Toby came over looking for the hand-held loud-hailer.

"It's only for emergencies," he reassured Ernest. "In case someone trips over that wire of yours and pulls the plug out. Or we get struck by lightning."

"Oh, don't say that," cried Ernest. "It's tempting providence."

"Where is it? In the pavilion?"

"Yes. On the hook. I've tested that too."

While the children were coming outside and the place was filling up with spectators, Toby gave the gathering of parents and friends a few recited poems learned by heart as a child, just to check the loudspeakers' acoustic he told Skip, although she believed he simply enjoyed hearing the sound of his own voice echoing round the neighbourhood. The poems kept everyone amused while they chatted and scanned the program for their child's name, or put up umbrellas to ward the sun off the youngest babies in their prams. Toby was on event announcements and Skipper and Dora were putting the various scores up on the cricket scoreboard, a bright idea Colin Wright had come up with the day before. Mrs Clark had her box of numbers and letters on the grass at her side, and Dora sat smiling at the children from beneath a scarlet parasol.

On the dot of ten, the fun began. There were sprints of various lengths, high and long jumps, discus and javelin throwing, a gym display involving the oldest children leaping over boxes and springboards, and all manner of novelty races including the popular 'Stokes' Steps' where contenders had to make giant leaps across a set of stepping stones represented by artfully placed hoops. The races – even the slow-bicycle race – went beautifully and nobody collapsed from sun stroke, much to Jean's relief, but it was hot and the excited children grew thirsty. Luckily Ivy and Sally had squash and some biscuits and apple slices available for those who needed a little sustenance before lunch.

"Keep them bees off that juice there, Joey," ordered Ivy as she handed out the beakers of drink. Joey obediently flapped his long-jump winning ticket. He needed a drink before taking it to the scoring table where Mr Henshaw and Mrs Smith – Zoe's mother – were busy adding everything up.

"It's one of Mr Wichelow's, I expect," he said, talking about the bee.

"Well, they ought to stay in their tropical jungle, not come bothering us," replied Mrs Green. "Me and Sally's enough to do without having to ward off swarms o' blessed bees. Wasps is bad enough. And lunch won't make itself. There's strawberry shortcake and ice cream for dessert today, so we gotter get a wriggle on."

"Would you like us to go in and start the tables, Mrs Green?" asked Joe.

Ivy gazed at the lad. "I would, Joey, if Mr Green says it's alright. Bless you. That would be a big help."

Joey grinned and galloped off to hand in his ticket and then ask permission. He took his mates Edwin, Jago and Stanley with him. Joe secretly did not care very much which house won the Inter-House Sports trophy. He was sure someone would come and tell them soon enough. It was much more fun to be doing the lunch tables indoors out of the sun.

The boys were just sauntering into the hall when Stringer dashed past with a dead rat in his mouth.

"Looks like even Stringer's taking part in the relay race," grinned Edwin. "Gor, it's hot."

Outside, the clouds gathered and they heard thunder in the distance. Inside, the hall was cool and shady, with a pleasant Summer breeze wafting through the open windows and lazily billowing the curtains.

"Coo," said Jago, wiping his sweaty brow. "I believe I know why they call them running races 'heats' now.'

Lido Day

After all the intense and steamy running about, many of the children thought Swim Day at the Lido the following morning much more fun. Today – as a special treat – swimwear did not have to be the regulation black, but could be any type of garment, as long as Mrs Clark pronounced it decent.

Little Zoe Smith could not help admiring Dean's neon yellow swimming trunks and sidled over to tell him so. She hoped he found her navy blue costume with its tiny skirt equally attractive.

"Hello Dean," she beamed.

He turned and saw her round freckled face looking up at him. The sun shone on her water-splashed skin, and glowed through her dark red hair.

"You wanna be my girlfriend, Zo?" he blurted out.

Her green eyes grew rounder, like a cat's. "Really?" she breathed.

"Really. Properly. You can have my St Christopher's." Dean unclipped the St Christopher medallion he was wearing (unknown to Mr Denny), and put it in her hand. "Just don't tell." He leant down and quickly kissed her cheek.

"Alright," she smiled. Her head was spinning and she could barely believe it. "Thanks. I do love you," she added as an afterthought.

He whispered in her ear, "I know. And I love you too. That's alright then."

Dean stuck his hands in the pockets of his natty swimming shorts and mooched off to find Jim Fisher who was helping Mr Denny line up the floats for the first race. Jimmy was not swimming today. His usually serious countenance broke into a broad smile when he heard Dean's news.

"You going to get married then? Like, one day?" he asked.

"Yeah, prob'ly. She's a really good singer." Dean helped with a few floats.

"Zoe's good at music. That's what you like too, isn't it?" said Jim.

Dean suddenly realised it was. Music was what drove him to dance and what made Zoe sing. Music and rhythm together – just like bangers and mash, or oranges and lemons. "S'pose. I'm in the first relay," he said. "I better go. Wish me luck."

Jim nodded and surprised Dean by shaking his hand. "I think you already got it, mate," he said.

Dean disappeared off in high spirits, leaving his diminutive chum to continue arranging the floats.

Now if only Gwennie would grow up to be mad-keen on gardening, he would have a ready-made plan of how to proceed. Jim thought it was time to begin saving for a St Christopher.

Founder's Day

Sir Garnet Broadstock, the school's wealthy founder, had set Mayflower up for two reasons. The first was to provide a good basic education for the children of the town he loved, and the other to give his only daughter, Mabel, her heart's desire – a school of her own.

Mabel was a pioneering female graduate, a blue-stocking idealist who cared deeply about the notion of eradicating the fundamental causes of social inequality by developing children's natural intellects in an environment that encouraged them to think for themselves. Deeply influenced by William Morris, and to some extent by Maria Montessori, she believed in a wide-ranging academic and practical education based on the arts, not only for girls but also for boys. She rapidly established the school's high academic standards and caused its name to be respected throughout the neighbourhood, and indeed throughout the county, although she fared less well when seeking to introduce simple furniture-making and handmade book printing and book-binding classes, which critics suggested were three steps too far. After the school's initial years, the rising importance of balancing liberal arts with sciences became a feature of the Mayflower curriculum, although mathematics never sparked Mabel's attention to the same extent as poetry. Still, she continued to strive to develop happy, resilient spirits in her young students. She aimed on dispatching young people of excellent character out into the modern world, with minds well-able to deal with anything life might throw at them. Mayflower children should reach for the stars, yet keep one foot firmly on the ground. And in order to learn how to be properly grounded, she encouraged them to embrace all manner of traditions, including an annual prize-giving named for her revered and benevolent papa.

Miss Broadstock's principalship was a tough act to follow, as Skipper Clark discovered during her first few years. However, although it was straightforward to carry on what had already been so carefully established, Skip found it an uphill struggle to introduce her own ideas. She was not aiming to make changes for change's sake, but wished – understandably – to set her own seal upon her tenure. Undaunted, Mrs Clark plugged slowly on.

Founder's Day was a simple and pleasant tradition, one she heartily applauded. Skipper particularly welcomed it as it afforded her an opportunity to take a good hard look at her entire world after another jam-packed year. See the panorama for what it was, and what it now required.

This year, despite its many ups and downs, she was relieved to be able to pronounce it thriving.

Cups and trophies were brought out and polished, new ones added and defunct ones mothballed. Long ago there had been a prize for needlework, another for handwriting and so on, but since her arrival, alongside those for individual achievement and team excellence, Mrs Clark had introduced one very special trophy to be presented to the child whose personal character had somehow blossomed during the year. It was called the Founder's Cup.

"Who is receiving the Merit and Character Founder's prize?" asked Ernest as he helped Toby set out the newly-polished trophies on a table on the stage in the hall. Last year it had been awarded to Ryan Hale, a lad who had entered the school virtually illiterate in his final year but who left well able to hold his own at secondary school.

"Well, it isn't Joe Latimer," grumbled Toby. He and Joey had had another run-in that morning. "I swear that boy has a self-destruct button. If he gets through secondary modern without being expelled it will be a miracle. He'd pick a fight with a paper bag."

Ernest sighed. Joey had indeed been a thorn in their side all year. Doctor Legg had had a long conversation with Mrs Clark about her suspicion that the boy's anger was based on some kind of sexual misadventure when he was younger, but there had been no follow-up. Mrs Latimer had refused to discuss it, and Joey himself could not or would not say there was anything troubling him. It was a stalemate. In the end, all the doctor and the headmistress were able to do was pass on what little they gleaned to the next school in the hope that someone there might be in a position to provide some kind of counselling one day, if Joe's behaviour continued to decline.

"It's a pity we can't solve every problem," agreed Ernest, with a deep sigh. "I sometimes think we're a little like the vicar's land yacht – tacking this way and that across a field of hazards."

"Lor," said Toby. "Don't go all philosophical on me. Latimer simply likes to slug first and think afterwards. He'll probably grow out of it when he's fifteen."

That shows what you know about children, thought Ernest. No one grew out of anything in his view. This issue will still be buzzing in Joey's head like the curate's bees under a jam jar when he's ninety, he thought. It was a great shame. Ernest considered fear, anger, and control were like a threefold cocktail mix that was shaken up every so often in some people, and poured out in such a tidal wave it could drown them. Only by facing what up-skittled him, and taking a cold hard look at it with someone who cared about him, and who he trusted, would Joe ever begin to deal with it, Ernest thought. As a child he had not been immune from unhappiness and confusion himself.

Chivers left Toby to it and went back to his library where a box of withdrawn books was waiting to be shipped off. He sat at his desk and wrote the overseas address label, still thinking about Joey Latimer.

Perhaps it was simply living *beyond* a bad time that gave one strength. No courage involved. No psychoanalysis, just straightforward plodding on. Planting one foot in front of the other, step by slogging step. He had watched Chloe Shaw do it after Max died. He had done it himself. No – but it *wasn't* just that, was it? There were two parts to getting over some traumatic kind of event. Two sides of the coin. One was facing what it was, the other thing was to draw a line in the sand and take personal control of your future. Say Right, *I'm* dealing with this. From now on it's up to me. That Alamo moment had to happen.

That was the action that saved you.

He looked up as someone entered the room.

"You coming to this shindig or what?" asked Mike with a grin.

Ernest grinned back. There was his own salvation, right there. "Yep! Lead on, McDuff. Where's my hat? Do you know who's won the Character cup this year?"

"I think it's Lulu Diaz from Charlie's class. Something about helping to get the first Brownie group started."

"Oh, good girl. Who is their Brown Owl?"

"Mrs Tolland, Ronnie's mother. The girls dote on her, by all accounts. She's in the audience."

They went down the steps into the assembly hall. Every window was open wide and all the children were sitting in rows – parents at the rear – waiting for the last big event of the year to begin with keen anticipation. It was already hot. Charlie was playing his usual medley of tunes in a calming, time-whiling way.

Mrs Clark and Mr Tremayne, resplendent in caps and gowns, ushered in the guests of honour, Dr Legg, looking colourfully exotic as usual, Rev Bill in a surprising safari jacket, and Mr Henshaw – chairman of the PTA – dressed perfectly normally and looking slightly embarrassed.

"Good morning girls and boys," began Mrs Clark. "Another Founder's Day has come around and here we are, ready to hand out some well-deserved trophies. Now, where's our school mascot I wonder? Time is pressing and we need to make a start. Has anyone seen Stringer?"

Exactly on cue, Stringer cantered in through the open french doors at the back, down one of the side aisles and up the steps onto the stage where he shook his head vigorously, causing the little handbell he was holding to ring loudly. The children shrieked with joy.

Mr Tremayne stepped forward, retrieved the bell and sent the dog to sit on a special chair to one side.

"*Bonjour, mes enfants,*" called Mr Tremayne, as was the custom.

"*Bonjour, monsieur,*" they shouted back.

"Stringer est sur sa chaise et nous allons commencer," continued Toby jovially. "Alright, alright, back to English. Now then, Mrs Clark, if you would be kind enough to introduce our special guests to the children, I will check that no pirates have crept in to steal our treasured silverware. Did you see anyone, Mungo? Did you see anyone, Lisa?"

"No, Mr Tremayne," returned those two very little ones. A kindergartener, Jason Brown, was so excited at talk of pirates he could not help himself. He jumped to his feet yelling "Arrrr!", which made everyone laugh. He sat down again with a sheepish smile.

The introductions over, the wonderful morning went swiftly by. There were prizes for Maths and English and Composition and Science, PE, Gardening, Swimming and every other aspect of school life there was. Mungo's mother was thrilled when he received a prize for English composition, and Lisa Rockwell's mother was gloriously proud of her daughter's award for PE. Mick McDonald shocked his dad by carrying off the Maths trophy and Joey Latimer took the football prize. Lulu Diaz was overwhelmed when she received the prestigious Founders Cup and wept tears of happiness when she was cheered by the whole school. The final award of the day was the Inter-House Challenge Trophy, which this year went to the yellows – Cook.

By the time all the awards had been given, and even Stringer had a yellow ribbon tied on his collar, everyone needed a breath of fresh air.

They filed out onto the field to let off some steam. It was a mere half an hour before a salad lunch, then a do-what-you-like-afternoon indoors or out. The teachers had plenty of puzzles and colouring and games for those that wished to sit quietly in the shade even if others preferred to spend a couple of hours on their allotments or running around in the wilderness. It was free-choice. Stringer scampered out after the children to discover where Nicky had got to, while Reg cleared up the hall.

The honoured guests enjoyed their lunch and a wander around the school afterwards. After the children had gone home they joined the teachers in the staffroom where the doors had been flung wide to allow a cool breeze in. Tea and cakes were the final delight of a long day.

Dr Legg plonked herself down on the old sofa next to Miss Fisher and patted her knee affectionately. Each appeared to be the complete opposite of the other at first glance – one distinctly pastel-coloured and composed, the other a vivacious chatterbox. One calm and attentive, the other dramatically expressive. But the two ladies were completely on the same page when it came to friendship – and children, and schools, and life in general. They were good friends.

Dora York pottered in from the patio with a half empty plate of cakes.

"Anyone for a do-dah?" she asked.

"Now that's what I *call* a prize-giving. A *proper* reward for a mornin's hard work," laughed the doctor. "Oh yes please, Mrs York! Over here. I can share mine with Miss Fisher if there aren't enough to go roun'. Half each. It just would not be a proper Mayflower get-together without one of your really *special* prizes, now would it?"

* * *

24.

Breaking up

The last day of term had arrived – the last half-day, to be precise. It was a sad time for most of the children in Form 6 who were leaving to go to secondary school, but a mere end of episode for everyone else. Including the staff.

Ivy and Sally only had to make some sandwiches for everyone's lunch today. They had spent a morning a few days before, picking soft fruit at a local 'pick your own' smallholding and had come back with baskets of fresh raspberries. They aimed to provide everyone with a taste of summer for dessert.

"Although," said Ivy, as she spooned raspberries into little dishes "if we manage to keep the flies orf this lot I'll be satisfied. Where's them clean tea towels, Sally?"

"Are we doing a cup of tea and a biscuit this afternoon during the cricket match?" asked Sally.

"Well I am. You don't have to stay, me-duck. You get on home and enjoy the sunshine. Start yer holidays proper."

Sally nodded and said she would. No point staying when you weren't getting paid, was there? It was different for Mrs Green.

Jim Fisher looked in at the kitchen door at break time.

"You wantin' a snack, young Jim?" asked Ivy. She always had something put by that he could eat without getting the collywobbles. She had always looked out for him, ever since he had been in kindergarten. She handed him an apple and a few raspberries.

"Thank you Mrs Green," he said and gave her a rare smile. She had helped him when he had fallen out of the tree and nearly froze to death that night last Winter, although he could not remember a single thing about it. He had been told Ivy and Auntie May had warmed him up with blankets and hot water bottles, for which he would be eternally grateful. She had helped save his life. He pulled an end of term gift for Ivy out of his pocket. It was a little paper packet with some seeds in.

He handed it to her, explaining that hollyhocks would look lovely round her own kitchen door and these would probably turn out to be white or yellow. Or pink. You couldn't tell. The little seeds would lie asleep until next year, then surprise her with a lovely cottage garden display.

"Well, ent that kind? Thank you, Jimmy, that's lovely. Mr Green don't do much in the way of flowers, as you know, him being so set on growing veg all the time. I will really enjoy these. They from your own garden are they?"

"Yes. And the man from over the allotments gave me some of his too. The association's going to buy that bullock field and extend the 'lotments he says, and maybe I might get one. Not a cow, a plot. I'm on a list."

"Oh, won't that be nice? Right up your street that'll be. You could just hop over the hedge every day then and dig your own potatoes. Or make a little gate and come and go as you please. Or have a stile. Reg'll help yer build it."

"You still got that contraption?" asked Sally.

Jim nodded. "Yep. You need anything carrying, Miss Turk?"

"Well, I'd be very glad of a hand with one thing, if you don't mind. It's a sewing machine that Mrs Nesbit's given me. If you could help me with it down to the station, I can take it home tonight. It's only one stop is Weston. Dad'll help me the other end."

Jimmy knew Weston was only one stop. He wasn't a baby. "Of course I'll help," he said. "I'll come round when the cricket starts shall I? I expect Auntie May will be staying to watch."

"Well, that's very kind. Thank you Jimmy. And I'll lift it. It's far too heavy for you to manage."

People were always saying that – as if his bad leg stopped his arms working. But it would be rude to contradict her, so he nodded and left.

Last man in

"Out!"

The batsman held out his arms in silent query. Mr Green, the umpire, solemnly held up a finger and the batsman walked away, wiping his brow.

Kay Fordam whooped with delight and performed her team's little war-dance, as did the rest of the children's side.

"Not bad for a girl," acknowledged Toby, winking at Guy as he strode passed him. Guy could barely believe he was out already. Again. Not exactly for a duck, but close enough. He glared at Toby.

"Who are you calling a girl?" he growled in mock anger.

Toby patted a few this way and that for a splendid ten minutes, then skied ball with a wild wallop high in the air.

"That's a six!" yelled Ernest, jumping up. Reg had raised his hands above his head. "*Yes!*"

The miraculous ball flew between the shady horse chestnuts over the fence and landed with a thud on top of the milkman's new electric milk float, beside which a very surprised Alf Rose was deep in conversation with Percy Watson the postman.

"What the hanover was that?" asked Alf, rather shaken. A falling sputnik?

Percy could hear the cheering coming from the field. "Looks like Mr Tremayne fetched a six," he said. "Hope he ent dented your roof, Alf."

"I'll dent *his* ruddy roof," stated Alf. He clambered up to retrieve the ball. "Here, you chuck it."

Percy set down his postbag and took the ball over to the fence where a sweaty-looking fielder was jumping up and down trying to find it. "You looking for this?"

"Oh, gosh, thanks, Mr Watson," said Dean. "That really was a brilliant boundary wasn't it?"

"It certainly was," replied Percy. "There." He threw it back over the fence to Dean, who caught it, and continued its journey back over the mown line to the bowler. "No harm done."

"Good job it weren't a cannonball," joked Percy. He picked up his bag and plodded on.

Contours

Early in August, Mrs Clark enjoyed a day alone in Fenchester. She travelled there by train to spend a few hours completely by herself, browsing in the bookshops and visiting the museum at her leisure. In the afternoon she returned on the bus and, feeling the sudden desire for a breath of fresh air, she alighted at Christmas Farm and climbed up to the very top of Holly Hill.

The higher she climbed the happier she became. Life seemed to flow up through her from the very chalk. Up, up it came, through the roots and stalks of the plants into her feet and legs, and rose higher into her shoulders, her ears, until it exploded like a firework out through her hair and on into the sky. The breezy breath of the world susurrated all about her, fluttering the beech leaves and singing through the stems. Everywhere was tingling with energy and she was part of it.

She found a fallen log and sat inhaling this intoxicating life, gazing north towards the distant place she called home. Below, stretching far away into the blue, her world unfurled like a painted map.

Green – it was green.

All shades of green and gold and blue in pastel patterns and hazy textures, with threads and ribbons running across and between its parts, defining some areas, closing others, linking them all together. In her imagination she floated bird-like over its surface swinging first left then right, higher and lower as the wind took her. Like a land-yachtswoman borne into the skies.

Open land and enclosed pasture jigsawed themselves together. Woodlands, forests, brushwood and scrub. Commons, marshes, islands. Gardens, vegetable plots and a complete almost pristine wilderness of which she was the current custodian. The green was complemented with houses, cottages, farms, sheds and even pavilions. Safe areas, wild places, forbidden zones, some that warmly welcomed the exploring wanderer, others that bade you leave. Tame places, cultivated and cultured parts where civilisation flowered. The old town was itself curled sleepily beside the glittering river. She half expected to hear its busy sounds, but there was only the wind sighing past her ears.

Side by side and locked together, each little space was a world unto itself, glued to the next and the next, each dependent upon the other, yet entirely separated by roads and paths and tracks and trails, the rail-tracks, the skeins of the river, the hedges, fences and walls which ran between. Natural and man-made liminal impositions defined differences and set thresholds that were sometimes boundaries, sometimes barriers – sometimes welcoming, sometimes not.

Some were clear lines, hazardous and dangerous. Others were merely broken, hazy suggestions that merged mysteriously into the next gentle area without any trouble at all. A few ended in abrupt darkness. Most she could recognise easily, while the existence of others she had never even suspected. The known and the unknown, the surface and the often complicated, unpleasant undersides. Below lay lies and sordid truths. Phoney friendships and self-serving deceit.

There had been plenty of both landscapes in her Mayflower days. Parents and children, sadness and delight, the old and the new. Cat and dog. She had believed she was living in a pleasant, predictable little humdrum world, but it had certainly held unsuspected secrets. Such as the people who would go to any length to protect those they loved, and others who thought nothing of wiping a person out. It was a looking-glass, chessboard world down there. Those never-ending lines, those sketchy marks only suggested where you might be. You could never be completely sure. Some indicated you were safe, but others marked bottomless pits.

Mrs Clark sat and dreamed, as she always did. As she always, always would.

Had she helped at all? Had she made any of this roughly laced-together little corner of the world any better? Any worse? She had done her best – was still trying to do her best – but was that enough?

The smell of the earth came to her on the breeze. A rich damp scent of beech mast, chalk and vegetation warmed by the sun.

She had planted a few tiny seeds in this corner of the world, tended them and encouraged them towards the light. She liked to think that mostly she had been successful. The school was thriving. She had fixed some parts, tended everything carefully and added a few extras. Maybe she was doing alright.

Mrs Clark stood up and brushed her skirt free of twigs and dirt.

Mayflower was still alive. Its heart beat, its voice was strong. School was a whole huge jumble of people, little and large, old and young. Nothing important was ever simply up to just one person – one middle-aged, imperfect headmistress – to decide. There was comfort in that. There were lines to follow, routines, putting one foot in front of the other, systems, yes. But there were also people to link arms with, to hold hands with, to join in your dance, and to lead forth to the call of its voices, its bells, whistles, and constant music. There was always shelter to be found somewhere within the gentle, quirky old building. It covered a multitude of sins. It forgave you your transgressions and suggested you try again. You had to take somewhere like Mayflower with you in your heart when you moved out into the coloured map down there. Mayflower was the key to the map.

Skipper smiled. It might look a little quirky, but she wasn't going to go by what she saw any more, was she? She was going to listen.

And suddenly she wanted to hear the voices again. Voices calling encouragement, telling her jokes, asking if she'd take a look at a painting or a poem or a plasticine dinosaur. Always and everywhere there were the voices of children laughing, talking, asking, singing, shouting, chattering, crying. She missed the sound of their voices. The world of her school.

It was down there, waiting.

And so, just as she had done long ago when she had stepped over the sunbaked threshold on her first ever day at Mayflower School, Mrs Clark knew it was time to begin again.

* * *

The Mayflower Trilogy

Book 1   Mayflower Days

Book 2   Testing Tides

Book 3   Crossing the Line

Printed in Great Britain
by Amazon